Meri,

Daniel Pascoe

---

deadline

Limited Special Edition. No. 21 of 25 Paperbacks

Best wishes

Dan Pascoe

(14: 6: 2019)

Daniel Pascoe was brought up on smog and boiled cabbage in London many years ago. He worked in the Health Services in the northeast of England for thirty years as a cancer specialist. Now retired, he lives on Teesside and spends much of his time writing, far from the hubbub of city life. His wife is from Hungary. As his two daughters contemplate their own futures, he worries that our political elite have not the faintest ability to make sensible progress within our sadly divided society. He has two children and three grandchildren from before. He also lives with a black cat and two cute Pomeranians.

He has had two intelligent commercial thrillers published already: *The London Sniper* in 2015 and *Dead End* in 2016. *Deadline* is his third novel.

Dedicated to three elegant women, urbane and hip, who are the present and the future:
Anna, Jessica and Francesca.

Daniel Pascoe

deadline

AUSTIN MACAULEY PUBLISHERS™

LONDON • CAMBRIDGE • NEW YORK • SHARJAH

A CIP catalogue record for this title is available from the British Library.

ISBN 9781788238670 (Paperback)
ISBN 9781788238687 (Hardback)
ISBN 9781788238694 (Kindle e-book)
ISBN 9781528953900 (ePub e-book)

www.austinmacauley.com

First Published (2019)
Austin Macauley Publishers Ltd
25 Canada Square
Canary Wharf
London
E14 5LQ

THE POLICE SHOOTING INCIDENT AS DESCRIBED HEREIN ACTUALLY HAPPENED, IN THE EXACT SPOT ON PEMBROKE ROAD, IN EARL'S COURT. BUT FOR THE NAME CHANGES AND TIME SWAP, THE SEQUENCE OF EVENTS THAT LED UP TO AND FOLLOWED THE INCIDENT ARE REPRODUCED FROM FIRST-HAND ACCOUNTS, MORE OR LESS, AS THEY HAPPENED. THE STORY THAT EMERGED IS GATHERED TOGETHER AS A WHOLE IN THIS VOLUME, WHICH MADE USE OF THE REPORTS AVAILABLE, TO ATTEMPT TO BRING SOUGHT-AFTER CLARITY TO THE TRAGEDIES OF THIS CASE AS A MATTER OF PUBLIC INTEREST.

Other books by the author:

The London Sniper: A Fictional Tale of Alternative History Set in London...

Dead End

Contents

Initial Police Report of Shooting Incident, Earl's Court

OFFENSE/INCIDENT REPORT	1.TYPE		
HAMMERSMITH METROPOLITAN POLICE 226 SHEPHERD'S BUSH ROAD W6 7NX	a.ORIGINAL b.CONTINUATION c.SUPPLEMENT or FOLLOWUP		
	2.CODE NUMBER		
	3.CASE CONTROL NUMBER		FH 007498

4.NAME OF OFFICER REPORTING DI Michael Sanger	5.SPECIFIC LOCATION Pembroke Road, Earls Court W4

6.DATE OF OFFENSE/INCIDENT Friday January 16 2015	7.TIME OF OFFENSE/INCIDENT 15.45 hrs	8.DATE REPORTED 16.01.2015	9.TIME REPORTED 17.45 hrs

10.PERSONS INVOLVED

ID	LAST NAME	FIRST NAME		
	PITSAKIS	HUGO		
ADDRESS – NO STREET (121/122) 36 Butler's Wharf Terrace, Bermondsey, London SE1		TOWN	POST CODE	

ID	LAST NAME	FIRST NAME		
	SOAMES	LILLY		
ADDRESS – NO STREET 18a Ingersoll Road, Shepherds Bush W12		TOWN	POST CODE	

11.VEHICLE

STATUS	YEAR	MAKE	MODEL	COLOUR	REG NO

12. OWNER

13.DESCRIPTION/NARRATIVE *(for additional space, use blank sheet and attach)*

As part of an on-going police search for known criminal on the run with a history of violence, namely Mr Midge Martin of 84a Adelaide Grove, Shepherds Bush, W4, believed to be armed and dangerous, officers from Hammersmith Police Station, together with colleagues from Shepherds Bush, were called during the morning hours of January 16 2015 to join an overnight stake-out of said property, following a local tip-off. Detective Inspector Michael Sanger was officer-in-charge, accompanied by Detective Constable Peter Finch, the only officer present who could make a positive identification of the suspect, having been the arresting officer of said Mr Martin following a previous robbery at Marylebone Art Gallery on December 18 2014.   Officer Ian Wade, on driver duty with DI Sanger and DC Finch in unmarked stake-out vehicle positioned on Adelaide Grove, had confirmed the presence of the suspect in the two-bed ground floor flat that Martin shared with girlfriend, Ms Veronica Secola.

At approximately fifteen-twenty hours (15.20), the suspect accompanied by two young women left the flat and climbed into a yellow Mini car parked outside, which then set off with Ms Secola driving and Ms Lilly Soames in the back, down to Uxbridge Road and then easterly towards Holland Road and the Shepherds Bush Roundabout and then in a southerly direction towards the Earls Court area. Three unmarked police vehicles, two following and one ahead, and an unmarked motorcycle outrider, were involved in tracking the said Mini, with DI Sanger coordinating by two-way radio communications.   At a set of red traffic lights on Pembroke Road at its junction with Earls Court Road, the Mini was stationary in a start-stop queue of cars when the suspect unexpectedly began to climb out of the vehicle. DC Finch advanced with caution along the pavement from the trailing car in order to identify the suspect, who was disguised in a raincoat and under a hat. DC Finch discharged his weapon twice to prevent the suspect making his escape and drawing out of the vehicle an object he was reaching for inside, that DC Finch presumed was a firearm. One other armed officer, DS Eric Jardine was involved in discharging further rounds at the suspect as he made to escape from the other side of the car and he was then apprehended by officers without any further mishap.   No police officer was harmed.

At this point, DC Finch realised that the wounded man from the Mini was not Midge Martin but a gentleman unknown to the police; in due course identified as Hugo Pitsakis, of 36 Butlers Wharf Terrace, Shad Thames, who is understood to be an artist of Greek extraction. An emergency ambulance arrived at the scene within fifteen minutes, and the victim was transported safely to a local nearby Casualty Department.

The whereabouts of Mr Midge Martin remains uncertain. The police have issued a warning that this man is armed and potentially dangerous and members of the public should not under any circumstances approach him but report any possible sightings immediately to their nearest police station.

14.NOTIFICATION	15.EVIDENCE
Other services - **ambulance**	Attachments Tag number

16. TIME/DATE _17:45 hrs January 16 2015_	REPORT BY _Detective Inspector Michael Sanger_ SIGNATURE

London Evening Standard, Friday, January 16, 2015

A man has been critically injured in a police ambush in a West London street in what may be a case of mistaken identity. Witnesses said marksmen surrounded a car in a traffic jam on the Earl's Court Road and opened fire. The driver was shot several times in the head and body. Scotland Yard said the ambush was part of an operation to recapture escaped prisoner Midge Martin.

Martin absconded from custody at Marlborough Street magistrate's court last month where he was due to face a charge of attempting to murder a police officer. But it remains unclear if the man shot was Midge Martin. Two senior Scotland Yard officers have already been appointed to investigate the incident.

One of the first witnesses on the scene, Secretary Jane Lumley, who was queuing in the car immediately behind, said the man seemed very badly injured. 'He was about 30, I would say, but I couldn't even see the colour of his hair because of all the blood,' she said. Another witness, Mrs Helen Westhouse, saw some of the incident from her home which overlooks the scene. She said: 'Whilst I was watching, I heard one or two more gunshot cracks, but I couldn't actually see where they came from. Then I saw that the driver of the Mini had sort of fallen out of his car, he was hanging out from the waist with his head on the road.'

The man is being treated in the intensive care unit at Chelsea and Westminster Hospital in Fulham Road, Chelsea. Two other women were passengers in the car; one ran off, and the other was taken to hospital by police officers for treatment of what are believed to be minor injuries.

Part One: Olivia Truelove

1

Saturday, January 17, 2015

Olivia is agitated and awake unnecessarily early. Habit, mostly, as she is normally up at the crack of dawn during the week, but the news reports from last night are nagging at her. Leaning against the kitchen sink at the window in her pyjamas, she nurses a mug of tea. Her mouth is dry and stale from last night, an empty ache in the pit of her stomach: too much alcohol, too little to eat. The street lamps are still bathing the empty pavements with their tenuous orange light. She pulls on a baggy tracksuit and trainers to brave the ugly London drizzle. Outside, the darkness has barely begun to seep away, while a joyless light tries to penetrate blankets of low cloud. The surprising chill hits her cheeks like a slap in the face, and she pulls her hood up to press its woolly softness against her skin. There is nobody about as she jogs carefully along to Broadgate to fetch a couple of the day's early editions. Neither have the story as front-page headlines, which are still shouting about the awful terrorist attack in Paris, even though that was ten days ago, but inside the *Telegraph*, she finds some bold paragraphs and a couple of pictures that grab her attention, as she ambles back home around Finsbury Circus:

Mystery Shooting by Police in Earl's Court

A man was gunned down yesterday evening by armed officers of the Metropolitan Police in Earl's Court – by mistake. He is said to be in a critical condition in the intensive care unit of Chelsea and Westminster Hospital, having had extensive trauma surgery. Hugo Pitsakis, originally from Greece, an artist and many years a London resident, was mistaken for a dangerous man on the run from the Police, Midge Martin, who escaped from Marlborough Street magistrate's court over three weeks ago, where he was on remand for attempted murder of a police officer during an armed robbery that went wrong at the Marylebone Gallery.

Cut down in broad daylight like a matchstick man, an innocent artist was rushed to the nearest emergency hospital for treatment when it was realised that he had actually survived the onslaught of a dozen high-velocity 9mm bullets smashed into his body. He was receiving emergency treatment throughout the day and night and was said to still be in a critical state. He is likely to be transferred to the Charing Cross Hospital for specialist thoracic surgery later today. A young woman companion had also been injured and taken to the hospital; she had received emergency treatment and was described as stable.

The photographs are crap quality snaps, one of a yellow Mini car at the side of a street, lopsided with its back tyres flat, its doors wide open and some hefty figures in black gear and helmets and hi-vis gilets standing around under street lights, behind blue and white incident tape. The other, a police mug shot of a youngish clean-shaven man with long wavy hair and a crooked mouth, staring wide-eyed into the camera, described as the elusive and potentially dangerous Midge Martin. There is practically nothing about the victim, matchstick man.

The *Daily Mail* has the headline:

Man in Car Not the Armed Robber That Police Suspected

with the same thin story details and photographs but an additional quote:

"It can be hard to identify some people from a distance," said a police spokesperson, "especially in the dusk when you suspect he may be armed, we could not take any risks. He was disguised in a coat and hat. If it turns out that an innocent man has been injured, which rarely does happen under the circumstances, then there will be an internal inquiry, and we hope the victim and his family would be able to accept our apologies."

Blithering idiots. How can they be so stupid? The man was shot twelve times, how can that be an easy mistake to make? Mind you, he was disguised in a coat and a hat. An inquiry and an apology? My God, are we safe on the streets of London these days? Olivia pauses along the pavement for a moment, glancing around, up and down the near-deserted street to see if there are any men disguised in coats and hats, armed policemen hiding in parked cars. The solid outlines of brick and glass buildings that rise on either side are strangely reassuring, castle-like fortifications for the capitalist elite, a demographic she realises she is in danger of joining herself. The mood among the confident and well-heeled city folk she knows is of reassuring continuity, reliable entrenchment, barricades built to last, and she gains some comfort from all that. But this shooting in the open streets in daylight involving the heavy forces of the law, normally there for our protection, sounds like madness. Or is there something else rather more sinister behind all this that is yet to be revealed?

She slips through a gate and strolls through the courtyards to her staircase, climbing to the second floor, her apartment reassuringly private and tucked away. Inside, she kicks her shoes off, cleans her teeth and splashes her face with cold water. She makes herself a black coffee and spreads the papers over her breakfast table, searching for more information about the condition of the poor, innocent Greek. This *is* the main reason for her keen interest in this incident, after all.

Whereas normally she would quickly pass over such stories to get to the business and financial news, today she is trembling slightly with nervous tension. Friday's police operation was headed by DI Michael Sanger, a mid-fifties near-to-retirement officer of over twenty-five years' experience with the Met. According to *Express* reporter Richard Armstrong, the police were all acutely aware that Midge Martin might be armed, having already nearly killed one of their fellow officers, and they were extremely frustrated and trigger-happy.

Shooting by Police in Earl's Court a Mistake

Detective Inspector Michael Sanger has revealed that the shooting incident of a man suspected of armed robbery by several officers of the Metropolitan Police on Friday afternoon on Pembroke Road, a busy thoroughfare in the Earl's Court area of west London, was a case of mistaken identity.

It all started from Adelaide Grove in Shepherd's Bush, where a police stakeout suspected a criminal on the run was holed up in a flat with his girlfriend. It was a drizzly late afternoon, the light beginning to fail when the suspect, his face obscured by a grey fedora, was seen by watching police officers to climb into the front seat of a two-door distinctive yellow Mini, which was parked outside, accompanied by two young ladies, both wrapped in hooded jackets against the weather. The girl driving was Veronica Secola, 29, from Serbia, and the girl in the back was a friend, Lilly Soames, 25, both described as models. The suspect was Midge Martin, 36, wanted by the police for robbery and assault, known to be dangerous and possibly armed. Police teams from Hammersmith and Shepherd's Bush Stations in unmarked cars, headed up by DI Sanger, tracked the Mini in the slow-moving rush-hour traffic as they negotiated through Shepherds Bush and the Roundabout and proceeded down Holland Road heading south. At a set of traffic lights on the corner of Pembroke Road and the Earl's Court Road, the Mini waited in a queue on the red light. The face of Lilly Soames appeared several times at the rear window, apparently speaking to her companions, and she seemed to be acting as a lookout.

The man in the Mini suddenly opened his passenger door and prepared to get out of the stationary car. Sanger assumed he had spotted the police and was about to make his escape. DC Peter Finch, who had been the arresting officer when Martin had committed his original crime, armed robbery of a Marylebone Gallery four weeks ago, and therefore the only officer present who could make a proper identification, climbed out of his vehicle and proceeded along the line of cars towards the suspect. The traffic lights still on red, Finch shouted to the man who he believed to be Martin, to step out of the car, with his hands up and be identified. He made it clear that he was a policeman and he was armed. The suspect reached for something inside the car.

DC Finch was convinced that he had a gun, given his past record, and was determined to stop this dangerous villain. He did not hesitate to draw his own Glock 26 pistol from inside his jacket and to fire a few warning shots, as he came alongside the Mini, also firing at the tyres of the car.

Miss Secola opened her driver's door in an effort to scramble away to safety. Another armed officer, Detective Sergeant Eric Jardine, approached the Mini from the roadside and fired shots through the rear window and then at the injured suspect who had scrambled across the front seats to escape through the driver's side and was hanging out of the car, head down in the road. DC Finch came forward to make his identification and only then realised that it was not Midge Martin as he had thought, but someone quite different. The innocent man was eventually helped into an ambulance that arrived later and was whisked away to Chelsea & Westminster Hospital for emergency treatment. He was later identified as Mr Hugo Pitsakis, 34, of Bermondsey, an artist. A hospital spokesperson later described his condition as critical but stable.

- Bermondsey, and he's 34, Olivia notes to herself. The remaining printed accounts give no more detail than she had already gleaned from the internet news last night. The *Mail online* has some extra clips, which she finds laughable:

A local elderly couple walking their dog, who had witnessed the entire episode, was seen to be standing stock still on the pavement nearby. On being asked their reaction, the man said the police had acted with superb speed and efficiency in apprehending the villain and his wife added that they were ever so grateful. DI Sanger confirmed that the victim did not act in self-defence and that he was unarmed. The unfortunate episode had been a case of mistaken identity, he said. The poor visibility on such a dull day had compounded to the difficulty of making out the exact features of the man hidden under a hat and in a long coat. On behalf of the Metropolitan Police, Detective Inspector Sanger offered the victim their apologies.

A senior officer of Scotland Yard issued a public apology within hours of the incident for this "tragic case of mistaken identity" and an immediate inquiry by the Complaints Investigation Team was underway. The Home Secretary Theresa May also promised a full report would be passed to the Director of Public Prosecutions and that all steps would be taken to ensure that such an incident could not happen again.

The idiocy of the incident, the inexplicableness of it, is clearly not to be explained by further delving through poorly informed news reports. She watches an out-of-focus video sequence with poor lighting and definition from a mobile phone currently running on *YouTube*, presumably obtained by the same on-the-spot journalist sometime after the event, alongside minimal details and of course no source quoted. The canary yellow Mini sits lopsided under street lighting at a kerb side, both doors wide open. The road seems to be clear of traffic. Armed police in black headgear and reflective vests are yelling incoherently and randomly moving about in the confusion. A blurred view of the presumed victim crumpled under a blanket on the pavement beyond the car comes up, although nothing close or identifiable, and then a crowd of officers hide the view as the wounded man is carried into the back of an ambulance, lights flashing. It finishes with wobbly close-up images of the roadside gutter and pavement, a reflective stain spread over the edge of the kerbstones and on the asphalt.

Olivia finishes her coffee and slice of toast. In the half-darkness of the bedroom, she strips off and goes through to shower away the fetid effects of her poor night's sleep. A rerun of the miserable images that she has just been watching plays through her mind. She rubs herself down vigorously, to feel purposeful but achieves only a partial reprieve. She lets the bath towel slip off to the floor in front of the mirror and watches her reflection, as she perches her bottom onto a stool. She has fine straw-blonde hair, which drapes neatly around her oval face in straight lines from a left-of-centre parting and reaches collar length, curling inwards. She likes it covering her small ears although she's aware of an irritating habit of hooking it impatiently behind both ears with crooked fingers when she's working. She is naturally fair, with a smooth complexion and thin feathery eyebrows that curve over bright eyes that her father always said were as pretty as bluebells. She has an honest appearance that sometimes gives the impression of an easy walk-over, but she can do serious when she wants, with a certain set to the jaw, a levelling of the eyes. She has a determined obstinacy that few have learnt to overcome. Her nose is a little too snub for her, but, otherwise, it's an intelligent face and when she smiles, her cheeks softly dimple, while the teeth she reveals are even and pure white. She can produce cute little wrinkle lines as well across the bridge of her nose when she scowls, like now. And she sometimes talks out loud to herself.

- I do not need that look of disapproval today, thank you.

Olivia without clothes arches her back and straightens her shoulders, pinching at her waistline, as she studies the figure that she finds pleasing: everything curves and shapes in all the right places, without sag or obvious excess. She feels good about herself. Her body, like her mind, is healthy, no question. At 33, she knows she is attractive, although she worries sporadically about her diet and her weight and wishes her legs were longer, just like all the other girls she knows. She lives alone by choice and wants for nothing, really. Work is busy, but the experience and the money are good, so she accepts the rough with the smooth. She has to fight to keep on top of the job, but promotion opportunities are always dangling a little ahead, so she has everything to play for.

Although today, change seems to be in the air, with all its disruptive possibilities to her meticulous routine. She feels like an actor being pushed out onto the stage for a first performance before she has properly learnt her lines. She sets her mind on her planned skiing holiday that is only a few weeks away, running through the chores she still has on her list, knowing it will be a fun chance to get away from the drizzly drawn-out London winter that makes everyone so gloomy.

But it's not the weather: there's an uneasiness stirring within, like a warning to tread carefully. Last night she had broken one of her unwritten life rules about not socialising during the week, but as it was Friday, she made an exception to meet with someone new and exciting. She can still feel the remains of their chaste goodnight kiss, as they departed with a promise of meeting again. She cleans along the inverted edges of her lips with the tip of her tongue, anticipating another encounter with a sense of vague longing.

She grips herself between her legs, tingling like a nervous itch. She senses an awakening of something unfamiliar, a feeling she may never have had before, at least not so intense or urgent. She returned home last night in a taxi and crossed the courtyard by the fountains with a skip in her step and a whole raft of fanciful ideas in her mind. Even the night sky had looked clear and interesting. She was tired but not ready for bed. She clicked on the 24-hour news on the internet and caught sight of the reports of this ridiculous shooting incident earlier in the day in Earl's Court. She continued searching for more details for half an hour and her sleep had then been disturbed by a mixed bag of confusing memories and dreams.

Hence, the heavy head and inner tiredness this morning. There's an anxiety in her stomach, where she presses a palm while holding her breath for more than a minute, like trying to stop hiccoughs.

- Just because I have no clothes on, does not mean I am without principles. I like looking at my reflection, it reassures me that I am one of God's children.

Olivia gives herself a slow smile and pouts into the glass.

- I believe in free spirit. I live in a madhouse world of continuous work and stress. My life is controlled by the business mammoth that turns everything upside down for its own purpose. I have no time to myself, I am a slave of the City. I have to find other ways to express my sensual being, that's all; even if that means something a little out of the ordinary.

Olivia had always struggled as a child to find ways to express herself; there never seemed to be anyone listening or interested. So maybe something unconventional has more possibilities for her, something she has been keeping from herself but waiting for, all along.

- I'm trying to be honest with myself.
- Yeah, right. Perhaps. Whatever floats your boat, girl.
- The novelty factor at the moment is compelling.

She is not going to let her routine and well-controlled emotions be disturbed, but a little fraying at the edges might not be a bad thing. Everything is bobbing along steadily: the office team seem to be working together in harmony, with the boys on the top floor sending messages of encouragement; her magazine column apparently receives lots of encouraging letters and twitter feed. Her social life is pretty average: she goes out occasionally with different men, no one in particular, doing the usual things City men like their women to do, which is mostly about conceding to their basest requests and playing to their alpha egos. None of which engages her, especially the physical stuff which she finds generally boring. So she lives a contented life alone, which suits her best. She can choose her own activities and live the way she wants without having to pander to others and their artificial desires. She can go out with girlfriends when she wants, invite them in to watch a TV box set of their choice, she can eat what she wants, when she wants, or read a trashy novel sitting on the toilet, if she wants. She can spend her money how she likes.

Thus has her life been trundling along expected lines, when all of a sudden, bump: she meets someone exceptional, attractive and without apparent demands; which has initiated a surprising change of direction in her thinking. Amazing.

And then, another bump: she is hit by the news of this nonsensical shooting in Earl's Court. And is faced with the disturbing sight of Hugo Pitsakis, a man she once fell in love with a whole lifetime ago, lying bloodied and dying in a London gutter; and now fighting for his life in an intensive care unit.

Two bumps out of the blue, one after the other; but sort of at the same time.
- Coincidence?

Olivia's Saturday mornings usually pass slowly and lazily. The bedroom curtains are left half-closed, the unmade bed ignored, the shadows undisturbed. In crumpled pyjamas and bare feet, coffee is made, bread is toasted and buttered, eggs and bacon may be fried. She dawdles through the hours, lounging from one settee to another soft chair, enjoying a slow-read of the newspapers or a glossy magazine and with the soft sound of radio chatter or music in the background. Eventually aroused, she might stare comfortingly through the wide windows of her lounge out over the dark-tiled forecourts and fountains of her estate and the concrete jungle of the city beyond. She will put on make-up and dress with a casual fastidiousness.

But this particular Saturday she feels different. She wants to be on the move, doing something. She applies simple foundation and dresses distractedly: blouse, sleeveless cashmere top in pink, tight navy slacks and flat white slip-ons, a Borden casual weekend girl. She places gold studs in each pierced ear, and around her neck, a chain with amethyst pendant, a present from her mother last Christmas.

Over the front pages are pictures of the protest marches and the politicians linking arms on their walk through the streets of Paris. Both horrified and fascinated at the same time, she is unable to concentrate. Instead, she is planning an extravagant shopping trip to the West End in the afternoon, her little reward for all the hard work, and a childlike thrill of expectation is starting to ripple down her spine. Despite feeling guilty, her plan will go ahead, and she will ring for a minicab.

She checks the internet news again for any fresh reports, a medical update, perhaps. She has the forlorn hope that she will find reassurance that the unlucky man was not the Hugo she had met years ago, the painter with the stunning first exhibition that she had stumbled upon in Camden Town; the sensitive, brilliant and artistic Hugo who had for a brief period filled her entire life, the Hugo she had wanted for her own and hated for his rejection, who had trampled ghost-like through her damaged mind; the Hugo she thought was clear of the sticky recesses of her memory; that "her" Hugo was not the man in a critical condition fighting for his life in an intensive care bed in a Chelsea hospital. Or if it had to be, that he was really making a speedy and complete recovery and would be out of hospital in a day or two, back to normal, unaffected, painting with his usual brilliance to win the public's approval and the art establishment's disapproval, probably both in equal measure. And that she could quietly forget about him, knowing that he was recovering and safe, and continue to trundle along her chosen path, perhaps with her newfound love, perhaps to reach new peaks, her ambitions undiminished.

The news media, unfortunately, are all too vague and distracted to provide her with that satisfaction. The *Independent-online* carries a little more detail about the victim and his injuries. He had arrived by escorted ambulance in Accident and Emergency at Chelsea and Westminster Hospital, Fulham Road, barely conscious, losing blood from several wounds, including a head injury, and in respiratory difficulty, according to a junior doctor interviewed at the hospital, and it was thought at first that he had a dozen bullet wounds. And yet, somehow he remained alive, and she is thinking that was a bloody miracle. He was admitted under the trauma team and needed several emergency procedures and blood transfusions. A casualty nurse quietly pointed out that the poor man had significant facial cuts and bruising around his eyes and his nose, which was bleeding so much it needed immediate packing to staunch it, which, she added with a knowing look, was all unexplained.

From a high bookshelf Olivia stretches for a scrapbook with pretty pictures on its covers, bulging with cuttings and photos poking out from the edges, and "Olivia Truelove – from my father, October 18, 1999" scrawled in a flowery style on the cover-leaf in confidant black ink. She used to keep it neatly in order and up-to-date, with articles from newspapers or college magazines placed squarely on the pages, photos trimmed and pasted in with childlike care. But of course, in later years, when just too busy with other things, notes and cards and old tickets, all relics and mementoes of an earlier life, were stuffed in loosely between the stiff pages at the back, with the intention of tidying them up at some future point. There are concert tickets, wedding invitations, front covers of programmes of student theatre productions from her university days and more. She finds the programme for Michael Frayn's "Noises Off" revival at the National, October 2000, the most hilarious play she had ever watched; a black and white photograph of a group of her student friends laughing in front of the college entrance; a coloured picture of friends on a ski slope waving their poles in the air, which looked like Val d'Isere, winter 2001; a receipt from a ladies' dress shop in Kensington, May 2002, which must have been her graduation ball gown, all of £240; a ticket to the Edinburgh fringe festival, a night of stand-up comedy, August 2002; an order of service for the funeral of Arthur Truelove, at St Alban's Trinity Church, September 8, 2012.

And there she finds a creased white leaflet, for the Camden Gallery, December 2–8, 2004, a first exhibition for young artists.

- So, it's ten years since I travelled down that particular road, can hardly believe it.

***

The memory of that chilly December evening a decade ago easily floods back: she was searching for an estate agent's place along Camden High Street among the jostling crowds Christmas shopping, glittery decorations jingling everywhere, a sprinkling of snow on the ground. She was young, impulsive and short of money in the Big Smoke, having just returned from three months' work experience in the Big Apple, and had been tempted out to hunt for a possible flat to rent, to improve on the hovel she was sharing with a couple of girlfriends in Kilburn. It was just getting dark, the foreboding sky heavy with more snow and she was running a bit early for her meeting. She was wearing a black woolly jacket with frilly fur around the hood that was hopeless at keeping her warm, tight black jeans and clomping furry boots. Her toes were freezing as she leant into the biting breeze, her gloved hands thrust deep in her pockets. She passed a brightly lit gallery with colourful pictures in the big glass windows: an exhibition of new work from local artists at reasonable prices, it said on a board. The doors were open and it looked temptingly warm inside.

She stepped into a bare space painted black, walls and ceiling alike, that went back a long way from the street and bright spotlights from above picked out the paintings hanging at regular intervals. She took a leaflet at the door, joining the few onlookers shuffling around in their heavy coats and boots, leaving wet trails over the wooden flooring. Sounds were hushed and thankfully there was no irritating seasonal music playing.

Years ago, when she was small, her hair in plaits, her father would take her to art galleries on a Saturday morning, which relieved some of the boredom of school holidays. Just the two of them, although it was only the sit-down tea and iced buns in a café afterwards that she could recall, not the Grand Master paintings at all. Here, amateurish local street scenes, common landscapes and a few average portraits were the order of the day and nothing struck her particularly. She nodded and checked the artists' names on the cards stuck on the walls, although none of them meant anything to her. After a while, she was ready to move on to her meeting but caught sight of something more interesting in a hidden alcove towards the back, where there was a small gathering two or three people deep. She edged closer and was amazed by the colourful images that confronted her, three large canvases in bold acrylics that were such a contrast to everything else in the gallery. These were action pictures of battle-scenes, industrial processes and human conflict, that at first made her think of boys' comic books, until she looked closer at the details. The realism was extreme, human faces substantive and alive, living skin with tone and texture, divine materialism portrayed with confidence and honesty.

The pictures covered the walls completely. There was so much activity going on in them, it was difficult to catch it all: in one, army soldiers on the move, nineteenth-century battles on a hillside, agonised expressions on the faces of wounded men, horses charging, explosions, cannon fire and gunshots and general mayhem; in another, dirty sweaty faces of labourers in an industrial complex, bulging muscles and gritted teeth, you could almost hear the noise of their grunting effort, the anxiety and grief palpable among the left-behind women. And in the middle, an explosive dust cloud enveloping a modern city, erupting, moving and clogging everything in its way, surely a 9/11 New York disaster picture, with the centre of attention drawn towards escaping victims fighting their way clear along a street towards you.

The three pictures were stunning in their reality, their perspective, the movement of people, animals, dirt and dust captured brilliantly, and Olivia was mesmerised by their sublime tactile nature. They were fast-paced and real: here was physical triumph, despair and agony, there was hatred, fear and longing. They were photographic in their exact detailing but were compelling, for the very fact that they were canvas paintings, bursting with tension and emotion, passions expressed boldly in the faces and postures, presented for the audience to share. As the other watchers gradually moved away mostly with expressions of amazement, Olivia was able to take a step back to study them better, feeling certain that she could have identified with her eyes closed the individual fabrics of the characters' clothing, cotton or velvet or silk or leather, by mere touch of the oozing canvases.

The artist was one Hugo Pitsakis, a name she saw for the first time on the little white cards and checked in the leaflet.

On either side were two more pictures, smaller but equally striking, portraits of a fulsome woman. In one she had just stepped up from the water's edge of a lake and was drying herself with a fluffy towel. A bare breast was bursting free as she tried to cover herself, a quizzical look towards the painter glancing over her shoulder. The smooth sweeping curves of her body were flecked with water drops, glistening on her back and bottom. Her auburn hair was flattened and sparkly wet. The towel had buffed up the skin of her thighs. There were tiny puddles at her feet which felt wet. The mimicry was superb. She was lovely, voluptuous and whole, her movements easy and coy. The scene was so three-dimensional, the perspective so wonderfully captured, that Olivia found it quite erotic.

The second was a portrait of the same woman, her back to the painter again, this time leaning forward over the balustrade of an open balcony with no clothes on, looking down into a sunny alleyway, probably Italian. The sole of one foot was moving up the back of her opposite calf, along the ridge of the Achilles tendon, the toes curled and its underside dirty from the floor, the skin roughened. She was balanced on one leg tip-toe, craning to seek signs of her lover returning from a day's labour and ready to surrender to him. There was exhilarating tension in the poise of her body, silken hairs down her back caught by the slanting light, on edge. In the distance, her man had eyes for her alone and like Romeo would probably climb the olive branches that groped over adjacent stonework to reach up to her. She looked wholesome, representing everything that any man could desire. The audience was drawn in by her impatience, knowing that she would soon be as one with her lover, as in real life she would probably be as one with the artist. The sense of the erotic was palpable.

Olivia was smiling, her ponytail swaying with her nodding head. She wiped perspiration from her neck with cold fingers, feeling an excitement of her own; a discovery, as if she had come upon some private pictures that she was not supposed to see, peeping at personal images. She looked around to see if anyone was watching her, but the area was deserted; she had been staring at the pictures for over half an hour. She felt a strong desire to meet this Hugo Pitsakis, wondering where on earth he had popped up from.

She meandered back towards the front entrance, thinking she had identified him, a clean-shaven tallish man with unkempt black hair being congratulated by others, some shaking his hand, someone calling him Hugo; he looked so young. She waited politely to one side for an opportunity to step into his circle and introduce herself, although not exactly sure what she was going to say. Anyway, it did not happen and she left, after another distant look at the paintings in the far gallery, wishing for a return visit some time to see them again. She drifted out into the street in a semi-dream, but the cold wind woke her suddenly to the fact that she was now running late for her appointment with the estate agent further up Camden High Street.

She never did move into Camden, in the end renting a room in West Hampstead, which was slightly less trendy but no less expensive. And she never did get to return to that gallery either, as she had promised herself. Quite soon after that she was embroiled with the new intake of two hundred budding banker hopefuls, like herself, and had to adjust to a new environment off Lombard Street. Despite having to work among the predominant breed of alpha males with their fierce competitiveness, she settled in quickly, becoming a devotee of the hectic almost unreal existence.

***

On another wintery evening twelve months later, newly promoted to assist the assistant to assist the senior analyst on the foreign exchange desk at Emerson's, having jumped over some other boys with high expectations, Olivia had no spare time to think about paintings or London artists. Until Sarah, a fellow traveller and general good sort, had suggested a visit to an exhibition of local talent at the Whitechapel Gallery, just up the road really, on the last day of the year. She had thrust a stiff white invitation card under her nose declaring that she could do with a modern piece of art in her life, something contemporary to counteract the staid and conventional pieces along their workplace corridors. 'Liven up the office or your flat, darling, about time. A glass of bubbly and a finger buffet awaits every visitor with an invitation,' she cooed, studying the blurb, 'and "you will be amazed by the talent on display from a clutch of young up-and-coming artists of the day," so there.'

'But it's New Year's Eve,' Olivia had protested feebly. The whole team were under the usual pressure at work, end-of-year positions to worry about, constantly needing to justify the upper floor's faith in them, there was so little time to indulge in such frivolity. So, when was it any different?

It was the last day of the exhibition, early evening and there was quite a crowd in, nerdy young socialites, arty-types with straggly beards in duffle coats, young businessmen in pin-stripes, the odd trendy couple, sipping at their flutes with exaggerated poise and educated accents, hoping they would be noticed. *Time Out* were sponsoring and occasionally there was a flash of photography and laughter among the punters. And a few casual wanderers like Sarah and Olivia in their thick coats, trailing scarves and wet boots, milling around the brightly lit rooms clutching a paper list of exhibits, vaguely looking at the names and the asking prices. Not many had that bright red round sticker of success on the bottom right-hand corner of the label indicating a sale.

Most of the paintings were insipid and uninspiring; the few sculptures on the floor or placed on wooden plinths for everyone to trip over were ordinary and meaningless. There was no one there she knew or wanted to talk to. Sarah wandered off to fetch another drink while chatting to some bloke in a leather jacket.

Olivia's world of business and finance dealt with real value assets that were tangible with measurable parameters, not pretentious coloured musings on canvas or board framed and hung on large bare walls with unaccountable price tags. Some of the things on display she would willingly have paid someone to dispose of, amazed at how gullible folk could be when it came to art. She looked for some hidden talent or originality, but after half an hour she was feeling hungry and thinking more about a freelance piece she was working on, about how technology was changing the workplace for many people; she just needed the chance to submit it to the senior editor of a finance magazine she had her eye on.

In the next room plonked awkwardly around the floor were raw metal objects welded together into weird shapes, with titles like "Industrial Landscape, Part VI". Backing away from one such contraption she almost knocked into a rather charming clay and copper sculpture of a young girl on a swing, only about two feet high, that reminded her straight away of Degas. It stood on its own plinth that raised it to waist height. She turned to admire it: she liked it, she could understand it and bent forward to look more closely at the detail, searching for the name of the artist. Staring straight back at her from the other side through the space behind the body of the sculpted girl and a post of the swing, was the friendly face of a man with a serious chunky appearance, who was also leaning forward. Olivia was startled and straightened up in surprise.

'Excuse me,' the man said, stepping backwards. 'Sorry.' He had a twist of a smile on generous lips, his chin darkened with shadowy stubble and he was looking at the figure on the swing with his head bent to one side, fingering the stem of an empty glass. He gestured toward the object between them. 'Good, though.'

'Yes,' was all she could say. The man, in a crumpled tweed jacket and brogues, seemed vaguely familiar, with rugged good-looks and black curly hair that was brushed casually behind his ears and flopped uncontrollably over his forehead.

'I like the flowing hair behind her head. And her smile. It's a happy piece,' he concluded. He had friendly brown eyes and a quiet rumbling voice that she found pleasing, an art teacher probably, the splashes of paint on his corded trousers giving him away.

Olivia cast her eyes down at the swinging girl and shyly smiled in agreement. 'Which is more than can be said for the rest of this stuff,' sweeping an arm vaguely around the room. 'Actually, it's probably the only good thing here,' trying to sound knowledgeable.

'You reckon?' He tilted his head slightly the other way, both eyebrows lifting a notch, with a quizzical smile and perhaps some laughter in his eyes. A name label swung around his neck on a blue lanyard but she was unable to read it.

'Do you know the artist?' she asked, looking blank, Sarah having taken their only programme.

'No, not really. Have you been in the far gallery, through the archway?' He half turned and pointed behind him. 'You might enjoy those.'

'No, I hadn't got that far.' Olivia was in two minds, about slipping away when she had found Sarah or staying to chat to this man in his crumpled tweeds, who was already turning away from "The Girl on the Swing" and engaging with other people around him. Now she felt obliged to explore the rest of the gallery.

'See what you think of those,' Olivia heard him call as she drifted towards the back, raising a gloved hand over her shoulder in a sort of acknowledgement. She jostled with the crowd into the last gallery and found herself standing next to Sarah and the man in the leather jacket. They said 'hi' and craned their necks, stretching on tiptoe to get a view at whatever seemed to be grabbing so much attention.

She was immediately stopped in her tracks, her jaw dropping open and her eyes widening, as she recognised the style, remembering the pictures in the gallery in Camden the year before. Drawn in, she elbowed her way closer. These canvases were large and busy with detail, bursting with life, with stories to tell, just like those others. Bright acrylics and oils, no static still-lifes or abstracts here but dramatic events: battles, weather storms, marching crowds, police forces. Full of tension and fury, violence and noise, with that unique tactile quality she had grasped before. The sheer vividness of the images spoke volumes of the talent behind them, stamping these pictures with a style that could only have meant one artist, Mr Hugo Pitsakis and she almost squealed with delight on seeing his name in print on a white card stuck to the adjacent wall. She wanted to tell people with pride that she knew the artist and had actually discovered him last year.

Sucked into the imagery as if by some magic attraction, Olivia completely lost her sense of awareness of everything around her. The characters seemed so real, with expressions of pleasure, triumph, jealousy, fear and panic. In one picture, a white horse and uniformed rider, both wet with perspiration, their faces etched with effort and fear with nostrils flared, were leaping out of the canvas over the heads of a crouching group of soldiers, hooves dirtied by mud and blood, with dust kicked up around them, the movement of the story captured in glorious colours. Olivia stood transfixed, tempted to duck, to save being kicked in the head.

The centrepiece was the most stunning of all. A huge portmanteau of impending disaster, as a tsunami wave from a vast ocean stretching as far as the eye could see rose hundreds of feet above a shoreline, dwarfing a city built for modern times along the beaches with its concrete and glass, its highways and skyscrapers. Already lorries, coaches and several cars were swirling chaotically within the on-rushing wall of seawater, its mountainous crest bubbling with white frothing surf just tipping over, curling in, while at its base, the water seemed to be sucking back under itself, revealing all manner of everyday human activity awaiting unaware its fate, the entire scene about to be swept away within a moment. The tension was unbearable; the longer you looked the more convinced you became that the massive wave of water was alive, edging ever closer, about to thunder down on the innocents below. The audience could hardly keep watching the scene, knowing what was about to take place, but at the same time trapped in the drama and wonder of the spectacle.

Olivia blinked several times and moved backwards to lessen the tension. She noticed a small round sticker in brilliant orange at a corner of two of the paintings, but there was no price attached. She turned to another smaller, calmer work, a delicious portrait of a woman, caught in private intimate pose, yet warm and non-intrusive. The same beautiful model she remembered from the Camden exhibition, judging by her wholesomeness. The audience was watching her, rising from a double bed, stretching upwards towards the ceiling, her lithe body poised, balanced, rust-coloured hair swept back from her brilliant face. There was passion and desire in her movement, her brows arched and lips parted. Shards of daylight from above glinted across her hair, the tops of her shoulders, the convexity of a breast, the ridge of a strong thigh, and illuminated the middle of the dishevelled bed, surely the scene of recent coupling. A simple image of a mature woman, in perfect shape, unashamedly exposed, glorying in her recent triumph without a hint of embarrassment, and immaculately represented, painstakingly real in her longing and affection. Entitled simply "Sam". The artist, Hugo Pitsakis.

Olivia stayed, fascinated and absorbed, uncertain of the time passing. But then she went in search of the artist, working her way back towards the front entrance, determined this time to find him, talk with him and to share her feelings with him. By now most people had left, including Sarah, a few stragglers milling around the glass doors wishing farewells, buttoning up thick coats before braving the wintery conditions outside. There was a group of young people standing together in casual dress and one, the dark swarthy-chinned man she had spoken to earlier over "The Girl on the Swing" sculpture, was in the middle of them, shaking hands, thanking people for coming, wishing good night and seasons' greetings. Suddenly it dawned on her that that was him, the man she had inadvertently insulted earlier with her clever comments.

Someone called him Hugo. She was determined to talk to him properly this time and to apologise. She hovered close by to catch his eye. Blessed with those deep brown eyes and good teeth, he seemed male model material without being pretty, square-jawed with the right amount of bristle and muscle, a hunk in a baggy polo-neck and those brown leather brogues and paint-splashed corduroys adding a nice bohemian touch. When he noticed her, he stepped forward, blotting the others out, almost shouldering them aside as he focused his attention solely onto her, like a spotlight. Quite tall and broad, he loomed in front of her, making her feel small by comparison. 'Well, what did you think?'

'Fantastic,' she stammered, trying not to stare at his sensuous lips and teasing smile, and thinking that he was in need of a haircut. Looking back, should she have sensed the dangers then, backed away, realising what she might be getting into? The trouble was when he spotted her coming his way, his face visibly brightened, and he took her hands in his own with such warmth and gentleness and he spoke with that rumbling voice that felt so welcoming, it was as if she had lost all strength to resist. She was hooked.

**

Olivia is home, exhausted by her afternoon shopping and flopped in an armchair, with the TV playing and a couple of DVDs in her hand, undecided: *Breaking Bad* season three or *Grey's Anatomy* season ten. On the floor around her, her purchases flowing from their New Bond Street bags. A successful trip, satisfying and expensive. She savours the tops and the dresses and a trouser suit and three pairs of shoes, all tried on and fitting. She muses over her ideas for possible accompanying make-up and appearance for each outfit, in particular, her flirtatious self in the tight purple velour with bareback and deep cleavage for her next date.

She has a simple supper, an omelette with smoked salmon and a glass of Corbieres. Another glass half-empty sits beside her computer as she does a rapid edit of an article explaining what effects a first rise in bank interest rates may have on the overall UK economy. But her concentration wavers, recalling all too easily episodes of her life during her "Hugo era", as she now calls it. The possibility that she might have played it differently keeps haunting her, even though she was only twenty-three and so impressionable at the time. Things might have turned out better. For both of them.

**

'Hello again. I'm Hugo. So, you enjoyed them?'

Olivia felt stupidly speechless for a moment, uncertain his was a statement or a question, and pulled her hands away, holding them up to her open mouth. 'Those paintings…' she stumbled, 'are fabulous, fantastic.' Hugo seemed pleased, she noted. His hands were large, and she pictured him scrubbing vigorously with carbolic to get them acceptably clean before turning out for the occasion. She had to double check that she was truly talking to the artist, the creator of those powerful, erotic pictures. That one man was capable of exhibiting such passion she found extraordinary and it aroused a sense of longing within her. She felt like a schoolgirl on her first date, her voice dry and body shimmering with nerves, her heartbeat racing. 'I am so impressed. Did you, I mean, really paint all those?' she smiled with a crinkle in her nose.

'Yes, your humble servant.' He seemed relaxed and made easy eye contact, holding her gaze for a few moments. Was he serious or amused, happy to hear her compliments, although he must have been basking in acclamation all week? She looked away, he retreated, others butted in. The moment seemed to have passed, lights were being switched off around the gallery, people calling, making arrangements. A scrappily dressed group stood together for comfort just inside the front glass doors, preparing to depart into the chilly night, as security stood waiting. 'I'm Olivia, by the way,' she called across towards his back, but he did not appear to have heard.

Just as she was about to slip out through the exit herself, she felt a hand on her arm and his unmistakable voice. 'Olivia, look,' he was saying, 'we've done for the night, it's our last night, it's New Year's Eve – so we are going around to a Greek restaurant at the back here, why don't you come along. I'll tell you about the paintings.'

Olivia's young heart tripped up for an instant and she decorously nodded her agreement without thinking, thanking him profusely. Just as quickly she was surrounded by half a dozen lively people, artists and assorted friends, she presumed, perfunctory introductions offered and soon forgotten. A broad woman in a huge duffel coat and woolly hat, whose name she missed, put her arm through hers and pleasantly whisked her outside onto the cold pavement, and, as they jostled along shoulder to shoulder up Brick Lane, leading the trailing party, she chatted about the group and the exhibition and the genius of Hugo Pitsakis, all the way to the restaurant in Brushfield Street. There they crowded in, all of them squeezed together around a line of tables.

Recalling the rest of that evening with any detail was tricky. Drunk with the excitement of being with go-getting trendy sorts and tipsy from the wine that flowed, sitting enthralled under a mural of Mykonos, Olivia was struck by the apparent free-and-easy way of their lives, their struggles and bourgeois tales of fun and debauchery. She could remember no one else in that company with anything like the clarity that she could picture Hugo, a larger than life character who took centre stage opposite her to entertain with his stories and explanations. He disclosed the driving forces behind his paintings, his ideas for further work, the commissions that were coming in and his grand plans for a commercial project that would take London by storm; he talked grandly about establishing a new painting academy that would redefine the meaning of art. He wanted contemporary media to express social and political issues, to communicate with a working audience, reflecting real people's everyday concerns. The establishment was terrified, he said, salivating at the mouth as he downed another glass of red wine, that he would be able to popularise his work, canvas it in front of the public and make enough money to challenge their centuries' long rule. He spoke perfect English without accent with a rumbling laugh like rolling thunder, but when he sang in a wobbly baritone in response to the stirring folk songs played in the background, his words were Greek, his accent pure and everyone in the restaurant joined in.

Olivia was taken in by Hugo's plentiful schemes and enthusiasm, listening attentively and asking supportive questions from time to time, always impressed by the earnestness of his vision: here was a man who knew his mind, knew where he wanted to go and how to get there, and she admired that sort of certainty in anybody. Whereas she was reluctant to share with others her own ideas and ambitions at the best of times, for fear of ridicule.

Hugo was generously courteous throughout, enjoying the adulation his followers obviously showed him, although he did not particularly seek it out, while they all hung onto his every word. Sitting at the far end of the table was the glamorous beauty with the auburn hair and classic bone structure, whom Olivia repeatedly glanced at in sheer admiration, recognising Hugo's loving muse and model, the divine Samantha. With her dazzling smile and cruel eyebrows, she had the exotic allure of a Cossack warrior queen. Her influence within the group was obvious and she would be quite unable to blend inconspicuously into any background, Olivia imagined. Hugo did not appear to speak directly with her during the course of the evening, but she could still sense something between them. Everybody around that table was the most talented, interesting, intelligent and attractive in London, but their faces and their stories were just merged into a noisy blur of friendly chatter and laughter and drunken silliness, outdone in every respect by the mighty Hugo, the central star.

He was keen that she stayed with him as they sought taxis outside to take them all to Trafalgar Square for midnight. Hugo was having fun, encouraging Olivia to snuggle up to him, both engulfed in their fur-lined coats, with others crammed in the back of a cab, laughing along together. They were all so friendly with a lot of hugging and handholding as they stumbled through the crowds filling the Square.

The air was freezing; the sky was black and translucent with millions of twinkling stars. Close to midnight, spotlights played over the crowds and sometimes they were caught in the white beams and for an instant everything was as bright as day. 'We're going to lose your friends, Hugo, among all these people,' she shouted into his ear above the noise of the chaotic rejoicing. Revellers sang and shouted, drank beer and jumped into the fountains or screamed at the fireworks exploding over the Thames and the massive Government buildings. A little drunk as they danced around, they managed to avoid a soaking. Shortly after everyone had stopped to sing the countdown, Hugo urged Olivia away with him, as he was bored and tired and wanted to talk to her alone. She remembers feeling elated and unaware of the icy conditions as they drifted away from the milling crowds along Northumberland Avenue and crossed over the Thames on the Hungerford Bridge.

'So, is this what you normally do on New Year's Eve, Hugo?'

'No, first time, actually.' They stopped walking at the end of the bridge sobered by the thrashing cold wind that swirled along the river. They leant against the wire-mesh railing side by side to watch the shimmering lights playing over the water's surface below them. 'Last year,' he revealed, 'I took a girl from college to a dance club and we joined in and sang *Auld Lang Syne* very loudly; and then later we joined in with some warmer private activity of our own, which felt good at the time.' He smiled innocently and she punched him playfully in his chest. 'But I was young and optimistic in those days,' he rumbled on mournfully. 'What do you normally do?'

'Me, oh, New Year's Eve is most often spent at home, alone, watching a weepie with a cup of cocoa and a glass of brandy,' Olivia admitted with a giggle. 'It would be *Love Actually* this year, I suppose. Sometimes I go see my mother.'

He guided her gently toward him with an arm around her shoulders and their eyes kept a sparkling contact as they rubbed their cold noses together. Then they both jerked away with awkward looks. They set off down the metal stairs holding hands and worked their way along some shadowy back streets towards Waterloo Station. 'Have you had an interesting evening, I hope it hasn't been too boring?'

'Oh, gosh, it's been wonderful,' Olivia gushed. Despite the freezing winds whipping around them, Olivia was floating along on a high, buoyed by the warming effects of the alcohol and her throbbing heart, feeling the joy of his solid bulkiness next to her.

'Yes, there are limitations to New Year's Eve,' Hugo continued. 'Whatever you plan, you are always in for a disappointment, I find; particularly if it's romance you're looking for. It's better to have no expectations at all.' He gave Olivia his most nonchalant and suave look as if he was not thinking about how to bed her at that very moment. And she was uncertain whether to take his admission at face value or as a challenge. She tried to look intriguing on the other hand, a woman of experience who expected nothing and was happy to take life as it came, or to leave it, whatever.

'Surely it should be the night for lovers?' she teased, as they strolled along an unfamiliar narrow and poorly lit street of plain terraced houses on one side and dismal workplaces on the other. 'A regular high point, second only to the irksome Valentine's Day, surely?'

'Here we are,' and Hugo fumbled in his coat for keys, in front of wrought iron gates that he slid sideways to allow them into a bricked courtyard. 'New Year's Eve is the night when all your demons come home to roost. The failures and humiliations of the past year stare you in the face. It's when I am reminded how useless I am.' They crossed over towards a squat brick building with tall rectangular iron-framed windows with wire gratings and heavy double black doors, while Hugo continued in conversation without any explanation as to what she was to expect. He ushered her through into a cool space that felt like a warehouse in its bulk and she moved forward into the pitch darkness ahead of her. There was a strikingly pungent smell of paint and turpentine. She heard the door behind her close and suddenly the lights came on, bare bulbs around the walls and suspended from beamed rafters high above. She stood in wonder in a cavernous primitive bare brick-lined space, with a few dirty rugs thrown over a concrete floor, staring around at a jumble of canvases and boards leaning against the walls, easels and trestle tables along one side bending under the weight of stuff, bottles of brushes, paint pots and tubes and piles of paper.

She delighted in the experience, of being in the middle of the artist's workshop, with its characteristic odour, its half-finished paintings and drawings scattered around, dramatic bright works in progress, and smears of coloured paint on everything, the tables, the carpets, the floor, even the brick walls. At the back was a wrought iron staircase ascending steeply up to a sort of gallery running along one side, which overlooked the main ground floor from above.

Hugo had put on a genuinely gloomy face and stood still amongst the exhibits of his life. 'The suicide rate is always highest at this time of the year, you know.'

'Hugo, don't talk nonsense.' She started to pull her gloves off and hat and scarf and then her coat. 'You're just seeking compliments! That exhibition of yours, that was fantastic.' She wandered around among the paintings, like a child in a toy shop, eyes feasting on this one and then that one, not knowing where to look. She dumped her things onto a stool and returned to stand directly in front of Hugo, stationary in the middle of the room, staring up into his young unshaven face. 'What an achievement, like nothing anybody else could do. You must be so proud.' He was trying to look modest, a little hang-dog, with a shake of his head. She turned her attention to the toggles on his coat and helped him off with it. She was wondering whether Hugo might be too good to be true and was, in fact, incompetent with women, and that she might make him angry. And whether she was up for it. The coat dropped onto the floor. She raised herself on tiptoes, arching her back while he bent his neck down towards her. The cracked surfaces of their pouting lips were momentarily pressed together in a dry kiss. She searched the depths of his shadowy eyes, wanting to discover a message in them. They moved apart.

'And they will all sell, you'll make a fortune.' Olivia joked, Hugo laughed and soon they were running their cold hands around each other's waists, pressing themselves a bit closer for more warmth. She pulled at his jacket, he pulled at her jumper, as he lured her up the noisy metal stairs to the gallery above and into a makeshift bedroom, where an unmade king-size took up a central position, and they feverishly undressed themselves in the chill air, although before Hugo dived under the freezing unwashed sheets and blankets he strode stark naked across the room to switch on an electric radiator.

They became lovers through the night, their bodies greedily and repeatedly engaged in passionate coupling, and she was not disappointed. He was heavy and clumsy, his body covered in dark hairs; she was svelte and accommodating and perfectly smooth. He bombarded her lustily, his thrusting vigorous and sweaty, his groaning loud and explosive. She played a more passive role, grateful to be sharing his bed. He was good, he was insatiable, each performance completed with a flourish before throwing the sheets off so he could cool down more quickly, before curling himself around her into a silent pose of exhaustion. Olivia uncovered, shivered non-too satisfied but elated, just that this amazing man was sharing his intimacy with her, had filled her, was inside her. What it meant to him she had no idea, he did not express any feelings, then or ever.

They slept intermittently through what was left of the freezing night, their bodies close, and when they stirred late the next morning, with feeble wintery light dabbling through the drab nets, they held each other in a warming penetrative cuddle. She was desperate for a pee and some respite and carefully tucked him up lying on his stomach to drift into sleep once again; while she darted out to the adjacent bathroom, a damp confined space that had a clicking light-pull like the crack of a pistol, and where unaccountably she found several pairs of lacy knickers lined up along the edge of the bath to dry.

Wearing only an oversized man's shirt, hair a mess and no make-up, she fiddled about in his tiny kitchen, downstairs behind the workshop, looking to construct a late breakfast, wondering if she was embarrassed. Having sex with a man on her first date, that was not quite Olivia's style. Hugo sat wrapped in a woolly dressing gown and they had tea and toast and fried eggs together, as if the most natural thing in the world. She apologised for her appearance, but he seemed not to notice and resumed his meandering thoughts, while inhaling deeply on his Rothmans.

During the night, somewhere between fornication and oblivion, she remembered him rumbling on about his disappointments. 'What I really want to achieve,' he murmured, lifting himself up on an elbow and pulling the covers off her chest once again, tracing his fingers over her cooling breasts, as she twisted her sleepy face on the pillow towards him, 'is difficult to explain: to pursue a message, to reach out further to people, oh I don't know, something about the broader society. And awareness. And perfection,' he hummed, reaching down to stroke her furry fleece, like it was a small domesticated cat.

'You're sounding like a Conservative politician,' Olivia had remarked wearily, squeezing her thighs tight, realising that Hugo had never once asked her what she was doing in her life or whether she had ambitions.

Gobbling down his eggs and toast, slurping on his tea, he was just getting into his stride, it would seem. 'We live in a world of disillusion and creeping cynicism,' he complained. 'I mean the politicians, whatever party. We don't trust our governments and our institutions, like the army, the police, the newspapers, the BBC; we don't trust any of them anymore, not in the way we used to. The old order has let us down, the corruption. Politics is changing; young people want different things. We need more influence, artists, I mean, but our circle is so small and we are so powerless.' Hugo appeared genuinely torn by his ideas.

'But that hasn't changed, Hugo, it has always been thus. The millions of poor people dominated by the privileged few, the elite. You cannot change that, whatever you did, however good your paintings and whatever you promised.'

'There is so much pointlessness and hopelessness in the world. I want so much more; there must be more.'

'Hugo, you cannot take on all the burdens of the world. You're a painter, an artist, you show people beauty and emotion and powerful stories, that's your talent. A fantastic talent.' She reached for his hands across the table and squeezed them generously, which rather surprised her, that she would show him her feelings in that way, so soon.

Hugo said he had some people to meet at another studio and Olivia remembered she was visiting her parents that afternoon and needed to get home to change into fresh clothes. So, they left all the dishes and the bed unmade and exchanged telephone numbers and parted soon after midday, wishing each other, with a firm hug and a lingering dry kiss, a happy and prosperous 2006.

***

Hidden in the back of a wardrobe, she finds the dusty unframed canvas that she has not looked at it since she moved in. She had forgotten about it, until all this recent kerfuffle. It is twenty-five square inches, just on its stretchers, and she replaces a photo print of the London skyline hanging in the hallway with it, the only portrait of her he ever did. She steps back to admire it, a head-and-shoulders view drawn in soft lead with only a light colourwash and minimal detailing picked out in subtle oils, quite restrained really. She had not sat for him specifically, but he had sketched it over a period of a few weeks while she was there, doing other things. It catches her beguiling look at the time, a young woman biting her lower lip in bewilderment, some loose strands of blonde hair blown across her face, with those bright blue eyes focused on the viewer from under soft brows, and if the truth be known, she thinks it is rather good. The skin tones are delicate, the eyes have a sparkle, and although it was never quite finished, she was touched at the time when he presented it to her on her birthday, that March. She cried, actually, but failed to see where the two of them were heading.

- You see, I was hooked from the start, blinded by him, by his strength of character, his charisma, his lust, I admit it. I was blinded by his genius and hunky manliness; I came to worship him, like every other woman that met him before me, and after me, I dare say.

What could more effectively turn a girl's head, but an artist with magic in his fingertips and mystery in his brush strokes? Any girl would have responded the same way to his brilliance, his intense conviction and unfailing honesty, his vulnerabilities, his rumbling voice with its hypnotic quality, and the chance to be captured on canvas, looking for exotic self-glorification. His love of the fairer sex was obvious, but he valued their inner beauty and saw them as sensitive living creatures to be admired and respected; objects of desire as well but presented as strong and purposeful. His images were not exploitations but celebrations of beauty and form, freely expressed in their abandonment and wonder at Nature's perfection; he explored their sexuality, capturing the passion and fantasy of their lives. His versions were as much the truth as the spoken word or photographic record. His "Sams" were authentic sequences of her natural womanhood revealed in all its buxom glory.

***

Through the early months of that year, Olivia came to know Hugo better and she thought she came to love him, although she had not found it easy. His was a complex character: devoted to his draughtsmanship and painting, with his continual search for improvement, there would be provocative outbursts of unconstrained energy, when nothing would ultimately distract him, not leisure time, nor visitors, not a bomb exploding in London and it appeared certainly not the love of a woman. He would be gripped vice-like, locked in his studio in Theed Street sometimes for days on end, with history and art books as reference, helpers and models at his beck and call, obsessed with achieving the right colour or texture, or correct line of costume or angle of body poise. His pictures told stories, of rebel actions in the desert, soldiers in full cry in blood-stained uniforms, retreating street protestors in colourful disorder caught in chaotic movement, of post-tsunami destruction across once idyllic beaches. Hugo would lose himself in his own world, his rooms strewn with drawings and sketches, half-finished paintings, pots, bursting tubes of paint and unwashed brushes, the disorganisation overwhelming to any normal social life. Boards and canvases and old easels were leaning up against walls and cluttering the corridor to the kitchen, and even upstairs in the bedroom, she might find pots stuffed full of upturned brushes, old rags and bottles of opened turpentine and oil on window ledges. It was difficult to move around sometimes without stepping on wet paint or tripping over a wooden frame and Hugo would shout frantically to be careful.

Olivia can well recall that untidy bedroom, having spent plenty of nights occupying the massive bed, and she had washed and ironed the sheets more times than she cared to count. Lying on her back in the mornings bracing herself to get up at the first sign of dawn, while Hugo slept solidly like an exhausted dog after his usual late-night stint, she would trace the lines of the cracks in the plaster ceiling, imagining having the place properly decorated, or promise herself to take down the cheap nets at the dirty windows sometime and replace them with something a bit more elegant. A Victorian wardrobe along one side was always bursting open and men's clothes were strewn about carelessly over the floor, the bed and chairs, shoes and boots discarded randomly anywhere, with the ever-present smell of turpentine and oils. There was a couch that was positioned across the end of the bed, facing an open area he called his lounge, where there was an old bulky television in one corner and stacks of DVDs and history books and encyclopaedias. The familiarity of their love nest, its curtains forever undrawn overlooking someone else's backyard, was little comfort to her now.

- You see, Hugo had a way of hooking you without actually touching you or proposing anything. It was no good thinking you might change all that, that he might wash his own sheets sometime.

Hugo seemed to sense a woman's desire. He never conceived of a woman not wanting him; but he played the innocent, the boyish looks intent on working his art. He nonchalantly managed to keep the circling brood at arm's length as far as anyone could see, while tempting them ever more. He was like a rock star with his groupies. And Olivia had joined them. When she and Hugo found time to be alone, he would pay her rapt attention. Once he had explored details of her life and career, which took some weeks of their being together, he became animatedly interested in the financial and business world. He came to realise he was dealing with someone intellectually his equal and showed her due respect. He never once asked her how much she earnt or whether she had money, this did not seem to interest him, but they would argue ferociously well into the night with a bottle of wine over vague philosophical points, the definition of true socialism or the function of capitalism.

Hugo regularly dismissed any notion of Olivia's investment banker friends having a sort of moral compass, an altruistic side. 'They just want to make money, period.' He became fascinated by the huge sums of money that were entrusted to some pretty ordinary people every day in the financial play areas of the City of London.

'Other people's money, note.' He liked to be provocative and would argue a case forcefully but with care, always leaving her to have the last word, or at least to make her feel as if her opinion had held sway.

For the four whole months Olivia was seeing Hugo, or more like chasing Hugo, a whirlwind that sometimes felt like chasing shadows, she imagined herself in competition and tried desperately not to make a fool of herself. Events and people seemed to take over much of Hugo's spare time. He liked to move among a crowd of assorted artistic types, theatrical eccentrics and performers; some were dancers, some were singers, actors and painters, some seemed to do nothing at all, while still appearing extremely talented and most of them drank too much, smoked or snorted too much and were outrageously promiscuous. This was his permissive society and he was seldom alone, there always seemed to be people wandering about the workshop, some homeless wannabe often to be found sprawled out on a mattress overnight on the studio floor, a floozy expecting to share his unmade bed above. There was a young photographer always creeping around with his long-focus lens pointing at everybody who decorated as much wall space as he could find with his enlarged prints. Eddy, she recalls, gay she thought.

Hugo was able to sail on, focused on his artistic projects and driven to succeed. Meanwhile, Olivia remained uncertain of his true feelings toward her and she dared not explore the depths. He never committed himself, not in so many words, unambiguously. At no point did Olivia actually move into his life, although she frequently shared his bed. An occasional article of her clothing might be found at his place, some make-up or a toothbrush, but you would not have found a discarded bra draped carelessly over a kitchen chair or a row of ladies' underwear drying on the side of the bath. There were few signs of feminisation in the predominantly male spaces of Hugo's life.

She never obtained a key to his Theed Street studio abode, as far as she could remember, her visits were always more by chance or invitation and she never really felt that she ever gained the exalted status of Hugo's partner, official or otherwise.

Of course, she remained in awe of Hugo's talent, how he could bring a reality to a flat canvas in a way that she had never thought possible. Just as she would never question his technique, she accepted wholeheartedly the company he kept. She expected the typical behaviour of an artiste: bad time-keeping, lack of social graces, excessive drinking and smoking. But Hugo seemed a man apart, with a superhuman drive for perfection. He was often unbearably difficult to live with. You might find him slumped in his studio in such an agony of despair and self-recrimination that rational conversation became impossible. He might wallow for days in a fog of dense gloom until his extraordinary willpower was able to impose its vision and his talents revealed themselves with a swagger, his creative juices flowing once again; culminating often in a display of trenchant copulation while basking in your adulation for the master craftsman that he was.

In many ways, he seemed to be entirely self-sufficient, not even needing to eat apparently for hours at a stretch. He drank modestly, except in celebration or during long sessions, when a bottle of wine was always open, and anything from Dvorjak to Crosby, Stills and Nash would blare out at high volume across the studio. He seldom drew figures from imagination but preferred to use models for constructing his action scenes, in mock-ups of background, costume and make-up, to create the historical contexts and realistic settings.

Sometimes days would go by and she could not find time for them both to be together on their own. She knew he continued to see other women, although she was never sure how physical he was with them, and she was not prepared to challenge him. It was not just Sam; there were paintings of other models, nudes and private pictures scattered around the studio or in his collections, and so she knew he spent time with them, presumably alone. Was she hurt that he had not considered her as one of his subjects to sit for him? She never challenged him on that point, although promised herself that one day she would.

The truth, of course, was that neither of them was ready for the sort of commitment that would cement them together, that might drive a compromise that might alter the direction of their life ambitions: they both kept their own self-interests preserved and intact.

***

One weekend, lying on a trestle table in the studio she found a cheque for several thousand pounds made out to Mr Hugo Pitsakis and signed on behalf of the Whitechapel Gallery. 'Yes, I sold three of the paintings from the Christmas exhibition,' he explained, 'and then had to pay the gallery 12% commission. Don't forget income tax, etcetera.'

Relieved that he was getting paid, she had been wondering how he covered the costs of overheads and materials, especially with the frequent deliveries of paint and sketch blocks. She assumed that collectors and art lovers were buying his stuff, it was certainly good enough, although most of them were large pieces, five or six feet across and would not suit every home. She heard talk of commissions and teaching at adult evening classes at Camberwell Town Hall. Everyone knew how precarious the life of an artist could be for the majority, never sure where the next sale might come from. His other friends who were always loitering about the studio were all in that category, struggling to pull together enough to live on, although they all seemed able to top up their supplies of hash and alcohol whenever they wanted. Black market, she presumed. She might have bought one of his paintings herself if she had had the space to hang one or the spare money. But then, there was no need, if she was to spend time at his place, where they were on display all around her all the time and she could watch the master at work.

'I don't worry about things that like that. How bourgeois, I know,' Hugo would exclaim. 'I have people, Jake looks after the money side.' Jake Preston was his trusted friend from school, who acted as his advisor and helped him find the work. Olivia had met him, odd little man, a bit of a grafter with a facial twitch. There was an argument one day when Jake was trying to persuade Hugo to adopt a cartoon drawing style of political characters or recognisable celebrities, which Jake could then get reproduced onto greetings or birthday cards, a growing market that sold well. Hugo said they would be regarded as too commercial, a sell-out that would not be considered proper art by the connoisseurs or the academic institutions; the Royal Academy would reject him as a popular painter, an entertainer, commercial low brow, especially if he sold to the masses in bulk and made a fortune.

'Does that bother you?'

'Not really, just so early on in my fragile career, I might want the support of some of these institutions to help me; I don't want to antagonise them unnecessarily. Just keeping options open.'

Although there were times when Olivia had the urge to show off her charismatic artist partner and hero to the outside world, to reveal the modernist approach of their relationship, to admiring workmates and friends, she always showed restraint in the end and kept much of her life separate from his. There were odd occasions when he stayed at her West End Lane flat, but generally she was well used to waking there in an empty bed, and mostly enjoyed the benefits of morning preparation time unimpeded by a half-asleep boyfriend who needed her attention and organising abilities and would kick his heels and otherwise get in her way. However sometimes, just sometimes, when she was missing the reassuring pleasure of waking alongside a warm manly hunk that she wanted to wrap her arms around, for a moment of affection and intimacy before the day began, she wondered what it would take for her to immerse totally her life with his.

She used to stare through the dirty windows of his bedroom at the lilac blossom and yellow forsythia swaying in the breeze and spring sunshine in the enclosed patch below that was their neighbour's garden. It reminded her of her mother's colourful walled garden. The blossom made her think fresh thoughts and she began to rehearse on early morning tube journeys to Bank what she might say to Hugo if he ever asked her to move in with him, permanently. In practical terms, she would hesitate; in emotional terms, she was warming to the notion that Hugo might be the one to fill that gap in her life. But while waiting indefinitely for Hugo to make his move, she supposed she might meet someone else; she worried that one day Hugo might be immensely disappointed to find that he had missed his chance.

She was poignantly aware that if she wanted to share time and experiences with Hugo, she would need to put up with his style and his behaviour and accept him as he was. She was insidiously strengthening her position as time went on and had stopped feeling jealous of others who continued to be overfriendly towards him. At the same time, she was herself an ambitious woman who worked in a ferociously competitive male environment, where women were lucky to gain any sort of an edge. She needed strength and resolve to fulfil herself. She believed in self-determination and hard work, that her destiny and ultimate control of her life were in her own hands. She was not going to flop down and worship in front of Hugo, slotting into a position as his muse and concubine. No, Hugo was going to have to fight for his right to claim her as his own.

So, a reciprocal arrangement seemed to work well at first, whereby they persisted with their individual activities and kept up with their own circle of friends and family, while enthusiastically sharing what was left of each other. Each was allowed to maintain their own control and character without compromise, apparently without being challenged by the other.

It was not a scheme, however, destined to last for long. Especially once Olivia had been introduced to Dominic Lebelov, a brilliant but unpredictable Ukrainian ballet dancer, who succeeded somehow over a short period of time in disrupting everything she and Hugo had achieved.

2

Monday, January 19, 2015

The Monday 7.30am headlines meeting at Emerson Smith's, known as the Bill and Ben show, is presided over by William Spencer and Benjamin Hexler, blue-eyed boys from the top floor. It covers the previous week's trajectories, the early trading trends, and financial news and media items. Despite dubious attempts at humour and much rivalry, it is taken seriously by all and it runs over time. The terrorist attacks in Paris are on many people's minds; concerns over the slowing Chinese economy and potential property bubbles, especially in London, are earnestly expressed. Olivia speaks for two minutes on the last quarter performance of the European special opportunities fund and someone talks earnestly about the latest developments in the robotics industry. Other themes for the week are established and the assistants are allocated their research projects.

Olivia quietly stretches her aching limbs at her desk. Colleagues in shirt sleeves and red braces are studying their screens with headsets on, assistants are moving around the open office between rows with the post and messages, dropping papers or reports at various desks; phones are ringing, people chatting. She can see her boss behind the glass in the far corner in a one-to-one with Toby Warrington, whom she knows is desperate for promotion. They both started at the firm the same day, almost three years ago, and although she would wholeheartedly agree that he works so dedicatedly hard that he deserves to go far, she remains annoyed that he seems to be currying favour with the management team over her. Not that she has the time to worry about the likes of Toby right now. With a skinny latte on the table, she turns her attention to the seminar slides she has been preparing, while a jumble of other personal thoughts keeps bubbling up to the forefront of her agile mind.

First, she trawls through some of the day's newspapers that Robby, one of her junior office boys, has piled on her desk, to quickly catch up with the latest comments on last week's Earl's Court shooting. She keeps seeing black-and-white mug shots of Midge Martin, and in one it is set beside a picture of Hugo Pitsakis to show the similarity of their appearances, similar ages, both clean-shaven with unruly hair as if the police could be excused for making a simple mistake. The tone of the reporting seems to have taken a more forgiving stance over the police action. Martin was dangerous, had used a firearm in the past; the police were naturally jumpy, it was dull and drizzly on that late afternoon, so you could understand how mistakes happen. What Olivia has been struggling with, and none of the reports have addressed this, is what was Hugo Pitsakis doing in Midge Martin's Shepherd's Bush flat in the first place? Was there a connection between Hugo and this Martin, a known violent man, who had already attempted to murder a police officer? Hugo had been with two young women described generously as dancers, but one of the red-tops in front of her is clearly delighted to reveal that these two were dancers of a particular kind.

Serbian Stripper Girl-Friend Confesses All

was the headline, after one of their reporters had managed an exclusive interview with Veronica Secola, visiting her friend with the shoulder wound, in the recovery ward at Chelsea and Westminster Hospital. Veronica (who liked to be called Nika) and Lilly were models and posed as pinups for men's magazines. They worked regularly at a topless nightclub in the East End, where clients were coerced into pushing folded twenty-pound notes under the elastic of their suspenders, the report said. Hugo Pitsakis was in the flat to paint their portraits and had spent the night with them. They were giving him a lift in their car when all hell was let loose. Nika had been terrified and screamed a lot but managed to scramble free without being hurt. Her car was a mess and it had been taken away and she did not know whether the insurance would cover her for a new one and what the police were going to do about it. She said she had not seen Mr Martin for weeks, he was away travelling. 'Mr Pitsakis very sweet man and lucky to be alive, after the vicious scum police shot him through with lots of bullets, again and again.' Hardly a confession, but it was exclusive.

What was Hugo doing, mixing with these sorts of people? What was he doing in their flat, overnight? Searching for authenticity, she imagines, whilst thinking the worst. She studies the photographs again, unconvinced that Martin looks anything like the Hugo she remembers: Martin with his lighter brown hair and Hugo's so obviously black. Could they not have seen that Hugo was not the man they were after? Olivia is still struggling to understand how the mistake could have been made. But nevertheless, it was and Hugo is suffering and is still critically ill.

Hugo used to speak so proudly of his Greek origins and his love for his father; and how he had adopted his new country with enthusiasm, how he loved London, where he had been schooled and had lived most of his life. Wonder how he feels now. Wonder if he is even conscious.

He had shown her over his friend's houseboat once, on the Limehouse waterways where he had lived as an art student with Gareth something. Gareth was a funny bloke, loyal to Hugo, intense when it came to social issues. He used to scream vitriol at the local council action over waterway rights. She remembers him grilling a fresh carp in tin foil over hot coals that they consumed outside on the deck, watched by amused passers-by walking their dogs or cycling the towpath. A few weeks later Hugo had produced a stunning picture in oils of the whole scene using blissful colours: shapely barges moored in rows, a boat ploughing sedately through reflected light, green algae-covered waters, an oasis of late evening calm; the familiar modern skyline rising in the distance against fading vermilion streaks across a translucent powder blue sky; a thin plume of smoke veering skywards from the well grilled carp.

Olivia is supervising the first seminar slot after the tea break, in the grand London Chamber rooms in Queen Street. She is faced with a room full of earnest post-graduates in economics and politics, all keen to be the next generation of wealthy investment bankers.

'Just because we have a new Governor of the Bank of England, Mr Mark Carney, do not for a moment think that we are going to hear any more of the truth about the British economy or its implications for society than we ever have been told before.' Olivia speaks with confidence and clarity, that's always rule number one. She needs to sound intelligent but with just a hint of scepticism, indicating that she is on the same side as her audience, just a bit further advanced in her fledgling career. She has moved around from behind the desk to be closer, more friendly. She has tried to appear relaxed, in a conservative navy blue dress and matching sensible shoes, unfazed by the overwhelming male presence; lipstick a restrained matt carmine, every blonde hair perfectly in place.

There are twenty of them, all excited by the enriched possibilities of City life, having sat through talks from Treasury officials and professors of economics all day. They have just heard from a Bank of England official about its commercial role in business, so it is not surprising that they are wilting just a touch in the warm atmosphere and at this late hour. Olivia wants to give them something lighter to think about and maybe achieve some rapport before the afternoon concludes.

'The new man may look like George Clooney and speak with an endearing North American accent, but believe me, he will be spinning his yarns as all have done before. Politics rules, remember.' She sees a few heads nodding, a few faces creasing with smiles of acknowledgement. 'Britain's future stability is intricately linked with its economic progress, but there are many unpalatable truths that we will not be told about with the unveiling of a new BoE strategy. The 2015 election campaign has already begun.' She pauses smoothly, well versed in the subject matter.

'First, interest rates of 0.5% are an aberration, they have never been this low for any length of time in four hundred years. At some point, they will rise. Second, the British Government is hopelessly in debt, with the biggest current account deficit in the developed world. It has promised us a range of benefits, from pensions, healthcare, education, even support now for buying our house. But it will not be able to deliver on any of these promises; it simply will not have the money. For two decades, Britain has consumed far more than it has produced, and we continue to do so, despite the credit crunch, austerity, dire warnings from Greece and Cyprus. This kind of behaviour is not sustainable. There will have to be a fall in the value of sterling.'

Olivia had written about the risks to the value of the pound and the dangers of allowing inflation to help Government meet its debt burden in her monthly column in the magazine, *Money Made Simple*. She is not expecting any of them to have read the piece, but she has brought a printed handout for them which explains it all, and she distributes it along the rows.

'Thirdly, and this is definitely something Mr Carney will not be mentioning. The recent growth in our economy has been based on debt, almost wholly, and lots of it. The only real source of growth nationally comes through productivity, but there has been scant evidence of that over twenty years. The result is that we, you and I and all our loved ones, will have to work harder and for longer, and save more and spend less for decades to come.'

A sharp young Asian-born man in the front row, one of the few still looking fresh, raises his hand and looks at Olivia with keen deep-set eyes. She turns towards him with a simple smile, 'Yes?'

'Surely the coalition government has set in train measures to do just that, to spend less taxpayers' money and rake in more with higher taxation?' This interjection alerts some of the others and there is a general murmuring and shifting in the chairs, especially in the front row, where they all start sitting up a little straighter.

Olivia is standing not far away and delivers a slow blink before replying. 'Austerity, you mean? What austerity? The UK State is bigger now as a proportion of GDP than it was in Denis Healey's time in the mid-1970s. It costs the UK forty-three billion pounds' sterling a year just to service its debt (despite our historically low interest rates) and we have those debts because there is a ceiling on the level of tax receipts that the Government manages to take at around 35–36% of GDP. It does not matter what level of income tax it sets, top rate of 50% whatever, the proportion of tax take always remains about the same. But spending averages out per year at more like 42% (and is relentlessly drifting upwards year after year). We have to borrow that 6 or 7% difference of GDP every year, and so the bill keeps on getting bigger. We never pay off the debt itself, just keep feeding the interest demands.' She looks at the questioner, leaning a little forward, 'how much were those debt repayments again?' just to see if he has been following her argument.

'Forty-three billion pounds, in the last year,' a girl sitting next to the Asian boy interjects, almost under her breath.

'Precisely. And there is no socially democratic system in the world where that is sustainable. The basic numbers just do not add up. We need economic growth to help the deficit and reduce the borrowing requirement – but economic growth begins with investment and ends with consumer spending. Not the other way around. Policy makers are confused on this point: governments all over are trying to conjure up consumer spending without the investment, which simply encourages more debt. So, no surprise that we have low economic growth rates. This Government, as so many before it, is desperate for a little bit of inflation to reduce the value of the debt; and in the meantime, it continues to put off for another generation the difficult decisions about reshaping the economy. The reason – politics and the next general election only four months away.'

She stretches herself upright and starts a slow walk along the front line, looking over their heads at the people sitting attentively behind. At least no one seems to have actually fallen asleep. 'No party in office has won an election on the back of falling real wages, and the average real wages across the country are set to fall 10% by the end of this Parliament – so Ed Miliband is to be our next prime minister.' She looks glumly at the audience and generally gets a slow nodding reaction with frowns across their faces.

'OK, we don't want to stray too far away from our subject. Just to say that we have a problem with Miliband at Emerson Smith's, which is that he is practising third-world politics: capping prices. The UK has some of the cheapest energy prices in Europe, but that didn't stop Miliband displaying his socialist dogma with plans for price controls, and price controls always cut supply. Price freezing is a stunt – just like the coalition's Help to Buy policy in housing, which is equally crude. Capital investment is what is wanted, but it is pitifully low.'

One of the other girls in the room mutters from the back, 'it won't build more houses and builders will want to keep the price of housing up, won't they?'

'Precisely. It's a populist move. As you all know, prices are set freely in a competitive open marketplace, which leads to the best allocation of resources: this is vital to prosperity. All parties look to control prices one way or another, by rigging the markets, but that always fails disastrously. Britain faces some extraordinarily tough social problems but none of them will be solved through price controls.'

Olivia encourages more comment from the students and the discussion goes on for a little while longer, but soon she has to cut them short as time runs out. She promises them next time she will talk about the broad questions of governance and how governments work to deal with some of society's burning and changing social problems.

Olivia leaves with her handbag over one shoulder, her coat pulled tight around her. She is feeling smug, the students' well-meant thanks ringing in her ears; some had even clapped. On her way out of the building gliding on the down escalator, she hears her name called from behind.

'Miss Truelove, sorry.'

She stops at the bottom and steps aside for others to pass. Feet together, she turns slightly towards a young man in a grey suit, open-necked white shirt, thick trimmed reddish beard. 'Hello.' Her voice is flat.

'Hi, I'm Edward,' and he is slightly out of breath. 'I am listening to you in the tutorial, it is excellent.' Olivia tries to place his accent.

Edward is fair-skinned with a broad face and a high forehead exaggerated by an early receding hairline. She remembers him from the seminar room, sitting almost unnoticed at the back, staring at her intently without taking his eyes off her, throughout the whole forty-five minutes. She found him a little creepy and wondered whether she had ever come across him before. Closer to, he does look vaguely familiar. From Eastern Europe, she decides.

She remains expressionless and suspicious. 'Yes, indeed.' She waits. People are streaming past them across the black-and-white marble tiled floor in their outdoor coats, hurrying to get through the glass exit doors.

'I think you were brilliant. I am wondering whether I can talk with you some more. About your ideas and things. Maybe I buy you coffee?' and he hesitates, with a raised arm pointing vaguely towards the exit. 'I'm on internship, Swiss Bank. Erm, I love your approach and just want to talk to you about how you made it and managed. It's so competitive and…'

'It's exciting, isn't it, but very hard work. You must be one of the clever ones. Anyway, I'm in a bit of a rush just now, sorry.' Olivia twists her wrist to catch sight of her watch in a gesture of being late. 'Maybe another time.' She smiles coolly and takes a step away to join the crowd. Edward is left standing mouth open, obviously hoping for more, watching Olivia's blonde hair bobbing as she moves through the open doors out onto Queen Street.

She joins the evening rush towards tube stations and taxi ranks, but cannot keep memories of Hugo away. Like a persistent gut ache, dull and relentless, there is a desire dragging at her. However reluctant she may be to admit to it, she has to justify it to herself and then cave in, as she knows she eventually will.

- All right, all right, I know, I admit it. It's overwhelming. I must go see this man, this Hugo. It has been a long time since we last spoke. I have not even thought about him for years. But I just need to verify that it is the Hugo I knew and that he is recovering. Courtesy, that's all, common decency towards a person I once loved.

- And hated.

***

If she needs any justification for visiting Charing Cross Hospital, where the papers have said Hugo Pitsakis has been transferred, beyond a morbid curiosity, simple courtesy will have to do. She does not necessarily have to speak with him or hear his voice; she just wants to see that he is recovering. It is more an intellectual thing; her heartstrings remain untouched, she reassures herself.

On her way across town to Fulham, she has the day's paper with her and she has another look at the photograph of Hugo: taken goodness knows when, on a dark street with no lighting by the look of it, but it is Hugo, she has to admit. Dark unkempt hair, clean chin for once and a cynical expression on his full lips, cheap creased white shirt. There is also a picture she has not seen before, of the street scene, taken from quite a distance, again dark and shadowy, poorly focused, but there is a definite bundle of a man lying across the pavement by the Mini. There is a figure in a raincoat standing over him and others milling around in their yellow *Day-Glo* vests. Olivia can feel some of his pain for sure, violent and humiliating, a hell on earth for poor Hugo. What can

48

he be thinking, if he is able to think at all? Who was there to comfort him? Sam perhaps, the loyal and beautiful Samantha.

She enquires of a West Indian woman at the reception desk: ITU is on the fourth floor, near the main theatres. It is early evening, the corridors upstairs are quiet, near the end of visiting time. She notices a clutch of men in coats standing outside the entrance, talking with the bulky figure of a policeman, nobody taking any notice of her, edging closer. Someone in scrubs with an ID tag swinging around her neck emerges through a heavy door with glass panel and security locks, and Olivia slips easily through the slowly closing gap, wandering a little bemused along a corridor of offices, under dimmed overhead lighting: Doctor Shah, Doctor Patterson, Sister, bathroom, sluice, dry utility, all labelled on the doors, towards a more open area, equally subdued. A dozen beds evenly spaced are raised for the staff's convenience, most patients intubated, unresponsive, barely visible through the charts, the screens, the pumps, the monitors, the tubes and catheters; their identities obscured, each with three nurses detailed. The voices are hushed, the movements are quiet and deliberate, nurses with drip stands, young doctors in shirt sleeves checking data on their electronic pads, others at the main desk staring at computer screens or writing reports, heads down, shoulders hunched.

Olivia looks smart, professional, in a dark dress, matching shoes, leather bag over her shoulder, coat over an arm. Eyebrows slightly raised, 'Hugo Pitsakis?' she asks an oversized ward clerk at her own desk, who wrinkles her face without actually smiling. 'Came in over the weekend, I'm a work colleague?' Olivia continues to hold her sheepish expression of innocence in this other professional world.

The clerk calls in an undertone to a nurse half way down the ward, 'Cath, all right if this visitor sees number 4?'

Cath is a staff nurse with boyish hair and a sky blue uniform, run off her feet by the look of her and longing for the end of her shift. She is about to change a drip bottle at a bedside, but she nods across, consenting and directing at the same time the visitor wordlessly to the bed opposite. 'Fourth on the left there, dearie, can't stay long,' the clerk concludes, returning to her keyboard.

'Hope it's all right,' Olivia murmurs, darting a quick smile at Cath, who nods again. She approaches slowly and reads his name in big blue felt-tip on the whiteboard at the end of his bed. Standing anxiously, she peers through all the paraphernalia around an unrecognisable body slumped under rumpled white sheets, and she covers her mouth involuntarily with the shock of his appearance, her eyes frowning. Arms limp either side, his face and chest are exposed, with plastic tubes, feeding tubes, intravenous lines and sticky monitor leads running chaotically in all directions. There is a plastic mouth piece tied around his neck and connected via reinforced tubing to a ventilation machine at the side making sucking and blowing noises to a regular rhythm, two drip bags brooding together above, a dark urine bag hanging heavy at the side, while blood is transfusing drip by drip into the IV chamber that runs in a line in his neck. His nose and mouth are scabbed.

'How's he doing, generally, actually?' her voice hardly audible, hoping someone will come to her rescue.

'You can pull up a seat, if you like. He is sleeping the while; recovering from a long theatre session this afternoon,' the nurse reassures her from behind. 'Still some way to go.' And with that Cath moves on to the next lifeless bundle in the adjacent bed. Olivia subsides into a chair and shuffles it a little nearer the side of the bed; placing her hands on the frame which is raised so high that her own head is at the level of the mattress and Hugo's body, if indeed behind all the technology it is Hugo lying there. She cranes up at the motionless figure. She does barely recognise him, lips swollen, everted grotesquely around the wet mouthpiece, his head partially shaven, the hair greasy, the skin waxen and lifeless.

She sits clutching her bag on her lap for comfort, unprepared really for what she is seeing, uncertain what to do; indeed, now feeling unsure as to why she came in the first place, so soon. Poor Hugo, eyes closed and apparently unconscious, will not know she was here.

A young ward sister in navy blue passes the end of the bed, looking busy. Olivia half stands, imploring, as if she wants to ask a question.

'Sister Williams, can I help?' and she offers a hand to shake. She steps nearer, and Olivia notices her prematurely lined face.

'I'm Olivia Truelove, a close friend. I was desperately upset by the news, I was wondering how he was doing?'

Knowing the acute sensitivity of the circumstances and with a suitably grave expression on her face, the sister, still hanging onto Olivia's hand, draws her away from the bed, as if anything she says might be overheard by the unconscious seemingly lifeless man lying inert in bed number 4. 'You're not family?' She is shaking her head. 'No. He is very ill. He was in surgery yesterday, most of the day, and again this afternoon; he will be in ITU for some time.'

Olivia looks downcast. 'But he will...you know, make it, all right, will he, in the end?' She tries to clear her dry throat.

Sister puts on her seriously worried look, well-rehearsed over time, a little furrowing above her brows, a little narrowing of the eyelids, a twist of the thin mouth, head tilted a touch to one side and with such concern in her eyes. She places her other hand lightly on Olivia's forearm. 'He has had seven or eight bullets removed, has liver and lung injuries, skull and vertebral bone damage...you know, there was a great deal of blood loss. He was in a state of shock when he arrived; he's been through a lot, so we just have to wait and see. Day at a time, yes?'

A friendly smile is attempted. Olivia feels upset and not particularly relieved by what sounded like a preparation for the worst, a preliminary explanation as to cause of death.

She stays only a short while, sitting still amidst the sorrowful but somehow impressive environment, the care and devotion of the staff obvious to observe. She could hear her mother scolding her for getting involved in the first place, for not being stronger, an artist, what were you thinking? Her father had lain helpless in a hospital bed for days before he died; she had sat silently for hours at his side awaiting any response, with her mother in a state of dignified delusion: overly chatty and ridiculously cheerful on their way home each evening, she would prattle on about all the places she and her beloved were planning to visit and all the things they would do when he came home, right up to the fatal moment. That was her way of coping, but Olivia knew things were much more open these days, with family fully informed and involved throughout.

She wanders slowly away towards the entrance in a state of confusion, not knowing what was the right thing to do, shocked by the sight of so many sick people being kept alive by machines and clever medicine.

Along the corridor an elegant lady with striking hair in a red coat passes with purpose in her stride and walks directly through to bed 4, where Olivia can see her reaching for the inert hand and stroking the bare forearm, leaning forward over Hugo's face and murmuring to him. Olivia lingers momentarily at the exit to watch from her distance before realising exactly who the new visitor is.

Against all her practical reasoning, Olivia returns to the ITU daily over the week that followed, to be informed each time that Hugo remained desperately ill and that further surgery was planned to repair this damage or that damage; one day it was his liver, the next his bowel, or some other drainage procedure was required. His kidneys were "playing up", causing havoc to his electrolyte balance and he needed intravenous antibiotics and further blood transfusions. According to Jim Easton, an earnest young doctor in short sleeves and open shirt, a stethoscope around his neck, a particularly tricky procedure successfully removed a lodged fragment from deep within the liver earlier in the week, and he happily started to explain the technical details reaching for a pen and paper with a series of firm nods of his head, as if that is what she needed.

Olivia chooses evening times mostly when fewer people are about, usually just as visiting hour was ending around eight o'clock. She would hover outside the ITU entrance, waiting for staff members to come or go with their security badges passed over a sensor, and she would slip through sometimes chatting to a nurse she had come to recognise. Each visit she would be relieved to see Hugo still in the same bed, his appearance unchanged, until one evening another name was written on the board against bed 4 and it was definitely a woman's head that poked out from among all the tubing and equipment.

Olivia's heartbeat suddenly jumps with worry, wondering what has happened. 'He's been moved to an isolation room now, eleven, right at the end,' calls another nurse. Along the corridor, just as a nurse is leaving, she passes his door, which is closing slowly on delayed hinges, and in the space of those few seconds she catches a glimpse inside the room, of an unshaven ghost with an old man's face, lean and pasty, bare torso and shoulders, semi-propped up on pillows, looking vacantly across the room. His face seems a little less angry, the healing scabs drying across his nose. There is an oxygen line trailing across his chest dividing into two for his nostrils. He barely has any hair, his eyes are sunken and dark and with all the ravages of his assault and subsequent procedures to his body, she struggles to recognise the man at all.

He does not look her way. The door closes with a clunk and she retreats distraught, lacking the courage to approach his room and unable to face him. Olivia feels curiously cold, thinking about his pain and indignity, so forlorn, so fragile. Is this what a dying man looks like? What would she say to him: how are you, Hugo, trying to sound cheerful? How would she explain herself to him or anyone else, or suppose she bumps into Samantha?

It takes considerable determination for her to return to the hospital the next day. She chooses an earlier time in the afternoon when there is lots of distracting activity around the unit. Outside his door, Hugo, looking so haggard with his shaven head, is slumped on his back on a trolley with his eyes closed. A bundle of notes in a buff folder is balancing across his lap, his hands casually crossed over them. The ever-present drips are connected to his arm and right neck, the bags of clear liquid hanging from a pole attached at the end. A porter is collecting a rug to tuck around him.

She turns her back pretending to read a notice board as he passes behind her, the porter chatting away in cockney. She spots Nurse Cath at the desk and learns that Hugo is off to Radiology for another CT scan; he may need yet another operation to remove more lodged metal fragments in his vertebral column, close to the spinal cord, which seem to have been causing residual pain. But otherwise, he is making some positive progress, Cath confirms.

She notices the elegant Samantha in her red coat emerging from Hugo's room with a clutch of newspapers and she watches her approach. She remembers the face she first saw at Hugo's exhibition, even if she does look a tad older now. Sam walks and dresses with style, upright in small heels, shapely legs, rich auburn hair tumbling in waves to her shoulders. She seems broader and taller than Olivia remembers, and even with her coat on, belted and buttoned up, there is the hint of that healthy wholesomeness. She passes without looking Olivia's way, her mind obviously preoccupied, and engages in a hushed conversation with the nurses at the desk. She had been his muse and the images of intimacy and closeness in his pictures suggested they were lovers, at least until Olivia made her appearance and occupied his bed, when Sam became a more distant figure in whom Hugo appeared to lose interest. She had no idea what might have happened between the pair of them since, but obviously Sam is much in the picture now. She wonders whether she would remember her, without resentment.

On her next visit, Olivia is surprised to find an armed policeman standing outside Hugo's room. In black uniform, with bulging pouches around his waist, he wears a flat cap on his head with police in white letters across the front, just in case you had not noticed the truncheon in his belt or the dangling handcuffs or the holster ominously placed at a handy level on his right side. His legs slightly apart, his hands hanging loosely together in front of him, he looks steadily ahead, grim-faced and bored.

Olivia nearly panics, but the ward clerk comes up behind her and whispers breathlessly that a couple of detectives were here earlier and advised the police presence, just to be on the safe side, and Sister Williams agreed. All fairly routine, she reassures her. The lady in the red coat is not here just now, apparently she has gone downstairs to the cafeteria for some refreshments.

Olivia retreats to the ground floor herself and follows the signs to the Lavazza canteen, for Italy's finest coffee, and sees Sam in her familiar coat sitting with an elderly grey haired lady towards the back, with white coffee cups on the table in front of them.

It always seems strange to confront someone in real life you have only seen in pictures or on television, yet whom you almost feel you know and are inclined to call out "Hey". To view Sam's features at close range and in reality, so substantial and vital, is a joy to Olivia as she approaches with her tray. She looks as if she has stepped out of one of Hugo's great canvases. Even in the horrible light, the auburn hair is gleaming around her smooth complexion, with its minimal foundation. There is a look of tiredness about the eyes, her brows a little neglected, although the deeper shadows smeared underneath may be an effect of the harsh neon strips above. She has applied fresh lippy, a glossy crimson emphasising the scallop of her upper lip, but it is the width of her mouth that still so dominates her face.

The older woman sitting opposite Sam wears thick spectacles and by contrast is squat and rotund, with fatty flesh hanging around the angle of her jaw. She has a colourful silk scarf around her neck, and, despite the warmth from the kitchens, is still wrapped in a thick winter coat with fur collar. Sam is looking at Olivia without any recognition, waiting, head tilting to one side.

Olivia smiles nervously in return, appreciating the harmonious contrast between the emerald eyes and the red, in her lips, her dress and coat. 'Hello. You don't remember me. I'm Olivia.' She steps closer, lowering her tray onto the limited spare space at the table. 'An old friend of Hugo's. Well, not so old, ha. Knew him a while ago. May I?' and she places out her coffee and a plate of cellophane wrapped cookies, disposing of the tray on an adjacent empty table.

She proffers a hand, 'Olivia Truelove.' She looks first at the older woman, realising from her appearance that she must be Hugo's mother.

'Yes, of course, how rude of me, please join us,' returns Sam after a fractional pause. 'I think I have seen you before, a long time…? At a gallery, perhaps? This is Bernadette.' Sam's clear educated voice is thick like honey and without accent. She touches Olivia's hand and shuffles her chair a bit. 'I'm Samantha Little.'

'Sorry, to disturb you.' Olivia sits down between them. 'Bernadette, hello.' Bernadette glances back at her with a rather vacant expression, and Olivia wonders whether she understands English.

'Olivia, it has been a few years, hasn't it, yes,' Sam murmurs, looking at her with astonishment, probably just dawning on her who this blonde upstart is with all her old memories of that difficult time with Hugo flooding back uncomfortably.

Turning towards Sam, she notices faint freckles sprinkled over her nose and cheeks. She dares to ask, 'how is he, do you think?'

Some waves of wayward hair waft across her face, which she spreads aside with delicate hands. 'Oh, he's coming along, slowly. He sleeps a lot still, but they managed to get him up yesterday, walked a couple of paces.' Sam tries to sound reassuring and nods to emphasise the progress the patient four floors above them is making. All three women sip politely at their coffee cups.

After a pause and leaning a little forward, Olivia cannot resist in seriously revealing her bewilderment. 'I just don't see what it was all about, how did it happen, like this?' She fixes her gaze on Sam's lovely mouth but Sam says nothing, as a pained expression slowly forms across her face involving her eyes mostly. She looks carefully into Olivia's for a second, emerald green clashing with bright blue, before darting down to her hands wrapped around her coffee cup.

'It was a mistake. The police got it wrong. Well, it's a complicated story.' And she inhales deeply, elevating her glowing bosom which peeks over the front edge of her dress between the lapels of the red coat. 'Hugo was being driven home by a couple of his models, from a flat in Shepherds Bush. They were held up in traffic, and he decided he would walk down the Earl's Court Road to see his agent. As he got out of the front seat, the car was surrounded by men in plain clothes approaching with guns and shouting and they started blazing him with bullets for no reason. He was gunned down in the street in daylight and collapsed in the gutter. One of the girls in the car was also hit. They checked Hugo and decided he was the wrong man but alive. He was bundled into an ambulance eventually once it got through and whisked away to the Casualty at Westminster and Chelsea, down the road.' Restraining her obvious anger, Sam has clenched her teeth a little at the reciting of this sorry tale, which she must have gone over with others a dozen times. While Bernadette, slumped with her elbows on the table and broad chin resting on her podgy hands, continually shows her distress with twisted grimaces and brow knitting. Olivia finds some anger mounting within herself at the unjustness of it all.

'He had fifteen bullet wounds, entry and exit, and three bullets recovered from his body at the last count. In his chest and abdomen, one in the liver had just missed the hepatic artery, I mean he is so lucky to be alive,' Sam continues. 'He's had operations in theatre and other procedures, drainages, transfusions, most of the metal bits are out now, they think. It was a miracle none of them actually penetrated a major vessel or his spine. He was in theatre all afternoon, with the cardiothoracic surgeons and they removed a bullet from the muscle of his heart.' They both look aghast at the uncomfortable thoughts conjured by Sam's words, as she gesticulates with her hands to emphasise the confusion and mystery of it all.

'Another fragment has lodged in the vertebral muscles and bone at the back of his chest but has not gone through to his spine; I mean about two millimetres away apparently, anyway that's to be removed tomorrow, I think, I lose count of the days.' Sam lets her shoulders slump. She finishes her coffee and crunches delicately into a gingery biscuit that she does not want. At this close range, she does look weary, her lids heavy and cheeks a little slack.

'He lose so much blood, is terrible,' mutters Bernadette, who has a Mediterranean skin complexion like olive oil and an accent to match.

'Some of the procedures were just to close wounds and drain blood from the chest,' continues Sam, 'and then he had a kidney operation to repair some damage and a stent inserted – that will need to come out at some point. He is artificially fed at the moment. He is on IV antibiotics all the time. He recovers from one procedure and then they do another – but it just seems fantastic that he has survived at all.'

'A miracle,' murmurs Bernadette.

'He's had marvellous treatment here, that Sister Williams is wonderful.'

'Wonderful,' murmurs Bernadette, like a parrot.

'But they're all good, so caring and kindly,' Sam concludes.

'So kind.'

'Um, good, that's good. They do seem nice,' Olivia agrees. Silence follows for a while, as Sam and Olivia absorb the meaning behind the words, realising that they have been talking about someone dear to them both, not just relating a story from the newspapers. 'And the police guard on duty?'

Sam slowly turns to Olivia. 'Just a precaution, against some idiot or journalist trying to get near him, you know,' Sam explains.

'But why, what was it all about?' Olivia pleads again, creasing the skin tightly between her eyebrows while discreetly sweeping her tongue to clear away any residual biscuit crumbs sticking to her lips.

'A miracle,' murmurs Bernadette once again, this time shrugging with both hands outwards and palms upwards. Sam explains a conversation she had a day or two ago with a police inspector, who had talked to her while Hugo was in the theatre and had apologised and said it was all a case of mistaken identity. 'He was very embarrassed, as well he might be, he said they had staked out this girl's flat expecting a man called Martin (her ex-boyfriend) and they thought Hugo was him for some reason. When he got out of the car, they thought he was armed and was making a getaway. This man Midge Martin had already shot a policeman, had escaped from custody, was known for his violence and so they were not going to take any chances, but decided to take him out when they thought they saw him. But they got it wrong.' Olivia likes the quiet and syrupy sound of Sam's voice, somehow reassuring, but as she has been speaking, she has developed a fine tremor, shivering.

'Are you okay, are you cold?' Olivia asks in sympathy.

Sam shakes her head, her lips quivering. 'No. I'm just nervous, thinking about the sequence of events. Hugo's wounds. This horrid man, Martin. So pointless, the whole thing, as you say. If we believe the police,' she adds enigmatically. Her glowing irises have a way of turning to steely blue in moments of intensity and then of fading gently to the colour of soft bracken, enough to reduce any man to helplessness, Olivia imagines.

'And they were talking to Hugo earlier, were they? Just routine, the nurse said?'

'Well, he was sleepy, almost unresponsive, they got nothing out of him.'

'You must sue them, this is absolutely disgraceful. We can't have our police going about London willy-nilly shooting suspects. It's unbelievable.'

'Disgraceful,' mutters Bernadette under her breath.

'The Inspector said Hugo was wearing a long coat and a hat, so his features were disguised and that's why they mistook him. They took no chances.'

'Shoot first, ask questions later,' Olivia interjects, with genuine disgust.

Sam suddenly looks desperate, lines on her face appear with her anguish. 'You must remember Hugo, such a peaceful man. He would not harm anybody; he never hits out, I've never seen him angry. He stood up for the common man, the underdog. And now he's gunned down in the street, by the frigging police!' A faint blush has appeared on her smooth cheeks as she clenches her teeth again. 'Sorry, Bernadette.' She looks lost, uncertain how to explain things, not knowing how to accept the events that have happened to her man, to whom she is clearly devoted. She looks as if she wants to cry and Olivia feels uncomfortable for a moment.

'It's all right, my angel,' and motherly Bernadette reaches out with her crabby hand to grip Sam's forearm through her coat. 'He will get better. God, he makes sure,' she adds, her eyes momentarily flicking upwards to the ceiling, just in case God is watching.

3

Saturday, January 24, 2015

Some of Olivia's football-crazy workmates had been talking about the weekend Cup match and had asked her to Stamford Bridge but she had too much on her mind, preparing for the evening, worrying about what was to come. She preferred the afternoon alone rather than watching Bradford City among a seething crowd of boisterous Chelsea supporters. By way of explanation, she had lied that she had a family function to attend that could not be missed. So instead at midday, she finds herself trying to lie still in the altogether at her local spa off the Clerkenwell Road at the mercy of a small muscular beautician from Thailand.

The late morning has passed pleasantly enough with hot baths, mud slings, exfoliation with a sloughing mitten, massages and a manicure, and now she is trying to relax under a single sheet while much-needed depilatory work is attended to; the end is in sight, as it were, her legs baby-skin smooth, with just the torture of her nether regions to deal with.

'You have husband?' Nicole asks as she rips off a hot wax strip.

'Oooh,' Olivia gasps, 'sorry, no.'

'You have boyfriend?'

'No, not really.'

'How long no boyfriend?'

'About two years,' she replies doubtfully. Nicole, in white cotton top and navy slacks, looks sad, her thick eyebrows wriggling together as she applies more wax to Olivia's bikini line. Olivia reciprocates: 'do you have a boyfriend, Nicole?'

'I have husband,' she says with pride and a satisfied smile, in her mixed cockney Oriental accent.

'Lovely,' she yelps as another strip is yanked off.

'Arranged marriage, five years. Now I will have baby.'

'Oh, congratulations.'

'Now we bend knees, butterfly.' And Olivia dutifully bends her knees up and outwards, feet together. Nicole continues with the waxing.

'Christ,' as first one side, 'ouch,' then the other is stripped in turn. 'That's so painful!'

'And soon you have babies?' Nicole asks, surveying Olivia's bristle.

'No, I don't think so, thanks.' She gazes nonchalantly down towards her toes and then flops back onto the towelled bench. 'Just a trim, Nicole, I don't want the plucked chicken look all over, like a porn star.'

The work is completed with a neat electric trimmer. 'Is good, no?' showing Olivia the finished product in a hand mirror. Nicole giggles: 'You are ready for marriage and children now.' She was starting to sound like her mother.

'No, not yet, please. I value my freedom for a bit longer. Now would not be a good time.' Olivia cranes her neck to stare down at her tidy threadbare snatch. Swinging her legs off the couch, she pulls up her briefs at last, reaches for a hooped rugby shirt and tight skirt, before slipping into flat shoes. Nicole gives her last minute advice about aftercare and they exchange a friendly hug, agreeing to meet up again in a month or two. After about four hours, and feeling hungry, she is relieved to be leaving; she reaches for her credit card at reception.

Back home, she is pleased with her own foresight in avoiding attending the match, which Chelsea had unexpectedly lost, as her colleagues would have been unbearably gloomy in the pub afterwards.

As Olivia readies herself for her Saturday night out, she thinks about her promised visit tomorrow to see her poor mother; she would get her some flowers to cheer her up, and those spicy cashews and Italian cheese from the corner deli in Upper Street that she liked so much. She had better get some flowers for her father as well. She had a powerful image of Hugo backing away from her suggestion that she should introduce him to her parents, all those years ago, over tea on a Sunday afternoon. He found countless excuses, too soon in their relationship, pressure of his work. She can laugh now, realising it would have been a mistake, especially for her father who would have found Hugo's chosen lifestyle rather disturbing for his daughter, although she thinks her mother might have appreciated his maverick attractiveness.

***

At Tatania's, just off Neal's Yard, Olivia has arrived early, away from the City where people might recognise her, and is clutching her gin and tonic, sunk deeply among dark velour cushions in the subdued and hushed atmosphere of its cocktail bar. Her keen eyes dart from the gelled hunk behind the bar in white sleeves and mustard silk waistcoat, to the Philippine waitress in white lace and short black skirt, who has a red ribbon bouncing from her bob as she moves around with her silver tray; across to the glass entry doors which periodically swing open to admit young punters nipping in for a quick drink before conspicuously dashing off to their next date. Sharply dressed in rich velvet of plunging purple and a face made up for an unpardonably wicked night out, she glances down at her cleavage remembering the old adage that a little can go a long way, especially on a first date. The dress is tight, backless, sleeveless and short, leaving uncovered lots of sheer nylon leg of elegant shape from mid-thigh down to tapered ankles, drawing the watchful eye to her expensive pair of magenta suede strapped heels that match her clutch bag. There is not a blonde hair out of place. Her lashes are thick with mascara and the manicured nails, like her lips, are a deep rouge. A dual eyeshadow of silvered lilac and blood rose, combine with glittered orange highlight over her cheekbones to confer a look at once fabulous, inviting and quite out of character. A high-class consort you might think, but Olivia would be most upset if she gives that impression. It is more an expression of defiance, an overwhelming desire to act out a new role, to show confidence and of course to be unrecognisable.

This is not strictly their first date, as they had met last week, the night Hugo was shot, as it happens. It was a quiet introduction over drinks in a bar, around the corner from the Leisure Centre, where both of them, they discovered, had been fencing competitively for over a year without ever conversing. They shared small talk about city living and the cost of renting in London, and in hushed tones swapped gossip and frivolities about their likes and dislikes. With a slight flirtatiousness, they had warmed to each other. Olivia had returned to her flat after midnight with the taste of their fleeting kiss lingering across her lips and not really understanding where the whole evening had gone, feeling electrified. She knew they would meet again and would want to explore way beyond social pleasantries.

For a City employee of some years, Olivia is unusual. She has all the educational background you would expect, with certificates and degrees aplenty to cover the entrance walls of her smart apartment. She is bright and strong-willed, with bags of energy and possesses ambition equal to any of the boys in the firm. But most of all, despite the muted attempts to push for equality of opportunity among the overwhelming presence of a testosterone-dominated workforce, Olivia is that rare thing, female, and unmistakably female. Attractive too, if you like your beauty in perfect symmetry and doll-like clarity. But, as a few brave men have found, Olivia's confident demeanour hides a strong protective tendency, not to deceive necessarily, but to divert. Her courage so often fails her when she is preparing to take the honest route with another drooling utterly convinced lover and reveal the few skeletons she might keep hidden in her closet. Indeed, she has tussled with her conscience so often over the need to be honest with herself before she could ever be honest with a prospective life companion, that she has almost decided that she should remain forever single and private.

After all, a drive for perfection, engineered by a social-climbing mother and an obsessive bureaucratic father whom she once doted on, has all but made quiet self-satisfaction impossible even for a fleeting moment. There are ever more goals to reach, targets to achieve, new levels to surmount. Her mother had once been beautiful, her father had been brilliant; how was an only child expected to react, but through relentless and restless striving, which could ill afford distraction?

She sips at her glass, the ice clinks. All of a sudden, she panics about whether they will recognise each other; after all, a week is a long time. She closes her eyes to concentrate. Chinese Asian, smooth complexion, an open face, with an English education. Her stomach gives out a distant rumble as she remembers she has not eaten all day; she presses the flat of her hand firmly against tight abdominal muscles, sits more upright. And then all desire to burp is instantly forgotten with a sharp in-drawing of breath, as her eyes alight on the raven-haired classic Oriental in red stilettos veering easily towards her around the noisy crowd at the bar, like a predatory cat on the prowl.

She stops a stride away, towering in front of Olivia's seated figure, and drops a black coat across the next seat, revealing pressed black trousers and a white blouse nipped in at the waist. Simple and elegant and everything Olivia wants her to be. Black hair severely sweeping away from her shallow face, silky skin pure coffee cream, glossy almond eyes in shape and colour, a cute nose and so much more besides.

'Hello, Olivia.' Her small mouth smiles serenely, not wanting to crack the glossy lipstick, making immediate eye contact. She lowers her taut bottom gracefully with knees together onto Olivia's sofa. 'I'm so solly I'm a liddel late.' She flutters mascaraed upper lids, which exaggerate the narrow slits of her eyes. 'I was worried I would not recognise you. You look so stunning.' Her English matches her grace.

'Louise, hi.' Olivia's nervousness begins to fade at the sight and smell of the licentious beauty beside her.

Leaning across, Louise mimics a kiss on both cheeks in welcome, with a small gloved hand placed imperceptibly on Olivia's shoulder. Their knees bump together, without embarrassment.

'Thank you, you are too.' Olivia recognises the easy manner that she so admired. Instantly captured by the perfection that is Louise's countenance, she watches the way her lips ripple, creating a tiny dimple in one cheek. There is a scent like sweet magnolia.

'So kind.' Louise is poised and upright as she removes her leather gloves with deliberation, finger by finger, popping them both into the top of her handbag.

'I love this,' Olivia says, touching her blouse that has broad flowing sleeves, neatly buttoned cuffs and classic lace design lapels plunging vertically in front. A green gemstone hovers from a fragile silver necklace between the slopes of her breasts and silver hoop rings dangle from her earlobes.

The waitress comes quickly to her side to take her order for a vodka Martini, which Olivia thinks is cool. 'Have you had to come far?'

- Oh, come on, was that a question? You're not the bloody Queen.

Olivia needs to relax, to stop worrying about her own ability to deal with one so confident.

Louise discretely touches Olivia's thigh with her fingertips. 'No, just a short way, I took a cab; traffic slow, sorry.'

'No, no, I've only been here a few minutes myself. It's nice, fun people, coming and going. I've had such a busy week it really is lovely just being able to sit with a drink and not have to rush anywhere. Watching other people rush about.'

'And just be yourself. We relax, yes.' She is not requesting, it is Louise reassuring her. Now she places her fingertips along Olivia's bare forearm, like hands to a keyboard. 'I have busy day too, teaching kids, six/seven-year-olds; they are quite handful.' Her speech is so middle England, she could have been to public school, although Louise had told her that she was brought up in Hong Kong.

'Teaching Mandarin in Hampstead, you said?'

'Yes, you remember. The Hua Hsia School in Trinity Walk.'

After a while, the waitress returns with a tall glass, clinking pink with lime and lemon slices perched across the top, and places it on a coaster on a low table. Louise takes a few pristine sips by straw and asks secretly, 'Have you done this before, Olivia?'

'Erm…you mean gay bar dating?'

'Well, I mean lesbian dating,' and she tips her head slightly to one side with a coy look.

'No, not really, sort of experimental,' Olivia confesses, knowing there is no point in trying to behave as if she is a dab hand when she feels pretty sure that it will emerge later that she is obviously not.

After more conversation about nothing in particular, they both flop back into the cushions, barely able to take their eyes off each other. In contrast to Olivia's dramatically painted face, Louise is sophisticated by her simplicity: minimal foundation on a clear complexion and a light turquoise eyeliner, neat curly lips a glossy crimson. She keeps remarking how she loves Olivia's appearance, so classy, so come on, she breathes. And she continues with her light touch, a tickling fingertip running along Olivia's forearm, the fine hairs sensing the direction of travel putting her on alert stations. Olivia wants to close her eyes and dream but fixes Louise with a meaningful stare from under her brows.

'Do you mind?' Louise whispers.

Olivia doesn't and wants more.

Louise leans closer, imprinting her fingertips on Olivia's bare thigh for support, to whisper into her ear. 'I will teach you. Show you special senses, release of tensions. You will like.' Her warm breath rustles through strands of her hair, tickling Olivia's cheek. Olivia gawps down the front of Louise's blouse, wondering at the firmness of her bosoms nestling in their black silk cups.

'I want you to, show me; oh yes, I want you to.'

And so later, their drinks replenished, their senses honed, they drift away from all the gay people at the bar and in the lobby, to ascend smoothly to the fifth floor. The rented room is warm and the lighting subdued. All is lush, the dark walls, the thick carpet, the quilted double bedspread, the velvety lamp-shades. Olivia is wafted on a favourable gale of heightened nervousness and looks to her companion for guidance. Louise carefully balances on one stiletto as she bends so flexibly to undo the other, and steps down in her stockinged feet. She drops her trousers, flicking them over the back of an armchair. She carefully unbuttons her blouse, while Olivia kicks off her pumps, mesmerised. They face each other, Louise a touch taller, a little giggly, perhaps nervous too. She reaches up both hands to Olivia's face and as if cradling something precious she draws her closer, with a serious look of joy. 'You are so enticing, exotic, sexy,' she breathes. Olivia cannot help being infected by Louise's sense of pleasure. She slides her fingers around the other's tight waistline, feeling silk and cotton and warm flesh. They softly collide, pouting lips barely brush, a sticky peck so as not to smudge, and they move apart. Louise wants the curtains drawn, the lights off and their drinks to hand.

By the flickering light of a few candles placed on ledges, they peel their remaining garments off their own bodies, under each's watchful eye, velvet dress tossed aside, tights and underwear discarded, lacy piles at their feet on the thick carpet. Obedient and unflinching, Olivia stands stark, arms loose before her admirer, as she rotates saucily on her spot for inspection and Louise does the same. And then they fall into an embrace, slightly breathless, kissing and touching, not caring about smudging their lips, pressing warm plump breasts and firm bellies against each other. They edge towards the bed.

Louise whispers, 'I'm wet for you.'

Olivia whimpers. 'Come.'

With trembling anticipation, they slink over the crisp sheets and luxuriate in their deliberate discovery of their bodies, the shapes and the textures, the angles and the curving slopes. They each marvel at the shameless beauty of the other, their lustful eyes glazing over with pleasure, watching for the response. Using the pulps of her fingers like brushes, Louise expertly strokes Olivia's sensitive surfaces, her outer arms, her under breasts, her inner thighs and around her bottom. Using their tongues and lips, they lick and stroke and tickle, and they suck and smear, their vital senses bristling.

Louise has modest breasts that harden with Olivia's attention and her nipples are peach-red and velvety, in stark contrast with her untanned skin, as white as porcelain. A red and green dragon-design tattoo adorns Louise's side, that spreads over her loin, its long tail trailing down to her pubic hairline. Her belly button is shaped like a keyhole and has a tangy taste of salt on Olivia's tongue. Her smell is of fresh spring flowers.

Olivia smoulders beneath Louise's natural touch. They straddle their legs like open scissors, whilst grinding their moistened lady gardens together with repetitive toing and froing movements that rasp with rhythmic urgency. After some effort, they squeal uncontrollably and grab each other in a tight embrace, before lying back panting and hot. Olivia has never realised that such shared ecstasy was possible between women and remains eager for more as she floats through such unknown territory, still uncertain as to where exactly her true self resides.

'I have never done this before. I never knew how sensuous it could be. You are so expert, Louise. How long have you, you know, been involved like this?'

'Oh, I a bit mixed, I like a man sometime.' She chuckles wickedly. 'I have had both same time once, actually not so good. Boys always want it rough.' Louise carries on for a while and then lies on her back closely tucked up to Olivia. 'At work, I am straight woman. This is gay club but many are mixed now, sometimes a man is wanted, sometimes a woman; some like it fluid.' In her dreaminess, Olivia does not have a problem with any of that; she recognises the potential attractiveness. Quite how relationships develop if attachment begins, she is not sure; there are many things she needs to learn, obviously.

After a period of calm, Louise fetches from the bathroom several small glass bottles. Crouching, she drips a few oily scented drops across Olivia's belly and chest, which she then massages joyfully, encouraging further feelings of complete relaxation. 'The most sensational cosmetics in the world,' purrs Louise, 'extract of starfish, snail slime and sea-kelp.' She giggles outrageously and is soon working on Olivia, sending her into sleepy dreams. With more subtle finger circulation between her legs, she slowly brings Olivia to a frenzied contortion, spasms that tense her whole abdomen. It is like an out-of-body sensation to her, a free-fall of bliss, that she wants to last for ever. She moans a muffled scream and clings around Louise's neck, wanting to kiss her.

Olivia flops back again like a rag-doll, running her fingers through her hair, feeling damp perspiration over her forehead. Louise fetches a face flannel and wipes her lover's face with warm damp movements, refreshing her.

In the really small hours of Sunday morning on her way home in a black cab, she feels cold despite being wrapped inside her long coat, hiding the skinny purple evening dress underneath, and not wearing any underwear. She slips her shoes off and, clever girl, finds the plastic bag in a pocket to carry them in. She hops out at the Barbican in her bare feet and darts happily through the courtyards to her block, taking the stairs two at a time to the second floor.

Although she only slept intermittently, disturbed by the strangeness of everything in the bedroom, Louise's presence, her low breathing, her scented beauteous body, sensitive to her every movement, she feels remarkably awake. She keeps seeing Louise unreservedly naked and exposed, fetching drinks, a damp face-cloth, even some fruit to eat at one point. Olivia's mind is working so actively with uncontrolled thoughts running amok, she wonders whether her drink was spiked or something. Examining herself, her motivation, trying to place her emotions and desires in some sort of context, has become a major issue.

- So how come you like Louise so much, when you've never mentioned anything about this before? How did relaxation come so easily, the release of your inhibitions with such wanton abandon? Such private acts and emotion, Olivia; you've never done things like that with other men, have you?

- Well, not quite like that, she was exquisite.

Olivia strips off and slips into a warm shower stream, sluicing away with fresh gel all perspiration and residual scent of Louise. She lathers herself with gentle care. Is her sexuality so much of a mystery to her, has she really been hiding these tendencies all this time or is it just that she fancies Louise because she is so obviously attractive. A protest against all those soggy domineering men that have tried to bed her over the years.

- Just being fluid, in your sexual choices, then?

Out of the shower and drying, she acknowledges she cannot remember ever feeling attracted to any woman before. It is lust, pure and simple, a deeply physical thing, without commitment. Or is there something more from inside, with Olivia lonely and vulnerable? Is she about to transfer her desires and want sex with every woman she meets from now on? Gosh, what about all her girlfriends, are they fair game, or can she continue her usual relationship and friendliness with them, as they will expect? She doesn't fancy any of them, she is sure of that, but will she want to tell them that she enjoyed physical sex with a Chinese woman?

- I'm not really gay, I just fancy Louise. Okay. It will pass. I still want to be in a relationship with a man, sometime. Don't I?

- Don't be daft, you can't have both.

- Can't I?

***

On her way to Islington, her thoughts are bugged by the highs of falling in love with Louise's perfectly shaped body, and the dreadful lows of the Hugo Pitsakis saga, imagining his withering tortured one. She wonders where his extraordinary talent and strong personality had taken him and what he had achieved during the years since they were last together. She is convinced it is right for her to meet with him again, to talk with him face-to-face, to help him regain his belief, his confidence. Sam had referred to him as a peaceful, good man, fighting for the underdog, always looking for ways to help the needy. Olivia sympathised with those sentiments, seeing herself as a thoughtful and kindly person, especially to those less fortunate than herself.

She likes Samantha, is not afraid of her and would like to get to know her better. She is interesting in her own right, sensible, dignified, not just as Hugo's muse. Hugo must have tagged her along for years without ever committing himself to her and yet she had remained loyal, single and waiting, a rather tragic figure, considering the central role she must have played in his formative years. Olivia was not sure where she lived, or whether she was now living with Hugo. If Hugo has not realised by now how devoted to him Sam was and that she loved him, well, someone ought to tell him straight; it was about time he did the right thing by her.

Just then, that little voice inside Olivia's head whispers:

- Only, I *could* have been in that position; perhaps I *should* have been in that position, but I failed to pull it off. Didn't I?

She walks purposively up Highgate village hill under a dull sky with a bunch of freesias, alone, her mother preferring to stay at home. In the cemetery Olivia stands forlornly still and straight in her black coat in front of the dark headstone, which is starting to look weathered and stained. Last month's flowers are long dead in a metal bowl and she replaces them on bended knee, happy that there is enough rainwater at the bottom. She screws up the wrapping paper, stuffing it into her pocket.

Bittersweet memories crowd in as she reads the inscription carved on the granite for the hundredth time. It was three weeks after the closing ceremony of the London Olympics 2012, well over two years ago that her beloved father died. Her firm had made a contribution to sponsorship costs of the British athletics team and she had complimentary seats for the middle Saturday. She had managed to drag both her parents along with her, on a day that GB won three gold medals, which made everybody in the stadium and throughout London ecstatic. They had struggled even then to get her father up the steeply raked steps to their seats, but once in position he stayed put throughout the warm rainy afternoon and he had seemed quite happy. But a significant exacerbation of his illness began within a few days, that involved his heart failing and his chest bloating and being unable to breathe comfortably. It was an unpleasant spectacle and ultimately an unsuccessful battle, and her mother had suffered since with depression and loneliness.

They were never really friends, Olivia and her mother, never had been. Not like some girls say they are with their mothers. Both her parents seemed so busy with their own lives to pay her much attention, she was often left to her own devices and felt unfairly ignored; and after Arthur died, her mother had become even more hopeless than usual, withdrawn and edgy. She was unpleasantly moody at times and would not listen to anyone. They never talked to each other, not openly about the things that troubled them or that really meant something to them.

Olivia had carefree ways, habits and manners, apparently, kept unsociable hours and unsuitable men friends, and her mother saw all of these things as irresponsible. Martha could not understand why at 33 her beautiful daughter had not already married some wealthy banker and settled down in the Home Counties with a gaggle of little children. She would often accuse Olivia of being scared to make grown-up decisions.

- Oh yes, she always called me beautiful.

Even if that was debatable, Martha would naturally claim all the credits she could, like all proud parents for their personal aggrandisement, in the way that they bask in the glory of their children and think that they produced the most amazingly gifted offspring anyone had ever known.

An only child, she was now the sole survivor of the family after her mother, apart from a wayward distant cousin living somewhere in the West Country whom they never saw.

- She always presumed to know how I felt about things.

"Loving husband and father, devoted to country and family", Olivia reads, remembering her mother once insisting that her dear father did very important work in the Diplomatic Corps, not to be talked about. Olivia in all honesty was never sure if her mother was exaggerating or whether her lovely dad really did do top notch work for the State. Olivia had been her father's treasure, in the early days, she knew that, and he had spoilt her something rotten, always giving in to her every wish, especially if she bowed her head with a severe pout and slowly bit at a corner of her lower lip, then her father would smother her with hugs and promises to stop her crying, all much to her mother's annoyance. She looked forward to his bedtime stories and special cuddles that followed before being tucked in. She would fall asleep with the self-satisfied smile of the only child in the centre of attention. She was his absolute princess and always indulged her with a surprise new book or a Barbie doll at the start of the holidays. He insisted she went with him, holding hands, dressed in her prettiest clothes, along the high street to the library or the supermarket, so that he could show her off and beam indulgently with hidden pride, even to complete strangers.

Until she started to grow up. In her early teens when her body began to change shape and appearance, she swiftly became taller and thinner, with a nipped-in waistline and a consciously swollen chest that seemed to embarrass him. He stopped hugging her in case he pressed against her, and they gradually stopped talking to each other, as he no longer could relate to girlie subjects like fashion and celebrities, clothes and diets; and she could not explain to him that her love of Cole Porter or Gilbert & Sullivan was waning and nowhere near as adamant as his.

Olivia's teenage years had not lacked love; it was just that love mostly passed by unexpressed. Her father did serious work with the civil service, she was constantly reminded, all to get her through her education and so at home, he needed peace and rest, as his health was not as good as it should be and she must not keep disturbing him. Latterly, as he became more ill and slower over time, his heart, her mother explained, he needed more rest. At weekends, he preferred watching television from the sofa than joining in with any family activity. She had to be quiet in the house, keeping her music sound down low and her mother frowned on her bringing any friends back to the house complaining that it gave her father a headache. Olivia found herself increasingly isolated lounging in her bedroom, the walls covered with pictures of George Michael and Robbie Williams, where she would dream of a handsome pop star falling in love with her and whisking her away. At the time when she was struggling with exams and career choices, when she might have gained most from wise advice from her parents, she found they were at their least receptive or sympathetic to her needs, her father too busy or too tired, her mother forever nervy about his condition, anxious about what might happen next.

- Yes, and he survived another ten years, mostly ill and bedridden at home, poor sod, with mother full-time nursing him; it's no wonder she was left bitter and depressed.

Her father's health prevented his attending her Cambridge graduation day. In fact, since her first day at Emmanuel when they had driven up the M11 in steaming late summer sunshine through crowded one-way systems, for a splendid tour around the college and strawberries and tea on the lawns, he had not ventured back once in three years. The time had passed quickly and Olivia developed a strong sense of self-reliance, determined to show her father what she was capable of even if he would not appreciate it.

She could not remember him congratulating her or anything like that, although he did apologise for not being well enough to attend. By the time she took up her apprenticeship at one of the big American banks in London she had departed the family home, renting in Kilburn, and she seldom saw her parents, sometimes only pitching up late to their home with a gift offering on a birthday or just before Christmas.

And then he died, not unexpectedly, but shocking when it happened, and she rushed to comfort her mother with a sense of guilt in her soul and need in her heart. It was Olivia that needed her now. There was some hidden relief and hope that perhaps their relationship could improve, her exhausted mother now having the space to free herself from the shackles of chronic ill-health, to live an easier existence.

The poor man was at rest; all things must pass, after all.

She had stared at his coffin top as it was lowered into the ground, imagining him within, his stern expression of disapproval masking his own fear and inadequacies. She had had a mad desire to prise open the lid and one last time to touch his cheek and apologise for being such a disappointment to him. She had had to choke back a gasp and her mother had turned to grab her arm, her agonising face full of venom.

She watched the attendants in black start to shovel earth into the deep cut-out in the ground. She had the courage to step forward onto the mound of surrounding dug earth, where her pretty clad foot had sunk down in the sticky soil when she grabbed a wet handful of the stuff to toss down onto the polished wood below; together with a long red rose stem. Stupidly symbolic, she knew, but something her mother expected of her. She had felt as if a heavy blow had knocked everything she valued out of her, a horrible sense of being left a vacant and empty shell – something that she had experienced once before, in those dreadful weeks after Hugo had left her, something she was hoping never to experience again.

Her mud-stained black shoes were thrown into a bottom cupboard when she reached her mother's home after the ceremony and she never wore them again.

- Probably still there, for all I know.

A lone tear slides uncertainly over the contours of her cheek, to be caught at the corner of her mouth, warm and salty. Olivia turns to depart the deserted graveside with a sense of relief, that the tensions and pains of her father's terminal illness are indeed over, but unable to suppress a powerful recall of the bond that she imagined she had had with him, now broken.

- I want so much to talk to you. You would listen, wouldn't you? You might even understand. Not like your dear wife, you know.

A sudden lurch catches in her chest. She is grateful the churchyard is empty, the damp weather keeping people away. She notices the weeds and mould running in the cracks of the concrete blocks under her feet, the unkempt wet grass along the edges, the bare winter trees looking haggard; the forlorn appearance that for a while matches the gloom in her own heart.

Olivia is saddened by her cemetery visits, stupidly feeling unfaithful leaving her father to be alone for a few more weeks, until her next time. She wends her way out, wondering whether there might come a moment when she would share her secrets with her mother. She wishes she had a sister, preferably older, and decides that if she ever started a family of her own, remembering Nicole and her happy pregnancy with an ironic smile, she would always have at least two, for friendship; being an only child produces too much isolation and loneliness.

- I need someone I can trust. Maybe Louise can be that person.

***

In the confined ladies' changing room, with its smell of warm bodies, soap and talcum, Olivia drops her mesh face helmet onto the floor where it rolls from side to side for a while. She hurls her right-hand protective glove, a dirty white leather, onto the wooden bench and flops down to rest. She is still panting from her exertions, perspiring heavily inside the thick jacket. She closes her eyes and stretches out her aching legs whilst rubbing at sore muscles around her shoulder. Her foil has been stashed away in the cupboards at the side of the arena.

She is annoyed with herself and sure that her face looks red and angry. Everything was rushed tonight and the odds stacked against her. She had arrived barely on time, had missed the chance to encourage Louise before her match, and had skimped on her warm-up and stretching exercises. She had only herself to blame.

She hears her fencing opponent, an older Polish woman, panting with obvious joy, the other side of a row of wooden lockers. It had been a close fought win, three-two in the end, but in the deciding bout, she had been charged down, unfairly she thought. The Polish fencer with the right of way had bundled into her, her leading foot catching Olivia's toe and she had retreated as elegantly as she could but not quite fast enough; their fists had clashed, the foils bent up towards the roof. Olivia had tried to keep her stance and balance, flexing low on her leading right foot, while her left leg stretched correctly behind her, but moving backwards she lost her footing on the edge of the piste and toppled sideways, twisting an ankle and landing on her shoulder. She had had to take a penalty point into the bargain, which had tipped the score in her opponent's favour, and now she had a sore head from upset pride. The end of the match salute had been grudging, their hand-shake perfunctory. Everyone knew her match would be tight, but she had come so close to reaching the next round; team-captain Margaret had commiserated with her in the arena, still resounding with some echoing boos underneath the overall applause.

She kicks off her sports shoes, peels the heavy jerkin off over her head and unstraps the inelegant white plastic moulded chest guard all women competitors have to wear. Off come the knee-length trousers and white socks. She grabs a towel and sponge bag and pads off into the steamy shower room. Other naked women are lathering and glistening under the sprays, soapy suds running out into a central channel. The water spray is strong and hot over her face, soothing, body and mind. She replays her lost match point by point in her head and realises she had enjoyed the encounter, coming close to beating an obviously stronger player. Soon she will regroup with the team and supporters probably waiting in the café; they will congratulate her and commiserate with some group hugs, and Toby from the office will try and make out with her and joke with her and touch her arm, while being unutterably self-satisfied at his promotion-inducing performance earlier in the week.

In front of a wall mirror, she twists around to inspect the back of her shoulder, seeing reddish bruising appearing. She creams herself and starts to dress slowly. Louise, already changed into slick trousers and a loose cotton shirt with upturned collar, walks in and leans provocatively against a pillar, watching with pleasure. Olivia had only seen the end of Louise's contest, which she had won, with a place in the semi-final next week.

'So sorry, you fight good match. Unfair point lost at the end.' Louise speaks clearly without any effort to lower her voice. 'I thought you were better fencer, overall.' Olivia smiles back at her, feeling better for seeing her and quite happy to be watched. She looks so playful that Olivia pads over to kiss her briefly on the lips.

'You're very kind, sweetheart,' she whispers.

'More skilled player, definitely. It was just the Polish woman was bigger, more muscles than you, that was all.' She notices the bruising on Olivia's shoulder and steps over to gently soothe the area. 'This will be so sore; and stiff tomorrow, I think.'

Olivia wriggles into her bra adjusting for a snug fit and then slithers into a tight pair of black leggings, stretching them over her bottom. Wincing she pulls on a cotton shirt, buttoned but not tucked in, and then a white hooded Holster jacket. She forces her feet into ankle boots while Louise wraps a scarf around her lover's neck.

'I could take you home and give this shoulder some massage with special oils,' Louise whispers huskily. Olivia gathers her other things. She smiles gratefully and says that that would be really nice, but she must not stay long, early start tomorrow.

'Can we nip out the back and avoid the café crowd, do you think?'

On their way out she picks up a crumpled edition of the morning *Express* discarded on a nearby bench.

Slopping around her apartment later that evening, after returning from Louise's place in St John's Wood by cab, Olivia reads again the newspaper article about the mistaken police shooting. There is a bold sub-title on an inside page, and she splutters over the short piece by that same reporter bloke quoted in the original newspaper article last week, which had included those amateurish pictures that found their way onto *YouTube*:

Victim of Mistaken Identity Says He Will Sue Police

Richard Armstrong, journalist extraordinaire, reports on an exclusive interview with the innocent victim of the police shooting in Earl's Court, Hugo Pitsakis himself. "I just happened to be passing along Pembroke Road at the time of the shooting when I used my smartphone, as anybody with awareness would have done, and snapped a few pictures," Armstrong said.

Olivia wonders how he had managed the interview, as she had never seen him in the hospital and nobody had mentioned a reporter at any time being allowed onto the ward. It must have been early one day when Sam was not around, as Olivia could not have imagined Sam allowing such a thing. Especially as the tone of the piece shifted from general sympathy towards Hugo, to being downright hostile, questioning what a wealthy controversial artist was doing staying overnight with two young ladies of dubious reputation, in the flat belonging to a known criminal on the run, even suggesting there might be a link between the two and wondering what role Hugo had been playing in this charade. Armstrong implies throughout that Hugo was in the wrong, that he failed to give straight answers to many of the questions; that he should have known better and had only himself to blame!

She is fuming at the sheer prejudice of the reporting; and comes to the conclusion that Armstrong must have collaborated with the police over the article, had probably not interviewed Hugo at all but had simply taken comments from that Detective Sanger, a man desperate to protect his own reputation, knowing that he would have to face a complaint and an enquiry in due course, that would be in the public eye, just at a time when he was hoping for a gentle run-in to a peaceful retirement.

And what was that comment about Hugo being wealthy?

***

Two days later, on another late visit to the ITU ward, the nursing team reassure Olivia that all procedures have been completed and that Mr Hugo Pitsakis is on a slow road to recovery. Through the narrow glass panel in his door she catches a fleeting glimpse of him: pale and emaciated, sitting up in bed, dozing, with dark stubble and his head half shaved, he looks like a criminal, in his prison cell.

'He's still on IV antibiotics,' Nurse Cath tells her at the nurses' station, 'but he's off the oxygen; he has wound dressings that need changing, but the drains are out, so that's good. Generally speaking, he is recovering. Should be trying him out of bed soon.' She tosses a not unkindly smile across at her, before strutting off to another bedside along the hushed corridor. A junior doctor glances Olivia's way and winks at her.

She cannot rely on second-hand stories from the papers or others and there is little point in her speculating. She is desperate to speak to Hugo directly, but still, this is not a good time. If she is to gain any understanding of the reasons for the shooting mistake by the police, she will need to find time to talk over the events with him. She would prefer that it was out of hospital, somewhere private, maybe at Sam's place when he is better.

Just as she is leaving the ward, Samantha bustles in wearing her usual red coat and they greet each other in a friendly manner. Olivia explains that Hugo is asleep and repeats some of what the nurse has just told her. Sam looks relieved. They decide to go for a coffee as before, only this time they will be alone, no Bernadette to be listening in.

In the canteen, they settle at a far table, their backs to a huge mural of an Italian hillside, almost side by side and it feels cosy, Sam appearing more relaxed than before. They chat easily about the cold weather and the chances of snow, the cheap tactic of piling all the sticky buns for sale at the counter and the disgraceful number of sweet drinks dispensers around every corridor of the hospital. Olivia mentions her looking forward to her skiing holiday in two weeks.

'Switzerland, Zermatt, should be good.'

'Lovely. I have never been skiing,' Samantha sighs. 'Don't fancy it, really, a bit cold for me. Would be nice to get away though. Would love to take Hugo somewhere, away from all these people and prying eyes.'

'And did you read that bit in the *Express* by that dreadful Richard Armstrong? Two days ago, it was. Apparently, he interviewed Hugo first hand. Is that true?'

'No, don't think so. He's not responding coherently or talking much. The journalist must have made it up or created the "interview" from what he was picking up from the police.'

'It is so biased.' Olivia creases her brows and sounds indignant. 'He almost says it was Hugo's fault. That he was staying with unsavoury characters and then disguising his appearance with a hat, you know, no wonder the police were suspicious. I mean, it's outrageous.'

'He never spoke to Hugo.' Samantha is calm, reflective, pursing her lips for control. 'They keep out reporters if they can, but you see them in the corridors snooping around sometimes. One tried to talk to me a few days ago, a pushy little man in a grey raincoat, but I walked away, ignored him. I prefer to ignore these articles as well. I don't listen to what they are saying.' She leans forward, speaking directly at Olivia, with a quiet determination. 'I wonder sometimes

71

whether Hugo is safe here in this hospital. The police presence has been withdrawn.'

Before they depart, Samantha to return to the ward upstairs to be with Hugo and Olivia to return alone to her apartment where she will wallow on her bed still nursing her sore shoulder and dream of Louise, they exchange mobile numbers, with promises to keep in touch.

'I will mention you, Olivia, to Hugo when I get the chance, if he seems receptive. I'll tell him of your concern and that you would like to come and see him sometime, I'm sure he would like that. Although how much he remembers is in doubt, when he's awake he seems quite confused. We don't know what his mental state will be really like.'

Olivia switches the television news off, the screen so filled with depressing stories of terrorist shootings, murders, child abusers, economic woes and other hard luck stories that she does not want to hear any more. She is thinking about Hugo, now that it would appear safe to assume that he will survive and recover from his injuries. She can contemplate events with a little more freedom, perhaps with more optimism. She is surprised that her thoughts begin to mirror those of that dreadful man in the paper. What *was* Hugo doing in a criminal's flat in Earl's Court overnight with two young ladies, of questionable professional employment? And other questions flooded her mind: where does Hugo live (although the first report quoted Bermonsey, which could mean anything)? Sam mentioned she was in Muswell Hill, so did Hugo spend time with her there? Olivia had not dared to ask. Did Hugo know this man Midge Martin? Was he aware of his criminal activity, and was not one of the girls supposed to be his girlfriend, so did Hugo not realise the risk he was taking? The obvious risk that Martin might return to find a strange man staying in his flat with his girlfriend, rather than the less likely risk obviously of being gunned down in a London street in broad daylight by the police?

- Is it actually anything to do with me?

Should she not be leaving him alone, to go back to doing whatever it was he was doing before, living with Samantha, sleeping with young women, whatever? Does Olivia have any claims on Hugo's behaviour? Of course not. She feels moderately outraged that Mr Clever Armstrong got in first with his so-called exclusive interview and ends up printing probably a whole lot of ill-conceived supposition and guesswork, besmirching Hugo's reputation and character, for the sake of a story.

- It gives me an excuse to pursue the story myself, though.

She recalls Samantha's remarks in the canteen about his safety and how she would prefer him to be in a private hospital that would be more secure, to continue his recovery; he could certainly afford it, she had said. Really? How does a simple artist, however popular and talented Olivia is thinking, plying his trade in painting pictures in oils, afford private in-patient care in the 21st century? And Armstrong referred to him being wealthy. Sam had also mentioned his agent, Jake needing to reorder a whole raft of bookings, indefinitely until further notice, and how that might adversely affect the summer business; and she asked whether Olivia had ever met Jeremy, his business partner, "Jeremy Ashcroft, lovely man, you would like him." Olivia remembers meeting Jake once or twice, way back; but is wondering what functions these two men have in Hugo's life. So his agent finds him galleries and exhibitions to work with, but what does he need a business partner for?

The more the questions mount up, the less likely she is to leave it alone, the more Olivia is intrigued. In the intervening nine years since she knew him, Hugo has maintained an aura of mystery around him that seems to involve business and wealth. She feels drawn towards his story, wanting to find the explanations and to be involved.

- God damn it, don't you see what is happening? Precisely what happened last time: you get hooked, with Hugo, and you cannot let go.

Suddenly a plan comes to her in a moment of inspiration while lathering herself dreamily in the shower, washing away the day's effort. Mr Hugo Pitsakis, *artiste extraordinaire*, needs some good public relations. She will research him and write a biography, presenting his genius in a stunning written account of his life.

She almost laughs as she steps out of the hot water, reaching for a bath towel. She starts to hop around the flat, looking for her iPad to write notes and looking at calendars to plan her way through the maze of her work and social life, such as it is. The seed of the idea must have been growing inside over the last couple of weeks, but indistinct and only becoming brighter with her recent discussion with Samantha. Now it is pounding through her grey matter, ideas spreading in all directions. It is so obvious. She would write an in-depth portrait of Hugo Pitsakis.

She would need to interview a host of people, family and colleagues, to get the story first hand. She had always been keen on writing from childhood and a career in journalism had crossed her mind seriously while reading business studies at Cambridge. Somehow, she had moved into the finance world and ended up in the City, where all of the brightest young minds were headed these days and she had no regrets, not in the slightest. She was satisfying her writing urge to an extent with her magazine column, where she tried to demystify some of the money topics that confused the public, by bringing simpler explanations for the ordinary person's understanding. She was also an occasional invited columnist in a well-known Sunday newspaper, so her name was getting about; actually, she thought people found the female voice on the subject of money quite refreshing, a change from the male-dominated viewpoint. But this writing a biography would be a stupendous challenge to her abilities and so excited is she, that she cannot wait to sit at the table with a blank sheet of paper and a pen and to list the section and chapter headings that are already forming in her mind.

She had never wasted much time on domestic chores and her sporadic social life was as full as she wanted; so here was an opportunity to concentrate on something else. She might have to take a short sabbatical, three or four months, she could afford it. She will talk with Charles next week to explore the idea. She might be able to concentrate on Hugo for the biography and Louise for the emotional satisfaction. The thought brings her to a standstill in front of her mirror, where she sinks gracefully onto her stool, feeling an immediate longing in her loins, such urging, almost painful. She has to touch herself, running the pulp of a finger like Louise had done, gliding along roughened folds, feeling for some moisture. With closed eyes, she is almost aware of Louise's presence and her whispering voice, marvelling at her skill in stimulating such pleasure. She desists, frustrated.

- You need to take care, girl. Just what are you taking on board? In this competitive world, you can ill afford to let up; you have been earning some respect, establishing yourself, beginning to show what you are capable of; don't risk it all with this project, that will take you out of the system for a time during which you will be forgotten and all your contemporaries will relish the chance to jump over you in the promotion stakes, in the pecking order.

The wide-eyed expression that reflects back at her in the glass frightens her for a moment.

- You're right. I want to be a success, at everything. Work defines me. I cannot afford encumbrances, obstacles like Louise or Hugo to get in the way. I need to break through in terms of promotion: senior fund manager, with its extra perks; it cannot be far away. These are not things I am prepared to jeopardise, even temporarily.

A harder, more determined appearance spreads across her face, looking at herself eye-to-eye, square on. Her jaw is set firm, her eyes narrowed and focused. She can do serious: her pupils are dilated widely in the shadows of the room, the encircling rings of bright blue have paled in accordance with an altogether cooler expression.

She sleeps fitfully through to the small hours and wakes with a shudder, rolling onto her back, her shoulder aching. She stares out into the darkness, her face hot, tacky perspiration around the back of her neck. All is quiet. There are no sounds outside that might have disturbed her. Her dreams had transported her to West End Lane and her old pokey one-bed flat over the laundromat, with its exposed copper pipes and leaking windows overlooking a bus-stop. Hugo had mysteriously disappeared, been gone three weeks or more without a word and nobody sure where exactly he was or when he was getting back. Jake mumbled something vague about family matters in Greece and Samantha confirmed he had shot off to Athens to help his mother during a family tragedy and that he was not expected back for some time. But where exactly and how she could contact him, she had no help. At the studio, all projects and painting had come to a halt, unfinished work left drying on easels, brushes caked in paint lying on surfaces, unwashed, everything abandoned as it was, ominously quiet. Anxiously waiting to hear something from him, she tried to understand the situation. She was bereft, hiding alone in her own flat, jumping at every sound of a telephone or a knock at the door, her work disrupted. She had heard that the police had visited Theed Street once in their search for Dominic Lebelov, the ballet dancer, reported missing; someone with a key had let them into the workshop, but they had stayed just long enough to satisfy themselves that he was not hiding under a couch or something. Olivia had nervously expected the police to pay her a visit in West Hampstead and was prepared for it, but they had never called. She kept herself to herself, kept her head down.

She became increasingly conscious of how much she missed him, the pain of separation surprisingly strong, pulling at her guts and affecting her whole day. She was as patient as she could be, quite against her nature. She had tried several phone numbers, including Athens, but was always cut off or left hanging. She lost weight and became a sad shadow of her usual cheery self. She dreamt of his dramatic return and dashing down to Gatwick to meet him, their crashing into each other's arms in the arrivals lounge and their clinging onto each other in the back of a cab all the way to Theed Street, where they would wallow in the warmth of their double bed in contortions of energetic love-making that would last for days without stopping.

Day after day she waited for a message, rushing to the front door first thing to look for a letter, jumping hysterically whenever the telephone rang. But there was nothing. All she could do was worry and wait, her dreams feeling increasingly stupid.

And then one morning, still dark and quiet outside, before the buses had started up, she was lying unexpectedly awake on her back looking up at the ceiling with her hands grasping the edges of her duvet, desperately longing to be cosying up against his warm body with his smell of turpentine and to be gazing into those deep wells of dark brown that were his eyes, with reassuring feelings of shared love, when she realised she was feeling dreadfully sick. She had to get up quickly and go the bathroom.

It did not take her long to realise that she was pregnant.

4

Saturday, January 31, 2015

On the packed flight from Gatwick, Olivia, sporting a new short haircut for the holiday, rests her head back with her eyes closed for short periods and shuts out all the irritating turmoil of petulant passengers and aircraft noise, allowing it all to wash over her. Her mind wanders over her plans: they are lying in a pile on a table top, like irregular cut wooden jigsaw pieces. Her task is to slot each in a position that fits comfortably, in order to view the whole picture. She is worried that she may not be able to fit all of them properly, not without trimming the shapes a bit or discarding some of them. And what if, when she is finished and she steps back, she does not like the picture she has created. The fit may be poor and there may be contradictions, leading to confrontation. She hates confrontation. She sees Hugo singing his Greek folk songs and laughing with his mouth wide open, spilling crumbs and a tipsy waiter sprinkles shavings of guilt from his grinder over the whole thing.

She jolts awake. 'No, thanks, I'm fine.' Lotte is prodding her arm, asking if she would like a drink from the trolley. Olivia is wondering whether Hugo had ever felt disconnected like that about a painting of his, having invested time and emotional energy on a picture, had he ever stepped back from the finished product only to find he disliked it, for some reason? What would he have done: scrubbed it out, discarded it to one side for later, thrown it on a skip? Or would he have worried about it, tinkered with it, painstakingly tried to make it work?

Charlotte, her workmate from Emerson's (one "m", darling) and one of her three travelling companions, has been moaning about the ridiculously early hour, the crowds packed into uncomfortable surroundings, and the lack of a proper breakfast available. The other two are sitting in the row behind. Beverley is Olivia's friend from school, the organiser of the trip, just like last year and Zermatt is her favoured destination, sophisticated, smart and expensive. Grace is the quiet one, once mistakenly married for a sadly short time to a handsome rake, and probably the intellectual one, as she is bound to demonstrate later with all her clever answers on quiz night. They are all buoyed up for a wonderful girlie week in the romantic Swiss Alps, in search of the right snow conditions, the right ski instructor, the right bar full of the smart set among the loaded, the amorous and hopefully the eligible. None of the foursome is married or even fixed, although Charlotte recently came close, with a near-miss engagement to a literary agent that faltered over the historically old-fashioned argument of sex before marriage: he wanted it, she didn't, which surprised Olivia for one, as Lotte had always seemed most

76

adventurous and had surely lost her virginity way before Olivia, back in the days.

Olivia relaxes, lost in the spell of her time with Louise, the sureness of her voice, the texture of her flesh and her smell, so rich with certainty, conjured so vividly. She is toying with the idea of confiding in Lotte or Bev about her new-found love interest. Will they be scared off as friends? They might feel vulnerable to the desires of a dyke in their midst. Olivia will keep it to herself, for now.

Yesterday, she asked Charles Treadwell for an extra two days of holiday after her week away, telling him she needed to spend some time with her mother, who had not been too well lately. He was actually nice about it, was sorry to hear of her mother's difficulties, and with a twist of a smile, commented on the board's general satisfaction with her work.

She visualises getting involved with her plans, making some first steps towards exploring Hugo's world. She is convinced that she must pursue it or she will forever regret it. She will keep it completely separate from her work commitments. She will bring the man, the professional artist, to life for all the world to examine, the good and the bad, playing on his extraordinary talents. It will be insightful, edgy and revealing, exposing the source of his genius. She will be able to lay to rest some of the uncertainties of the past, provide her with some justification for her own actions. It would be a way of rooting him out of her system, and at the end, she could perform a cremation, the episode of her life boxed and sealed, and pushed on a line through the heavy curtains into the certainty of an all-consuming fire. Done.

It seems to her the most obvious thing in the world. It carries risk, that while pursuing the professional life of the artist, and writing the definitive biography, she becomes diverted away from her chosen path, her City career. But she would never be far away, and it would only be for a short time. She will give herself six months, take it as a sabbatical, and if the firm disapproved she would resign. She would have no difficulty coming back to another firm, even though she might have to accept a lower starting point. And with a bestseller under her belt! Perhaps this has been her vocation all along, to research well-known characters and become a literary star.

The journey seems endless, slow-moving through Geneva airport, the bags taking ages to turn around their carousel, and then finding the right coach for their destination. The two and half hour trip takes them through a wintery landscape of brown and dull flats and valleys, before the gradual climb over the lower slopes of the mountains. The warmth inside and the rhythmic rocking set her nodding off again, her private images spinning around in her head, her puzzle pieces moving about on the table top.

The coach is soon twisting its way up slopes of cleared roads following a recent snowfall, and through the smart outskirts, they reach the Hotel Schonegg, nestling invitingly below mist-cloaked mountains, its window boxes stuffed with drooping geraniums. Sunshine is sparkling off the surrounding whiteness, but the air outside is remarkably chilly. There is snow lying in thick layers on the roofs like caster sugar on a giant cake and the stunning pointed Matterhorn rises dramatically in the distance beyond the rooftops and spires of Zermatt. Everyone tramps inside with their burdensome bags and clomps off to find their rooms; to unpack and to meet up later in the bar. The girls wander around the immediate environs of the town for a while before daylight starts to fade quite suddenly and they return to shower, makeup and dress for an early dinner. And early to bed that night, as they are expected to be at ski school the next morning prompt at 9 o'clock and will need to get kitted out at the hire shop in the basement first.

The week progresses variedly: some days are wonderfully clear with blue skies and glorious sunshine, others dull with threatening low cloud and then the occasional white-out. There was an overnight fall of snow in the middle of the week covering the resort and mountain slopes with perfect soft whiteness beloved of all skiers. The girls work diligently throughout in their colourful one-pieces with a humourless blond Swiss instructor called Gabriel, who enjoyed putting them through some tough routines. After six days, they have all shown mastery of the perfectly arced turn. Even the slightly cumbersome Charlotte, who is a touch overweight (although Olivia always claimed it was relative and a matter of weight transfer), achieves a certain elegance with her parallel skis.

Evening times are shared with the other residents, eating veal, morels and soft smoked cheeses, and drinking plenty of wine, with sing-songs around the wood fire later on. A few local farmers with clay pipes and ruddy complexions are on the lookout but largely ignored by the English girls. On the second night, Grace proves her worth once again at the quiz, knowing all the general knowledge and politics questions, as well as much of the film and sport. Olivia and Charlotte are pants, but fare better the following night at the karaoke, when Olivia gives a moving rendition of Don McLean's "Crying", imagining Louise's confident face throughout and having to wipe away a tear or two while trying to laugh it off.

On other occasions, they explore the town and eat in different restaurants, where they compare their day's bravery on the slopes or amorous encounters in the cable cars. One afternoon they go shopping on the Bahnhofstrasse and buy silly things like German sausage, Pellegrini truffles and a Zermatt bobble hat. They return to the spa, for massage and sauna, finishing with a splash in the hot and steamy pool, more like a giant bath.

One day they take the railway up to Gornergrat and eat a pasta Bolognese lunch in blazing sunshine sitting on the open decking that pokes out over the slopes. Gabriel is keen to take them up to the Plateau Rosa glacier and Testa Grigia at twelve thousand feet, where they enjoy some challenging red runs and the best skiing of the trip. By the end of the week, they have all come to like Gabriel and club together to give him an expensive bottle of liqueur brandy as a thank you.

At odd spare moments, Olivia works on an article for her magazine, based on her seminar to the post-graduates, discussing all the promises of Government that cannot be kept and the many more that will be presented to the gullible public ahead of the election due in May. Entitled "Promises, promises", she shared a draft copy one evening over supper with her companions.

Beverley was particularly enthusiastic. 'I love the line: "The Government derives its authority from the extraction of £680 billion of tax a year from the British people and then spends it in the way it thinks most likely to perpetuate its hold on office. This is referred to as 'democracy in action'."' Beverly reads on. 'And then: "In the political life cycle, politicians in opposition promise the earth, get elected, fail to meet the expectations they have created and are promptly replaced by the next opposition promising even more." How true is that? Excellent.'

'And then you talk about liberal democracy. I've never heard it called that,' muses Charlotte.

'Yes, the problem is so short-term, politicians never think long-term,' comes in Grace. 'It's no wonder that they will never face the reality of climate change, or environmental pollution, or being able to feed everybody; or the healthcare issues in increasing elderly populations. You're so right, Olivia, I see this all the time.'

'Popular democracy is a big part of the West's problem – to win votes you have to give more and to beat your opponents at the next election you have to promise to give away even more, so it is a never-ending process of auctions, with the cost and debt levels passed onto the next generation. That's the theme anyway. I want people to look out for the wild promises to come in the electioneering before May. Honesty won't win seats. The toxic by-product is debt – Britain is almost the most indebted country in the world – personal, corporate and government. Politicians just tinker with this at the edges; nothing radical is proposed, and so bold action is impossible.' Olivia was quite pleased, her audience seemed to like the punch-lines and the tone; all she needed was to tighten it a little into less than 600 words and hopefully her editor would like it too.

Later, over coffee and chocolate cake, the four friends are celebrating their week, regretting that the time has passed so quickly.

'It's been so lovely here, girls,' smiles Bev, raising her cappuccino in salute to the others, and they toast themselves with clashing of china cups. 'Thank you, all.'

'But still not found Mister Right though, have we, Olly?' Charlotte murmurs with regret. 'Not a shag all week! Never mind, maybe next time.' And they all laugh.

'So, are we going to do this again next year?' Olivia asks.

'Why not?' Bev challenges, 'the cake is delicious.'

'Well, we might be hitched and have some hunk around our necks, who won't let us out of his sights,' Charlotte chirruped, unusually optimistic for her.

'Olly, I fail to understand why you are still alone, dear, honestly. You make a fortune in the City, you're quite the most beautiful creature on the slopes and the brightest. Why is there not a queue of soppy males lining up behind you?' Bev looks at her dear friend straight in the eye, but gets no answer, just a coy smile and a slight shrug. 'Um? I read your column every month, by the way. Very intelligent.'

'Oh, thank you. I was not sure anybody read it.' She carefully brings a small forkful of the shared cake to her lips and smiles with pleasure as she compresses it around inside her mouth before swallowing slowly with closed eyes. 'Mmm.'

'Oh God, back to work Monday morning,' Grace moans. She is a pretty brunette who works as a researcher in a well-known charity organisation but seldom speaks about it. The others join in with the general dismay at having to return to their ordinary lives again.

'Well, I am having a few days off to do some research of my own.'

'Oh,' says Charlotte, 'first I've heard of it.'

'Well, I squared it with Charles before I left. I've been thinking about it for a while. I am studying an artist that I know, a genius really; want to write a biography of him. Try my hand, writing a full manuscript, as it were, instead of just short analysis papers.' She is not getting much of a response from her friends and so her voice drifts away, as she looks down at the remains of the chocolate cake.

'Sounds interesting. You mean you have a publishing contract?' Bev asks.

Olivia shakes her cropped head, delighted at the lack of stray hair around the sides to irritate her vision. She has pale goggle marks circling her eyes, but otherwise her face is impressively tanned. 'Not exactly. I will take the risk.'

'Do you have a personal stake in this project, by any chance?' Bev asks with a slight raise of her eyebrows. Bev knows nothing about her time with Hugo nine years ago, but Charlotte does vaguely remember the period and the misery that Olivia went through. She had never met Hugo and he's a subject they neither ever refer to, in a sort of unspoken agreement of mutual understanding.

On the flight home, which is as packed as when they came out and just as uncomfortable, Olivia and Beverley sit close together and share some personal moments. Bev talks about a new bloke in her life but is wary not to risk spoiling it all by presuming anything, which is why she has not spoken of him before. 'Promises, promises,' she jokes with a knowing look. 'It is early days, just now,' she smiles nervously, but Olivia squeezes her arm in her excitement and whispers how pleased she is.

'When am I going to meet him?'

'Oh, he might turn out like all the rest. Why is anal sex so important to most men? I can't stand it.'

A full-length nude image of Louise crosses Olivia's mind, dark hair shimmering, breasts bobbing as she clambers on all-fours over her. She comes close to confiding in Bev about her Chinese heartthrob and the wonderful sex they share, but her cautious reluctance prevails, as she would hate to risk their friendship. She is desperate to see Louise again and show off her new look hairstyle and suntan. Instead, she drags her mind over to focus on her other plans.

'I've been thinking about writing a biography for some time, perhaps it is what I have always wanted to do.'

'You should, I'm all for it. You're a great writer,' Bev enthuses.

'What better way to explore the great themes of our times than through some of the people that have shaped them? Get close to someone and then place them in a story on the page, bring them to life. That would be really satisfying.'

'You might take it up full-time. You could pick a cabinet minister, or a senior civil servant next time; the governor of the BBC or an Old Bailey judge perhaps.'

Or the Bank of England Governor, Mr Mark Carney, Olivia thinks. The crisp chill of the Alps has helped to cement clearly the idea in her mind, and a genius artist would make an excellent start.

After a horrid bumpy descent through the low cloud of a typical English winter to land at Gatwick, they wander with relief through "Arrivals" at the North Terminal. There unexpectedly at the barrier among a small crowd stands Louise, cool and erect in a long leather coat and winter boots. Olivia is gobsmacked and has a panic about greeting her with a kiss in front of the others. She almost cries out with surprise but finds a way to suppress her thrill as introductions are shared. And then they are all hugging and saying their goodbyes. Bev and Charlotte are going on via train, Grace is met by her father, which is lovely, and so alone Louise and Olivia head back to London sitting respectfully in the back of a cab. Louise loves Olivia's short hair and suntan. They are hardly able to keep their hands off each other and both arrive at Louise's flat in St John's Wood in a state of desperation. They grab at each other, their fingers pawing at their coats, faces colliding, mouths open, their tongues lapping. 'God, I've missed you.'

'Shh, shh…we'll talk later, just get naked.'

The suitcase is left standing in the hallway, coats are dropped and boots kicked off where they stand, as they pull and pick their clothes off. Two lovely bare bodies tumble together onto a wide bed where Louise has arranged a ring of sweet-scented candles to burn all around. They are kissing lavishly, pressing together the soft flesh that they have so missed, stroking and caressing endlessly all their intriguing textures.

Olivia initiates lovemaking, squatting and entwining her thighs around Louise's, as she lays spread on her back. The juices flow and lubricate their neglected gardens, which flare open like petals. As the moment takes them, as the rhythms accelerate, tribbing and grinding, their breathing reduced to gasps, Olivia is the first to tip over the edge into free-floating oblivion. Climaxing with short whimpering sounds, she doubles forward to grip Louise tightly with affection.

They wallow in each other's warmth and smell, while Olivia quietly relates tales of the girls on the ski slopes and their evening activities. Louise equally fills in for Olivia her activities during the week while she has been away, admitting that they were nothing compared to Olivia's. 'My life is dead without you. Nothing happens but the drudgery of teaching little children.'

***

Olivia returns to her flat Sunday morning, her sexual appetite sated for the time being. She is feeling motivated and excited, on the edge of something new. She wants to clean everything around her and she whips around the rooms, dusting and mopping and hoovering; detoxing the sinks and the toilets, and the entrance hallway. She washes herself down, showers and dresses simply, all to prepare mentally and physically for the work in the days to come. She feels pressed, time is short.

In the middle of it all, a message buzzes on her mobile – the hospital, Sister Williams wants to talk to her. Thinking something dreadful must have happened to Hugo, she phones the number straight away and after only one ring, a female voice comes on: 'Ward 35, Sister Williams, can I help?'

'Yes, Sister, hello. I'm returning your call, it's Olivia Truelove.'

'Oh, good, thanks. It's just that Hugo Pitsakis has left the hospital. He apparently walked out during the night, unexpectedly. It was not noticed until 8 am handover and I have been ringing around some of his contacts to see if anybody has seen him or knows where he might be. Nobody at his home number and no joy so far. Any ideas?'

Olivia is stunned and cannot think straight. Her head is full of so many other things but the call brings her back to reality. Hugo disappearing, that is an unexpected turn. 'I have no idea, Sister. Have you spoken to Samantha Little?'

'Not getting an answer there either. I was wondering. Still, sorry to disturb, I'll just have to keep trying.'

In her underwear, gripping a mug of tea, she stops to study her portrait hanging in the hallway, the half-finished sketch of her younger self, and reflects solemnly that it was not quite true that Hugo had never asked her to model for him.

When Dominic Lebelov appeared in the studio, mincing his way around the bare floor, stripped down to waxed chest and unforgiving tights that hugged his buttocks like cling-film, it was Olivia who had to adopt a submissive role, Hugo bending to the demands of the Ukrainian ballet star. Well, not quite a star at that time, but no doubt destined to become the Bolshoi's leading man the following season. Touring Europe to gain international experience, the company had commissioned Hugo Pitsakis, through his agent Jake Preston, to create a memorable picture of the group, crowding in front of the theatre steps at Covent Garden or bunched together on the stage during a moment of climax, although Hugo had something more dramatic in mind. Over a number of days, he attended their rehearsals in Soho to watch and sketch the acrobatic man at work with his troupe, growing his ideas for the composition. Then he invited Dominic to the studios alone for personal sessions, to capture the dancer in dynamic pose. After some initial sketches, Hugo decided he would do better with a dance partner, to give a balance for his energies, and back he went again to the rehearsals in search of the perfect female ballerina, looking for the right face and shape.

Dominic always liked to draw immediate attention to himself, as soon as he was in company, and the more people in the audience the better. Like a performing circus animal, he would prance around the edge of the floor space, his lofted arse and envious tackle worn with pride, sublimely outlined in spandex leggings. He would leap and twirl in a display of perfect poise and balanced gymnastics. He had immense strength, especially in his thighs shaped like torpedoes, and his was an aggressive performance, that demanded respect. Wafting strong aftershave, he was attractively dark and swarthy and had a way of working his sensuous lips that Olivia found amusing.

Once Dominic had laid his eyes on Olivia, he instantly took a fancy to her and he would not listen to any of Hugo's arguments, but demanded that she was in the picture with him as his dance partner, his leading lady. They argued for a bit, Hugo wanting something more offbeat, Dominic wanting a classical ballet dancer's pose, in mid-flight or pirouetting.

Olivia pitched up from work one evening carrying plastic shopping bags bulging with provisions, prepared to cook for whoever was still about, and found Hugo in the studio, in a mucky vest, brushes at hand, drawing materials scattered around in a state of excited animation. The floor had been cleared in the centre where spotlights shone and Lebelov was exercising around the limited space as best he could, reproducing his stance for Hugo to sketch, bending forward here, at full stretch there, on one leg, prancing, leaping, spinning. He paused in his performance to bound forward as soon as she appeared, to help her, to flatter her. He was gentle and charming, contrasting with Hugo's brusquer impatient style, as he worked up his inventive juices, deep in thought or shouting instructions. Dominic, his smooth chest puffed out, a mock-up of manliness, with his lascivious little smile and soft handshake, playfully suggested Olivia might like to stand in just now for the star that Hugo was looking for. He spoke of her natural poise and aristocratic look, her dignity and dare he mention, her body beautiful. How perfect would the fit be with him in a pose for his Russian sponsors and fan-club?

And so, Hugo asked Olivia with amusing reticence one evening, when surprisingly they were alone, if she would be so kind as to help with his Lebelov portrait. 'He says you are a delicate beauty on loan from Heaven; a Helen to Dominic's Troy, of unsurpassed quality.' They both laughed at the absurdity of the man, but Olivia was flattered nevertheless. The man had prodigious energy, combined with remorseless self-discipline; not unlike Hugo in many ways. Dominic obviously envisioned some sort of soft porn imagery of loosely clad bodies in close coupling harmony, something commercially in demand in the glossies. Olivia stayed late the next evening to discuss the project with them, before making up her mind but sensed that there were dangers afoot.

With a pose of demure reluctance, she eventually caved in to their entreaties, squatting on the floor in jeans and a loose shirt, for Lebelov to dance rings around, while Hugo urged them on. A few other hangers-on remained to watch with amusement as Dominic grasped Olivia's hands and whirled her around him, and as they danced together, he hummed unrecognisable tunes. They circled the confined space, spinning and laughing, until she became dizzy. He suggested she change into something more comfortable, and she disappeared upstairs, catching her breath. After the two men had called her down, she stepped gingerly out in a loose tee shirt and skirt over tight sports bra and bikini briefs, and danced in her bare feet. He waltzed and spun her around and they laughed together, his hand around her waist, and her skirt flared; her bare legs were as much admired as Lebelov's balletic manoeuvres.

Olivia had danced as a young schoolgirl and possessed poise and carriage not to be sniffed at, and after a couple of evenings practising, although still a little rusty, she was able to pull off some reasonable pirouettes. After a few sessions, after work, with Lebelov taking the lead and guiding her with hands-on attention to detail, it became a regular thing for the two of them to spend evenings together posing for Hugo, performing arabesques and parallel grand jetés in their tutus and pointe shoes. Olivia, often out of breath and aching, would later cook for them and any others still in the studio, and would then retreat upstairs to bed exhausted to snatch a few hours of sleep before her early morning wake-up call.

Samantha was never around during this time. Hugo became increasingly difficult, demanding quiet from everyone as he forced his mind to concentrate and played the music of prominent Russian composers ever louder while Dominic would hum and sing with his booming baritone, laughing at the great romantic climaxes and forever extolling the virtues of Shostakovich or Rachmaninoff. They drank continuously during these sessions and sometimes with the help of a little snort of powdered lines of coke, they all lost their inhibitions. Hugo was working on three images, all sizeable works; one, a group picture with Dominic in the foreground poised in calm reflection; the second, a tragic pose of Olivia from a low angle making her look tall, with just a thin veil of light muslin draped over her shoulders, a hint of audacious breast beneath, while she turns away from her heart-struck fallen star imploring her with outstretched arm, his muscled legs firm in a low crouch beneath. The third was of the two of them gliding side by side in mid-air in pure white with a luscious azure blue background.

Dominic looked monstrously cavalier-like during these sessions with his slicked-back black hair and generous smile and rather out-of-place in Hugo's dirty old studio. But he radiated homoerotic narcissism with every self-adoring gesture, with an actor's awareness of the camera lens, his appetite for self-drama and passion for the limelight undisguised. And the young photographer, Eddy was there to capture much of it, leaving his developed blow-ups pinned around the studio walls.

However, all his magnificent attributes still did not make him as irresistible to Olivia as Dominic thought they should.

Late one night, being on his feet all day but close to completion of the Lebelov pictures, Hugo was slumped on a couch in the side shadows of the workshop – they had eaten a meal together and Olivia had tucked him up. Dominic, intending to find a sleeping place himself somewhere among the artist's paraphernalia, was wandering through the studio in his tight leotard tossing and turning in balletic steps. He found Olivia clearing up in the kitchen and sidled over to her. He smelt strongly of perfume, as he touched her cheek lightly with his fingertips, and she turned to face him, with a cool expression. He was a dangerously handsome man and she was alive to his attraction.

'You are most beautiful, you know, Miss Olivia. Perfect skin and perfect face.' He was studying her features with a close eye, roving over her like an art critic inspecting a piece of work. 'Truly I should have you as my lover.' And with that, he swayed a little closer, against her, and pouted to kiss the corner of her mouth. He was of the same height as Olivia and his warm hands came to rest easily on her hips.

She turned her face away from him, so his kiss came to nothing. He jerked her angrily around towards him. She could feel the heat of his pulsing muscled body, lean as a whippet. He pressed his groin up against her and she sensed his monstrous kingpin champing for release at her lap. He wanted more.

'You fuck me, Miss Olivia, you like? I have reputation for good lover. I have large penis which I am sure you will enjoy.'

Dumbstruck, Olivia for a moment was lost for words. 'Erm, well, not really.' She looked around her for an escape, putting her hands up between them. 'Listen, in England, we don't approach such things quite so directly. Custom has it that we take things a bit slower and don't introduce penises quite so soon in the proceedings.'

'But you want fuck, yes?'

'Actually, no, Dominic. I know that's hard for you to believe. I have Hugo to play with and his penis is quite enough for me.' And she applied concerted pressure to push him away with her fingers on his chest.

He resisted and Olivia was worried that he was going to make a fuss or even make a lunge for her. She excused herself saying she was tired and was going to bed; she was sure Hugo would be joining her just as soon as he woke up. 'Good night, Dominic.'

'You not know what you are missing, what opportunity.' He looked crestfallen.

'I can well imagine,' she murmured, glancing inevitably down at his bulging tackle, but she quickly looked away, 'I am sure I shall manage.'

Unfortunately, that was not the end of the matter, by any means.

Olivia saw Dominic as a media-savvy guy with the cool looks, the tattoos, the slick image and flash car, all he needed was the flash girlfriend. She was worried that he saw her fulfilling that role, at least for the weeks he was in London.

Over supper one night, Dominic challenged Hugo about his privileged life, his education and family upbringing giving him everything he wanted. Whereas Dominic had suffered a communist upbringing, separated from his family for special attention at an early age, undergoing state-sponsored schooling, which meant prison-like conditions and rigorous soul-destroying routine day after day, year after year. Dance was not necessarily his choice but the state's choice for him, and he was powerless to argue against it. He had lived with the strict routine of the national ballet school for over twelve years, his personal ambitions and desires solely focused on those of the troupe.

Dominic spoke movingly about his impoverished childhood and lack of any privilege, his parent's sufferings and the harsh light of unresolved turmoil. He spoke with honesty and talked of the craftsman's role in society, pouring unreserved praise on Hugo's artistic skills; he shared his frustrations in his struggles for recognition. 'Life is random and unsafe, there are many dangers in a world gone mad.'

It was shortly after this that Hugo disappeared. There was a single garbled message from him on her phone, something about his need to be away, confusion among the family, his father not well, things needing to be sorted. That was it. Olivia was acutely aware that Hugo had seen the way Dominic handled her, and in her politeness, at first, she was accommodating, but Hugo had probably misread her intentions and become jealous. What then happened was unforgivable, but it had a tragic inevitability about it, a certain Shakespearean twist.

And afterwards, Olivia stayed out of the way as instructed, away in her own West End Lane flat for days on end, to allow the dust to settle and she only returned when she knew the Dominic incident had blown over, not forgotten but blotted out of their minds. When she reappeared, she carried on with the usual routine for a while trying not to show anything but indifference, as they had often spent days and nights apart and Olivia had long ago accepted that she did not necessarily know where Hugo was at any given moment. She had noticed that a suitcase of his was missing from above the wardrobe. And as each evening darkness settled, and the studio stayed shadowy and unused and eerily quiet, she worried more that he had done something rash or had taken up a hiding position so as not to face the truth.

Jake called round one day, checking she was all right, suggesting he should lock up the workshop, while Hugo was away, better security. He said Hugo had been called to a family tragedy; his father was unwell, he had returned to Athens, Jake had even driven him to Heathrow. There were no further messages or other contacts.

Olivia had always wondered whether it was because he suspected Dominic had made advances toward her, that Hugo in his anger could only see running away as his solution. He had surely observed Dominic's behaviour, the lascivious way he looked at her, wormed and writhed his body around her, fingered her; suspicions must have mounted, that there was something going on behind his back. Although he pretended not to mind, priding himself that their relationship was solid and special, that he trusted her implicitly, enough even to leave her alone with that highly charged Eastern-blooded sex-maniac. Perhaps he misread her, and had to leave to cool off, could not face a confrontation. Dominic may have boasted to his followers about his imagined conquest and Hugo overheard, misinterpreted. Either way, Hugo's control had eventually failed and his temper erupted into feral anger in the only way it could. And Dominic was the loser.

***

Back in that spring of 2006, Olivia's mind was concentrated on one thing and she needed someone she could trust. Cosseted and protected through her adolescence and beyond, thrust out into the big wide world, expected to know how to behave, she was twenty-four years old, barely into adulthood. She had been with child, apparently abandoned, not knowing what to do. It was not all her fault.

She languished in an expensive private bed, watching the endless blank sky outside her windows. In the mirror, she hardly recognised herself: she looked pale, her hair lank, sticking to her neck and forehead. Her body was aching so, from deep within, gnawing at her insides and stretching into her loins. She clutched herself between the legs through the bedclothes or rolled away from the light onto her side, knees brought up together, her face buried in the crumpled pillows, not wanting to see anyone, or talk to anyone.

She felt sorry for herself, understandably. She apologised to the staff all the time, kept saying sorry for no reason. She tried to explain she normally looked better than this, better turned out; better company.

Olivia needed someone she could trust. A friend, to help her cry. She remembers a brief interval of bright sunlight, with shadows of raindrops running down the glass cast across her bare forearm and white sheets while she dozed and peace seemed to come to her. She tried ringing Lotte but obtained no answer.

Embarrassed to find herself in this position, she wanted to keep everything private, to herself. An overwhelming sense of loss tugged at her soul, a feeling of bereavement. The stuffing had been wrenched out of her; she was an empty shell, shaking with guilt, a sense that she had done something wrong and wicked. Although she had not come to feel any new life within, she felt sorely aware of its loss. She was a good person really; her decision had been right for her. Anyone could make a mistake, she promised she would find a way to pay back. Her mother, for all her misgivings, had instilled a true sense of righteousness within her, with Catholic overtones; there was a price for everything. But who was she promising? It was not all her fault, she should not have to take all the blame.

Her heart felt heavy; her body had been violated, scorched within like she had been turned inside out. Her face looked deathly. With no make-up or anything, her skin was dry, her lips cracked. Her eyes, normally the source of her vitality, her spirit, seemed to have lost their brightness, the blue had faded. She felt so tired. She could not muster a smile, the edges of her mouth were fixed in a downturn, even when that sweet Asian nurse brought her a tray with tea and a slice of bread this morning.

There was blood loss, the smell of it was stale and sickly. Not exceptional the gynaecologist said, it would settle. Rest and drink plenty of water. She felt feeble and trembling, swaddled in her thick woolly pink dressing-gown.

It should not have been such a big deal, any modern girl should have been able to take it in her stride. Just one of those things that can happen, that needs to be dealt with, a mistake routinely corrected. But Olivia had cold feelings of regret and guilt in equal measure, that edged their way through her mind, even though she felt herself to be the victim.

- But that had been no mistake, you see. That was entrapment, neither humane nor fair, more an act of gross selfishness. I can get over it. I will get back to work, back to what I know, back to my life as it was.

Of all the people she might have called to share her emotions with, to talk through her feelings, friends she might have relied on, it was her mother who came visiting the second morning and into whose ample bosom she did weep, buckets. The truth was, it was her father, with his soothing and reassuring voice, she might have spoken to, had he poked his head around her door; he had always made her feel safe and she would have been able to have a more dispassionate conversation with him, but it was Martha who bustled in, to hug her and to organise her, and to shuffle her down to the car for the short trip home to Islington. Olivia could not remember calling her. She had been thinking her mother to be unapproachable, but Martha was her saviour. She had explained to her father that Olivia was under the weather, a virus or something, and that she needed a little mothering for a few days.

Olivia was frightened, in danger of losing control and felt so alone. The warmth of someone else come to help her, to offer comfort and to make her decisions for her, even if that person was her mother, was so terribly welcome that morning. So she fell into her mother's generous arms, a feeble supplicant, willing to do whatever she was told.

'But I don't understand, Olivia, darling,' Martha kept prying in the car as she drove tentatively through the wet streets. She wore an artificial fur around her neck and smelled of Chanel. 'You seemed perfectly happy with Jonathon last year. Then you chucked him out. And now this.'

'This has nothing to do with Jon,' Olivia retorted wearily and returned to her reverie, the big Jaguar's easy motion lolling her into a sleepy state. She remained silent for the rest of the journey, just pleased to be going back to the family home to be molly-coddled for a couple of days, without complaint, with home cooking, warmth and security, her life on hold until she felt confident again to face the job and the people.

She longed to be settled with comfy cushions on the old wooden bench, worn and weathered at the back of the walled garden behind the house. It was out of the wind there and quiet. The sun always played across the brick paths and the ivy-clad walls, and the area was bursting with palms and fronds and leafy plants, dripping and climbing over everything. She would recoup her confidence in the spring sunshine that had appeared at last after the dreary wet winter. She would be able to think about her work and do some casual writing. She could forget about Dominic and Hugo, even if they appeared nightly in her dreams; at least during the days, she would be able to ignore them.

'But I don't understand, darling,' Martha persisted, helping her out of the front of the car. 'Was this really necessary?' Martha tried to hug her close and insisted she spent a few extra hours in the spare bedroom midmorning, while she prepared some hot soup and vegetables for when she woke later. 'I bet you haven't been feeding yourself properly.'

She sat with both her parents at dinner and they chatted about irrelevances mostly, and over the next few days she recuperated at her mother's pleasure in privacy, staring at the daily newspaper, gawping at the television day programmes, napping on and off through the day, pecking at her mother's fussy cooking, sleeping restlessly at night, listening to the sounds of the city beyond. Then she woke one day strong again and with an inner certainty that she was over the worst and was ready to return to the fray.

She went back to West End Lane and in a day to her City office, fighting fit, as if nothing had happened, pretending that all things were forgotten. Like Dominic's assault on her, that made Hugo seethe with anger; their complicity in hiding the truth about the accident; Hugo's disappearance from her life, as if it had all been a dream, especially as nobody could tell her where he was exactly and when or if he was coming back; the discovery that she was pregnant, just when she needed Hugo most; or the destruction of the life within, that Hugo was blissfully unaware of, that she alone had been responsible for.

***

- Please. Don't stare at me like that. You need to stop and listen.

Olivia is slumped in front of her mirror, hiding nothing, making a confession of sorts, even after all this time. With Hugo, she allowed chance to take its course. She knew he would not initiate a change, take a lead or make some sort of commitment – if she wanted a stronger union between them, she had decided, having his child was the obvious way to go. She let her discipline slip for a while without telling him and left it to the fates to decide.

- You look nice, I've always told you that.

- Thank you. You remember when I first started talking to you. Years ago, I was a romantic teenager; but I have always been faithful, have always shared everything with you. I do not hide anything from you. You are my trusty partner, you let me share my feelings with you. I mean I have other friends, girl-friends, but they'll just take sides and you always listen without prejudice.

- I don't have a…you know, a boyfriend, at the moment. God.

- Nine years ago: I still live with the memory, the anguish, every day. The thought that I did wrong; that I trapped Hugo, that it was all deliberate. And he defeated me cruelly, by simply walking away. But I showed single-mindedness, determination; I overcame many things. Although I have been left with a deep-felt distrust of men. Maybe that's why bumping into Louise has been such an antidote and so easy, to feel uninhibited with her because we feel an equality between us.

- I just need someone I can trust. You have always helped me to accept certain things in life. Things that cannot be changed. Like my mother, she is who she is. Things that happen, you have helped me to come to terms with them. So much in our paltry lives is fixed and cannot be altered by anything as trivial as desire or willpower. We cannot just wish things to be different. You help me.

Olivia lives with the blame, every day, although over time she has come to feel that Hugo should have taken some responsibility as well. Forgiveness lingers close by but has never been written off, closed; it remains incomplete, even now, even nine years later.

- I cheated for him and killed for him.

- You are in safe hands; there is no need to continue to chastise yourself. What is done is done. Do not judge yourself so harshly. Your journey continues and like all journeys, it is something of a discovery; discovering the nature of your own character, your own self. That is no bad thing. How else do we ever find out who we really are?

- I'm Olivia, by the way.

She smiles at her reflection, and it smiles back.

- But you knew that already.

5

Monday, February 9, 2015

Two mysterious figures in Hugo's life have been playing on Olivia's mind since her return from Switzerland and her overnight tryst in Louise's arms: Jake Preston, his agent, whom she has already met briefly nine years ago; and Jeremy Ashcroft, his business partner, whom she has never met.

Monday starts dull, cold and windy, and for Olivia's first port of call, she finds the office block she is looking for at the lower end of King's Road, behind the Health Authority buildings and a stone's throw from Chelsea's football ground. A most unprepossessing building, Preston Management Services appears in white lettering halfway down a long list of company names on a weather-beaten board hanging outside, third floor. Just as she is pushing through a set of grubby glass doors with relief to escape the biting wind ruffling her hair, her phone buzzes. The hospital again. She is standing alone in a dimly lit lobby with a low ceiling of discoloured plastic tiles, but at least it feels warm.

'Sister, hello, it's Olivia Truelove.'

The line is crackly and before she can make out who she is talking to, the surprise appearance of a dark male face popping up above the wooden countertop in front of her gives her a jolt. In his "security" uniform, he looks friendly enough behind a massive computer screen, smiling a lot, black eyebrows bouncing up and down his short forehead in his excitement at having a visitor.

She recognises Sister Williams' voice. 'Just thought I would let you know. Ms Little seemed to be content that he was making progress.'

'I'm sorry…'

'I was just saying Samantha Little phoned me yesterday to say that Hugo Pitsakis is safe with her, in Wales, Monmouthshire, I think she said. Mr Pitsakis had been desperate to escape the confines of the wards and apparently is feeling so much better now. Ms Little is ministering to him; he is catching up on his rest and regaining his strength. She said there was no need for us to worry. So, I've sent her his next appointment card, and she promises me that he will turn up.'

'That's good. Good. Wales, you say?'

'Yes, we have an address, a village called,' and she fumbles her pronunciation, 'Llandegveth, that's South Wales, isn't it? Anyway, yes, we were worried, but I think Ms Little is dedicated and will do a good job. Just hope they are not too far from a hospital, just in case. But she sounded confident.'

'Thank you for calling me, that's very helpful.'

They end the call and Olivia pockets her phone. She needs to think about what she has just heard, but the Asian guy is now standing directly in front of her, nodding his head with a big smile. 'Please,' he gestures her towards the lift.

Olivia had suspected it must have been Sam, getting him away from the hospital, which she thought was possibly unsafe for him. Recuperation and better safety, somewhere that no one knew about, away from prying eyes and journalists, and a small village in South Wales sounded ideal. So, this is a convenient time for Olivia to get to work on her background research, and she has these two days' leave for that purpose. Finding Preston's address had been easy, the website helpful, and she had phoned first thing for the appointment.

As the lift door slides open on the third floor, a short friendly looking man is waiting for her. He introduces himself quietly as Jake, with just a hint in his eyes that he remembers her from the old days. She hardly recognises him, with a florid goatee beard, deep brown like everything else about him, his tousled hair, his corduroy jacket and open shirt and casual moccasin slip-ons. She can smell cigarettes on him as he leads her through an open-planned office area, divided by cheap partitions, where several casually dressed workers are moving about with their tablets or ears bent to mobiles, clutching their takeout coffees. Jake points to a seat in his untidy corner office, and she sheds her coat, revealing a carefully chosen Marc Jacob V-neck jersey wool dress in tight, bright turquoise.

'Can I get you a coffee or anything?'

'No, no, I'm fine, thanks.'

'So, you were Hugo's friend, a few years back, weren't you, love?' Jake tucks himself into a space the other side of a wooden table, folding his short legs under him, revealing bright yellow socks. 'Terrible business, you heard?' He starts to stroke his beard, in the attitude of an older man. The rest of his tired face is unshaven, and he adopts a look of grave concern at the mention of his friend and client.

'Yes. I have been visiting him in the Charing Cross. But Sam has taken him off somewhere in Wales to recuperate.'

'Oh, I had no idea. I'm just the agent, not privy to the finer points of dear Hugo's friendships. I know Sam, of course, fine woman, fine woman.' He blinks his narrow, pale brown eyes repetitively.

'So, you remember, we met in 2006, once or twice? I was sort of going out with Hugo, the girlfriend?' she sighs, adopting a coy little smile just for Jake, which he obviously finds appealing.

Jake screws his eyes up for a moment in concentration, staring more closely at Olivia, better to study her eyes and suntanned complexion, putting on a fine display of slow recognition. His face is suddenly cracked in half by a tremendous smile showing uneven and stained teeth, as he waves his arms about. 'Yes, of course I remember, although you've changed a bit... Yes, Olivia, how *are* you?' he drools, 'you look, er, wonderful.'

'Fine, doing well, thanks. The thing is.' She is not going to dither, she wants to get on with it. 'I am hoping to do a piece in a magazine or even something weightier, a biography perhaps, I haven't quite decided. About Hugo the artist, the genius, his life and times, his influences and aspirations and so on.' Olivia sounds keen, and Jake seems genuinely to be listening, rubbing his hands together, presumably sensing income generation, eyes softening into something more fatherly. 'That's why I wanted to talk to you. Hugo's best friend. Background and so on.'

'Well. I wouldn't say that. Good. Sounds interesting. Do you have a publisher?'

'No, not exactly, although I already write a column in a City magazine, published by EMAP, I'm sure they would advise.'

'I wouldn't guarantee it.' Jake's interest in Olivia is warming, and he leans across his table towards her, the better to scan his beady eyes over her, from bright magenta lips down to neat navy shoes, via the tight body-hugging dress, well-appreciating what he sees. 'I might be able to help though, contacts and so on. Hugo and me, we were at college together, doing art and stuff.' He reaches for his cigarette pack at this point and, after offering one to Olivia, who shakes her head firmly, lights up with a satisfyingly deep inhalation, letting the smoke then drift out of his mouth and nostrils in little puffs as he speaks. 'He was good, really good, whereas I was a dabbler, had to work hard at it. Not a natural, like Hugo. Talented, what? I should say. I predicted then he would become a star. When I started this organisation, he needed advice about running some of the commercial stuff, so he decided to join us, and very pleased we were too. Good business is Hugo. Lovely man.' When he talks, Jake's upper lip twitches upwards, distorting the rounded shape of his mouth, like it was on a cotton thread, and his eyes cannot stop blinking. Olivia supposes a tic of some sort, which she finds distracting.

She starts to write in a small notebook fished out from a coat pocket and looks enchantingly straight into Jake's eyes. If she sits quietly prompting him from time to time, he will go on talking non-stop in his London street voice, with his idle collection of observations and comment, mostly concerning himself but with vague references to Hugo. Jake reveals how he spent time wandering about Europe in the mid-1990s after he left art school, hanging out with a hedonistic crowd flushed with recreational drugs, so he lost Hugo for a year or two. He started his agency with a few contacts he had in the art world and music business, looking after their interests, helping develop their careers, arranging deals, gigs, commissions, you name it. His group had a mixed collection of writers and poets, artists, a few actors, TV people.

'I want to move into the sports area, like the footballers, that's where there is a lot of money to be made.' And Jake compresses his lips into a strained look of determination with a couple of nods of his head as he imagines the riches piling up. His messy hair flops around as the tic speeds up, and he nervously wipes at his nose with a free hand.

'So, what was it about Hugo that attracted you, you became good friends?' Olivia realises that she has to improve her questioning skills, which will need some practice.

Jake pulls a leg up and wraps an arm around the knee, while he fiddles with the elastic of his socks, and he starts to rock back and forth. A smile develops over his face at some amusing recollection or other. 'Hugo is a big bloke, physically, but a gentle giant against my small frame, we were like Little and Large, an odd couple, but we both liked the same sort of music, went to plenty of gigs together, talked football. Punk was strong, and we wrote some stuff, a band we knew did a couple of our songs. He used to hang out late at night behind the scenes, clubs and that. But it was painting and drawing that he was most adept at, he was always sketching on a pad, listening to the music, or when he was out and about. He had a way with a brush, just the ability to create movement and shape with the minimal of stokes, you know, just a flick and a twist and he had the depth and the three-dimensions of a picture. His was a rare talent, but he was always getting into local politics and argument, with right-wing toffs and socialist union groups. Actually, I think he had taken politics and economics at University College for a year before he came to Camberwell. He was often quite outspoken. But he couldn't abide the politicians, he hated their hypocrisy. I often wondered whether he would be tempted, he was clever enough.'

'You mean by a life in politics?'

'Yeah, but he was an artist foremost, he believed in the search for beauty through expression. He painted as his emotions and feelings dictated. He did a few cartoons of politicians, New Labour, and some were put onto postcards, greetings cards, sold quite well actually, I got him some of those contracts, before Jeremy came along.'

Olivia is loving this, all the detail from the horse's mouth, and is scratchily scribbling down as much of Jake's words she can catch.

'I was busy expanding Prestons, we moved in here about five years ago, I had a grotty shop over a bookmaker's in Whitechapel before. And then out of the blue, he turns up here, few years ago now, and says he wants help, marketing and fronting, facing the public; he wanted a more public-oriented career, like a service he was offering. He didn't want to become a recluse like so many painters, hidden away in the shadows, lost in a messy studio so the customer never sees him. He wanted more interaction, taking a more active part, and that's what has driven his teaching and his work in the East End, in schools and that.'

'Ooh, I didn't know about that,' Olivia cooed, beginning to recognise some of the complexities of the man.

'Well, he wanted more control, so that a painting by him would not necessarily just be finished and sold and then lost to some home or institution; he wanted a private gallery to hang his works so that they delivered a story, a continuum. Obviously, he needed to sell them to make a living, but he usually made copies: he employed students to do the work. And he started taking commissions, retaining the copies – so that they were not forgotten. He preferred to sell to galleries, so he got paid, I got paid and the painting stayed in the public view. Win-win.'

'So he owns a gallery?'

'In Charlotte Street, it's private, by invitation only, but he does hold public viewing days. And every painting has a reproduction or a copy for sale and other merchandise, surprisingly lucrative. He came into some money, when his father died, did you know? Quite a lot, actually, like winning the lottery, although he never quite let on even with me how much – but you're talking millions. He created his Butlers' Wharf studios and apartment, developed the Charlotte Gallery, and he has a workshop at Elephant & Castle. And still has the Theed Street studios.'

'All sounds amazing.'

'You're talking an amazing guy, lady. And he has further ambitions. Well, he had further visions; we don't know how he will be after this shooting, do we?'

'He will take a long time to recover fully, I imagine,' says Olivia with a grimace and a knowing nod, visualising Sister Williams' sad expression on the subject when they first met.

'He was working on his First World War series: very ambitious. He has been over to Flanders several times, stayed there last autumn for a week. This is a massive work on behalf of the Commonwealth War Graves Commission. I've only had a glance, but, wow, they are good. He has had some special music composed by a modern cellist friend and the first showing is planned at the South Bank with a live orchestra of eight cellists (they're all from the Berlin Philly); it's quite heart-wrenching, it goes into The Last Post, with its single bugle. You must come along, well, it's scheduled for November, Remembrance Day, later this year.'

'Yes, I must.' Olivia's face is a picture, eyes wide with excitement, mouth in a slight grin, yet a look changing from admiration to disbelief that one man can be involved in so much. No wonder he needs an agent.

'So, Hugo happy with this, is he? I mean the biography? Doesn't sound much like Hugo: despite his approach with the public, he is not what you would call a celebrity type; he tends to shy away from all that, leaves it to others to speak on his behalf.'

'Oh yes. Well, when I knew him he certainly kept out of the limelight. I'm sure he would appreciate a good piece about him, to counteract the impression in the papers that he is a common criminal, the way the police have treated him.'

'No. Yes, oh yes, he must be feeling so angry. Lucky to be alive, though, perhaps he does not realise what has happened. Sam will tell him, she will fill in the details.'

'How long have Hugo and Sam been together?'

'Oh, they've known each other for ages, they go way back, well about the time I met him. I don't think they are together, you know, an item; although, he's obviously had her, I mean they have been, you know…' And Jake's voice trails off with slight embarrassment, his eyes swivelling over Olivia's shapely body. Staring at her bare knees, he blinks wildly and gives a little cough, his mouth twitching.

'Lovers, yes, I imagined so. But they don't live together then?'

'Well, not as a rule, not as far as I know. Hugo's love-life is no concern of mine, I hasten to add; although he is inclined to get up to some tricky things from time to time, so long as it doesn't interfere, we don't ask questions, eh?'

'I gather the two girls he was with, Nika and Lilly, were on your books. You introduced them to Hugo, is that right, Jake?'

'Yeah, quite. They are my girls, not exclusively, but we find them various gigs, quite legit. Hard working, they are. They do girlie jobs, you know, a bit of dancing, posing, a bit of arse and tit, pays well, even down Whitechapel.' Jake looks pleased with himself.

'But why was Hugo spending the night with them, apart from the obvious, of course?'

'Oh, Olivia, I would not be at liberty to say.' Jake is shrugging in all innocence, his hands turned over to face the ceiling as if to say don't ask me. 'Best left to Hugo himself to provide the reasoning there, wouldn't you say?'

'Yes, obviously I need to ask Hugo. So, when did his father die then, when he acquired all that money?'

'Oh, gosh, well, that would have been around early 2006, end of March or April, I think, I'm not sure of the exact date; it was just a few months after the Whitechapel Gallery success, which was his first breakthrough really. He sold three paintings at over six thousand quid apiece, it paid for his trips back to Greece and helped his mother move back to England.'

Jake suddenly jerks upright, slapping his hands on his thighs. 'I've been rattling on and on. Surely you would like some tea or coffee? We have water. Anything?'

Olivia shakes her head again and smiles, 'No thanks. You go ahead.' She rather likes Jake. He has a well-worn friendly face and seems to speak with honesty, not so common in his trade. She feels he would have Hugo's best interests at heart, which reflected his professional role in Hugo's life. And it is obvious they are friends. Olivia is dying to ask him if he is married, any children, but does not quite venture down that route. She glances around his busy office, every surface covered with unruly piles of papers, books and magazines and there are dozens of photographs of various personalities from the media world in frames, the walls covered in blown-up faces, but she cannot see a shot of Hugo anywhere. Nor does she see a domestic one of Jake with a woman and a couple of kids.

'You see, there is no picture of Hugo, he really does not like that sort of thing. But over here,' and he waves an arm for her to direct her attention to a small, black and white picture hanging by the door. Here was a group of three men standing together, quite clearly Hugo in the middle with Jake and the then

Prime Minister, Mr Tony Blair shaking hands in front of a large picture, a portrait of the PM himself.

'When was this taken?'

'Oh, about 2007.' Jake goes over to his desk and reaches for the mouse, activating the computer screen, which he studies for his other day's appointments.

'Sorry if I've kept you away from your meetings.'

'Well, I have a few today, but we're all right. Listen, the person you must see is Jeremy, he's the sort of brains behind the business. Works closely with Hugo. I'm just a marketing man, I organise some gigs, a few photo-shoots, explore the galleries. His business negotiations are with Jeremy Ashcroft and he is quite an astute chap. But he is also passionate about the art, you know? I'm not so appreciative, I mean I love the stuff Hugo does, it's the best and he is really talented, he deserves a knighthood frankly. But my talents are more the smell of the oily rag and the feeling on the streets, the mood of the times, you get me?'

As Olivia retraces her steps along the King's Road she is thinking back to the time of Hugo's sudden disappearance, which, according to Jake, coincides with his father dying in Greece, which is where he had gone to help with the family affairs, according to everyone she spoke to. Shortly after the Lebelov accident.

- So, that made it all right, did it?

- No, but it's corroboration at least, it explains what happened. It wasn't just Hugo running away from me, for no apparent reason.

***

The next morning, dreaming of Louise all the way, Olivia ambles enjoyably down from the hill-top at Hampstead, along Admiral's Walk, to find Jeremy Ashcroft's place, a modern narrow townhouse built over five floors of steel and brick with pine wood cladding, probably worth a few million. Jeremy is effusive in his welcome and leads her down a grey steel staircase to an open-planned living-area in the basement. Warmed by its traditional Aga, it looked out through folding windows onto a patio and a grassy patch, surrounded by high ivy-covered brick walls giving it total privacy.

His wife is away with their two children visiting her parents in Norwich, Jeremy happily explains. So they are able to talk with their mugs of coffee without interruption sitting opposite each other at the oaken family table, the rest of the house peacefully quiet. A few toys were arranged around the room, a small tricycle and upturned coloured trucks, bricks and cuddly toys.

It is not unusual to have a spare hour or so now that he works more often from home, he says and seems quite happy to talk about his mate, Hugo. They had overlapped at College, although they did not particularly know each other then, not like with Hugo and Jake, but the three of them had soon become acquainted, together with Sally-Ann, his student girlfriend at the time and soon-to-be wife.

'Did Jake send you?'

Olivia nods. 'Thought it would be a good idea.'

'Well, we must all wish Hugo a speedy recovery, poor sod. I visited a couple of weeks ago, but he was too poorly to see anyone. Sam was there, but she said he was not conscious most of the time and he had so many procedures carried out, he was always in the theatres.' Jeremy speaks quietly, with a rather public school accent, well-bred. He is pleasant-looking and manly, with a good head of mousy hair, plastered down and parted, a clean-shaven face and thick horizontal eyebrows that waver up and down and sometimes curl as the mood takes them. With talk of Hugo's injuries and tragic situation, they are generally drooped in a grave frown over deep-set eyes that look almost black in the shadowy gloom.

'Do you want to sit outside?' Jeremy asks, pointing to the wooden chairs on the decking, as a little shaft of sunlight finds its way between the surrounding foliage onto his strip of lawn.

'No, it's all right. Quite cold, actually,' she says with a shiver and pulls her coat she has not discarded around herself. She is wearing a dark trouser suit and sensible shoes, the professional look, which she thought would project the right image to a business manager.

'Would you like a biscuit?' In the corner a small TV, its volume lowered, is running through a Jeremy Kyle Show, the studio audience showing a mixture of tears and bile. Olivia's attention is distracted, but she declines his offer and launches in: 'I was wanting to chat with you about Hugo for background and stuff. I am researching him for a book I am planning about his life and works, and Jake particularly said I should talk to the brains behind the operation.'

'Is that what he called it?'

'Well, yes, he thinks of it as an operation; he admitted the artistry meant not so much to him.'

'Jake is a terrific organiser, but I don't think he has ever seen the beauty or meaning behind Hugo's works, a bit of a philistine actually.' Whereas Jeremy, of course, is the doyen of the modern art scene and enthusiastic supporter of Hugo and all his works, Olivia is thinking, recalling the large framed painting in the hallway of the house that presents any new visitor to the Ashcroft's as they step inside the front door with an image stunning and real enough to stop them in their tracks. A panoramic view of an Arabic city, under intense midday heat, a few spirited domes and pillars reaching for the sky out of the mass of its low-rise concrete buildings, riddled with signs of battle and grinding poverty, entitled "Aleppo 2014". There are groups of civilians, men and women with children, with fear and despair etched on their weather-beaten faces, tramping out of the city into the desert with their makeshift trolleys and bundles of possessions, their clothes dirty and torn, their shoes worn thin; as on the far side, an artillery and mobile force of soldiers with automatic rifles and coloured scarves over their faces sets up its position on some rising ground overlooking the city. In places, thick black smoke is billowing skywards from explosions across the city; ugly shell holes in the walls and fallen masonry speak of the on-going violence of the place. The focus though, through all this mess and mayhem, is directed onto a small boy sitting in the dusty road, his pitiable round face smeared with dirt and blood, crying, his arms raised towards the backs of the crowd walking away, as if forgotten or abandoned.

This colourful drama fills the wall across a small void of the stairwell, with a bannister preventing anyone reaching out to touch it, but equally offering protection as they flinch at the thought of being caught up in the impending action. Olivia had shuddered with wonder, almost hearing the screams of battle, the cries for help in her mind and seeing the texture of the clothes and the uniforms so vivid, so tactile, the movement so three-dimensional that she knew immediately it was Hugo's work without seeing his tell-tale signature in the bottom right-hand corner.

'I knew Hugo some years ago, actually, we were sort of going out together, when he was starting out as an artist, but we lost touch, you know, over the years and went separate ways. And then I heard about this shooting episode and I visited the hospital a few times and met Sam, she's nice; she's very supportive. I never actually got to talk to Hugo, and now Sam's taken him out of the hospital and away somewhere secret, in Wales, she was worried about his safety.'

'Really? You mean she thought Hugo was still at risk; might be attacked again, in the hospital?'

'Well, that's what Sam seemed to be concerned about, yes. I didn't think that was likely if the whole thing was a police error. Surely there is nobody out there with a feeling of hatred or a grudge against Hugo, is there?'

Jeremy looks thoughtful, puckering those mobile eyebrows as he sits heavily on his wooden chair, contemplating his white coffee cup and saucer on the table in front of him. He reaches for a sugar bowl and a small jug of milk and mumbles 'Help yourself' before returning to the unpleasant dilemma of explaining the shooting of Hugo. 'Hugo and I have known each other a while, and I think I know the man inside quite well. We are just now developing a number of things, in our favour, business and what-not. The whole episode is very odd. It feels so like a jealous opponent, or a lover, someone he has upset. You know, I don't buy the police story, not so easily; it just feels like some setup.'

Olivia is stirring her cup, but with thin brows arched upwards, she catches a glance at Jeremy, whose dark eyes are deep and hooded and difficult to fathom. She notices some hairs along the front of his neck, over his Adam's apple that have been unexpectedly spared, and a nick in the skin nearby, a thin dark line of clot over its peak.

'So, are you a writer, Olivia?'

'I work in the City, at Emerson Smith. Fund management, I'm on the European desk at present. But I also write a monthly column for "*Money Made Simple*", and occasional investment pieces for a Sunday column. I nearly went for journalism, but economics won the day. So this project with Hugo sort of deals with more than one skill set, such that I have. I think he is a wonderful subject for a biography, don't you?'

'Well, yes, I mean, I love the man. And I love his work and I love much of his philosophy. Writing a dense biography would be quite a different prospect from a newspaper column, I should imagine, not that I'm any sort of expert you understand.' Before Olivia could reply, Jeremy carries on. 'But we would need to deal with this in an ultra-sensitive way, I mean it's how it's portrayed that would be important. How much freedom are you going to have, I mean vis-à-vis the exact content and the editing, I think our team would want to be very much involved at the editing stage.'

'Yes, of course…'

'I mean Hugo knows about this, right, he has agreed, has he? Because it's not really like him unless it was all low-key, hush-hush; I mean, you won't get him into Waterstones signing copies.' Jeremy's eyebrows rise up sharply, accompanied by a knowing look, a sort of suppressed laugh, and Olivia notes his scepticism.

'The first thing is to get back to some sort of routine again with Hugo fit. We don't know how long he will need to recuperate, do we? I mean, he will regain his full fitness, won't he? He was a pretty energetic fellow, jolly difficult to keep up with most of the time.'

Olivia is slightly taken aback at Jeremy's bid for control of her project; she imagined something that would be entirely hers, with all the freedoms she wanted. 'I was wondering actually about these women in the flat. You know, what was Hugo doing staying at this place in Shepherd's Bush? Did he know Midge Martin, who sounds like a pretty unsavoury character?'

'The girls, Nika and Lilly, are models that he was using for one of his current works; both of them are on Jake's books and he had found them for Hugo, as I understand it. Hugo probably had a long session with them that ran late into the night, he slept over and left the next morning, needing a lift to wherever he was going.' Jeremy's voice fades out and now it is Olivia's turn to offer her most innocent look while barely hiding her scepticism.

She tries to keep a professional face but is beginning to be irritated by Jeremy's persistent claim to all of Hugo's thoughts and desires. After another half hour or so of comments and conjecture, with a top-up coffee and eventually a small cookie, Olivia comes away with the understanding that Jeremy approved in principle to her working on a Hugo biography and that she should start laying out her chapters with titles and pursuing her research as she sees fit, but that Hugo needed to recover fully and be totally on board with the idea for Jeremy to give the go-ahead. In the meantime, she might like to sound out a few possible publishers to gain a better understanding of the current market and what sort of commercial deal she might be looking for.

***

On leaving Jeremy's place, she takes the downhill routes from Hampstead village, along Frognal to the Finchley Road, crossing over towards her old patch and the West End Lane. She remembers some chilly afternoons among the local mums with their prams and little wrapped bundles sitting around the Green, under the leafy plain and chestnut trees. It is not as tidy as it used to be: there is an overflowing litter bin by the gate and last autumn's sodden leaves are still choked around the edges, swept by the wind and trapped against wire fencing and under the legs of the benches. Opposite on the island the old public toilets are still open, and over on the far side, the fire station looks to be still working.

The day has become gloomy and overcast, but the exercise has warmed her, so that she unbuttons her coat and loosens her scarf and finds herself a cafe to have a sit down and a cappuccino. From her seat in the window, she can just see the front of her old flat further down the lane, above the laundromat which is still there, its cracked paint and rickety looking window frames unchanged. She became fond of the area, even if the streets were overcrowded, the diesel buses noisy. The streets were always friendly and busy, the shops staying open late most nights to cater for the locals, especially the Greeks and Turks that rented here. The prices had always been high, but with City access reasonably easy, it was worth it; although since she had moved away the house prices had really rocketed.

She resumes her walk along West End Lane through familiar territory and passes the end of Lymington Road, which fires sudden memories of Andrew, dossing in her place, where she had moved to for a short while after the "Hugo" saga. She struggles to remember what she ever saw in him. They had bumped into each other, rather too literally, in a bar below Canon Street full of happy City types with their trainees in tow after a particularly successful coup on the trading floors one Friday lunchtime, when everyone was drinking too much and touching too much. Andrew had wrapped a large hand around her and was squeezing her bottom and whispering into her dainty ear that he wanted the best shag in the business and she had agreed, uncharacteristically but only because a girl from her office had bet her twenty quid she couldn't get laid before the weekend. Andrew moved in soon afterwards, partly on the strength of his good shagging technique and partly because she needed to take advantage of his knowledge in the firm to help her with her promotion prospects. He was a few notches further up the greasy pole than she was and far better-off and so a little help with the exorbitant rent would not have gone amiss either.

Following three days' staying with her mother after her father's funeral, she had returned one afternoon to find pretty-boy Andrew lounging about in a pair of dirty y-fronts. The combined pong of his socks and dried semen made her wretch and after opening a few windows to let out the unpleasant smells and let in some fresher air, she turned on him with a lacerating degree of frustration that even now she is ashamed to recall. 'I know you've been masturbating in here, you haven't even changed the sheets.'

'But where have you been, Olly, I was worried. I had no idea where you were or when you were coming back.' He was reaching for some clothes to cover his pale body, with a cigarette smouldering in an overfull ashtray by the bed, her bed.

'So you laze about making the place dirty. Have you washed up? Done some cleaning? What the fuck are you doing here anyway this time of day? What do you mean you've lost your job?'

'I was fired by that bastard Rutherford, four of us, for consistently sub-standard performance.' By then she had been getting the hang of life at Emerson's, whereas Andrew had sunk out of favour with the toffs: his job loss came as no surprise.

'Oh God. So have you been looking for another job?' Normally, during odd moments of affection, she might have called him Andy. 'You're disgusting, Andrew. You said you would not smoke in here. You are such a drip. I don't think I can have you living here anymore.' She threw him his crumpled jeans that were under a chair. 'I don't know why I let you in, in the first place, really. I took sympathy on you, but now, frankly, all the novelty has worn off.' She gave him a fiery look of disdain. 'And nobody calls me Olly. It's time to pack up and leave, Andrew, I'm sorry.'

And so on, she was unrelenting. An hour later he sloped off with his stuffed suitcases and a tacky raincoat, trudging along to West Hampstead station in the drizzle. She hated to be called anything but Olivia and was much relieved to see the back of him. He had not been there long and she really had not formed any attachment to him, thank goodness. She always thought he was unclean, but he was pretty looking and she had foolishly fallen for the forlorn look; he was quite obviously a mistake, a fill-in at a difficult time.

- Anyway, I really did not need a man at that moment. Who does need them, when?

A question she had asked herself many a time, usually with a little dismissive smirk, knowing full-well that she would inevitably fall for another pretty boy with a lean body, a clean pair of pants and a good story to tell.

She spent hours furiously cleaning the place, washing all the plates and cutlery, wiping down the floors, spraying the lavatory with bleach, putting the washing machine on, trying to wipe away all his traces. She changed the sheets, even turned the mattress over. Some smalls of his left in a drawer and a couple of his paperbacks were binned, photos removed from frames and dumped. She erased all remaining signs of the pathetic Andrew.

Only a few months after that, she made a huge leap, financially and socially, and moved to the Barbican estate, a rather more exclusive haunt.

She reaches the tube station and relaxes in the warm carriage on her way through to Baker Street and the Circle Line. At one point, she nods off, dreaming of meeting a perfectly fit Hugo and of being whisked away into his troubling world once again.

6

Saturday, February 21, 2015

The days go by, a week or more and Olivia has slipped back impeccably into her disciplined routine, the dawn starts and the frenetic activity through the day; and all the while, uneventful as far as the Hugo saga is concerned. She finds no other annoying little paragraphs about the shooting in the newspapers and hears nothing from Sam or anyone else. The story has gone quiet.

She keeps up with her foil fencing and saunters over to Louise's quite often, when she can resist the offers of comfort and sex no longer, even in midweek. Although aware that she has not properly started on her new project, she has been sufficiently busy to be distracted, content that Hugo is recovering in good hands and calm surroundings. She is pleased that he and Sam are spending close time together. He will be drawn back instinctively to London soon enough.

One day she decides to grab the bull by the horns: or at least to move a little further forward in her preparation, by visiting Hugo's mother. They had met at the hospital canteen the one time and she hopes that the old lady remembers her favourably. With Hugo out of the way, now would be a good time to talk to her in depth about her son. She finds her listed in an old phone book: Pitsakis, Golders Hill Park and over the phone they mutually agree a visit mid-morning Saturday. A coffee and a little chat in the warmth of her lounge in her fine house at its fine address are welcome on what is an exceptionally chill morning. There is ice on the roads and a thick laurel hedge out front is still wrapped in silvery crystals from overnight frost. No strolling in the garden later for Bernadette, she says, the chill plays havoc with her arthritis.

'I hate this English weather. I crave the Mediterranean sun and some freshly picked olives.'

From the little she knows about Bernadette, she had been a formidable Greek matriarch in her time and in some ways presents more of a daunting challenge for Olivia than the affable if sceptic Jeremy or easy-going Jake. How is she to avoid looking like a young woman on the make, trying to wheedle details out of her about her son's life; for what, a revealing article in a gossip magazine? She would not believe that it was a *bona fide* attempt to unravel the mysteries and the character of an interesting man of his time, a person of public interest, or that her writing might be of literary value and constitute a respectable tome on contemporary artists, who were shaping the modern world.

'Call me Bernie, won't you,' she confides with a motherly smile and a light touch on Olivia's forearm, as she leads her to a cane lounger with soft cushions, pink roses patterned on a green background which manage to match the décor in the room, 'all my friends do.' She has arranged some dark green olives in an oily pile in a glass dish, with some wooden picks scattered next to them on the table alongside a plate of shortbread biscuits.

'Ah, those times have long passed, sadly,' she continues to moan, as she pulls a bright blue cardigan around herself against the cold. Olivia gives her a reassuring smile. 'Have you ever been to Greece? The virgin olive oils are the best in the world; the olives of Lesbos are to die for, and they improve my joints, like magic.' She is of short stature, as noticed in the hospital, but here in her home she looks flushed, bustling and larger than life, if a little uncomfortably squeezed into a patterned blue-and-white dress that is too tight across her bosom and expansive bottom. She is holding up a tall glass bottle without its cork and the light catches its yellowish sluggish contents. 'I get these from a deli here, the next best thing, I suppose. The Kolovi olive tastes of pepper,' and she places the open top under her nose, 'but smells of artichokes and grass.'

She pours freshly made coffee and plonks herself down opposite, the low glass table between them. She rolls back on the deep cushions, rubbing her hands together in her expansive lap. 'You know I play bridge and backgammon; we have a club night every Tuesday. You play? My late husband was a devilish player. Hugo sadly is never interested. Always swishing a paint brush and wanting to show off.'

She laughs wearily and her jowls wobble. Her greying hair is pulled back both sides of her crumpled face and tied with a blue ribbon at the back. She appears quite sun-tanned, but Olivia thinks that maybe that is her natural skin colour. She has heavy bags under her eyes, with ageing brown spots around her neck. 'So what could you possibly want of my son, I ask myself? He paints pictures, big ones, but you know that, and tries to make a living from that when he should be running his father's business. That's it, that's Hugo.' Olivia is about to put in a word for herself, but Bernadette presses on. 'Perhaps you might be girlfriend, no? But of course, there is Sam, good old Sam, always there, but never they settle. I don't know.'

Bernadette shrugs in characteristic Greek style, as if the whole world is a hopeless case, which she cannot understand. She looks assertive, wondering if she has touched a sensitive nerve but Olivia can see that she enjoys saying controversial things.

'I wanted to ask you...' Olivia hesitates, waiting for her host to butt in and stop her.

'My late husband build big firm, work for thousands, Greek workers and trade he brought back to the mainland was something incredible. It was good. Good work, steady, it make profits, big. He provided good living. But all that is going, thousands in trouble. After all that hard work and build-up of an empire. And my son, what did he do but sell it all to private finance company for millions of dollars, for God's sake, so he can go on dabbling in his oil painting! And this shooting business, what is this? Some sort of trouble he is in?' She leans forward with a look of gloom to grasp her coffee with pudgy fingers and begins to slurp tentatively at the hot surface. She has a fine carpeting of dark hairs over both sides of her upper lip, which she wraps over the edge of the broad china cup.

Olivia decides letting her talk is the best thing, but to help her on at this point. 'Do you know where he is right now, Bernie? You know he has left the hospital? With Samantha.'

'Oh yes, I know, of course. Sam has taken him to her cottage in Wales, for recovery and that is good, although what is wrong with his mother's house, eh, where cooking is healthy, substantial? What can Sam provide that his mother cannot?'

'Oh, I can't imagine, really,' Olivia retorts quickly, looking around at the comfortable living style, the large kitchen with its plentiful piles of fruit and loaves of bread, and its wonderful smell of coffee.

'Sister Whatever phoned me, I said I know nothing, no idea.' And she laughs a full chesty roar, knowing that she has been a tad naughty.

'Bernie, you rascal,' Olivia exclaims, but rather approves of the older woman's approach. What does the hospital know, indeed?

Bernadette has a guttural rumbling laugh that reminds her of Hugo's. She is prone to dump her hands into her capacious lap and let out an air of exasperation at the actions of her son and the modern world in general. She has lost control of her bushy eyebrows that are greying and thinning at their outer ends and with her husky voice, Olivia is wondering about myxoedema and such. But Bernie is surprisingly agile: she pops up from her chair to reach for a bookbinder from the sideboard and Olivia realises she is about to be subjected to endless happy family photos.

'My other son you have not met, perhaps, he was here on Friday last, came over from Greece with Hebe. Knew nothing of this shooting, he is angry young man, he thinks Hugo puts his family and inheritance in danger and does not take proper precautions. I'm not certain what he means really, but Loukas is absolutely sure that Hugo has brought all this onto himself.'

'Loukas, the younger brother? And a sister? He never really talked about them. Do they live in Greece?'

'He is Greek. He has his family, his wife Salma and they have a baby girl. Runs the trading company, Pitsakis and Sons. Notice "and sons", but no Hugo. Loukas very cross, I think. Hugo gets the money and Loukas gets the hard work of running a failing business in Greece, where everything is broken, no one works anymore.'

'I had no idea.'

'And Hebe is 23, very attractive, my youngest, also lives in Greece, close to Loukas; wants to be actress, spends time waiting tables, poor girl.'

'So, there is resentment there? I mean rivalry, is it serious? Just Hugo never mentioned to me, I mean years ago, when he was younger. Before his father died. When was that exactly? Sorry.' Olivia is trying to be gentle while tying events together. She even brings out her little notebook with her pencil, holding them up for Bernadette to see and raises an eyebrow as a question. She realises she may be rushing her, but she seems willing to chat freely about her children.

'May 6, 2006. We have family home in Marousi, northern Athens. After the funeral and the reading of the will, there was confusion, but Hugo went off for two days somewhere, to think he said – I think he went up into the mountains on his own. He came back, with energy and force and he visit all the businesses, met the managers and agents, go into head office and speak with accountants and clerks and many workers and he decides he would run the show. He lived with me for two or three months and went into the works every day, worked weekends. Threw himself into the business, sat with the Directors. But,' and Bernadette hesitates here, with a look of despair, her unkempt eyebrows extending upwards with a sideways tilt of her large head, and those arms going up again, with the shoulders shrugging, 'after a while he realised it was not for him. We sat in the kitchen and he held my hands and said: "Mama, business is not for me, I don't think in the right way, I can't understand the ways they work, the unions, the demands, and so much paperwork, it drives me crazy." He wanted to be back with his paints and his friends and the life he had in London. So…by August, he was gone. I decided afterwards I would return to London house and make this my base for most of the year. I had some money, so I could choose. I have few friends here and sometimes I get to see Hugo.'

Olivia is scribbling notes, the notebook resting on her knee. After a tantalising pause, during which Bernadette seems to stare into the middle distance, remembering things that were perhaps a little painful, while she sips absent-mindedly at her coffee, Olivia almost whispers: 'Did he mention me at all, at that time, when he came down from the mountains or when he decided to return to London?' She really wants to know the answer to this question.

'Olivia, I have poor memory. He mentioned people's names, but…I don't know, I don't recall an Olivia.'

'Oh well. I would love to hear you speak about Hugo himself, you know, what sort of man he is, what was he like at school, where did he get his artistic talents from, that sort of thing.'

'I show you pictures, yes.' She pulls the photo album across her lap and pushes a pair of thick-rimmed spectacles onto her nose. 'Come, sit here,' indicating the space on the cushions next to her and Olivia hops across the gap to oblige. 'We need some more coffee, yes.' Bernadette pushes her frame up with her sturdy arms and waves Olivia to sit still as she reaches for the carafe and milk jug. It is a few moments before she plonks her weight back onto the double cushions again and Olivia bobs up and down like a floating buoy.

'Hugo was born in London, went to early school here. Hardly spent any time in Greece, didn't speak Greek well. The twelfth of March 1980 was his birthday, and I was in Queen Charlotte's Hospital. That was crowded and hot, I remember. Barnabas arrived just in time, mainly because Hugo was big baby and late,' she chuckles. She has opened the album and is pointing at a series of pictures of babies and young couples with smiling tanned faces. Olivia always remembered Hugo's birthday because hers was the day after, the thirteenth of March, but one year later, 1981.

'He loved his father, he was a good boy, did well at school, he was a big boy, no good at games, he studied well, he read a lot, always had his nose in a book, classic stories. And he drew pictures, with a pencil on scraps of paper. He did pictures of people, their faces, their movements.' Bernadette prodded her pudgy fingers onto certain photos, picking out a young Hugo in a school group picture. 'He was good, but Barnabas was disappointed with him really, he showed no ambition for business and he seemed uncompetitive. Whereas Barnabas liked to see youngsters with determination to win, to play games with strength and conviction. He had ideas that Hugo would come into the business, maybe at 16, but Hugo kept away and studied hard. Loukas was coming along but was younger by five years.'

'So where did Hugo derive all his artistic instinct, where did his ideas come from, I wonder?' Olivia recalled those first paintings she saw in the Camden Town Gallery, when she was unable to get to talk to him afterwards but leaving with such strong impressions in her mind that she could never forget.

Bernadette is constrained inside her tight dress and stretches her back with a groan and a grimace, raising herself a little, 'Have you seen the painting in Jeremy's house?'

'Yes, it's magnificent.'

'Jeremy paid Hugo a few thousand pounds for that. Hugo read a lot of history, he loved the old stories of the battles, in the European wars. Lately he very interested in First World War and the damage to the villages and the people. He stay in Bruges last year, went to Ypres, Mons, the Somme, stayed a week, like a working holiday. He go round the cemeteries and old battlefields with ex-Army people, so he try to understand the horrors of the war and the meaning. A lot of Greeks die in that war.'

It is obvious to Olivia that Bernadette has always kept a close watch on her oldest son, even if she rarely saw him these days, speaking of him with knowledge and pride.

'Hugo was shocked when his father died, early really, had a heart attack and then clots on the lungs. There was some nasty business with the Government, talk of fraud, Barnabas was angry. This upset him, affected his heart. Hugo seemed confused. He always said he did not want to follow his father into business and live in Greece; they argued and shouted about it sometimes, but he respected and loved his father, for his great success, in business. He built an empire, shipping, containers, transport, oil.'

'So how much did Hugo inherit in the end then,' Olivia tries casually.

'He sold out for sixty-four million dollars in the summer of 2008.'

'Wow,' Olivia is wide-eyed, her mouth open.

'He have lots of argument with tax people, in London, in Athens, but they decide, I think, they settle. I move to England after that; to be near Hugo, of course. I thought Loukas might come over, but he stayed to do his best, like Barnabas want. But they have not done well, with all the debt problems; loss of jobs, pensions stripped, no confidence. Is terrible. I was thinking maybe I should have stayed there, to help Loukas; and for better climate and for my olives.' She chuckles good-humouredly, her face brightening for a moment at the thought of blazing hot afternoons rambling through dusty mountain-sides of olive groves, but soon it reverts to its hangdog look. 'But they riot in the streets, there is anarchy and chaos, no one seems to work, the Government has no money; God knows what will happen.'

Her large figure slumps back on her cushions, in despair at the turn of events in her world. Olivia is quietly writing a few notes, watching Bernadette from a corner of her eye, in a state of total surprise by the sums of money mentioned. Bernadette starts up again in a hushed dreamy tone. 'Sometimes it is nice to live in one's own dreams and memories. Barnabas worked so hard to provide prosperity, for his people, to keep them in work, off the streets. He had a calling, I think; and maybe Hugo has the same conscience, the moral strength,' and her hands are quivering by her face, trying to find the right words to explain things. Hugo's motives and ambitions have obviously been hard for his mother to understand. 'He seems to want to help others. I hoping one day he gets the painting bug out of his system, he will return to his roots and his people.'

'His father would have wished it, I suppose,' says Olivia cajolingly. 'But his painting is so stunning, Bernie, it's majestic.'

'Ah, well, young men today, they have their heads turned by London, the big city and the business, the girls probably and they like the good life. Are you one of his girls, my dear?'

'No, Mrs Pitsakis, Bernie, I am not. Although, I did know Hugo briefly some years ago when he first started, and I loved his work. His paintings are monumental, they are important statements about our world. He will become famous for them and they will sell for big money, I imagine. Your son is multi-talented and I think he should use that talent to the best of his ability.' Bernadette is looking sceptical and is still shaking her head slowly, or perhaps it is more of a tremor. 'He communicates through his painting, Bernie, his influence *is* through the art.'

'Are you in love with him?' Bernie asked, intuitively.

'Heavens, no.' Olivia is shocked, definitely not wanting to give that impression. 'I am a journalist and an investment manager in the City. I want to write a biography about Hugo and about his artistic works. I think he is a great talent and the public would be interested.'

During another pause, it is so quiet around them that Olivia can hear the faint ticking of a clock and Bernadette's wheezy breathing. 'It will be illustrated, full colour, expensive? To appreciate the pictures?' she asks.

'Oh yes, absolutely, heavy and glossy, with first-rate photographs. I have all that in mind. A coffee table book.'

'Hugo was fond of politics before all this shooting business. Do you think there is connection? I suspect there is. What does Sam think? She is very sensible woman and very loyal. Why does he not marry her, they have been together for so long?'

Olivia says nothing, just nods her agreement, absorbing carefully all of Bernadette's words.

***

It seemed like an odd coincidence that later that same evening, a mobile message unexpectedly pinged in from Samantha herself to Olivia. She is back in London and would Olivia like to meet up, to talk about what was best for Hugo.

Samantha Little and Hugo Pitsakis: the secretive couple, with a relationship that Olivia does not quite understand. She the loyal and close companion, the reliable, tireless galley slave who takes responsibility for the man, always available when needed; he the creative spirit with deep passion for his art, needing a counterbalance for his inspiration and vision. Their emotional make-up and fit is hard to read, always was. Olivia recognises the importance of getting close to Sam, to gain her trust, to win her over as an ally, if she is to get close again to Hugo. She needs to hear the full story from her point of view. She imagines her as the ballast that maintained an even keel over all the years and kept their boat afloat. Sam would counteract Hugo's more eccentric side and his disorganisation. Being a conviction artist, he had his wild bouts of energy and drive, mixed with periods of despair and he needed his ego massaged, his spirits stirred and his morale supported through the bad times as well as the good. Sam would have had to ride through all these moods and keep Hugo sane, safe and normal. That surely took a strong character, with so much devotion and presumably love, and didn't Olivia know that? Has he just been taking advantage of her unstinting support or did he repay her in some way for all her hard work and dedication? Perhaps Hugo was her keeper?

Samantha Little was becoming a subject of interest in her own right, the focus of attention in some of his most brilliant portraiture, the model he had used most often. He captured the passion and lust in equal measure, the wholesomeness of the woman with her exaggerated curves, acres of enticing flesh but never blatantly rude, always tinged with a subtle twist or a turn, a veil placed here, a shift there, the light and shadow playing such important roles in drawing the lines; but the implications of her raw sensuality just there, under the surface nonetheless. There was always that question on her face, for the audience to ponder: had she given herself completely to him, had he won her over, had they achieved mutual satisfaction together?

Hugo's paintings asked his audience to view them from different angles; you could look at them like this or you could turn them around and look at them like that; you decided. The pouting of Sam's lips, the intense come-on in the eyes, an inclination of the head or an arching of the back, a playful lean forward of the bosom or a turning of the shoulder, all these could be interpreted as simple joy and pleasure at the human form or represented a powerful lust, an alluring invitation to wallow in her presence. Hugo would always keep both options in his mind as he painted. Just as he did when depicting any other scene; you could choose actions of self-defence or of vitriolic violence, self-protection or aggression. Right or wrong, he always explored polar opposites and left his audience to judge. Arrogance perhaps, but one way or the other you had to take part.

Hugo and Sam had been lovers, they must have been. Olivia is unsure whether they are cohabiting still. Would she describe herself as his "other half"? Was Sam wanting to nest, to develop a home with Hugo, have a family? Maybe Olivia should tell the whole story from Sam's point of view, a kiss-and-tell version? Might sell better.

A shroud is draped over the city this morning, spitting a fine drizzle over everything without interruption. Olivia under her umbrella finds her way along the wet streets of Muswell Hill, rows of three-storey terraced houses, brick-built between the Wars, solid and squat with stone sills, heavy guttering, large sash windows and wooden porticos with coloured tiles and the occasional flamboyant design on the metalwork. Next to a heavy door with its coloured glass panes at number 18 were three bells with names attached. Flat A – "Samantha Little".

Delighted that Sam had contacted her, she phoned her back straight away. A few days ago, Hugo had departed her Welsh cottage to return to London she presumed alone, and she had not been able to find him at any of his known addresses; he was not answering any of her calls and she was worried. She was unsure where he might be staying, or how safe he was. She sounded in some despair but did not want to talk about it anymore over the phone. Olivia simply assumed that Hugo would have found himself a bolt-hole somewhere, from which he will emerge when good and ready.

Olivia sees Samantha's shadowy image through the frosted glass in the door leaning towards a mirror on the wall in the hallway to check her appearance before answering the bell. Apart from her newly cherried lips, she has little make-up on and is dressed in crisp blue jeans and a simple deep green polo neck top that emphasises her heavy bust. Her feet are in flat slip-ons. The auburn hair, normally so gleaming and dominant in her portraits, is pulled back harshly and tied behind out of the way, making her face look narrower, pinched in the half-light. Her complexion too looks pasty, less than perfect and her face is tired and stern although she manages a welcoming smile at the door.

In her warm and shadowy high-ceilinged front room on the ground floor, they sit comfortably on a leather settee, while a Joni Mitchell CD plays Blue. There is an orange carpet in the middle of the floor, pale cream on the walls, dark drapes. A pleasant fragrance pervades the room and a collection of candles in a tray are burning peacefully on a sideboard, reminding Olivia of Louise. A fluffy black cat pads silently in through the gap in the door, to find warmth on the rug and then settles for Sam's lap. Olivia helps herself to a sparkling water while Sam drinks beer from a bottle.

Small talk about the flat and the weather is kept to a minimum and after complimenting Olivia on her hair and facial tan, Sam soon proceeds to outline her concerns for Hugo, although her thoughts seem to be out of sequence.

'It was never supposed to happen like this.' Olivia gives her a quizzical look. 'Hugo gunned down in the street, in broad daylight, by armed police. He is a peaceful man. He's not confrontational. He fights no battles.' She looks confused, astounded by the whole event. 'He has a life that is untouched by the ups and downs of modern living, with all its frustrations, that are thrown at the rest of us every day, that trip us up. Rules and regulations, queues, parking restrictions, bus lanes, bike lanes, no entry, no right turn, bureaucracy, etcetera; these do not trouble Hugo.' She leans forward, one hand firmly stroking the cat, the other holding her bottle and makes waves in the air for extra expression. She is frustrated that she cannot capture in her descriptions the full importance of Hugo's character, although Olivia well appreciates what she is trying to say. After a while she rests her chin on a hand in despair, an elbow sinking into the upholstered arm of the settee.

'You mean, you had been expecting something to happen, Sam, but not this violence. This surprised you?'

Olivia notices the red-rims around her green eyes, unusually dull in the dim lighting. Some strands of her hair have sprung free, wafting in front of her face, which she blows away periodically, just like in the hospital canteen. 'Hugo has fixed ambitions; he works doggedly and unmoved towards them. All the rest is just part of the mundane ebb and flow that seems to pass him by; he doesn't notice the passing of the day, the weather outside; no milk in the fridge, the light bulbs not working, council tax due, whatever, he has people who sort these things and he doesn't notice them or is untroubled by them. His productive artistic life has all the meaning he needs.' Sam is smiling at her own recollections which flow from her in a rolling low pitched rumble, unexpectedly fluent and dignified.

She tilts her head and presses her jaw against the heel of her hand, the fingers toying with the waves of her thick hair at the back. She looks reticent at divulging so much of her personal feelings about Hugo to a stranger and yet at the same time willing to expose those innermost thoughts, aware of a growing but sympathetic bond with Olivia, another attractive girl floating in the confusion of Hugo's wake.

She reaches for a pack of cigarettes on the table behind her. 'Do you mind, I'm sorry.' Olivia shakes her head and the perfect blonde hair shimmies as Sam fumbles with matches and then draws deeply, blowing a stream of smoke from her pursed lips towards the ceiling; she visibly relaxes in the process. The cat is disturbed and stretches its front paws out, before jumping off of Sam's lap to the floor and padding silently out of sight. Sam's fingers fiddle with the cigarette packet as she continues talking fast. 'Hugo has tried to create an ideal infrastructure to his life, using the money that came to him, surrounding himself with the beautiful things he loves in the world, the apartment with the city view, sculptures and nice objects; the people that take the stress out of life,

I mean he has a cook and personal assistant, sort of PR. And you've met Jake, he's such a good organiser. Hugo's innermost ambitions are centred on the spiritual fulfilment that he finds in creative painting and historical research. He has no arguments with anybody. But his relationships, he can be naïve sometimes, trusting in others and unintentionally he treads on people's toes.'

Sam pauses to take more puffs of her cigarette and another swig of beer, while Olivia merely sips at her water. The music has stopped and there is a quietness in the room, only the occasional passing of a car outside to disturb it.

'Maybe there is something else that we are not seeing?' Sam speaks quietly, twisting her mouth in genuine perplexity and looking towards Olivia, leaving the question rather hanging.

Olivia is quick to respond, feeling the need to be direct. 'You mean, these two girls that he was with that night, Lilly and Veronica?'

'Nika.'

'Yes, the one who is Martin's girlfriend but Hugo did not take that seriously; I mean, a known criminal, that didn't worry him?'

'Precisely. You know about this? What did he think, that Martin wouldn't mind that he was seeing his woman, in his flat, while he was hiding from the police somewhere else? But Hugo has no argument with anybody, he would not have sensed the danger. Naïve, yes. He's not a violent person, he never loses his temper. He might raise his voice occasionally, shout at Sunday drivers maybe – but he would not have thought anything of it: he was using the two girls as models, for his latest work and was helping them with some contacts. Lilly and Nika, they are on Jake's books, that's how they met.'

While Sam has been speaking, the bout of furious and uncontrolled temper that she had witnessed in Hugo the night Dominic had his accident vividly comes to her mind, but she says nothing. 'You know Nika, do you?'

'Yes, she's all right, hard working. Okay, she's a stripper sometimes, but she's trying to get into better modelling jobs and Jake's helping her. She needs money to survive like we all do. Hugo was being driven home, they were held up in traffic, and he decided to get out at some lights and walk down to Chelsea. There were no proper photos, actually not a complete story, just brief lines and innuendo in the papers. I was unsure what to believe. But Nika told me about it later, men in plain clothes approached from all sides with guns blazing, how Hugo was chopped down by a hail of bullets as he scrambled out of the car after her, and fell into the road, his body juddering like a ragdoll, she said. The girls were terrified, Nika and Lilly, they screamed; Lilly was hit in the shoulder. Glass from the back window hit both of them across their heads and necks. Nika had little glass bits in her hair and she cut her hands rubbing them out. She said the noise was deafening. But then it stopped and everything went quiet and nobody moved, and a cloud of tiny glass specks settled all around like falling snow. All the traffic was stopped; everyone mesmerised looking at the yellow mini. Even the policemen outside stood still, their weapons trained at arm's length on Hugo's body, motionless on the road. She saw Hugo's blood running over the asphalt, seeping from under him on both sides and mixing with the puddly rain. She was bundled away in a police car.'

Olivia is transfixed by Sam's story, being able to visualise the scene explicitly from Nika's description. 'Lilly was slumped in the back of the car for a while and was quiet but started screaming again when they tried to get her out. Nika had not heard the ambulance arrive and was wondering how it had got through all the traffic. She was kept at a police station for hours, in the Gloucester Road somewhere, had a medical exam, remarkably had no bullet injuries and was allowed to phone, so she contacted me. I went over to Westminster and Chelsea straight away. Hugo was unconscious in ITU, had lost a lot of blood, was on drips, a blood transfusion and they were planning to take him to theatre later to try to stop the bleeding, in his chest. He had a head wound, stomach wounds. Remarkable that he was alive at all. Nika was convinced by what she had seen that the police seemed intent on killing him, whatever he had done. To her, it was not self-defence, but a cold-blooded attempt at killing.'

Sam quickly assumed her dreamy pose again, as if she was talking to herself. 'It was all so pointless, one minute the police are gunning him down, presumably trying to kill him, the next the specialist surgeons and all their support teams are trying desperately to resuscitate him and save him and keep him alive. Hours and hours, repeated procedures. What was that for?' Her eyes are intense, her mouth pursed, angry that no one will answer her questions.

She veers off in a different direction. 'When he was recovering, about three weeks later, you know, after the Police had said sorry, they thought Hugo was someone else; when he was almost ready to go home, we stole him away, in the dead of the night. We struggled down the back stairs of the hospital, Hugo and me, his arm draped over my shoulders, he was walking with difficulty, but so brave. He was in pain, I know he was. Charlie drove us away to my place and we swapped cars. Charlie's an old friend of mine, he didn't know anything and had never met Hugo before. But he had some of his own painkillers with him, including some liquid morphine, that he let me have. This is what Hugo wanted, he had become convinced that leaving the hospital out the front door was asking for more trouble, that there might be forces waiting to follow him home and continue the work that the police had begun. He had become paranoid; I did not understand what he referred to, but the concern in his eyes, the way he implored me through gritted teeth convinced me that we had to help.'

'Maybe that was the drugs he was on, steroids and diamorphine can do that, make you paranoid, delusional,' Olivia suggests with apparent knowledge.

'Well, I drove and Hugo flopped asleep in the back, through the night away from the city, heading west, the M4 and into South Wales, through Cwmbran and up the Tre-Herbert Hills: I have a little place, my parent's old cottage, in Llandegveth. It's hidden away and nobody knows about it. And there I nursed Hugo, I fetched for him, and did for him and was there for his every wish; day and night I cradled his head, caressed his body and shared his pain.' Sam is weeping silently, tears building up along her lower lids, a few spilling over when she blinks to trickle down her cheeks; one or two drip onto her lap. She works her lips and then smears her mascara with a forefinger. She doesn't look at Olivia, tries to shrug it off. 'Sorry. I rubbed his sore joints and massaged him and dressed his wounds. I slept beside him when he wanted, I left him alone to sleep when he wanted.' She is whispering and her voice falters; she wipes her mouth with an open hand and then reaches for a tissue stuffed up a sleeve and blows her nose quietly. 'Sorry.'

Olivia moves nearer to place a sympathetic hand on Sam's arm, squeezing gently. 'You did the right thing, maybe he would have been still in danger in the hospital.'

Sam looks forlorn but not uncomfortable. She is in love with Hugo and devoted to him, of that Olivia is certain. Sam would have done anything for him and Olivia feels no pang of jealousy or regret.

Sam rises to wash her face in the bathroom next door. Olivia tries to visualise Hugo, as she has not seen his face properly for quite a few years, except the recent ghost-like images of him in his hospital bed, and she wonders whether she would recognise him if she did see him, walking into the room. There is no photo of him that she can see in Sam's lounge, in fact, there are no photos at all, which is unusual. Sam returns to settle again on the settee and lights another cigarette.

'One afternoon, quite late, I found he had left the cottage and wandered up the hillside behind. He was standing out of the heavy rain in a sheep shelter when I found him. "I love you very much, Sam," he said, "for doing what you have, for rescuing me. I don't know what I would have done without you." He was holding my shoulders at arm's length and looking into my eyes and basically saying he needed to be alone, he did not want to stay with me any longer; he needed his own space. Called me Sammy. I think he wanted to stay and support me, but...he is a driven man, he is restless, and the quiet of our valley for a few weeks had been too much, he now wanted to return to the noisy city life. He said he was ready to face it.' Sam gives a little whimper, a sob and she covers her mouth firmly with a hand to suppress her inner urges.

Olivia waits, engrossed.

'He slipped out of my arms, shaking his head, and stood outside in the rain, before retracing his way down the slopes, back to the lane which leads past my cottage and out of sight. I wanted to follow but knew I should not. I was rigid, I couldn't move.' Sam plays with her empty beer bottle, sucks on the cigarette, blowing smoke up over Olivia's head. She smoothes out the creases in her trousers along her thighs and wipes imaginary ash from her sleeve.

'And I have not seen him since, for a week, I do not know where he went. He took the train back to London, for sure, but I don't know where he is right now. There has been no answer from his phone in the apartment; his mobile is dead. I dare not visit in case he feels pressurised. But not a word from him. Just a bunch of flowers, white chrysanthemums and blue irises, no card, but delivered to the cottage by Jessie Evans, our local florist in Cwmbran. The day after he left. A phone call, from a Mr Butler, she said, and could she deliver tomorrow, as it was the lady's birthday, with a message: "Always in my thoughts." Hugo lives in Butler's Wharf, so he was saying thank you. Maybe a touch guilty that he had left me there? I couldn't face returning to London, I just wanted to be alone, in the peace of the valley. I was certainly feeling sorry for myself, although it was poor Hugo that had been shot, who had to recuperate; *his* confidence destroyed, *his* courage tested.'

'Poor you. Hugo must be better. He's probably staying with friends. It's you who needs the comfort.' Again, Olivia offers a hand on her arm and grips her in sympathy. Sam's gratitude for her listening and her smile are genuine.

Olivia herself has to suppress an urge to confess to Sam her earlier life and role in Hugo's life, when they had briefly lived together; when Sam must have felt excluded and pushed aside. She wants to tell her how much she admires his work and his talents. But she is conscious that if she is to gain Sam's trust, she needs to be seen as an outsider, unprejudiced by past events and not a rival or a threat. So she keeps her counsel and continues instead to entice more from Sam, while she is in her talkative sharing mood. From the sound of things, she and Hugo had never actually made any commitments to each other, not expressed in any formal way, but they had worked together for many years, had become friends and lovers. So much like her own short relationship with him years ago. It was obviously the dramatic shooting that had awakened Sam to her true feelings for Hugo, her innermost compassion rushing out towards a man in distress, his life threatened. But Sam is now thinking that Hugo must have scuttled back to London to be with someone else.

These were desperate times for artists, Sam was saying, which meant loyalties were tested to the full, while allegiances shifted and occasional rivalries got the better of them. The last few years had been desperate for some, although Hugo had been thankfully protected from all that by his healthy inheritance, the staggering details of which were only slowly filtering through to Olivia: millions of dollars, Bernadette had said.

'So, he has not been living at his old address?'

'Apparently not, or just not answering; switched everything off, for the moment. Someone will be looking after him; Jake or Jeremy, they are always sharing secrets. Or other possible friends. He can be a very secretive man, sometimes. He inherited all this money, but no one knew about it, he didn't talk about it to anybody; seemed rather embarrassed.'

After a moment, she jumps up, 'I'll make some coffee, shall I? Are you hungry? I could do an omelette or something?'

'We could do one together, could we?' Olivia suggests, with a helpful smile and they leave the room together through a middle partition to the small kitchen/dining room behind, with views over a walled-in garden, a neglected patch of grass. Sam finds some eggs in the fridge, Olivia puts a pan on the stove, with a drop of oil, and soon they are chopping onions and tomatoes and grating cheese and slicing ham. They sit at a wooden table and tuck in with a bottle of beer each and Olivia basks in the common warmth between them.

'You have not told me anything about you, Olivia, I have neglected you, I'm so sorry. You work in the City, that's right? Something about investment funds.' Olivia nods, while eating. 'And you write a column for a magazine, you said?'

'Pretty much, sums it up. I live at the Barbican, small apartment, work off Lombard Street, have a mum in Islington, no dad and no siblings. No boyfriend at the moment, which is fine.'

'So, are you the only woman, among all those bossy men? How do you manage?'

'Well, yes, we are outnumbered a bit, but that is slowly changing. There are some very bright women around and they compete with the men pretty well. I keep my distance, try not to get too close to any of them. I live alone. I foil fence regularly at the Finsbury Sports Centre and sometimes at a private club in Pall Mall. So yes, I write this column for investors in a money magazine and occasional articles in the weekend reviews. I don't know who reads them,' she shrugs, 'but it lets me do some writing, which is what I want to do. And I want to do a biography actually, this is my new passion. And something I want to talk to you about. I think Hugo would make a great subject for study. What do you think?'

Olivia's young features light up as she looks eagerly into Sam's face. Sam looks ruffled about the eyes and sounds a little surprised. 'Really?'

'Oh, yes. He's talented, dashing, a romantic.'

'He's all those things, all right,' agrees Sam, her eyes sparkling a touch, a smile spreading along her broad mouth. She finds yoghurt in the fridge and spoons some into two bowls. She makes more coffee.

'He's enigmatic. The public always loves an artist. He needs a face for the public to recognise. He's got so many sides to him.' Olivia is in danger of sounding overly enthusiastic and giving herself away, and she pulls back. 'I would want it to be authorised, you know, with his permission and help. I would make it sympathetic. I'm not looking for controversy.'

'We need to give this some thought, but I like the idea. He is certainly a very interesting man. You are talking about getting this published?'

Olivia is nodding. 'I don't know whether anyone would actually read it,' she half-joked, 'apart from his friends. But there should always be an audience for a good contemporary story of artistic struggle and romance and a little intrigue.' Olivia is smiling like a schoolgirl, trying to carry Sam along, with her positive approach.

'Intrigue?' Sam queries, head tilted again.

'Well, he has just been shot in broad daylight in the street by the police...you know, in Britain. I mean this is not Northern Ireland, but... The truth may be absolutely mundane: maybe it was a police error, mistaken identity. But what about all that money Hugo has: jealousy. Or he has put people out, unintentionally, you said he could be naive, maybe he's really upset someone? Suppose those men were not police at all, but some gang employed to kill Hugo, for whatever reason. This biography could be the vehicle for establishing what happened and why.'

'So you're not looking for controversy?'

'Well, only for the possible truth.'

They wander back into the lounge and the cat is sprawled on the rug in the middle of the room for Sam to fuss over. 'Have you seen these stories, they appeared last week,' and Sam hands her two newspapers that she had kept on one side. 'So far the papers have been pitiful,' she comments, as Olivia scans the stories, mimicking her thoughts precisely. One of them has spelt Pitsakis wrong, says he was a Russian émigré and that he was being sought after by the Police. The other had him cavorting with prostitutes when he was discovered and he was running away when the Police gave chase across Earl's Court. 'Ridiculous speculation, when the papers cannot build up a proper story. So a chance to write the truth would be welcome, to counteract all of this crap.'

'Precisely. But who reads the written word in newspapers these days, anyway? You know, the damage may not be as bad as you think. What we need is something on the internet.'

Olivia is perching on an armchair, watching Sam's friendly reaction with the cat, rubbing its tummy, her lovely auburn hair bobbing down her back. It is probably time for her to leave. 'He never painted me, you know, Sam, not fully. I was never immortalised like you. He must love you, the passion and beauty in his portraits of you are stunning, I love them.'

'You're very generous. What Hugo loves most is historical illustration; there's this First World War series he has been working on. And I know he was looking at the social turmoil in Greece, its historical perspective.'

'Yes, Bernadette told me. Sounds fantastic. He would have such great sympathy for the plight of the Greek people, I'm sure. A man of so many sides. I would want to concentrate on the artist, his background, his inspiration and describe details of his works. Illustrated, of course. Bring out his charismatic side. I'm sure there would be interest in the life and times of a contemporary artist, successful and influential. What do you think? Do you think Hugo would agree?'

'It sounds interesting but this is the thing, I wonder whether he would agree. He would be worried about privacy and so on.'

'I would need you to help me persuade him.'

'When was the last time you spoke with him?'

'A few years ago now. But, I don't know, often feels like yesterday.' She looks into Sam's eyes as if she wants to convey more meaning in her words, like a subliminal message. 'There are one or two other things I wanted to ask, do you mind?'

'Sure.' Their eyes meet and Olivia feels sure they could be friends.

'Have you ever met Loukas, his brother? I spoke to Bernadette yesterday and she implied that there was some animosity between Hugo and Loukas because of the difference in the inheritance and the money situation.'

'I haven't seen Loukas for ages, not for a year or so. He spends some time in London, I think, visits Bernadette, but he lives with his family in Athens. He did not do so well, he inherited the Greek businesses and what with the euro crisis and Greek's debt problems, his fortunes have not fared well; he's had to work hard to keep everything afloat. Whereas Hugo got the successful shipping business which he eventually sold, a few years ago, for this enormous sum. He is doing, was doing, very well. But we have not seen Loukas for a long time, I imagine he is a bit jealous, but it's not Hugo's fault that Greece has been through such a difficult time – those were his father's wishes. The money itself means little to Hugo, but the opportunities it brings is what excites him. So he used the opportunity to set up the perfect situation for himself. Most of the artists we know are poor, they barely make ends meet. He did not want this money to make any difference to the way he treated people or others treated him. He didn't want relationships with his artist friends to change, so they don't know the extent of it, but he has been helping some and the academy he is starting is for budding artists, of all media, not just painters. With Jeremy, he is into a few other business projects and charities. He has so many different lives, I am not up with all of it myself. He was beginning to see many projects coming good, and his life was near perfect – how many people can say that. He lived exactly where he wanted, how he wanted, doing what he loved.' Sam is smiling in obvious admiration. 'Amazing. That's what I mean by saying that it was never meant to be like this: shot like some common criminal or terrorist in the street.'

Sam is sitting on her haunches on the carpet. 'I admire him so much for sticking to his ambitions, and not letting the money ruin him. I mean, he never needs to work again in his life, he could live the life of a playboy, go anywhere, buy anything he wanted. But...' she pauses, leaving her true thoughts unspoken.

'But he has not chosen you... I mean to share his life with, to live with?' Olivia asks quietly, venturing at last onto sensitive ground, not meaning to sound at all cruel.

'Quite. I have not won him over. Perhaps he has found life with someone else, who pleases him more.' Sam has a defiant look, pursing her lips, but then it quickly turns to deflation. There might have been more tears at this, but she stoically presses on. 'You must talk with Jeremy Ashcroft.'

'I have, two weeks ago, in his house in Hampstead, but we only touched on the subject. You've told me much more. He sort of approved of my biography idea, but then seemed to want to control it and run it for me. I thought he was quite bossy.'

'He's very switched on. They've been working together on Hugo's career for some years now and he knows him as well as anyone. And will know a load of stories and secrets and things even I don't know. He may have some ideas about this shooting. There has to be some other explanation.' Sam's face lights up a little with a sarcastic smile. 'Perhaps your investigations and research will help us all get to the bottom of it; heaven knows, the police won't do anything, except try and suppress it.'

'Did Hugo have any other ideas as to what might have been behind it, I mean, when you were away together – he must have talked about it?'

'We talked about it, obviously. He said he was so pleased to be away, so no one knew where he was, he felt safer.' After a slow pause, Sam knits her brows. 'Maybe. I don't know everything about Hugo, I'm not married to him. Maybe there is someone out there who hates him. Jealousy could be behind this attack. He seemed to think it was possible, he certainly wanted to lie low, out of London. But he loves the busy city life; city life is a strong feature of his work. He is often out on the streets, near the familiar sites, or street markets, picking out people to talk to, to sketch. He travels to Europe – he was back in Greece just before Christmas with Jeremy to observe the changes there, with all the classic architecture as a background. Actually, you should talk with his PA, Alicia Arundale, she works in the office in Charlotte Street, lives somewhere out in Essex. Sort of superannuated secretary, nice girl. Getting married soon.'

'Yes, I have tried but no answer at the gallery, which is closed. She might know where Hugo is hiding?'

'You know, she just might. I had not thought about her really, but now, well maybe. I will ring her later, this evening, I'll try her home. Then I can let you know.'

'OK, sounds good.' Olivia decides it is time to leave Sam in peace. 'I'm sure he will be safe, Sam. He'll be home soon. He just wants some space. He has good resources and friends to fall back on. He nearly lost his…' but she does not know how to finish the sentence. 'It must have been such a shock, to him; and he is not sure how to handle it. He'll call you soon, you see.'

Olivia tries to reassure her, squeezes her hand and thanks her profusely for all her help. Sam offers to drop her down at East Finchley tube, save her the walk in the wet. They agree on numbers and they will call each other when or if there is any news. Then they could arrange a meet with Hugo to test out Olivia's proposal, once Hugo has emerged from his hiding place. They hug awkwardly in the front of the car and touch cheeks.

As Olivia journeys home on the Northern Line, she feels so eager to meet with Hugo, confident after her successful discussions with his mates, Jeremy and Jake and now with Sam, maybe the most important of the three; and that Sam will be on her side to persuade him to give the go-ahead with the biography idea. In Sam's hands, he sounds such a heroic figure. Will he be the same Hugo she had met and fallen in love with the first time when she was an inexperienced twenty-four-year-old?

Olivia transfers her thoughts to Louise, knowing that their secret meetings and manner will have to change at some point. She, Olivia, is going to have to share more about Hugo with her new lover; otherwise, she, Louise, will be confused by what is happening. The sinister side of Hugo's shooting, that maybe there was a conspiracy involved, and not just a police cock-up, a mistaken identity, plays on her imagination. Maybe Hugo's paranoia about his safety was real. Sam seemed to think it was possible. Or they are trying to cover up something else, a gang battle with the armed police that Hugo unwittingly walked into? Maybe his hiding for the moment is wise after all.

Sam had seemed interested in Olivia's potential role, as a biographer, which is good. She would want Olivia to produce a powerful riposte to all the negative trash in the newspaper reports, which would be one of Olivia's definite objectives. Olivia's memories of Samantha years ago were of a calm, elegant and commanding woman, in control of her life. The contrast with the woman she met at her home today, only nine years older, is stark: more the impression of a once-free spirit deflated by events beyond her control. Sam was desperately trying to keep it together, but real stress was not far below the surface.

'You've done this sort of thing before, have you, writing biographies?' Sam had asked in the car, just before she jumped out at the traffic lights.

'No, Hugo would be a first,' Olivia chirped, with an exciting smile that dimpled both cheeks. 'Hey ho!' she called, closing the door firmly.

7

Friday, February 27, 2015

Alicia Arundale has been hard to pin down, as she has always been out of the office when Olivia phones, and leaving messages did not seem to work. When at last they do speak over a mobile, she seems reluctant to want to talk or meet. But using Samantha's name as leverage she manages to get Alicia to agree to a meeting in a close-by restaurant down from Goodge Street, in a pedestrianised alley.

Olivia is drawn to the gallery first, a short walk from the tube station, taking a prolonged look from the opposite side of the road at the glass-fronted shop, Pitsakis Galleries painted in gold on a dark green background. She crosses over to take a closer look at the pictures on display from the street, through metal security gating, and has a *déjà vu* moment looking at two contrasting and colourful works that shout Hugo Pitsakis at her. One depicts street demonstrators fighting in Athens with the Acropolis ruins in the background, a scene of turmoil and anger, a blow being landed on a policeman's distorted jaw, spittle flying; the other shows a pretty semi-clad girl stepping barefoot towards you along a dry path through sun-dappled woodland alongside a trickling stream, her face a cherubic innocence, wavy blonde hair catching the bright light. Olivia is bewitched by both pictures, one a fierce tragedy in progress, the other perfect serenity captured in innocent youth – their contrast could not be more striking and yet they speak volumes about the genius of the artist. From her fresh perspective of fluid relationships, with an open mind, she stares admiringly at the attractive blonde in the painting. She can picture Hugo crouching at his easel revelling in the sheer delight of her perky breasts and ripe belly, capturing her movement with clever swirls of his brush with erotic perfection. Olivia swallows her dry saliva, a touch of embarrassment colouring her cheeks. Imagine just pitching up at home, with Louise in tow and coming straight out with it: I am turning lesbian, mother. I don't understand, dear, she would whimper.

- God, what would dear father have said?

Peering in through the closed glass door, she is unable to make out any detail inside the dark shop. Locked, viewing by private appointment only. An adjacent closed wooden door painted deep green to match has a label attached, Pitsakis Offices. 'Hours Mon-Fri 9 am to 6 pm; Sat 10 am to 2 pm. Ring for prior appointment.' There is no answer to the bell.

The day has been windy so far but gradually a weak sun has appeared and Charlotte Place is bathed in light that gently toys with the lunchtime strollers. There are people queueing onto the street at *Lantana's* and Olivia joins them, looking around for a woman who would do for Ms Arundale, remembering that helpfully she would be wearing black. Some people are sitting outside on the benches among a cheery atmosphere despite the chill, even shedding jackets and jumpers. Olivia is cool in a white blouse and leather jacket over a short cerise skirt and black tights; she has even found a pair of Ray-bans, and with her distinctive blonde hair she should be easily recognisable. Indeed, within moments a stocky young woman, probably late twenties, broad in the beam with generous bust, dark hair parted straight down the middle and splayed shapelessly down to her shoulders, appears in front of Olivia with a forced smile wearing the promised black. Black jacket, black trousers rather too tight around the bulging middle and black heels, contrast with her pale complexion and pink blouse. Her face is rounded and youthful, and she squints into the sunshine with crossed brows. When she stretches an arm out for a handshake, bangles jingle on her chubby wrist. Her left hand is clutching the shoulder strap of a leather bag that is bulging with all her PA accessories, and Olivia cannot help noticing not only the Rolex but a glitzy engagement ring. 'That's very nice,' she comments.

Olivia is still finding it difficult to accept that an artist devoted to creating images with paint, following unpredictable instincts and wildly varying moods from moment to moment, who already has an agent and a business manager, for Heaven's sake, needs a personal assistant. What does she do all day long? Although Sam said she only worked part-time for Hugo, about two days a week, Olivia is wondering what this girl has got that Hugo needs and how much he pays her.

'I'm Olivia Truelove, thanks very much for coming out on your lunch break.'

'I'm Alicia, Ali.' Glancing at her left ring finger, she carries on breathlessly, 'Yes, it's very exciting; we were engaged last month and the wedding is planned for Christmas in the Bahamas.'

'Wonderful. Lucky girl.'

'Rob wanted to have it in this country, but I don't have a mum, only me dad, and he wouldn't be very good at organising things. He lives in Basingstoke, so I said why don't we go away, somewhere exotic and Dad said he would go halves, if Arthur, that's Rob's father, would as well, and we said yes, so the Bahamas it is.'

They soon reach the till and order two white wines, and Ali fancies a caramelised onion tart with a salad and clearly has her eyes on the cherry ripe chocolate slices and cupcakes for afters; Olivia makes do with a carrot, spinach and feta salad. They find a bench to perch on, against a wall, but still have to raise their voices to be heard above the general hubbub of the place.

'We haven't sent out the invitations yet, so we don't know how many will be coming; maybe a hundred or so,' Ali giggled. 'It's going to be wonderful.'

Ali constantly flicks her hair out of her face. In the artificial light that glances unkindly across her doubtful complexion, Olivia can see the effort she has made with plentiful foundation to disguise the superficial scarring in her cheeks and surmises a hurried approach to her morning's make-up, the mascara unevenly applied, the eyebrows poorly plucked.

'Still, Christmas is a long time to wait.'

'I know, but…can't be 'elped, eh?'

They shyly sip their wine. The café is crowded and noisy, so they have to lean in closer. A middle-aged couple in matching anoraks squeeze onto the stools next to them, lovingly holding hands and staring into each other's faces across the table.

'So, Olivia, I've never met you, have I? You were asking about Mr Pitsakis?'

'Yes, I was,' she says, keeping her friendly smile, 'Hugo.'

'You heard about the incident, with the police?'

'Oh yes, I'm up-to-date, I've spoken at length with Samantha Little.'

'I mean, gosh, that was awful; so upsetting.'

'I remember seeing you once outside the ITU, actually. I didn't know who you were then. Sam told me about you. I never realised a contemporary London painter needed a personal assistant.' She keeps it light, but an inevitable hint of mischief colours her tone.

'Sorry, I've been away, staying at my mother's, it's been so upsetting. Well, he is an incredibly busy man, with so many projects and I help him with his diary commitments and travel bookings, that sort of thing. I'm a secretary really, as I'm sure you've guessed but, you know, with the internet and e-mail and stuff, I have not much traditional typing to do these days, although I did do his correspondence with the Houses of Parliament a few weeks ago complaining to the Secretary of Work and Pensions.' She snatches a wild swig of her wine and hurries on: 'The poor man, the agony of it all and all a mistake, I ask you. It's terrifying it is, it makes you wonder about goin' out at all.' With her rushing London accent she has a way a crinkling her nose so that three cross folds appear over the bridge like a ladder, whenever she applies some seriousness to her conversation; but when she allows her expression to relax to neutralise her face, Olivia finds her quite pretty.

'I used to know Hugo,' Olivia manages to get in with a quick parry, 'a few years ago; have not seen him for a while, but I'm intending to write a biography of him and I was hoping for some explanation about his activities, Ali, if that were possible? After all, you must know of his every movement at any one time, better than anyone?'

'S'pose I do. During the week, in the daytime,' she giggles. 'He's going to be all right, is he? I mean I'm worried, he looked so bleedin' awful last time, like death when I saw 'im in that hospital.'

'I think he is recovering. Sam's been looking after him. I'm sure he'll be back at work soon, knowing Hugo he will want to get back to normal. Is there anything important in the diary, on the horizon, coming up?'

'Well yes, he has a couple of teaching seminars at the College of Art, and a meeting at the British Library. He's missed a meeting with Finnegan, it's a TV production team working for ITV: they're making a film on the First World

War and following Hugo's work – he's in the middle of a memorial painting, a triptych for the Commemoration Exhibition starting in November. The National Gallery, he'll be behind schedule on that. He's having an exhibition in New York in October, Jake has been fixing that one. Vienna maybe, on the cards. And then there was his Greek project, he'd had a few meetings and was due to fly out to Athens again in June. He wants to see what's happening with the troubles there, you know the austerity marches and the elections; he wants to look at the social side.'

Olivia is genuinely impressed. 'So, you're right, he's a busy man.'

'As I said, I help out with booking his trips and getting visas and whatnot and where he might stay and so on, but for Athens, I have done nothing definite yet – waiting for instructions. No doubt he will have lots of strongly worded letters to write when he returns, to the Commissioner of Police for one, complaining about this mistake. The Mayor of London too, I shouldn't wonder.'

'Does he often do that? Write letters of complaint, like Prince Charles is he, writing to Ministers?' and Olivia chuckles, not quite being able to visualise the left-leaning socialist Hugo now with money to let him mix with the upper crust, writing letters to *The Times*: "Disappointed of Bermonsey."

'Oh, he's been getting involved you know with politics. He was asked to be an advisor,' she says proudly, 'for one of the independent parties, The Popular Front, The PPF, I think it was.'

'But they're a radical right-wing lot, aren't they? They wouldn't appeal to Hugo, surely?'

'No, he spoke to some rep bloke, but in the end told him to bog off.' And Ali cackles into her glass.

Their food arrives with the waiter shoving a wooden tray from his end along the table, between the other sitters. They start to tuck in.

'What I would like to know more about, Ali, is the day of the shooting, or the day before. What was Hugo doing staying at this flat in Shepherd's Bush? Belonging to a criminal, it turns out and his girlfriend. I mean what's the connection?' Do you know?'

'Mr Pitsakis always said to me he liked to get close to the action. He wanted to paint some girls from poorer backgrounds, and the like, struggling, maybe some rough types, in the raw like, and this was to be part of his Greece series. He asked Jake if he knew of any girls, models he could use for this painting who would sit for him – Jake has models on his books. He introduced Hugo to some girls, I didn't know who they were. Nika something, she's quite photogenic, I saw her picture. She does magazine stuff and works in some East End nightclub, pole-dancing and that. You saw the tabloid headlines about strippers, which I thought was a bit cruel. I mean she does soft work, quite artistic actually, some of it. Then there is a girl called Lilly, she's another of Jake's, he found her wasted in the East End somewhere and has been bringing her on. She and Nika are friends, often stays with her. She's lovely actually, quite young, figure to die for and Hugo liked her looks straight away. So they have both been sitting for him and he paints them with sketches in their own place, Nika's flat, rather than bring them over to his studio. Jake thought it better not to let them see what Hugo's got, you know, security and all that. And he's there with them, at the coalface, so to speak.'

The food is delicious and they drain their wines.

'Anyway, I knew he was spending time there, he was working against the clock on these projects. He did not know of Nika's links with this Martin character, I'm sure he didn't. And on the day before the shooting he was there late, well into the evening and the weather was horrible, he didn't have a car, he stayed the night, and the next morning the girls were giving him a lift back to his place, they were on their way to a modelling session in Hackney somewhere. They were stuck in traffic and Hugo apparently decides to get out and walk to Jake's office in Chelsea not far away, said he had some business there. And then these mad policemen were swarming all around him, shooting at random.'

'Wow, who told you this, was this Sam explaining?'

'Well, yes and I met Nika, Hugo wanted me to check them out, injuries and that. Lilly was hit in the shoulder, 'orrible scar. That's going to upset her modelling, poor thing. They were both shocked really but gave us their version.'

'So, Ali, do you think Hugo was sleeping with one of them, Lilly perhaps, you said he was smitten?'

Ali is quick to reply, sounding as if she wants to retract some things she has said earlier. 'Well, I wouldn't know; I said he liked her, her looks were perfect for the picture. He wanted the perfect face of innocence among the rubble and filth of a city in riot.' Ali is serious, although she struggles to look Olivia in the eye as she speaks.

'And he had never met this Midge Martin man, as far as you know?'

'I never heard him speak of any Martin, but…don't know. Clearly not his type.'

'But wouldn't he have realised he ran a risk of angering him by staying with his girlfriend in his flat, even if it was all innocent. I mean Martin wouldn't have believed him, would he?'

'This is all a bit beyond me, Olivia, I'm afraid – you'll have to ask Mr Pitsakis. I'm sure he'll have a perfectly good explanation.' And her chubby cheeks dimpled for the first time on either side of her forced grin.

'A bit above your pay grade, eh?' Olivia jokes. 'Does he pay you well, for being the secretary? Is it a retainer, or for hours done, how does that work?'

'No, he pays me well, monthly for two whole days per week or equivalent. He's a good employer, always asking after me circumstances. I was planning to invite him to the wedding,' she chirps.

**

126

The Uxbridge Road this Saturday mid-morning is crowded with traffic, the pavements busy with Cypriots and Asians wheeling shopping trolleys, buying fruit and veg from the stalls, stocking up, queueing at bus stops, young blacks on the make. It is extremely cold and overcast, and looking for Nika's road on foot, Olivia is dressed for the task in walking boots, warm trousers and woolly polo neck under a leather bomber jacket. She has been going over her chat with Ali in her mind and has decided she likes her. Although clearly not the brightest or most attractive girl in the office, she is making the most of her opportunities and she seemed honest; good for her.

By The Queen Adelaide gastro-pub, with its distinguished black windows, red brick and grey-green tiles, ironically just a few paces beyond Shepherds Bush Police Station, she turns into Adelaide Grove with purpose, counting the small two-up, two-down terraced houses on either side. Not all of them have their numbers showing, but halfway up, by a set of bollards, where the pavement on opposite sides pinches into the road to limit the width to one car, number 84a is over on the right, with its door painted puce and set back a couple of paces from the pavement. Immediately next to it is another puce door, number 84b, for the flat upstairs. The place looks uncared for, unlike some of the other houses along the street that have been done up with more than just a lick of paint. The window frames are peeling, gutter overflow stains the outer brickwork and litter is scattered about the concreted front, around the wheelie bins that partially obstruct Olivia's way, as she steps through a gap in the low brick wall, where a gate is missing.

Waiting for the door to be answered in response to her buzzing, there is not a sound to be heard from inside. She glances over her shoulder, seeing a young black man in jeans and a trilby slouching along the opposite pavement, who seems to be keeping an eye on her. She presses the button again and soon there is a tug on the door which creates a gap and the tired-looking face of a young blonde woman appears, looking confused, sleepy and pale.

'Hello. Is that Lilly? I'm Olivia.' Olivia, by contrast, is impeccably made-up, with sharp mascara and a fawn eyeshadow, her lips a crisp crimson. 'Can I come in? Is it convenient?'

Lilly is slow to react but then breaks into an embarrassed look, opening the door wider. 'Yes, come in. Sorry, I was expecting...well, I don't know, somebody different, anyway.'

'Oh, sorry, if I have disappointed you,' Olivia says in mock sarcasm as she follows the girl inside. In her bare feet, she is just shorter than Olivia and she is wearing a cream knitted sweater, oddly paint-stained and holey along the sleeves. Her right arm is encased in a muslin sling, the bare fingers emerging curled and cold.

'No, I thought you sounded a bit older, I was expecting an older woman, that's all,' and turning at the entrance to her bedroom, she looks suitably bashful, the fingers of her free hand stroked across her lower face. Olivia pushes the front door closed. 'Sorry. I've not made-up. Come in here.' She retreats into the first room on the right off the bare corridor. Her giant jumper has a generous neckline that leaves one shoulder exposed and reaches well below her bottom, but what else she has on underneath Olivia can only guess at. A fire with two short electrical bars burning orange is feebly trying to warm the cluttered space; on the tiled mantel sits a single sunflower in a narrow glass vase. The walls are shabby, the once-white nets grey, the cream coloured carpet sadly threadbare. The single bed along one wall is unmade and Lilly hastens to cover it. She grabs some used mugs on a side-table in her one hand and indicates a silky mustard armchair by the window for Olivia.

'Can I get you a drink, coffee or what?' Olivia can see that Lilly is certainly pretty with thick and tangled honey blonde hair that falls about her face and tumbles over her shoulders. She looks about twenty and has the innocent face of untrammelled youth, a fair and perfect complexion with surprisingly lime coloured eyes. Her lips are luscious, like plumped-up cushions, the philtrum scalloped, and her chin gently dimpled. She would make an attractive model for any male artist on the lookout, Olivia concedes.

'Coffee, yes that would be nice. No milk. Need some help?' Lilly retreats somewhere into the back of the flat as Olivia waits alone keeping her jacket buttoned up. Discarded clothes are scattered on the bed, the back of a chair, the floor and more are bulging out of half-open drawers of a chest in the corner, jeans, bundled pyjamas, women's clothes and undergarments. A bin in the corner is overflowing with tissues and finished make-up boxes. A few long strands of blonde hair are caught in the wrinkled folds of her pillowcase, still warm to Olivia's casual touch. There are no pictures anywhere but hanging on the wall behind the door is a striking sketch in charcoal and minimal paint, a full-length naked girl walking away along a dusty path through woodlands, her face half turned and a mass of tangled hair tumbling down her back. A thin lacy shirt trails from one hand. It must be Lilly, and it's unmistakably a Pitsakis, Olivia thinks to herself, sitting gingerly on the armchair, with an amused expression playing across her face. As she absorbs the detail, she imagines a barefooted Hugo prancing up the path behind the girl, reaching for her extravagant buttocks to have his way with her from behind, crouching on the verdant edges of grass. Olivia is blissfully castaway for a fleeting moment by the characteristic boldness and movement in the picture, feeling the light breeze that is catching at Lilly's hair, and imagining, almost wishing, it might have been her, Olivia.

- Really, you are too fanciful. And I have entirely forgotten what Hugo looks like in the buff.

Lilly quietly returns with one mug of swirling instant coffee that she plonks down on the floor by Olivia's feet. She shakes her mane of hair backwards and more of her pretty face emerges, washed and alive. She has nice teeth, two large front ones with the tiniest of gaps between and when she sits down on a wooden chair opposite and crosses her shapely bare legs, Olivia is able to confirm that she is at least wearing a pair of knickers. There is a silver chain around one ankle and a small flower tattoo just above; the toenails are painted purple, matching her fingers, but the varnish is cracked and needs attention.

Olivia coughs and focuses on the younger woman. 'I wanted to talk to you about Hugo.' She tips her head towards the hanging picture. 'I knew him well a few years ago, and I'm planning to write a book about him. Like I said on the phone, I just wanted to clarify some things about the shooting incident. Sorry to bring it up, you must have been quite upset.'

'Yeah, not 'alf. Bloody 'ell, don't remind me.'

'You were injured, I know, the shoulder?'

'Yeah, effing stiff.' She passes a hand up to her right shoulder, 'and I can't move it properly.' She tries to reach up with her right arm in its sling and winces. 'The stitches are out, an' that, but I still have a dressing over it, don't like to look at it.' She grimaces some more. 'This takes the weight of it, they say it will get better; I have to do these exercises every day, but it bleedin' hurts.' She is thumbing a spot at the front, just inside the shoulder joint. 'Bullet went in at the back and came out 'ere.'

'You poor thing. You must have been wondering what the hell was happening. How did you see it?'

Lilly tells Olivia what happened that morning in her faltering cockney, a version not unlike the ones Olivia had already heard quite a few times already.

'And what does Nika think? Does she talk about it?

'She's here, next door, but she's asleep with a bloke from last night. She was back late, it was half three or something.'

'Okay, don't worry her. I can always talk to her some other time.'

But just then they hear a voice in the hallway and Lilly jumps up to poke her head out the door. Some words are exchanged, a garbled sort of English. Lilly comes back closing her door. 'Yeah, she's coming. She's doin' a gig this evening, at the Palace in Wandsworth, rehearsal, it's a sort of fashion show, without the fashions.' She snorts. Olivia reaches for her mug and sips gingerly, not sure about the taste but grateful for the warmth. The pathetic fire is barely touching the chill.

'And you?'

'Me? Oh, I'm not working at the minute, damn thing,' moans Lilly, indicating her arm. 'Soon, I'll be back, I'll have to. Just grin an' bear it, eh?'

Just then another woman, older than Lilly, edges into the bedroom, in black leggings and a long baggy T-shirt. She looks thin, shallow cheeks under prominent malar bones, her skin sallow. She smiles faintly and speaks with an Eastern European accent, saying she is from Zagreb and sorry for her English, although Olivia readily complements her on it.

'That's Zagreb in Croatia, not Serbia.'

'Yes. I'm Olivia, a friend of Hugo. I wanted to talk to you about the shooting. Are you recovered now?'

'I was not hurt, I was scared. The police, like it was Zagreb, at home we have bully police. But I am OK. Is Hugo all right?'

'Yes, I think so.'

'I thought he was dead. I not see him for weeks. Sam said he is going OK, some weeks ago.'

Olivia leans toward her, keen expression of kindness on her face. 'So, it all started from here, yes?' Nika steps further in and tilts her bottom toward the fire, taking hissing breathes through clenched teeth. 'I was just wondering why Hugo was here overnight, that was unusual, was it? In this flat?' Olivia looks from Nika to Lilly and back, noticing their glance at each other and slight hesitation.

'Look, this not my flat, and if Hugo want to stay he can stay. He a great artist, wonderful painter, great man and he has lovely way. If he stay, then that's fine.'

'No, what I mean is I suppose, how did he get involved with this man Martin, he didn't know him, did he? He knew you and wanted you to pose for him, model, that right?'

Nika is lighting a cigarette. 'Midge is good man, sometimes bad man, he bully by police, I say, he is running; he not do anything, he is on run, hiding, I not see him for weeks. I pay rent now, total, and never have spare money. So I work. We both work.'

'Yes, I understand that. It must be quite difficult. Did he sleep with either of you, sorry to ask?'

They are both quiet, awkwardly looking away, at their feet and then at each other.

'Both of you?' Olivia asks, her voice faint. Still nothing, just a shrug from Nika and an apologetic look on Lilly's face. Nika stares at her younger friend with what looked like a mixture of anger and surprise. 'Okay. I get the picture. And you don't know where Midge is, you have not been in contact?'

Nika becomes more animated and seems a little irate, raising her voice. 'Are you work for police? This I get from them all the time. They watch this flat, they have cars in the street. I fed up. I tell them, not see Midge for two, three months he not been here, we are on our own.'

'Okay, sure. No, I am not police, definitely not. I want to find out why this happened and why the police got it so wrong.'

'If I contact Midge, this let police know where he is. No, no, he kill me. No, I wait and the police wait, they watch this place. I not know where he is.' Nika looks distressed and draws deeply on her cigarette; Lilly sits quietly watching her, deferring to her.

'So Hugo did not ever meet Midge, there is no connection, right?'

'No, why should there be?'

'So why did the police think that Hugo was Midge? Do they look alike? Something about a hat and coat, is that relevant?'

Nika shrugs, waves her cigarette around but says nothing. Lilly stirs, squeezing her free hand between her knees, and looks across at Olivia under soft brows. She looks pretty, her lips pouted, good legs. 'Hugo took the fedora and raincoat from the hall because the weather outside was shit; they were Midge's. So the police thought it was Midge. I mean they were not expecting another man in this flat, were they? It's what they were expecting.'

Bright girl, thinks Olivia.

When Olivia is leaving along the narrow hallway, thanking the two girls for their time and promising to keep in touch, through the open door of the room opposite, she sees a bare-backed man lying face down half covered on a bed, an arm thrown out and hanging over the side, a bare foot poking out at the end. On the far wall a huge poster of Elvis Presley, above the mantel. Nika murmurs something softly to the prostrate man, before pulling the door closed.

Olivia heads thoughtfully back to the Shepherd's Bush underground, longing to be with Louise again but thinking about Hugo at the same time, an interesting combination.

- Oh, naughty Hugo, sleeping with both girls. All three of them together perhaps? Running a bit of a risk, Hugo, with the girlfriend of a known violent criminal, or maybe it was just Lilly you were after. Although Nika seemed annoyed that Lilly had admitted as much, presumably Nika had not known.

Incidentally, Olivia looked carefully for any possible unmarked cars with watchers inside but saw nothing suspicious, walking the full length of Adelaide Grove, first up one side and then down the other – but maybe that was the point.

In the warmth of the underground, Olivia's wandering mind settles on a sudden unpleasant thought. The man in the bed at Nika's place – could it have been Midge and the girls were deceiving her? Or was it Hugo, hiding with Nika these past few days? Absurd ideas.

The man she saw was thin, smooth-skinned with short brown hair, not like Hugo at all. And Midge, well she had only ever seen an old black and white photo in the papers, so how could she be sure? It would be amazingly audacious, were Midge to be hiding out in his own place, and so close to the local nick. Another impertinent thought crosses her mind. If she pursues Hugo, recording the details of his life, his early years and development, will this worry him that certain events might come to light, secrets that both of them might prefer to be left alone? Hugo would be concerned that she might reveal too much about him, more than he would want, being such a private man; he would certainly want complete editorial control, or at least Jeremy Ashcroft would insist on it. That might not be too bad, so long as it did not cause conflict. The Dominic Lebelov affair was not likely to raise its ugly head, not unless they wanted it to – nobody else seemed to know anything about it, as far as she knew, but…?

***

'Tell me about the men you have loved before,' Louise whispers into her ear, in the steamy heat and peace of her bathroom. Sitting in tandem in the deep scented water, Olivia in Louise's lap, with her arms hanging over Louise's bent knees, they are enjoying some well-deserved intimacy after their usual busy weeks. Her slippery body twists and she nestles her face against Louise's neck.

'Wouldn't you like to know,' she murmurs.

Standing up together, causing tidal waves to crash up the sides, they cling to each other for a moment, exchanging a long full-on kiss. They step out to dry each other and slip on flimsy nightdresses. Soon they are snuggling side by side on Louise's big bed, talking in hushed tones, sharing secrets while sweet essences burn and wine is sipped. Olivia props herself up on an elbow, stroking her partner's hair and face, letting some of her inhibitions fall away in the easy atmosphere.

'I was in love some years ago, an artist, a genius with a magic paintbrush. I was quite in awe of him and we lived together for a few months. He was a rapacious lover, wanting sex two or three times during the night; and then for a whole week, he would work all day and flop into bed exhausted late after I had fallen asleep. And then he would want fucking all through the next night. And that was the pattern – it was very exhausting in its way.' Olivia seems amused at her own telling.

'And was he good? I mean, was he thoughtful, did he take you to heights? Or did he just satisfy his own lust, time after time?'

'Well, if I was perfectly honest,' and Olivia places a delicate forefinger onto Louise's lovely lips, 'a bit of both.' She looks straight into Louise's soft almond eyes and then snatches a kiss before sinking and rolling against her, squashing her breasts against her.

'Not like me then – I make it work, don't I?'

'Yes, oh yes. Hugo was great most of the time, but he could be difficult and his male passion was strong, very strong.' She rests her face between Louise's breasts, kneading them contentedly through her nightdress with probing fingers.

'And you didn't love any woman at that time?'

'Oh, no, it never occurred to me. I liked hirsute men because I wanted to think that the man I was dating had more testosterone than me. I had a preference for furry chests rather than waxed metrosexuals.' They both chuckle.

'So what happen with you and Hugo?'

'That's a long story,' Olivia mumbles, her eyes closed. She is feeling sleepy and warm inside, the fury of her passions temporarily calmed. She would be wonderfully happy just then if they both drifted into sleep, to dream of intimate unlimited romance in a faraway haven where nothing could disturb them.

'So tell me. I want to know. What happen that you turn to women after such a good man?'

'It wasn't Hugo that made me want to change. No, we had some difficulties and then he had to suddenly leave the country. He was Greek and his father was dying in Athens and he went home and I didn't see him after that.'

'What, just like that? But you live together?' Louise persists, trying to catch Olivia's eye.

'Yes – it was quite sudden.' Olivia is suddenly jolted by the image of Hugo shouting at the top of the studio stairs and forcing her back into the bedroom

132

with a vicious expression of pure anger. She buries her face into Louise's nightie, surprised by her own memory, and having trouble holding back the emotion. She feels sharp pricking over her eyes and would love to cry, to let it all break free. Instead, she smears her eyes in the soft cotton. 'Ooops, sorry.'

'You upset.' Louise turns Olivia's face towards her, holding her, 'you cry. Darling, why you cry? Tell me, I kiss it better.'

'Oh, Louise, I don't know. Silly.' Her body is floppy with despair and tiredness. She struggles to sit up, reaching for her bath towel that lies on the floor. She brings her knees up to her chest and hugs them, facing her experienced lover, propped up on the pillows.

'I was pregnant when he left.' Olivia cannot resist a sob. 'He never knew. I had a termination in hospital and I have always felt like a killer, I don't know why.' She quickly defends herself. 'It was absolutely the right thing to do, for me, I know that. But it saddened me so.'

Louise wraps her arms around Olivia's shoulders, hugging her with gentleness. 'You poor girl, poor girl.'

'I thought Hugo may have gone off to another woman, or something, but everyone said he had to rush over to his family in Greece, his father was dying, he had to look after his mother and sort out the business. I felt abandoned. I never understood why he could not get in touch.'

Sleep comes eventually. For Olivia, it is the restless kind, as she turns and tosses at the mercy of her vivid dream-world.

Something even more horrid had happened, just before Olivia discovered herself to be with child, but she was not prepared to share that with Louise, however trusting and honest she wanted her relationship to be. The prissy figure of that Ukrainian dancer bounced relentlessly across the complex labyrinths of her mind during the night, telling her how big his penis was and all but displaying it for her. Other images, like restless demons, reappeared and played themselves over and over, like a spool of music that starts again at the beginning within moments of completing, round after round. She was not prepared to share those with anybody.

It was Dominic, wretched man that he was. So full of himself, with his love of display, stretching gender roles with his ambiguity, always seeking admiration and an audience he could show off to. His dancing was dramatic and fluid, his body so expressive, his skills exquisite, no one doubted that. His strength was immense, torso and limbs shaped like a bodybuilder. He was capable of tossing Olivia through the air, spinning her around his shoulders only to catch her around the waist in perfect balance and poise. But God, his male urge was irrepressible and he had taken a shine to the young Olivia; more than a shine. The presence of Hugo did not seem to stop his determination, probably made it stronger, to demonstrate his superiority over his artistic rival, to show his better breeding, by stealing his girl away from right under his nose.

A few nights after his extraordinary proposal to bed her, when she had refused him without ceremony, he crept up to the bedroom late, seeking his just rewards. Hugo had gone off somewhere, to his other workshop probably to help others on some project and had not yet returned, and Olivia had gone to bed exhausted as usual and was soon asleep. Dominic had decided to take his chance. Olivia was woken in the darkness to find rough hands groping her, arms clamped around her from behind, her breasts squeezed, her nipples pinched. She knew instantly who it was by his sweet perfume and she could smell alcohol on his breath. His unspeakably stiff kingpin, that he had so proudly boasted about, was poking between her buttocks. She was repulsed and fought bravely, kicking out and screaming. She managed to bite his arm, breaking the flesh, which infuriated him so much that he hit her hard across the back of her head.

She caught his shin with her heel and managed to squirm her body free of him, keeping him out. She kneed him weakly in the groin and tried to kick harder, but, regarding her as a challenge, he was not prepared to give her up. The only illumination came through the windows, a mix of yellow street lighting and moonlight, which eerily played across their grimacing faces as they twisted this way and that. He caught her ankles, forced her legs apart and bent her knees up, her nightdress riding up, exposing her again. He came down on her with his full weight. She twisted and wriggled, and he let go her ankles to slap her face. She caught him again in the groin, feeling his testicles squash against the front of her foot, and he fell away coughing, tumbling off the bed. But he rushed her from behind, grabbing the cotton nightie, pulling it backwards and upwards, scrunching it up tightly around her neck, to restrain her, to strangle her. They were struggling upright, in the middle of the bed, her bare body pulled back against his and his erection jabbing at her bottom. He forced her to bend forwards, pushing her head down onto the bed and she struggled to breathe. Her attempts at screaming, to shout for help were muffled and useless. He was panting and wording obscenities at her, calling her a cunt and a whore. He was forceful and vicious in his penetration of her, with skin-tearing agony. Just as she came to realise that her attempts at stopping this rape were going to be hopeless and she would do better just to let it happen, she thought she heard a man's voice downstairs. For a second Dominic stopped thrusting, his grip loosened. She was suddenly hopeful of release and was able to lift her head enough to force out a muffled scream. A light had come on under the door and definite clomping boot-steps could be made out on the stairs.

And then the door swung inwards and banged against a chair.

The stark-naked Dominic had withdrawn and risen to face the intruder in the semi-darkness, grabbing some of his clothes, but his waggling penis was caught in the extra light from the hallway. Olivia, face-down on the bed with buttocks exposed, was coughing and trying to free her neck of the ligatured nightie. Hugo's view of events must have been shocking and he responded with an anger and a violence she had never seen before.

'No you don't, you fucking prick.' He charged at Dominic with flailing fists, catching him on the side of his head and again across his chest. He tried kicking out at him but only delivered glancing blows. Dominic, at a disadvantage naked and in bare feet, danced around and parried the blows as best he could. He went for the exit, deciding that escape was his only chance. But Hugo caught him with a leg as he passed and knocked him over by the door post. Hugo swung his right arm at full stretch towards Dominic's head, but the ballet-dancer ducked and Hugo's fist crashed into the edge of the door jam, which made him cry out. Dominic was stumbling to his feet half out on the landing, when Hugo still incensed, swung again with a booted foot. 'All right, all right,' Dominic shouted. 'No, it's not all right,' shouted Hugo in turn and lashed out again, catching Dominic across his thigh. He toppled towards the head of the stairs, catching himself on the bannister rail, where Hugo kicked out again across his backside.

Dominic Lebelov flew down the stairs backwards, tumbling without control. Olivia had warned Hugo on several occasions that those metal stairs were steep and quite dangerous, and that one day someone was going to fall down them and break their neck. Dominic bounced down with some force, head over heels, and crunched into a heap on the concrete floor at the bottom, caught in the studio's neon lights. He did not move: his neck was positioned awkwardly under his shoulders at an impossible angle, his limbs looked unusually out of place. Olivia heard the sounds, of something heavy banging down the steps, ending with a dull thud. But there was another distinctive bone-snapping sound that both Hugo and Olivia would be able to recall with nightmarish clarity forever afterwards.

'Oh fuck,' murmured Hugo, panting from the top of the stairs.

His knuckles were hurting and bleeding, he was breathing hard. He roared at Olivia in the bedroom doorway to go back inside. Slowly he descended the steps one at a time without taking his eyes off the naked bundle of immovable ballet dancer, his neck broken and dead as dead could be, his meagre clothes scattered about him.

Part Two: Police Shooting, Earl's Court, London
(Friday, January 16, 2015)

Hugo Pitsakis at 34 is built ample and broad. He has recently taken delivery of a bespoke presidential-sized oak framed bed with a thousand and one pocket-springs and smart fibre technology for his apartment on the river. Few people know about his lucky sanctuary, where he craves to be after another gruelling session. He is unable to settle comfortably in the narrow flimsy metal structure, so short that his feet are sticking out and freezing in the overnight chill, that Veronica from Zagreb insisted he share, with her. The mattress is lumpy and turning over is an exercise in itself, making the whole thing bounce and squeak under the strain of his fourteen stone. Nika's slim body is in danger of being crushed. Their points of skin contact are sticky and he repeatedly needs to adjust his position without disturbing her; restful sleep is all but impossible. The warmth of their earlier lovemaking has abated, leaving a stale aroma filling his nostrils, while he can only dream of thermal-filled goose down duvets.

Hugo is tinkering with the idea of slipping out into the bedroom opposite to find the delectable Lilly Soames, who would make a heart-warming companion just then, however flimsy and cranky her bed might be. They had already consorted a few times at his studios, unknown to Nika, and he is hoping that the Croatian will be gone in the morning, leaving them time enough for further lovemaking of their own.

Hugo has the carefree and generous attitude to life of his Greek inheritance, expressions beaming and hugs bear-like, but is driven by an incessant demand for maximum effort to achieve maximum results. He is a painter in oils, a supreme draughtsman, a magician with charcoal and brush, a creator of extraordinary movement and emotional realism. His genius is expressed on giant colourful canvases with large-as-life perspective and he has received some encouraging notices these past twelve months, with at least one commission from a well-known television chat-show host. His agent, Jake Preston is revelling in the way that his popularity is upsetting the British establishment, with his modern interpretations of social conflict and political vainglory. It is obviously Hugo's ability to make a bob or two out of selling direct to the public, his version of giving their lordships the middle finger, that most disturb the hierarchy at Burlington House, who regards his work disparagingly as rather too commercial to be called art.

His mind is juggling with the various projects that he is currently involved in, not least the preparation sketches he has been working on these last two days. He seldom draws figures just from imagination but prefers to use life-models in costume to construct action scenes, in mock-ups of the historical context and setting. He is relying on his little band of promising students to progress the background preparation and fill-in work on the Remembrance triptych and on his Greece series, and hopefully, they have been beavering diligently at his studios while he has been away. He needs to be back soon to bring it all together and to dedicate his time to the details that are so inimitable of his work.

Jake had brought the two girls, Veronica and Lilly, to his Theed Street studio last summer for the value of their unique beauty, and for small payments they had agreed to sit for him. They were both models, working the clubs and doing photo shoots for men's magazines and the like. He could see their potential straight away. They both had curiously attractive faces, that would draw attention in any crowd. Nika was from the Balkans and had presumably seen a thing or two. She had a line of barbed wire tattooed around an upper arm. She was dark and angular and rarely smiled, but applied a coquettish look when she wanted, moping and vulnerable, letting her brown hair fall untidily across one eye as she viewed you keenly with the other. Lilly was younger and more relaxed during her sessions. She had a charm of her own with dimples to match, a buxom blonde whose perfection startled Hugo at first, but he was soon taking his chances.

In truth, they are both grafters, prepared to do anything, with or without their clothes on, if the money is there. He has already drawn Lilly on a field trip (he called it), through some of the more remote pathways on Hampstead Heath, where he persuaded her to disrobe and walk away from him up a narrow tree-lined path, through the slanting dawn light of late autumn. He presented her with the full-sized canvas only a few weeks ago, as a Christmas present and helped her hang it in her small bedroom.

At the moment, Hugo is entirely engrossed in a heartfelt series on the current social troubles in austerity Greece, showing a demoralising hand-to-mouth existence, amongst the dilapidated ruin of a modern European city in a state of uncontrolled dysfunction. He needs the girls to depict certain scenes for him, to highlight the plight of women residents in parts of Athens, bullied and abused by police and other ruffians. Three full sized pictures of struggling life are planned, street scenes depicting demonstrations, battles at barricades and food hand-out huts and the immigrant crush at a holding station on the Macedonia border. The centrepiece depicts hand-to-hand fighting and poignant scenes of police tear-gassing crowds, the violence of blades and picks in shocking retaliation.

He had been dropped off on Adelaide Grove with all his arty paraphernalia to hand and had taken over the only lounge space at the back adjacent to the kitchen, where a skylight delivered natural light marginally more appealing than in the front bedroom. Here he had been able to concentrate his efforts away from the distracting bustle at his own studio and had already stayed two days, which meant two nights trying to sleep in Nika's inadequate bed.

Hugo had first checked on the whereabouts of her boyfriend.

'He been naughty, with police,' she had confessed. 'He on the run, don't worry. I not seen him for weeks. Don't know where he is; don't care.'

'What was his name again, Nika?'

'Midge, he called Midge, he handsome, long wavy hair, like you, big smile. He good actor, he work in Soho once.'

'So he won't be around, or anything, if we work at your place for a few days?'

'No, is fine, he has more sense, he won't be back.'

During a late session yesterday evening, Hugo had asked what exactly Midge had done. Nika was poised at full stretch, with one foot on the ground and the other above her waistline, leg bent at the knee stepping up onto a wooden chest, representing a wall in Hugo's mind, her arms reaching for the safety the other side, springing away from the danger stalking her. She was wearing a tight leotard, so Hugo could outline her form with accuracy, muscle straining sinews, clenched buttocks, sweat glistening across her shoulders. A uniformed policeman with plastic shield and teargas canister appears behind her, about to strike her with a truncheon. Hugo has used sweeping lines in charcoal to outline basic shapes of figures and then worked on the shadows and the three-dimensional perspective. 'Hold it there, just hold it.' Nika was struggling to stay still in her awkward position.

'He rob a gallery, jewellery, art relics and little treasures; police catch him, he shoot a policeman, in the leg, but he nearly die. Then Midge on the run, but they catch him again. He is in prison waiting for weeks, and then he escape at the Court, he break free and runs over the rooftops, Marylebone. Very clever man.'

'So he's clever but violent?'

'He is only when provoked.'

'But he used a gun on a policeman; that's violence, isn't it?'

Nika said nothing, concentrating on keeping her balance for a few moments more. 'So what do you see in him, Nika? Are you afraid of him?'

'He put down loads of money on me in the club. In Whitechapel. He put over a hundred pounds in my garter and promised to look after me. He generous but then I find out he make money by cheating and robbing. He's made lots of money. He has a flat in Edgware, as well. He bought car for me.'

'Sounds good, but now if the police catch him he will go to jail, for assault. What will you do then?'

'Look, he a boyfriend. I have boyfriends, I see you, I see others. He don't own me.'

'So he won't beat you up if he finds out you've been unfaithful…?'

'Look, I can do what I like,' Nika shouted. 'I earn good money. We pay rent here. He not boss me about, okay?'

'Okay. That's fine. Just checking, you know.' Hugo realised Nika was a feisty woman and could probably look after herself. Or was all this just bravado? He wondered what sort of bloke Midge was but presumed that he had the same approach to sex as she did: enjoy it with whoever was available, at the time, and pass on. At least Hugo was not thinking of maintaining any sort of ongoing deal with Nika. Now Lilly, she might be different.

As they ate some food in the dingy kitchen area last night, Nika had spoken a little about some of the hardships of her life, her mother being an asylum seeker to Europe, with her two young children in tow. Lilly and Hugo had listened attentively, in sympathy.

By midday on Friday, they decide that Hugo has done enough. They ravage greasy bacon and eggs off plastic plates and slurp from their mugs, slumped on the floor cross-legged, among the mess of brushes and paint tubes and semi-dry boards, with dramatic sketches on the fold-away easel and pinned to the walls all around. Outside the rain keeps thrashing against the windows, blustery and cold.

Nika stares out into the back yard with dismay, seeing the rain bouncing off the wet concrete. 'We have to be in Hackney by five o'clock, we're going to be soaked. Do you want lift, I will drive? I can drop you somewhere.'

'Yes, Nika, that sounds good. I'll gather the sketches. I'll have to come back another time for the rest of the stuff,' he mutters, wiping the back of a mucky hand on his face, leaving smears of charcoal and white paint across his cheek. He has not shaved for three days or washed properly for that matter. 'Anybody around on Sunday?'

'I will be,' offers Lilly, with a knowing smile and a playful rolling forward of her shoulders to offer Hugo a view of her tumbling cleavage.

'I must get these pictures pinned up for the weekend.' Hugo rolls up the cartridge papers to fit into a cardboard tube for protection and stuffs other things into a leather bag. He is ready in the corridor in what he had been wearing when he arrived, brown cords and boots and a cream thick-knitted jumper that has seen better days, baggy and paint-spattered, with some holes in the sleeves. He waits for the other two as they make themselves up.

Nika steps out the front, the wind howling against her and splattering raindrops across her face, before she forces the door closed again. 'You need waterproofs; you can't go out in that,' sneering at his paint-spattered top. 'Have you not a coat?' She shrugs contemptuously. 'Men, I don't know. Here, put these on,' and she reaches for a man's coat that has been hanging limply in the hallway, with a hat. 'Take this off, you have paint all over sleeves.'

Hugo pulls his jumper off, tossing it onto Lilly's bed through the open door, before donning the offered grey fedora and long trench coat, fastening the belt tight. He pulls up the collar, tugs the hat down low over his face, grabs his bag and picture-roll and is ready to face the weather. The two girls, made-up to the nines with wicked displays of black spiky eyelashes, are wrapped in winter coats with fur-lined hoods and knee-high boots. They file through the door, with Nika last in line to lock up.

***

It is way past lunchtime and DC Ian Wade has stuffed the cellophane wrapper from his earlier chicken salad sandwich into the driver's side door pocket, so

142

Sanger won't see it, although the lingering smell has already alerted him. They both have a cardboard carton of take away coffee that they nurse in their hands, to make them feel warmer than they really are.

A nondescript car-lined street of run-down terraced houses in Shepherd's Bush looking miserable in the winter drizzle, and Wade has been here overnight and all morning watching the rain bounce across the bonnet of the silver Vauxhall. Cold and sleepless, he is finding it difficult to keep his mind on the job; nothing of any interest has happened. He is sharing the watch with his mate Jones in the other car, and their only exercise has been alternating trips up to the end for a pee in the bushes along Sawley Road, returning rain spattered each time. And each time they have taken surreptitious glances through the windows of number 84. Wade is longing for some rest over the coming weekend, no more bloody watching jobs, freezing his bollocks off.

Slouching at the wheel, he definitely confirms the presence of a man in the house, far-side terrace, just by the bollards, sir, no side entrances or exits, together with a couple of young females. From the sneer in his voice, Wade imagines them up to no good. He has walked past several times, he says, and has clearly seen the tall figure moving about behind dirty net curtains, but dark-like inside, not a clear view. Not seen him arrive, no, sir, must have been before Wade had set up his position, which was at nineteen hundred hours exactly, last night. Been on watch himself ever since, front door never opened.

'Well, not exactly a direct vision, no, sir,' Wade mumbles on further questioning from the Inspector.

'It's him. The walk, those clothes, the hat. It's quite definitely him. It's Midge Martin.' So the petulant Mike Sanger alerts the backup teams from Hammersmith and Shephard's Bush Stations in their mobile positions, coordinating everything using short wave radio. 'He'll be armed. Consider him dangerous.' A long-serving plain-clothes copper, he should have known better. Joining Wade within the last hour, he has been sitting impatiently in the back of the unmarked saloon, parked thirty yards away up the street, toying with the idea of going in or waiting awhile. They needed DC Peter Finch with them anyway to make a proper identification and he has only just fortuitously slipped into the back seat.

The suspect, his face obscured by a grey fedora, folds his large body into the front passenger seat of a two-door yellow Mini, parked outside the house, pulling the door closed after him with a long outstretched arm. The two young ladies with him, in skinny jeans and trainers, fur-trimmed jackets with hoods, hurry around to the roadside and clamber in, heads first, one into the cramped back seat, the other dropping behind the wheel. The little car is seen to rock from side to side as all three occupants adjust their positions, tugging at their coats to smooth out creases and tuck away flaps, and wrap themselves against the chill. Sanger checks his watch: twenty minutes past three o'clock, rush hour.

The girl in the front automatically pouts her lips at the rear-view mirror, working them together to check her lipstick, admiring the colour-effects around her eyes. She starts the car and they move away from the curb with a judder as she struggles with the gearbox, never once using the mirrors to see what might be coming along the road. While in the back, her young friend, the prettier and smaller of the two, hugs her knees and shivers.

'The blonde one is Secola's friend, Lilly Soames. Secola is Martin's girlfriend, she's driving.' For a while, Sanger continues his commentary over the intercom, speaking cautiously, but unable to suppress an excited edge in his voice as they all follow on without incident, along the Uxbridge Road. They mingle with the congestion at the Bush roundabout and then along Holland Road. Progress is irritatingly slow. All three lanes are stop-start along Pembroke Road, where the Mini inches its way forward along the near side, towards the junction with Earl's Court Road at a set of traffic lights, with the dark red brickwork spire of St. Philips Church standing tall as a landmark ahead. Sanger, Wade and Finch trying to look inconspicuous in their dull raincoats, are three cars behind. Sanger mutters under his breath that they are bloody well going to get their man, there is not the remotest chance of his escape this time. The face of Lilly Soames, with stunning crimson lips and a puzzled look, appears several times at the rear window, apparently speaking to her companions. Sanger reported later that he was sure she was acting as lookout and had been asked inside the car to see whether the coast was clear behind them.

***

'This is so infuriating, this traffic. It's taking so long just to go a hundred yards. It would be quicker to walk.' Hugo's frustration is catching and he drums his fingers irritably on the dash in front. The car remains stationary. 'Look, I'm going to walk down to Jake's office, it's just down to the right, Earl's Court Road.'

'OK, Hugo, we see you Sunday, and we clear up the flat? And we get paid, yes?' Nika is looking sternly sideways at him with an eyebrow raised, her jaw jutting.

He nods and pulls down firmly on the handle to push the door open. 'Oh, yes, you bet. Thanks, girls.' He turns around to take a glance at Lilly. 'Could you pass me my tube?' And he reaches for his bag. They go through the awkward process of kissing cheeks.

'At least it not raining so hard now,' comments Nika.

***

From the trailing car, Sanger sees the passenger front door of the Mini open and a leg protrudes as the man he so desperately wants to catch prepares to get out. He is turning back to his female companions and appears to be giving instructions. Sanger makes the assumption that he has spotted the police and is preparing to make his escape.

'He's seen us, he's getting out,' another police officer calls over the airways. 'I've got him, I see him,' murmurs Sanger, and he pushes Finch out onto the pavement twenty-five yards behind the Mini. It has to be Finch, as he was the arresting officer when Martin committed his original crime, the armed robbery of the Marylebone Gallery, and therefore is the only officer who can make the positive identification. And Finch seems up for the task, climbing out with eagerness and spirit. The drizzle and the gusty wind makes him stumble awkwardly in his stiff black shoes, his open raincoat flapping around him as he advances by the line of cars towards the Mini, the traffic lights still on red. Unexpectedly a revolver comes out of its holster from under his left arm and he waves it erratically in front of him in his outstretched right hand. He is shouting to the man at the open door of the car ahead, although some of it is lost in the rush of chill wind and traffic noise. 'Armed police. Put your hands above your head where I can see them.'

The passenger in the fedora, who is just rising from his low sitting position, carrying a tube of something tucked under his arm, his right hand buried in his coat pocket, a leather bag across his lap, looks up in surprise towards the frantic man running along the pavement, trying to make out what he is shouting. In his defence, exposed to public scrutiny some months later, Finch said he was convinced that this was Martin and that he had something in his coat pocket, likely to be a gun, given his past record; that everything happened so fast, that Martin did not stop but turned to make a dash for it; that he, Detective Constable Peter Finch, inexperienced officer that he was, who had never actually fired a gun at another human being in his life, felt utterly determined to stop this man and not be shot at himself; and that he wanted to make a name for himself. The Police Commissioner commented later he had certainly done that.

The heavy snub-nosed Glock 26, set on automatic, sits so nicely in Finch's palm, so powerful that it makes him feel invincible. He does not hesitate but fires freely some rapid shots, almost out of control, as he comes up alongside. Two or three bullets sink into the bulk of the man at the open door, while others scatter aimlessly, bursting through the side glass and the rear window or miss the target altogether.

Twinkling pieces of splintered glass cascade over the pavement and asphalt in all directions. The sounds are of crunching fireworks and metallic cracks as bullets hit metalwork and glass, and screams come from inside the small car. An elderly couple walking their spaniel on a lead not ten yards away stand mesmerised, staring with disbelief at what they see, their mouths open, the dog cowering behind their legs, as clouds of tiny glass fragments shower down upon them.

At least three other officers are coming at the Mini from other sides, weaving between the halting traffic, running and shouting, their firearms poised and pointing. Officer Eric Jardine fires shots at the rear tyres to stop the car being driven away and several random shots through the back window.

The front passenger slumps back into the Mini, his door still wide open. Ms Secola has opened her door and is scrambling to get out in a forward crouch, falling and screaming in horror. Her injured male companion tries to follow her, twisting and crawling on all fours across the front seats, smearing blood stains over the new leather and falling out of the open driver's door face forward onto the road. Nika is grabbed by a police officer and half walked, half dragged crying hysterically to a nearby police car. Sanger, who followed gingerly behind Finch crunching over the glass splinters along the pavement, assumed that Finch was convinced that this man, Midge Martin, was their target, or he would not have opened fire with such exuberance. Jardine, who is a close friend of the officer Martin had severely injured at the robbery, sees the man crawling out of the driver's door and moves round to that side, firing two or three more shots into the groaning body in the trench coat. The man flops forward and rolls grimacing onto his back, the fedora discarded. Jardine gets down on his haunches, bending over him, placing his gun over the man's forehead and is heard to shout, 'Okay, cocksucker, this is it.' He appears to fire his weapon more than once but nothing happens, no bullet is released, the weapon seems to have jammed. Instead, he hits the man across his face several times with the butt of the pistol before another policeman pulls him up by the shoulders and away from the motionless bloodied figure.

'It's not him, boss,' exclaims Finch, panting and overlooking the apparently dead man supine on the wet road, realising that it is not Midge Martin as he had thought but someone quite different.

'So who the fuck is this, then, you idiot?' shouts Sanger, raising his arm towards Finch as if to strike a blow.

Detective Inspector Michael Sanger confirmed later at a hurriedly called evening press conference when asked several times, that the victim did not act in self-defence and that he was not armed. The whole unfortunate episode had been a mistake. The poor visibility on such a dull day had compounded to the difficulty of making out the exact features of the man hidden under a hat and trench coat. On behalf of the Metropolitan Police, Inspector Sanger offered the victim their apologies.

The victim of mistaken identity lies still, arms akimbo, with a fixed agonised expression, as blood from his nose and battered face washes across his cheeks in the light drizzle, dripping over his unshaven chin. Dark patches are seeping around the several torn holes in his coat and a ruby red puddle is spreading outwards beneath him. His head lolls to one side on the wet road, floppy hair in disarray, revealing another wound around the temple that is bleeding profusely. In his right hand, he is gripping tightly an oyster travelcard.

The innocent man is stretchered into an ambulance that arrives miraculously through the heavy traffic fifteen minutes later and is taken to Chelsea and Westminster Hospital for emergency surgery. A hospital spokesperson later described his condition as critical but stable.

Part Three: Hugo Pitsakis

1

Week Beginning Saturday, January 17, 2015

Hugo's mind is a mush. His body is not there. Connections are missing. He is aware of nothing and then something, but far away, not part of him. He is floating away from himself, out of control. He is screaming silently. He watches himself drifting aimlessly as an autumn leaf on a running stream, upturned and helpless and soon to disappear.

Hugo's mind is mushy like sludge, where thoughts are dropped in and mixed up with so much else. He makes no sound, although he wants to. There are human voices around him, but they are not his. Waves of pain, like burning fire, consume him.

Everything is fluid, moving; nothing is stable. A white canvas looms in front of him and giant paint brushes with broomstick handles are leaning against it, but the paint pots are small and the brushes will not fit through the openings. Pots have been knocked over, Prussian blue and cadmium red flow over the floor. He is on his knees with a scoop, until it all slinks away through gaps in the floorboards.

There is a naked body of a crumpled man at the bottom of the metal staircase, the neck twisted grotesquely and on its face is a smile. He stands over him and tries to kick him aside. He wants to hide him, cover him up. The dead man is calling someone, someone at the top of the stairs behind him. A distraught blonde woman he does not recognise in a ripped cotton nightshirt, whimpers behind him, eyes popping, voice failing.

There are noises in his head, sharp cracks, like someone hitting a metal gate with a hammer. He is suddenly blinded by paint thrown over his face and he is in pain; he reaches for the front of his head and realises the paint is a red running gush of blood that is so warm and must be his. The burning pain, like a dirt stain on a white cotton shirt, washes away, spiralling down a waste pipe. He is floating out through the open windows and above the buildings, where clouds envelop him. It feels cold and everything is in an empty space without walls. Time stands alone, without meaning.

He is bouncing in slow motion on soft expanded foam, and splashes of sticky liquid spray his face again and he wants to wipe his eyes. His nose is sore and scabbed. He sees a woman smiling above him, her bright lips moving, her mouth oceans wide. As he reaches up for her, there is no one there and her laughing voice fades away. A vast sheet of polystyrene plastic hovers far above him and soon turns into squares, like tiles in a false ceiling, hiding the watching demons beyond.

He is drifting in sleep, always in sleep, and he cannot hold onto anything. He tries to shape his hands so that he might grip something solid that will help him stop and see where he is. But everything is moving, the walls, the doorposts, the bannister railings, even the floor beneath him is inclined to open up so that he slides without meaning into blackened rooms of emptiness. Just as a thought pops into view and he is deciding on positive action, preparing his hands to catch it like a football, he is drawn away and his fingers make a hash of it. He cannot feel his body. People are touching him, turning him one way and then the other, but he cannot feel them. Their hands pass through him without hurting. He is moving through the air, travelling backwards under flashing neon lights that rush past him. He tries to concentrate on the white tiles that cover the ceilings out of reach way above him. Metal doors slide with a rattle, a bell chimes. He hears a siren's voice speaking to him, door opening, fourth floor, it says. Voice chatter is subdued. The rooms are packed with buzzing machines, motorized machines and flickering screens, robotic voices.

He lives here, he hides here, he is tortured here. He says nothing, he cannot speak, he screws up his eyes tight but the tiles above his head in the ceiling are moving sideways, making a scraping sound and someone is watching from above through the gaps. When he opens his eyes to look, the tiles have moved back over the gaps again and his view is blocked.

From behind his sore eyeballs, gloop oozes out under the lids. His throat is sore, he cannot swallow. His lips are caked and cracked; he feels thirsty and craves cold water rinsing through his mouth. But his mouth is jammed full with hard metallic objects, tied around his face, with sticky tape pulling on the hairs of his cheeks. His head is sore and throbbing. There are boxes on every ledge around him with luminous screens and moving green dots that beep. He cannot move his head but revolves his eyes around to count them and tries to speak to them. They are watching him. He sees flashing blue light across the room and the sound of tyres screeching. Someone is shouting into his face.

Out of the blue, his mind resting and listless with no apparent conflict, come sounds of glass breaking and firecrackers, and a girl is screaming. Something thumps his chest, more than once and he cannot understand it or how that is possible. The hits are numbing and take his breath away. Then comes a shearing pain and a burning thud into his stomach, with multiple hot stabs. Several tumultuous sounds of crashing burst along his ears, crackling into the drums. He must be dreaming, but the screams are real, he hears them beside his bed. He tries to sit up so that he can see who is screaming and where the blows have come from; only more blows come and he is knocked sideways, trying to lift his arms up across his face for protection. He cannot feel his body; he does not know where his legs are, they feel stupidly twisted. There are angry voices in the distance, men closing all around him, sounding aggressive. He is not sure whether he is wetting himself. He is on a hard surface, his face scraping the gritty path, his palms grazed. He feels cold and starts to shiver. There are more juddering thuds into his body and bruising hits across his face, but he does not feel these, they seem remote. He is used to them by now. He is drifting away again, feeling his life tissues draining from him. His nose is bleeding through his fingers, he is flushing along a river of viscous strawberry-coloured fluid, sucked through an open drain beside the gutter, dropping unimpeded into underground channels, like sewage. He is drowning in the mush, relieved, the suffering will soon be over.

He wakes exhausted and fearful. He has been floating along on the surface of a hot river, a river of lava, of blood, the burning pains always there. His body is quite alone, adrift somewhere, his legs lost to him, in a vacuum. All sounds have vanished. He lies on his back, wet with sweat, he cannot move. The pillow behind his head is flat and lumpy. He is repulsed by the pungent smell of his own body. He sees the chequered pattern of dirty ceiling panels above him. He waits for the slow agonising scraping of the tiles to begin, so he knows he is being watched.

Samantha is looking at him, her face close, he sees her lips moving. She has tears flooding her eyes. Her smile is wide and her voice friendly, but when he tries to touch her cheek, she moves away from him out of reach. There is a buzzing in his ears and it seems to blot out other sounds. He is being manoeuvred sideways by his arms onto a moving trolley by his gaolers who are not gentle people. His head is raised at an angle and he sees other inanimate bodies stretched out on beds neatly in rows opposite him, with forlorn expressions, uniformed faces. There are men in white coats around the end of the bed. His feet are bare and he sees them for the first time, exposed. Voices are bouncing around from one side to the other but he cannot make out what is being said. Samantha is in her red coat and is talking to the men in their white coats.

He thinks of Lilly, her screaming. He sees her on the path through the woods walking away from him and calls out to her to help him. She is looking at him over a shoulder offering him the come-on, her superb breasts in free motion, but he cannot catch up with her. She is wounded in the shoulder, a trickle of blood running from a black hole down her back. He is holding his limp penis, normally so proud, reduced to a soft insubstantial thing. He can hardly feel it, it is shrunken so, and Lilly is laughing at him. She lays down on the grass on the bumpy hillside, her arms outstretched towards him, mocking him, her thighs apart inviting him in, but he cannot find his penis. When he approaches, it is not Lilly at all but Samantha, who has caught him out, who is gleefully reclining on her back on the ground, tossing her mane triumphantly behind her, greeting him, admonishing him. He crouches down between her legs and lifts her skirt, and leaning forward close to her, he prises apart her labial folds with their fine orange covering, so that he can climb inside, head first. He squirms his way up into her pitch-black passageway with its wet walls that smell of dead flowers, into her sticky recesses, that are warm and secure inside, out of sight. He pulls his feet in and the entrance clamps completely closed after him, sealed.

'We have to take you back to the theatre, Mr Pitsakis, we need to do an operation on your chest, to drain some blood that has collected there and to remove some metal debris, if we can.' The voice is silky and compelling, a man with persuasive powers and Hugo's instincts are to reach for his hand, to be held reassuringly. The squeeze is taken as consent, he assumes. A kindly hand with soft fingers, he folds his arms across his chest, one upon the other. Are they preparing him, is he to lie in state, for all the world to pass by in quiet solemnity?

He is in motion again. Neon lights are whizzing past his head, blinking at him, and he cannot prevent them burning through to his eyes even with his lids tightly closed.

He is in pain when he breathes; needle-like explosions stab him every time he tries to move his chest. He coughs feebly, a grating in his throat, and pain strikes up his back. His abdomen is distended. He still cannot feel his legs properly. He has a round plastic knob in his hand the size of a ping-pong ball, attached to a flex; he can press the button on it with a thumb when he wants to, and the pain subsides and his mind swims through the mush. He is allowed to do this at will, as often as he wishes, which is often. The ceiling tiles directly above his head have been moved, swapped around, so the dirty marked one is now over to the left and a clean white one is immediately above his eye line. But it scrapes sideways, just like the others did, he hears it. Someone above is watching him, they know when he thumbs his pain button. He tries to call out but his throat is like an oven-baked tin, with his voice seized up inside. His teeth are bone dry and tingling and he wants to wash out the repulsive taste in his mouth.

Around his head all the time there are beeping noises that keep him awake. He tries to blot them out by pressing one side of his head into the pillows and then, as that makes no difference, the other side. He leans a little over to one side or the other, but stabbings in his chest are repeated and he needs more pain relief, so he uses his thumb on the rubbery knob in his hand, which feels like a gear-knob in a car, the old-fashioned type.

There is a new arrival in the bed next to him. A heavily-built man with greying hair at the sides and a deep-tanned face, which has been cleaned and shaved as best it can. He has all the paraphernalia of a failing mortal among the intensive care, with catheters placed in all his orifices. Slumped and immobile under countless drips and beeping machines with their monitor leads, a ventilation machine puffing rhythmically by his side, he looks just like Hugo. With all the trappings of a dead specimen on first admission, slapped in the middle of an experiment to keep a human alive, even if patently obvious to any casual observer the futility of it all, Hugo watches from the other side, with fascination, understanding the predicament. For hours, a sad-looking woman in a blue plastic raincoat stands head bowed at the end of the bed with a handkerchief to her face, eyes swollen with grief, hardly moving.

Hugo knows that the body belongs to his own father lying beside him under the single white sheet, suffering from his second heart attack, which would prove ultimately fatal. This within two weeks of the first, when he had collapsed at work, found distressingly with his trousers around his ankles while his young secretary composed herself, adjusting her clothing and smudged make-up in the ladies' toilets.

There is an admirable carpet of grey-white matted hair over the old man's chest poking above the edge of the sheet, but the body is not as robust and well-built as Hugo remembers from the past; there has been some deterioration, some weight has been lost, the face is less rounded, the jowls a little slacker, and the bags under the eyes are like the feeding nosebags the donkeys in the park are given while waiting in line for their next young customer.

He wants to ask him if he has spotted the watchers up above the ceiling tiles, which keep sliding sideways so they can see what you are doing. His father is not wounded but something has happened, he looks close to death. Perhaps he should talk to him, rally him, boost his reserves so that he would not die, but recover to fight another day, which is what Hugo always believed his father was capable of. He is a tough character, with enormous fighting spirit and as strong as an ox; "take more than a little hardening of my arteries to knock me out," he would roar at Bernadette when he saw the look of sad pessimism on her face.

Perhaps the old man is dead already, he has not moved since he spotted him; no eyelid movement, no grunting or snoring. Perhaps they are both dead, both waiting their turn to be admitted on the other side. The Greek doctors are murmuring heart attack, over weight, overstressed. They start barking orders and shouting out observations, more drugs, adrenaline, another drip, a cut-down, shock treatment, stand back. Through an internal window into the care unit, he sees his naked father shuddering with the passage of electricity, his body lifting up off the couch, into the air to crunch back down again, no luck. The process is repeated several times.

He reaches out towards him and wants to speak to him, but perhaps he will sleep first and speak later, after another push on his pain button. The gap between their cots anyway is not just a few feet, as in their local hospital back home, where relatives would bring all the patient's food in and sometimes cook it on portable stoves by the bedside, as the family crowds around. His father is many feet away, an unbridgeable separation that is widening all the time, as his bed slides sideways towards a shadowy archway in the far wall leading to who knows where. Hugo wants to speak, to call out, to warn him to take care. The nurses have turned away, they are not bringing him back. This is London, he knows that, he is not confused. He just wants to sleep for now.

He is clutching Sam's arm and she is leaning down towards him. He sees her buxom shape, her red coat open at the front, her lovely hair rustling against his face for a second. Is that outside air he can smell, sweet Coty perfume, her warm breath? She pecks at his cheek, murmuring sweet things at him and he drifts on a floating raft, languid in the hot glare. There is water running over his arm, cold at first and then it becomes warmer. He is blissfully unconcerned.

Later when she has gone he tries to remember the feel of her, the warmth of her against his cheek, the soothing sounds of her voice; but he is being watched from above, an impenetrable gap between the tiles in the ceiling has opened up. He pretends to be asleep.

Something sharp is poking into his side. He tries to inch away from it but the edge is so close, he might tip over. The light above his head is painfully bright; it bores through his tightly closed eyelids. He wants to pull a cover over his face but cannot get his arms to move; even his fingers seem only capable of wiggling where they are, by his sides. He concentrates, tries to visualise at least his right arm, sliding up the side of his hip. The skin is bare and it is warm, he can feel its bony shape and then the wispy surface of hairs over his stomach, which seems convex, bloated and tense. There is something rough across the front, Elastoplast strips and a netted rag, like a face-cloth. He feels a thin cord, a plastic tube that is hard, emerging from under it; he can roll it sideways but dares not pull on it, already feeling an odd sensation inside.

He recognises the unhappy lady standing by the next bed as his mother, in her younger day, her complexion smooth with no giveaway crow's feet around the eyes, her figure trim. But her shoulders are hunched, she is grieving so heavily, she seems shorter than he remembers. She has been standing there forever. Her face is dignified, her tears suppressed, and she has made her face up with a little colour and a pink lipstick. Her arms dangle by her side, the blue raincoat buckled at the waist.

Hugo is the young man making his ambitious way in the world now and his mother takes his hand; together they stare at the ashen white figure of the big man, her blustering hero to whose mast she had pinned her flag long ago. Hugo is taller but shares her looks in many ways, the arched brows, the deep-set dark eyes, the same sensitive mouth. His colouring is more of his father's, whose jet-black hair was always impressively greased and severely drawn back from his proud forehead. Barnabas Pitsakis in his heyday had had a neat electric-trimmed line of moustache, as brilliantly black as his slick hair, divided into two by an exact three-millimetre gap plumb at its centre beneath his typically prominent Greek nose.

They stand side by side, Hugo's warm hand-grip offering his mother some support. They walk with slow deliberation behind the plain coffin, carried on the shoulders of six trusted business colleagues who are strangers to Hugo, and with as much dignity as they can muster on such an occasion, they troop solemnly between the rows of black-dressed mourners lining the cemetery's pathway. His mother is in black too, her head high, her battered face obscured by a veil that flusters in the warm breeze and their shoes clomp on the gravel. She is gripping tightly in her other hand a small handkerchief and struggling within her core not to give way to her desire to weep, which would betray her dignity.

Hugo is grateful and Bernadette leans over him in the bed to wish him a speedy recovery; he sees that she has aged into an old woman, her face crumpled into lines of worry, her dumpy body listless and sagging. She turns away from him, looking more overcome and grief-stricken than he had ever seen her. A nurse reassures him in whispers that his mother will be back for sure and probably she will bring Sam with her.

Alone through the endless darkness, Hugo merely exists in some floating vacuum. His body functions are taken care of, he has no control or say in the matter. During brief moments of wakefulness, he is aware of nurses combining together to move him, turn him, wipe the warm sweat from his face, his trunk. They change bags, check drips, inject him and record measurements, and then they tell him how well he is doing, with cheery smiles before retreating to their own lives. Other less friendly beings stab needles into his arms, rip wound coverings off for inspection, of his scalp, his chest or abdomen, poking and prodding. The drainage tubes continue to splutter and yank him inside; his bladder seems to empty unnoticed; his bowels have not been opened for yonks.

Bright corridor lights are rushing passed over his head, his trolley is rattling and the woman's voice in the lift is sounding calm, fourth floor. There are masked people milling about around his head, leaning in and out of view, with halloed lights behind them. He can hear muffled voices and smell chloroform and lavatory cleaner. Another operation awaits, but he will sleep through on another drug-induced ride, sheer bliss and disconnection. He feels all right.

They are peering at the row of screens along a tabletop to one side, shaded grey images depicted in line, attracting all the attention. He recalls the surgeon telling him about the need to get inside his chest and clean out the rubbish and leave him with some drainage tubes to help clear the unwanted excess fluid from within. There were bullet fragments lodged inside somewhere; did he say, in the front of the heart muscle? That sounds hair-raising. He said they would go through the space in the front of his neck, in front of his windpipe, down behind his breastbone, which would mean a quicker recovery. The surgeon stood beside his bed a while ago, leaning his legs annoyingly against the frame which juddered, and Sam was there, holding his hand firmly. She repeated that it would be all right, this would be the last operation he needed, they hoped. Hugo strokes the front of his neck, protectively. Someone was whispering in his ear that he should start counting down from ten, nine, eight, seven...and he would be drifting off to sleep before he reached...six.

He hears a thump, against the far wall of his bedroom. There it is again. He is sure that he was asleep, but now a bleary-eyed little boy in blue pyjamas and bare feet, cautiously pulling his door open, looks out onto the shadowy landing and carefully threads his way past the pair of eighteenth-century mahogany wing chairs that are his mother's pride, towards her bedroom, his parents' bedroom, dragging along the floor a fluffy brown teddy bear for company. He knows their room is out of bounds. He is also aware that his father is away on his business affairs. He reaches the double white doors, with their brass handles and hinges, which open inwards onto a massive room of soft carpeting and luxury drapes, golden silks and rouge velvets, with a giant bed in its centre raised on a platform. There are gilt-edged mirrors and paintings around the walls and in the daylight, magnificent views over the wooded park; at night time, the grandeur of the Parthenon under floodlights can be seen in the distance across the roofs of the northern district.

Twenty child's paces further along is the next door that opens onto the adjoining bathroom suite, and the frightened boy with his ruffled black curls notices that it is slightly ajar. He pushes against it and sniffs at the familiar damp and soapy smell inside. He makes out the reflections across glass panels and mirrors, the shower cubicle and massive white bath, the low sinks and toilet. The inner wooden door, which leads back to the master bedroom, is also slightly ajar, and the boy creeps towards it, becoming increasingly aware of the mysterious sounds of human endeavour beyond, of moaning and gasping, and noises like when he jumps up and down on his own bed, producing those giveaway mattress-squeaking sounds. Trembling, he pokes his head ever so slowly around the edge of the inner door and looks across the darkened room towards the bed in the middle, where outside nightlight through undraped windows playfully reveals a naked hunk of a man on his haunches, working hard, he can see, but not certain at what. His bottom is taut and the fat rolls at his waist are swaggering up and down, as he repeatedly pumps his lower body backwards and forwards, slapping hard into the rear of somebody else he cannot identify. They seem to have their face down in the bedclothes and he is afraid that they might be hurt. He can see bare white legs caught in the swaying cross light and realises straight away that what they are doing is naughty. The man is white-skinned but covered in flurries of black hair, over his shoulders and across the middle of his lower back and down into the black slash between his buttocks. He looks old and has a big stomach and is shiny with perspiration and, at first, he thinks it's his father but cannot understand how that can be. The man's head is large and around his neck is a gold chain that flails about erratically with his movements, and he has unkempt black hair that normally, when attending the house as a guest, is swept back tidily off his forehead with gel. The young Hugo, for he remembers firsthand the exact episode, recognises with horror that this brutal beast is Uncle Nikos, although everyone about the house knows he is not actually an uncle but a friend and work colleague of his father. The two of them have done business together for years, although even Hugo is aware of the obvious rivalry between them.

The grand headboard thumps against the far wall, that is to say, the other side of his own bedroom wall. The two figures seem completely oblivious to anything else and after a while, it all seems to reach a peak, with louder wailing, grunting and a soft scream, followed by some breath-holding, the two bodies clamping together motionless for a moment by what forces Hugo cannot imagine, before the man suddenly drops like a felled tree-trunk, grunting noisily, and the woman, for surely the white-skinned figure with long trailing brown hair crouched face-down is a woman, her bottom momentarily exposed, rolls over to one side collapsing onto her back, and stretching her arms up towards the ceiling, lightly panting with the occasional burst of giggling. Hugo's eyes are fixed on her rolling bosoms that bob across her chest and the dark furry mass of hair on the mound between her legs, something which he had ever only seen once before on his mother when she had unexpectedly stepped out of her bath and pulled him into her side for a cuddle when he was ever so small.

He is in a strange room; the ceiling tiles are smaller and arranged in a different order. He is watching them carefully for any movement so that this time he might catch someone out. He is grateful that his mouth is free of any impedance of ventilation tubes, valves and masks; he has his own air supply piped through a nose-piece, one little upturned nozzle into each nostril and an elastic string holding it in place tied around his head. The noisy rhythmic pumps are gone, just the slight hiss of the oxygen. His bed is lower and he has several pillows, starched and fresh-smelling, although they are all flattened and hard. The mattress is hard too, with a dip along its body length, which makes manoeuvring difficult. The sheets are severely tucked in around the end and heavy blankets, laid across at night-time, seem to crush his feet under their weight. He feels trapped, movement causing more pains and severe aches, mostly inside him somewhere that he cannot identify. A few plastic tubes are still emerging from various places and when pulled, usually by accident, he knows about it. There is one particularly mucky-looking one, emerging from under thick layers of bandages across the front of his abdomen, right side, draining horribly discoloured gunk into a sealed bag hanging under the edge of the bed. Alongside that is another bag full of his amber-coloured urine. He feels the tug on that one, yanking at his penis but in a way he is relieved that at least he still has a penis and that he can feel it. He is holding it for comfort in one hand under the covers when a young nurse comes in, bustling around him, sticking an instrument into his ear, clipping something onto his finger and blowing up the pressure cuff around his upper arm. She listens with a stethoscope that was around her neck, reads a few screens and writes the results onto a chart which hangs by a metal hook over the end of his bed. She replaces her biro into her top pocket as she crouches below him to inspect his drainage bags. 'That needs changing,' she murmurs. She leans over him to check the drip and the blood drop-rate into his left arm, and for a fraction of a second, he is aware of the pressure of the front of both her thighs against his forearm. His eyes are closed and he has stopped playing with his John Thomas in case she notices and takes fright.

'Are you awake, Mr Pitsakis? Hugo?' and she rests a limp hand on his shoulder. 'You have a visitor. A policeman. He wants to have a few words with you if you think you can manage it.'

Hugo wearily flickers his eyelids and slowly prises them apart and then has to blink rapidly to clear the sticky fluid over the surfaces of both eyeballs. He turns his head towards the nurse, who has a sweet smile and plucked eyebrows and a sparse collection of the finest blonde hairs over her lower face, just caught in the glancing angle of some light from behind.

'Um?' He tries lifting his head which draws the nurse leaning further towards him while she places a helping hand under his nape. 'Do you want to sit up? I can get more pillows?'

She has no cleavage that he can discern, as he flops his head wearily back, shaking it slightly, but with a little twist of a smile to show that he appreciates her thoughts.

'Okay. I think lying still is best. You've got your pain pump?' and she taps his left arm that is by his side under the covers, 'and the call button is there,' making sure the remote with its electrical cord is placed on the covers also by his side. 'I'll get you some tea in a few minutes, so we'll allow the police gentleman ten minutes, shall we?' She has a quick smile and Hugo hopes she is making some young man somewhere very happy. He watches her leave the room, uniform dress at knee level, and then turns his head the other way, towards the windows, which are loosely covered by thin blinds to reduce the day's glare but giving sufficient light to enable the ghastly overhead neon strips to be switched off during the day.

A stocky man of medium height in a crumpled brown Parka slips into the room and steps towards Hugo's side, drawing a chair up with him. Turning his head back towards the door, Hugo has time to notice the short greying hair combed forward over a thinning pate, the clean-shaven face with extra concern etched across it.

'Detective Inspector Michael Sanger, sir,' reaching out with an open hand that Hugo has some difficulty grasping from under the bedclothes. Is he familiar with that name? He is feeling a touch dizzy and the man's features are not altogether in focus.

'I wanted the opportunity to apologise for the state of things. You being in here and all. It was a complete mistake. We had no intention of shooting,' and the inspector seems to have something distasteful in his mouth that he wants to spit out, 'of hurting you, we were chasing a dangerous criminal, someone quite different. We were mistaken.'

Hugo hears the inspector talking, a stuttering voice with a touch of Midlands, if he is not mistaken, but he does not understand fully what he is saying. Hugo is inclined to close his heavy lids again and drift off into a floating world of pain relief and clouded half-wakefulness.

Sanger stumbles on. 'I wanted to ask you, if I may: what do you know about the girlfriend, Veronica Secola? How did you meet her, sir, if I may be so bold?' He is leaning forwards on both his elbows from his sitting position to hear better Hugo's quiet mumblings.

Hugo notices the fraying edges of his shirt cuffs. 'Nika, Nika, and Lilly; don't forget Lilly. She is hurt, I heard her screaming.'

'Yes, unfortunately she was hit in the shoulder, but she is mending, she will be better and will be home soon,' Sanger reassures him. 'How did you meet these two girls, sir?'

Hugo takes in a slow breath. 'I am painting them, they model for me, beautiful, are they all right? Are they here, I have not seen them? I am a painter, I think I am a painter. The paintings, the drawings were in the car, they were with, I was carrying them, I must have them.'

'Yes, we have made all property available to a lady called Samantha Little. Said she was your closest, er, friend, I think she said.' Sanger looks uncomfortable. 'We're not married, are we, sir, is that correct?'

Hugo shakes his head with a slow conspiratorial smile opening up his face and he winks, 'Oh no, no, God no.'

'And you have never met Mr Midge Martin, have you, sir?'

But Hugo is swimming in a sense of euphoria, with a picture of a white-skinned bare bodied Lilly tripping before him, squealing at all the sharp bits on the pathway she runs over in her bare feet, reaching down to wipe her soles, before running away again, laughing seductively. 'There is no Martin here,' he murmurs and tries to curl up in comfort, feeling the warmth of his own belly under the covers.

Mike Sanger looks relieved and stands to leave, feeling he has done the necessary: he has apologised and asked a few questions, what more can he do? He has to face the press again first thing, but the interest in the police's role is waning the longer there is no sign of Mr Martin; the many and various stories surrounding the two models have managed to take some of the pressure off him, at least for the time being.

2

Week Beginning Saturday, January 24, 2015

Periodically, he slips away on his own, into a land of floating dreams and misty images, scenes from his life bubbling up in muddled sequences. His body is detached, not part of him. Sometimes he is free-falling and has to pull up with his arms, grabbing onto anything solid that will help keep him level. More than once he has slipped helplessly through cracks in the ground that open up, pulled through by inexplicable forces, hands or tree roots about his ankles. His cries are unheard and unanswered.

He is returning to his new room; the walls are a pale cream but the windows are bigger and there is another door to a toilet in the corner. The trouble this time is further chest pain, with the drainage tube towards his back, uncomfortable to lie against. There is a wide-bore plastic tube emerging from between his lower ribs and a bloodstained murky fluid is filling the see-through drain with black bits floating along for the ride.

The ceiling tiles are neater here and they seem to be fixed; he has not yet noticed any gaps appearing, but he must be vigilant. He sleeps through the daylight hours and wakes so dry he cannot open his mouth. He cannot sleep at night, his mind is racing through his projects, worrying about the rioting in the streets, feeling desperate to be there to observe and to help. He is wondering where his team are with the Remembrance pictures. He is scheming and planning his next moves and wants to talk with Jeremy as soon as possible.

'It's probably the steroids,' the registrar explains at the early morning ward round when Hugo complains he is so awake and agitated through the night. 'We need to continue them for a while, I think, helps reduce fluid pressure in the head and elsewhere.' She is from Korea, apparently, one of the nurses had told him, very bright lady.

'And the noises in the ward all night long, it sounds like a lunatic asylum in here,' Hugo continues, 'with interruptions every ten minutes, so just when I might be nodding off, in comes night sister with her blood pressure and heart rate and temperature measurements. Are they really necessary at two o'clock in the morning?'

'We're running the IV antibiotics to prevent an infection but we still must be rigorous. The op went well yesterday, Mr Pitsakis.' She sits gingerly at the foot of his bed. 'We removed two pieces of metal: one was a complete bullet tip, from the muscle over the sixth thoracic vertebra and the other was a fragmented piece lodged in the muscle of the left ventricle. It had ruptured the outer covering, the visceral lining, and was deep into the substance of the muscle, but had not penetrated the endocardia, into the cavity. That was lucky.

Equally the vertebral bullet had penetrated into the bone but had not pierced through to the space around the spinal cord, so again, very lucky.'

'And you got them out. So, no more metal around?'

'Yes, all gone, we think. We will need another CT scan later today or tomorrow but should be fine. The chest drain needs another 24 hours and the biliary drain through your liver needs another five or seven days in place. But good progress.' She rubs her hands together, giving him the briefest of smiles and departs with her small retinue of sycophants. The last to go is his flat-chested nurse and she says with a tiny wink she'll be back in a bit when she has a moment for his belly injection and is sure she'll be able to find him a chocolate biscuit with his tea if he behaves himself.

The childhood dreams return. The bemused seven-year-old boy hiding behind the bathroom door; seeing the expression of joy on his mother's face; feeling the tears beginning to course over his young cheeks. He pulls his teddy up to his chest but then discards it with petulance onto the tiled floor, thinking only a baby needs a teddy bear at this point. His mother has reached across for her beastly assailant lying next to her, to hug and kiss him with obvious affection. A shock of misunderstanding sweeps through the loyal little boy and he wants to shout out: stop. And when his tears turn to anger, he pushes at the door and runs into the centre of the room. 'Leave her alone,' he shouts, 'she's *my* mother.'

Hugo is lying awake in the gloomy night-time of his room and can see the exact look of amazement on his mother's face and of niggardly annoyance on Nikos's. Bernadette springs up into a sitting position, pulling the sheets over her front, and grabs the small boy as he runs into her arms. Nikos stark naked has rolled off the bed the other side and remains lying on the carpeted floor out of sight until Hugo has been lead away by his mother back to his own room.

Hugo is wondering whether his mother ever recalls that night of infidelity, of being found out by her young son; and how many other nights and other men there might have been. Tucking him back up in his bed very firmly after that, she had made him promise not to tell anyone about what he had seen, she and Nikos were just having a bit of fun, she explained, no one was hurt. She kissed him firmly on his cheek, while he wished he had picked up teddy on the way. To this day he can recall the slightly moist feeling of his mother's lips on his face, which he had wiped off crossly with his fingers, inexplicitly not wanting to be touched by her.

Hugo loves his father, admires him as the greatest businessman in all of Greece. He would do anything to win his approval. He tells his friends at school that he is a very important powerful man. His friends beat him up for being the son of such a powerful man who does not come down to the school and help fight for his son.

Barnabas is short and stocky with massive fists and a broad face like a boxer, his nose somewhat flat, with protuberant eyebrow ridges and a wide intelligent mouth. He has large ears with grey tufts emerging from them and the young Hugo always believed he used them to fly off to work each day. His nostril hairs often need a trim. He is clean-shaven mostly, except at weekends, when he works in his shirt sleeves in his study with Greek folk music playing on the radio and his chin, with bristling overnight shadows, is left unattended. Until the Saturday evening, when he and his mother dress in their best outfits for a party or a function in town. It is then that Hugo feels most proud, when his father is washed and shaved to perfection in a slick bow tie and shiny dinner jacket that obscures his paunch and he really looks the part; his elegant mother is equally shimmering in something tight and covered in sequins with golden shoes. A black limousine whisks them away to some smart place and only returns them when it is very late, well after he has gone to bed, although not necessarily after he has fallen asleep.

One weekend in the summer holidays, long after the naughty bedroom episode with his mother and Uncle Nikos that he desperately tries to obliterate from his mind, his father has him trapped downstairs in the boot room, where stacks of all the family shoes and trainers and boots are kept in rows by the back door, while they are preparing to go out for an early morning forage at the Monastiraki market together. His mother is still upstairs with toddler, Loukas, and Barnabas is already heavily perspiring in the day's heat. Hugo is aware of his strong body smell, as he is drawn closer into his father's arms. He begins to whisper into Hugo's ear while holding him affectionately around the waist. Hugo is eager to go play outside in the sunshine, in his tee shirt and shorts and red leather sandals, but his father wants to share a secret with him.

'You listen carefully now, my boy. Won't you? When I am away from the house, always on important business, when I am not here, you are in charge, okay? You are the man of the house. The servants do as you say. You look after your mother, with your life, you hear? You make sure she has your best behaviour and that she can rely on you. It is a responsibility, but I think now that you are nearly eight, you are ready for this. Yes? But there is one thing I want you to do for me. When I am away and you are in charge, I want you to keep an eye on your mother and let me know when I return what she has been doing and who comes to the house, or who she goes to visit. You hear me. You understand?' He wipes the moisture from his upper lip, his big fingers rasping across the unshaven skin and suddenly smiles a big smile. 'I know you can do it.'

And so of course, feeling so proud of his father's faith in him, feeling so puffed up in his chest with the importance of his new role in the house, although he was not yet eight, Hugo gushes forth with the very story that he has bottled up inside for so long but that he has promised his mother faithfully not to divulge to a living soul, especially not his father. He tells Barnabas exactly what he saw that night, what Uncle Nikos was doing to his mother. Barnabas is red and incensed, and perspires even more, pumping Hugo with lots of questions, most of which he cannot answer. Hugo starts to cry, with shame and sorrow, scared that his father will punish him for telling such stories. He wants

162

his mother to be free and not hurt by his uncle. He does not know what to say but desperately wants his father to put it right, put a stop to it. He wants his father's approval.

For weeks afterwards, Hugo tries to keep out of the way, tries to avoid talking to his mother or father if he can, in case the subject is brought up and he has to answer more questions. He observes the mood of the house and can sense his father's simmering anger and his displeasure with his mother. He worries that he has put his mother in trouble and that perhaps his father's anger will erupt in violence against her, when she will hate him for evermore for his disloyalty to her.

But of course, Barnabas's anger is not directed at his beautiful wife, but at Uncle Nikos, her lover and his ex-business partner and it is Nikos's bloated water-logged body that is recovered from one of the far reaches of the reservoir at Lake Marathon, his ankles and wrists tied with plastic flex and a heavy weight attached, his mouth gagged. Barnabas expressly takes Hugo out in his car, driving himself east out of Athens up to the mountains to the scene, where the local police have made their discovery. He drags the reluctant boy by his hand over towards the water's edge, where a plastic sheet covers a body-shaped mound on nearby ground. Here a police officer, who greets Barnabas with familiarity, peels the sheet back for Mr Pitsakis to identify the blue-grey swollen face of his past associate.

'Found under the footbridge, over there. The water is deep at the edge there but it's clear and a works engineer had seen the submerged body. Been there a week or so, I would say.'

Hugo wants to be sick. The face is hardly recognisable at all, bruised and swollen out of shape, but the deep black hair is familiar as is the gold chain around the neck.

His father bends low to speak into Hugo's ear. 'Let this be a lesson to you, my boy. Stay true, stay faithful, to your friends and your family. Deal?'

And Hugo nods automatically, too utterly scared of his father to dare ask how Uncle Nikos had found his way to the bottom of the reservoir under the bridge and who may have put him there.

***

Outside his window, the rain is thrashing against the glass and the views across to the roofs of other buildings and rows of housing are bleak and misty, with low cloud. It is London in January and he is indoors in the warmth, best place to be. He remains supine in his bed, hard and back-numbing. He has no mirror to check himself but feels his facial swelling has subsided and some of the crusty scabs over his nose and upper lip have dried and dropped off.

He is slowly recovering and now has been sat out of bed in an uncomfortable armchair, facing the window and the afternoon weather. The room is bleak, grey lino floor, pale walls, a dreadful reproduction water-colour of a country scene on one wall. Many crazy ideas and images have been spinning through his mind, he wants to capture them; like a street juggler of softballs, hand to hand in rhythm, he has to keep them in the air for fear of dropping one. He needs absolute concentration. He wants to sketch and play with colours. Although just as quickly his energy wanes and he much prefers to nod off to sleep, his head lolling against a wing of the chair. Leave them alone for now, they can wait; let them blossom inside undisturbed and then later, if they are any good, they will be expressed, instinctively and freely without corruption.

His bottom has become numb, dozing on and off in the same chair all afternoon, his drips of saline and antibiotics still running. The blood transfusions have finished, thankfully; they gave him hot feelings and temperatures. Earlier he was helped by two physiotherapists on either side to stand and walk three paces before he felt exhausted. He had had some lunch, he remembers, a bowl of thin vegetable soup and a slice of white bread.

He looks down at himself, his loose hospital leggings, white top with a depressing green check that matches the colour of the corridor outside. He notices the recent bruising under the skin across the front of his lower abdomen where the nurses plunge their anticoagulant injection every day. He is wondering what his face must look like and wants to get over to the mirror on the wall above his basin a few paces away. He casually picks off another bit of dried scab from his nose. He has lost much weight, he knows that. Yesterday he saw his thin legs when he was bed-bathed; there was no muscle on his thighs, no wonder his legs feel as weak as jelly.

He is grateful to the nurses who comb his hair and tidy his face with a disposable razor most mornings. He tentatively feels the left side of his head, which was closely shaved around the scalp wound, and the hair is beginning to regrow. He just wants to look to see if he recognises himself and what sort of shock his friends will get when they see him. Sam will help him; she may have one of those small palm mirrors that women carry in their handbags.

Sleepy in the gloomy room, the outside light fading, he dozes on his bed, coiled up with his hands clasping the corner of his pillow to his mouth. The ugly face and damaged body of Nikos Sergianopoulos keeps returning, even though that was all of twenty-six years ago. He has doubted not for a moment that it was his own father who had been responsible. He can feel his silent tears drying on his cheeks and his father's tight grip of his hand in the heat of that Greek afternoon.

He dreams of his father's illness and his ultimate passing. His half-naked frame seems a relic of his old self, lying and waiting on his deathbed. Hugo has difficulty recognising him, on a flat mattress, with a saline drip inserted into his arm and numerous monitor leads attached across his chest among the thick pile of curly hairs now turned white. His once sturdy body with sagging breasts has lost much of its bulk and he looks pale and close to death already. His suffering is etched across his face, in his sunken cheeks and dull eyes, he can read his fear. The room is stuffy on a humid day, on the top floor of a University

Hospital, where the doctors and nurses are doing their best. Hugo sympathises with their struggle, with few staff and proper facilities, the lack of easy funding obvious in the neglected and dilapidated state of some of the building. His father, normally so garrulous and full of life, always colour in his cheeks as he relentlessly chewed gum, with his commanding way of speaking, not a man to argue with; and today, he looks like a ghost. But he wants to speak, secretly for Hugo's ears only and Hugo sticky with sweat leans over him to bring him closer to the old man's dry lips, to listen. Is it a confession? He is murmuring about all sorts, mistakes from his earlier life, his behaviour as a father and as a husband. Hugo cannot decipher it all.

'The business, your mother would never manage. I want you, dear boy, you are fine handsome citizen, from the top city in the world. You must take control. Look after them, the business, nurture them. You have responsibilities. You make lots of money, so it will be all right. Deal? Don't let your brother into the Corporation. Your brother is not your real brother, you understand me, he should not have a Corporation job. Share the other businesses with Hebe, I give him something. Don't forget your responsibilities. Bury me here, Hugo, in Athens, the grand city. Deal?

Hugo is not sure what all the rambling means, but he knows the main business that bears the family name, Pitsakis Corporation, is all about shipping and freight, with its dockside container and storage business, road haulage and oil transport and tankers. None of which he knows anything about. He is surprised that his father wants him alone to take it over and confused with what he says about Loukas not being his real brother.

All that was such a long time ago. Leave it alone, let sleep wash it away. And yet, it seems it was only yesterday, he has the odour of the laying-out room in his nostrils, with the open coffin and the decrepitude of the body disguised with a lavender air-freshener. Arriving in the midst of his family's grief, a potential scandal with official accusations of fraud and corruption, finding out what kind of man his father really was, his bullying, his womanising, seeing him collapse from his second heart attack and not recover, the family in disarray, his mother near hysterical; it was all quite shocking. The great Barnabas Pitsakis was not the idol he had unreservedly worshipped, his hero who did no wrong, the model of fortitude and courage, but someone buffeted by the corruptive forces of the day, willing to risk his business reputation for gratuitous rewards of the flesh. The shock of it all, still lingers, nine years later. As it happened, the case against him never materialised, his name was preserved for posterity, the businesses survived, probably because the Greek authorities had more pressing concerns to attend to, and the family came through, even if there remained just a faint whiff of something rancid. After all this time, faded memories have left him with a sense of disappointment: that his image of his father is tarnished a little, his love for him weakened a little, his regard for him a little bitter.

It had all happened so soon after that other wretched incident in London, with that annoying little ponce of a man, Lebelov. God, how did he ever get so involved with him? He started off loving that man, his artistry and beauty as a dancer, even his charm, exaggerated by his foreigner's way with the language. Hugo had created a couple of terrific works, big paintings with passion and movement, showing off Dominic at his prime, in mid-flight, his face handsome in concentration, his graceful body beautiful in shape and strength. Eventually, he did complete the commission, about a year late, showing the entire troupe in rehearsals with Dominic in the foreground, which hangs in the Bolshoi Concert Hall in Moscow above the grand entrance on the first landing; and paid handsomely he was too. The second picture of Dominic the artist also sold and Jake was especially pleased, as he had won the commissions in the first place. It was Jake who introduced Dominic to him and they liked each other straight away. There were another two or three paintings, he forgets, still unfinished and somewhere among a whole stack of half-finished works, mistakes, rejects that are in his studio at home. One of them features Dominic dancing with Olivia, Olivia Truelove. He has always promised himself to return to them one day, but over the years he has not felt inclined to risk rekindling all those memories.

That charming Ukrainian who slyly wormed his way into Hugo's life had begun to irritate him, had started to cause distrust in the people around him, with his precocious and demanding behaviour. It brought its own tragedy eventually, not unexpected perhaps, to a man who lived on his artistic wits and high emotions and valued their unimpeded expression beyond anything else. He turned out to be a randy little sod, like so many of them. A man of outward high ideals, broken in the end by his own uncontrolled lust for selfish adulation and dominance.

Hey, this is Dominic we are thinking about, is it? Hugo, half dreaming, stretching his aching limbs on his stiff hospital bed, chuckles easily at his own self-deprecating tone, realising he is getting back to his normal self.

***

Hugo has poured a generous glass of red wine for everybody and they were all arraigned around Bernadette's large wooden dining table at the comfortable family townhouse in Marousi, their home for twenty years or more. The kitchen next door with its flagstone floor was cooler, protected from the direct relentless sun by the outside trellis draped with mature vines and already beginning to show this year's new growth. The dining room had the bigger table and the solemnity appropriate for the occasion and Bernadette was sitting heavily and bereft at one end, being comforted in her grief by Hebe. The French doors to the outside garden were open for a little breeze and long nets rustled on either side. A bedraggled and elderly German retriever was slouched on guard at the entrance, keeping a beady eye on both the outside and on the gathering within.

Hugo has been briefed by the lawyers before the funeral service and was well versed with what was to come; he sat in silence at the other end of the

166

table, while the rest of the family gathered forlornly with their drinks. Bernadette was wailing softly, asking all the time what she was going to do without him, how would she manage?

At sixteen, Hebe, still at school then and living at home, had a small olive-skinned face, a sweet girl, unassuming and gentle, her eyes red-rimmed from her crying. She was crouching by her mother with her arm around those broad shoulders, quietly trying to stop her thinking bad thoughts, reassuring her that she would always be there to help her get over her loss.

'I will never get over it, Barnabas was my life, my whole life.'

Along one side of the table was Loukas, six years younger than Hugo, short and dark, with emphatic black slashes for eyebrows and a face that even then needed shaving twice a day. Loukas was just twenty-one and had been learning hotel management under Barnabas's team, and had often proclaimed how easy and straightforward it all was and how one day, if he took over the business, he would expand into the luxury end of the resorts along Greece's southern coastline. He had pretensions of success and, despite the sadness of the day, seemed eager to talk about how his late father's company should be divided up between them.

On the other side of the table were two men with suitably sombre and sympathetic expressions on their faces, hot in their black suits and tight white collars. The family lawyer was Andreas Giannopoulos, who had been retained by the Pitsakis family for over twenty years and knew the businesses backwards, having been the shared architect and legal adviser with Barnabas for most of them; next to him was Dimitrios Kokinos, one of Barnabas's most trusted and leading business partners.

Bernadette's younger sister was there as well with her two sons, and several cousins and nephews, almost complete strangers as far as Hugo was concerned, all crowded around the sides ready to listen with interest in the details of a family dynasty in difficulties. Hugo sat fiddling with his glass, watching and reflecting on how family tragedy appeared to bring everyone together, while loyalties can be tested. He was already missing the presence of the big man: his father would dominate such occasions with his brazen opinions and loud laugh, making sure the wine was flowing, always generous. There would be back-slapping and hugging and the sharing of cigars and a late glass of spirits for his special friends, drunk outside in the shadowy darkness of a humid summer evening. He would often sit out there alone in the dying heat of the day, reflecting on another deal, another clever piece of business, another win over an adversary, further swelling of the family coffers.

'Mrs Pitsakis, Madame, are you sure you want to go through these papers now? And the figures?' Mr Giannopoulos, known usually to everyone present as Andy, was asking considerately. 'Or shall we do this tomorrow or the next day – give yourself a little bit more time?'

Loukas almost jumped in too soon. 'Oh, come...' but then stopped.

'I'm fine, Andreas, thank you.' The whining and sniffing stopped as Hebe settled in the spare chair next to Loukas.

'Well, if everyone is happy for me to go ahead.' He looked around the small group of faces, all of whom were looking back at him, nodding a little with their attention. He reached into his floppy leather briefcase to draw out a thin green folder, with a red ribbon threaded and knotted along its spine. 'I have the will and last testament of the late Barnabas Berenike Pitsakis, in front of me here, signed and dated the fifteenth of April 2006,' and he laid it on the table in front of him. He opened it, fanning his thin fingers out over the pages to hold them flat. He was a wiry parsimonious-looking man, his gold-rimmed spectacles and rapidly receding hairline giving him an intellectual air. Neat and clean-shaven, he spoke slowly and clearly. 'Barnabas had become aware of his weakened heart and fearing that something dramatic might happen to his health, last year, he worked with me on updating his will and this is the result, redrafted and signed, and here we are, sadly gathered six days since his sudden and tragic death, this day the twelfth of May 2006.'

He adjusted his glasses and focused on the page in front of him. Next to him, Dimitrios, having taken a generous swill of his wine, leant back in his chair and studied the ceiling, while stroking his silky greying goatee beard with a generous hand. Hugo presumed he knew the contents of the will as well, but his real interests would be in the company businesses, in which he held a considerable personal stake, worth a great deal of money. 'Now I don't want to bore you with the usual preamble and other certain particulars and legalese that pertain to this sort of document and fills the opening page and a half, but I will move into the meat of the issues, if that suits everyone.'

There was a general shifting of positions as they all adjusted themselves for more comfort. Loukas, whose anxiety was in danger of getting the better of him, was a particular fidget and had also taken a large swill of his wine. Hebe sat back properly in her chair, looking at her mother who seemed to have resigned herself to the present situation, with a scrunched handkerchief pressed across her nose. They all turned their attention on Andreas and his green file.

'So, firstly, there is an important statement, a tribute to his family for their loyalty and support, and especially to his long-serving and trusted partner in life, his wife, Bernadette. To whom he entrusts all the residual artefacts and effects of his life, including his good name and reputation. To whom, he asks his family to pay their due and special respects for the rest of her life.' Everyone smiled deliberately and agreeably while giving gentle nods in the direction of first Bernadette and then in answer to the lawyer.

'Secondly, he asks that all his worldly goods listed as assets be transferred to the aforementioned Bernadette Pitsakis, to cherish and utilise as she sees fit to ensure her comfort for the rest of her life. This includes all wholly owned properties, bank accounts and investments (listed separately) and all personal chattels.' Hugo feared at this point that Andreas would be inclined to read out the extensive lists of all the assets and chattels of his father and indeed he began to do just that. There was the house in Athens, the cottage on the Argolic Gulf at Porto Cheli, the apartments in Chelsea and Paris; the bank accounts, the investments and savings, even a pension fund; there were the cars, the furniture and jewellery, some antiques, the knick-knacks, the books and clothes, the list was exhaustive, and he spent over fifteen minutes detailing them. Then came the special exceptions, separate sums of money that he awarded to his children and two nephews, who would be informed in good time. These were tokens, gestures in their euro thousands, but nothing compared with what was to come. And as Hugo had been informed, the Corporation (the shipping, storage, dockyard servicing, freight and transport) was to remain intact, with the Pitsakis family continuing with their major share, which was around 80% to be transferred in its entirety to Mr Hugo Pitsakis, his first-born son, and the rest remaining with the business associates, represented in their absence by the trusted and professional, Dimitrios Kokinos.

'The businesses comprising several hotels and retail outlets are to be split equally and transferred to his other children, Loukas and Hebe on reaching the ages of 25 and 21 respectively, and that in the intervening years, they are to be run by appointed managers who will undertake to train and support Loukas and Hebe in their preparation for their future roles.'

Loukas dropped both his hands onto the table and forced himself into a half standing position. 'What...? I only get half? And Hebe gets half, but she's still at school.'

'Loukas, Loukas,' Hugo butted in, 'please sit and listen. Wait until Andreas has completed the reading of our father's will and then we can have a discussion for clarity and understanding.'

'Thank you, Hugo. Loukas, we will discuss details in a moment.' Andreas groaned on about the various divisions and the list of properties and hotels and shops and it all sounded like such an empire. Hugo had had no real idea how wide or extensive his father's business interests were and the whole scenario was becoming a bit scary. No mention was made of any corrupt deals or accusations or official investigations into any of Barnabas's business dealings, and Hugo did not expect any.

Hugo knew he could not run a freight business or an oil transport network. Why would his father do that? Hugo was an artist, pursuing a professional life in London, he had no interest in business, especially in Greece. But then what alternative did his father have, if he wanted to keep his legacy within the family? And this way, he brought Hugo into the business, away from the distant and abstract world of art, something he knew his father had always disapproved of. Hugo would need all the existing managers to be in place and work with him, instructing him, just as Loukas and Hebe would need that support.

Andreas Giannopoulos went on to explain the debt and tax situations and the inheritance tax laws. It was also clear to Hugo that when Bernadette succumbed, which, Heaven forbid, no one envisaged for at least another twenty years or more, there would be a lot more to inherit, not least of which was the Athens townhouse, when the division of the spoils could turn out to be even more tricky than the current will, especially if Loukas was going to act all stroppy.

There followed a general rumbling conversation among everyone, but Bernadette, who had by now controlled her tears and had taken on a more serious expression, looked around the company with a severe expression and demanded hush and respect for her late husband's will.

The brothers confronted each other the next day, once again in the family dining room with the remains of a prolonged breakfast still scattered around the table and Hugo finishing his coffee with an English newspaper across his folded legs. There was no one else around. They talked amicably enough, as Loukas seemed to have calmed down from the previous day. Hugo asked him what the real trouble was: the value of the businesses he would have at the age of twenty-five would be wonderful, and by then he will have had the expertise and training of some of their father's best officers and associates, that would improve his efficiency and ensure his success. 'You can expand as much as you wish after that and make your fortune.'

'Meanwhile you walk away with millions of dollars' worth of international business. The Corporation name and value is ten times, twenty times the value of the hotels, or more. Is that fair? And I have to halve what I get with Hebe! That is ridiculous.'

And so on. Loukas and Hugo had never been the best of friends, there was too big an age gap between them to be close. And Hugo had spent most of the latter twelve years or so in England at college and then working in London, whereas Loukas and Hebe had stayed in Athens with their parents. Hebe looked up to Hugo almost as an uncle or father-figure, eleven years between them. She thought he was wonderful, loved his paintings whenever she saw any and always followed his work and career as best she could, as best as he would allow, from such a distance away. She believed in him and everything Hugo said she listened to and followed with a devoted diligence that always surprised him.

Loukas on the other hand had always felt that his older brother got the best deals and the favourite's attention, whereas he always got the raw end of the deal. He had little interest in Hugo's painting career. And Hugo perceived that that view would probably fester for always.

He almost stopped listening after a while to Loukas' stream of objections, mumbling that he was sure they could work it all out. He was musing to himself about what he could possibly do with the Pitsakis Corporation and all that money, not sure what quantum of money he was really contemplating, but aware that he was about to inherit not just unimaginable wealth but the power that would come with it. He would be able to do whatever he wanted, whenever he wanted. And that realisation was shocking, numbing, almost frightening.

He was telling himself that he would not be overwhelmed by it, that he would take great care over his decisions and would always take advice from the experts. He would love to open a gallery in Athens, to attract and support local artists, and maybe discover some special talent that he could nurture; he would be fascinated to see what local interest there might be. He could start a new academic art school in London, establishing a new focus on realism and returning to basic artistic skills of illustration and draughtsmanship. His dreams started flooding through him, but he knew he had some hard graft ahead over the future of his father's legacy, which at that moment was the most responsible task he had ever been set.

Undoubtedly his father's last desire was for him, Hugo to lead the family Corporation, his precious business empire for the continuing benefit of his widow and family and for his country; and from his grave, he would be demanding hard work and commitment, to stay loyal to the company and its people, to stay loyal to Greece.

3

Week Beginning Friday, February 6, 2015

In the dead of the night, when the ward is quiet and only a few nurses remain on duty, one semi-slumbering at the middle station, one in a bay with an elderly lady unable to sleep, another in the sluice tidying up someone else's mess; when the few lights are all turned down and the long corridors are draped in shadow; when there is barely a security officer to be found, there is Samantha encouraging Hugo to shuffle the short distance from his room to the emergency exit and a back flight of stairs. They stutter down the dimly lit echoing stairwell, enclosed by ugly breeze blocks, stopping at each level for a few moments for Hugo to regain his breath, to a side door that opens into an unlit passageway between buildings, where Charlie has backed up his Vauxhall estate. How she has organised this little escapade Hugo dares not ask, but Charlie is an old friend of hers and has enacted some sort of distraction at the main door of the ward as the two creep out the back. Hugo is in pyjamas with a belted coat over the top and a small workman's cap and rubber-soled shoes.

The trouble Sam had trying to get his socks on at the edge of his bed, tickling him and both prone to nervous giggling, will be one of her lasting memories. Sam had tried to sound stern. 'This is all down to you, Hugo, you wanted to leave, so stop laughing.'

At the bottom of the stairs, he is sweating with the effort but shivering with cold. Sam pushes hard on the barred fire-exit door and there is Charlie like a magician waiting for them. Hugo has been constipated for weeks and his lower abdomen feels bloated. His chest is hurting, despite the extra painkillers Sam has fixed for him. They bundle him into the back seat, where he lies flat out of sight, and Charlie drives slowly out of the gate onto the Fulham Palace Road, with Sam in the front like any innocent couple. They head for North London and Sam's place, where Hugo is transferred into her smaller car and Charlie wishes them both well before driving off.

Sam has suitcases in the boot and provisions in a plastic bag inside. She drives carefully through the empty streets along the North Circular, heading west for the M4 and South Wales. Hugo sleeps fitfully in the back during most of the trip, and by the time first light is spreading through the murky skies behind them, they are well on their way up into the hills of Monmouthshire, taking the smaller roads and bends with care.

Sam is relaxed and takes Hugo into her cottage on the village outskirts for the first time. He has to bow his head at the front door to avoid cracking it on the low lintel, and take care in the lounge with low ceiling joists. She settles him in a high-backed armchair that had once been her father's, where he slouches into a further sleep. There is a massive old fireplace dominating one side, where she plans to light a wood burning fire, and they can snuggle up together later enjoying the cosy warmth and safety.

If he were not so tired, he would be fascinated by her anecdotes and childhood memories of life here with her parents. He knew of her hideaway, although he had never visited, but she raised the possibility last week in answer to his paranoid feelings about being in the hospital.

'I don't want to walk out of the front door to be seen by anyone watching. I don't feel it's safe. And the apartment, I would rather lie low a bit longer, somewhere else. Just see how the land lies first.'

'You are worrying unnecessarily, Hugo, I am sure. This was a police mistake, they've admitted as such, and there is nobody else interested in harming you at all.'

'So how did I get all these bruises around my face, the bloody scabs over my nose? Answer me that. They fucking punched me, whipped me, that was no mistake. That was an ambush.' Sam had heard Hugo mouthing off his worry several times and admitted she was unable to answer his questions. As the time to his discharge from the ward drew closer, Hugo worried about it more, so often that she had begun to believe that his paranoia might be justified.

Sam had brought all the newspapers she had collected since the shooting, those with any account of the event, in the boot of the car, and later she hauls them out to place them on a side table in the lounge for Hugo to read at his leisure. She is sure that he will want to update himself on the manner of the reporting, even if most of them were inaccurate.

Sam also has Hugo's cardboard tube, containing the rolled-up drawings and sketches from his work at the house in Adelaide Grove. She had not apparently even taken the lid off to peek at them.

'My God, you're brilliant, Sam. How did you get these?'

'The police had everything in the Hammersmith Station and I visited Inspector Sanger there to pick them up. I've got your bag at home. He kept the coat and the hat you were wearing, said they were important items of evidence; they were Martin's apparently.' And Sam has a quizzical look on her face.

'Yes, I had to borrow them, they were all we could find, against the rain. Full of holes now, I should think.'

Despite Hugo's obvious relief at having his work back, he seems reluctant to want to open the canister and extract the drawings. Instead, he changes the subject. 'I have a follow-up appointment with the trauma team in a week and the chest surgeons the following week.'

'I will get you there if you want to go. Or leave it a further week and re-appoint. I can ring them up. Whatever?'

Hugo manages a smile for the first time since the shooting. He reaches for Sam's shoulders, bringing her closer and kisses her mouth briefly. 'Thanks, Sam, you've been marvellous. Appreciate it.' She hugs him, just so pleased to have escaped London with him safely and without apparently alerting anybody.

One morning, when Sam is out at the local shops, Hugo, still in his pyjamas, gently brings the roll of drawing papers out of the canister and spreads them over the floor, using spare books from a shelf to hold down the curling corners. He studies them, perusing pictures of the two girls at the flat, liking their beauty, especially Lilly, who appears near-nude in several. One of his best is a portrait that he has started, of Lilly squatting cross-legged in a deep stone window alcove of an old building, with glancing sunlight coming through the leaded glass and playing on her tangled blonde hair that she has flipped forward over her face, where it hangs partly covering her chest, with an eye peeping through at the painter. Intriguing innocence captured with subtlety, he thinks. He wishes he had his brushes and paints with him, so he could finish it.

He returns the pictures carefully to their cardboard roll for safety before Sam returns.

Hugo spends his time resting, sleeping often during the day, taking a few gentle walks around the village or over the fields at the back of the cottage. Sam feeds him well on pastas, fish, fresh vegetables, soups and plenty of fruit. His recovery is slow but genuine. He still needs his pain tablets regularly, his codeine and sometimes he sips liquid morphine. He has stopped the steroids, which is a relief, as they were responsible for such ridiculous highs, his mind racing into action all the time, especially in the middle of the night, driving him to want to start a new canvas after midnight. He inspects his wounds, the bullet holes and the surgical scars when he showers, sometimes with Sam.

One afternoon they drive over to a massive reservoir where they quietly watch small boats setting out from the Sailing Club jetty and a few keen water-skiers in wetsuits trying their hands, but it is so cold, Hugo could not imagine them enjoying it much. Dozens of fishermen were lined up along the shore, despite the temperature and wet weather, sitting at neat, silent intervals, some under umbrellas and waterproof capes. 'The fishing here is reputed to be good, excellent pike,' murmurs Sam from the warmth of the car. 'Dad was keen: he had a little boat here and would row out on his own and sit there in the middle for hours; he would catch a bit, throw most of it back, and then bring a respectable catch home for supper. We never went with him.'

Hugo has been drawing with some pencils he has found, signs of his rehabilitation. He misses his charcoal, but there are sketches lying on the floor and on the kitchen table, landscapes and cottages, the neighbour's golden retriever, Sam with a bunch of flowers. Sitting at the dining table, freshly washed, in a clean white tee shirt and jeans, three days of growth on his chin, he seems more cheerful and positive than Sam has witnessed since getting him out of hospital. Earlier, he had been playing with the next door's genial dog and had walked with him to the top of the garden along the far hedge and down to the village road.

'I love being here, Sam, in the country, everything so peaceful and quiet. With you.' He has his arm around her waist, and they are surveying the outside weather from the comfort of the front room, with its roaring fire. 'I had forgotten how I loved dogs. We had a terrier when I was young, and my mother had an old retriever of some sort, which survived for years. I've missed having a pet around; they can be so comforting.' Sam is happy, pleased with Hugo's progress. He had watched her chop some wood logs earlier and carried them in for her.

They make love in the late afternoon in the upstairs bedroom with the low beams and dusty smell and fall asleep afterwards draped over each other. She had been gentle and indulgent, allowing him to find his rhythm. He had been shy and slow, easily tiring. She had coaxed him, gently received him and, when he petered out early, comforted him and cried for him. They are relaxed, unbothered and they doze together.

A little later she wanders downstairs in a loose gown to fetch some tea and then, with the tray within reach, sits on the edge of the big squeaky bed watching Hugo on an elbow sip gratefully to wet his dry throat.

'Do you remember Olivia, Hugo? Olivia Truelove?'

'Yes, of course,' he says after a moment's hesitation. 'Why?'

'I have seen her since the shooting; she came to the hospital, quite a few times, actually, she was worried about you.' Hugo looks up and is searching Sam's immeasurably calm and beautiful features, wanting to slip his hands inside the open draped gown. 'She read the accounts in the papers, saw the news, recognised your name and was concerned for you. She came over the next day and most days in the first week, but you were either asleep or in theatre. She talked to me and Bernadette. I like her; she is very attractive. Such neat, classic features, perfect blonde hair. Just as she was when we knew her before.'

Hugo is taken aback, surprised to hear Olivia's name again, after so much time. He dribbles tea down his chin and wipes his beard with the back of his hand.

'How is she?'

'She was worried and looked anxious, but she is well; she works in the City, doesn't she?' Sam slips out of her gown and Hugo watches with fascination as she slowly dresses herself, stepping from one foot to the other, slithering underwear over her thighs and around her bottom, wriggling into tight jeans, pulling a cotton shirt on that barely covers her breasts and then sitting at her dressing table with a hairbrush.

'Married or anything?'

'No, don't think so; she didn't speak much about herself, more concerned about you and the circumstances of the shooting. Thinks you must sue the police for their incompetence.'

Hugo strides as carefully as the wind and his healing wounds allow, out alone over the back fields, past some grazing sheep, taking a hop over Sor Brook. He had been there almost two weeks, living the slow-paced existence of a retired old man, with nothing to do all day but sit around, read the newspapers, sleep, go for gentle walks, eat without hurry. He is feeling frustrated, he feels a calling. He makes his way steadily over the Tre-Herbert Ridge leaning into the driving rain along well-worn paths and past Ty Capten Farm, after which the sloping hills give a view of Llanhennock valley and in the far distance the outskirts of Newport. That is if the low cloud will allow for any reasonable view this day, which he doubts. It had been wet on and off all week and he is wearing a greatcoat and heavy walking boots with a fisherman's waterproof hat, which had belonged to Sam's father. He takes shelter under the corrugated roofing of a crofter's sheep hut, leaning achingly against its solid stone walls. Inside it is at least dry although it had been heavily trampled underfoot turning the floor to mud.

Hugo is feeling increasingly restless. Sam has been brilliant, so loyal and devoted. So loving, always there when he has wanted her. Everything he has wanted she has provided, all the food and comfort of every sort, she has made available. They have shared her bed each night. She has listened to him, cuddled him, bathed him, massaged and soothed him. And he is not ungrateful, but he is grown restless with his recovery: two weeks out of the limelight plus his time in hospital have amounted to a massive loss of active time for work, as he thinks of all the jobs he has waiting, for the projects that need his attention. His sleeping is better now, the nightmares have calmed and his mind is easier. He feels ready to return to London life. Ironically here, in rural Wales where nobody knows him from Adam, he feels increasingly trapped; he has a need for his own space.

It is Samantha, of course. Despite her best wishes and gentleness, it is her constant presence, her tending to him, her control over him that he finds clinging. He feels guilty for such thoughts, as she has been so good to him, giving up so much of her time to protect him, but somehow he needs to tell her, he needs to break away from her.

Although his scars are many and deep, and nothing will hide them completely, they are all healed or granulated with crusting, and only the drainage wound under his right ribs from his liver still needs a small dry dressing changed daily. He studies them in the bathroom mirror when he can and probes the deep depressions with his long fingers. His hair is growing more evenly on his scalp, where he still has a short haircut to make it look more natural. There are scabby marks in the skin along his right neck and down his arms where the multiple drip needles were sited. Although he remains stiff and lacks a lot of his energy, his walking has become steady, much to his surprise, with almost complete return of feeling in his lower limbs and feet. He realises how bloody lucky he was, so many bullets coming so close to structures, like his spinal cord and heart. He will regain his energy in time. Back in his apartment, good food, regular exercise, the smell of the river again, and he will be fighting fit in no time.

'Hi, I thought I might find you up here,' Sam calls, approaching along the muddy path through the drizzle. Hugo's watchful gaze has been following her progress in her see-through plastic cape as she passed the farm and around the edge of the adjacent field; he is not displeased that she has come after him. She steps into the shelter dipping her head under the old metal roof. They embrace easily, their wet clothes clashing against each other. He kisses her rainy cheek. She tries to wipe her face dry and shakes out her hat.

'I've been here nearly two weeks now, Sam. I must not take up any more of your kindness and time. We've both got our own lives to get back to, you know.'

'You can stay, Hugo, as long as you like.'

'I know. You are so kind and I love you for it.' He bends down to kiss her floppy lips tenderly. Her chilly face is slightly flushed; without make-up, she looks natural, so fresh. Anticipating what is to come, she remains sombre and her lips do not respond to his attention.

'I have seen your case packed.' The rainwater is pattering over the corrugated roof above and dripping off the edges all around. There is a pungent damp and rich smell, of wet straw and sheep's dung, as exhilarating as it is powerful. Rainwater dribbles over his face glistening through his beard.

'But, you know, I need to get back to work. I need some sort of proper routine. This is all pretty heavy for me, Sammy, I mean I love being with you and making love with you. But I need time and some space to think.'

'I would like us to build our lives together,' she says, her voice trembling.

Sam has always accepted him as he was, even without an expressed commitment, and he has always come and gone as he pleased. She was weak, as far as he was concerned, but she could not face the possibility that Hugo might reject her. And he rather took advantage of that, but it seemed to work well for both of them: they had remained friends for many years. She was always going to keep the door open, as it were, as if at some point he would wilt under the pressure and agree for him to move in. She had never gone down on bended knee and begged him, thank goodness, he could not face such a humiliation. He needed still to feel that it was his choice.

He runs his fingers through her hair, wiping water over her face and speaks kindly, softly, there is no anger in him. They clutch at each other, bringing them closer through their wet coats and Sam is willing this moment to last longer. She wants to say that they are good for each other, that she cannot live without him. Is it something she has done or said or not done? He shakes his head and says no, no, it is all down to him, he needs to be back in the studio and doing his thing.

'I don't know if we should be together, all the time. I am impossible, I know. I don't want us to fight or lose what we have.' Hugo seemed to have thought about the possibility, it was his constant restlessness that drove him. Village life was too slow, he needed the hustle of the city.

'I have a taxi booked for the station in an hour.' He pats his pockets. 'I have money, and the keys for the apartment. So, Sammy, I will be in touch and will see you soon.' After a long hug, as they rocked side by side, he touches her lips with his forefinger and they look into each other's eyes and exchange smiles of melancholy. She wishes him well, dreading the loneliness she will feel later when the house is darkening and empty. He slowly turns away from her, taking his eyes away, and places the droopy hat back on his dark head. The rain has reduced to almost nothing. He starts back along the field, the path by the hedge to the road and past the farm and out of sight. Sam can only crouch against the roughened stones in sad contemplation, realising she has to let him go. And praying that it will not be for always.

4

Week Beginning Thursday, February 19, 2015

Hugo arrives into Paddington late but Garry is there waiting for him. He takes him back to his house, canal boat living now replaced by a grand three-story Victorian semidetached on Clapham Common. 'This is what we call success, boyo.' By the time they creep quietly through the front door, his wife Angie has retreated upstairs to put the children to bed.

'Listen, I'm really glad you've come here. Angie will be fine, you can stay as long as you feel necessary.'

'Thanks, Garry. I want to have a look at the Wharf sometime, sneak around the place, see if there is anyone suspicious about.'

'I want to come with you, I love a good snoop. Cloak and dagger stuff, eh? Are you thinking police watch or something more sinister?'

'Is there something more sinister?

Gareth Webster, a Welshman with sticking-out ears, red hair and freckles, had been the first bloke Hugo had bumped into at college. Everyone called him "Ginger", even the tutors, and he had a way with girls. He was outrageously anti-establishment and funny, Hugo the more serious and hard-working who regularly helped him with his studies. At eighteen, they became instant friends. He was always up to some little scheme to raise money, selling cheap postcards of rock stars, doing a bit of security work on the doors of nightclubs or working in the vegetable markets at Cheapside, and always had a pretty girl hanging on his arm. He bought a long boat barge on the canals of east London, moored mostly in the Limehouse basin, using some money from his father, which he shared for a while with a local girl. There Hugo and Jake among others would meet up for weekends, and a small crowd of art students inevitably gravitated to the canal towpaths, to meet in the tight confines of the hold, or to lounge around eating grilled fish, steaks or Chinese noodles from the wok, cooked on deck if the weather allowed. Later they resorted to card games or baccarat, betting sums they could ill afford while drinking, smoking or snorting anything available into the small hours. It was a wonder that Garry ever came through with any worthwhile degree, but he survived and mucked about on his own for years until finally, he fell on his feet with a publishing venture, mostly left-wing and mildly revolutionary material, that he expanded rapidly with numerous fashion and youth culture magazines that paid him whopping regular dividends.

Garry is anticipating an interesting May election, seeing a real opportunity for the minority parties to make significant inroads into the established two-party scenario. 'Young people are so turned off by our modern politics, the two-party system, and quite rightly. Why should someone find the policies of only one party sufficient for what they want in a single package – much more likely that they would want multiple parties offering a variety of policies that suited a more portfolio view of society, a mix-and-match sort of thing. Then you would get them voting. Coalition has been good in many ways but it's time that other parties got a look in. It makes for a more exciting time, don't you think?'

'It won't happen, Garry, not in the UK, it's too establishment-fixated and the electoral system is not designed for the smaller groups.'

'I know, but this time, there will be more pressure for change. So I've been working with the PPF, they want us out of Europe, to concentrate on our loyalty and patriotism. They would stop all immigration, which believe me, Hugo, is going to become the big story in the next few years.'

'I'm an immigrant. What, are they going to chuck me out?'

'No, daft, you're already here, established. No, but they would stop more coming. These inflows of migrants and refugees destabilize communities, lower pay rates and put pressure on housing, schools, the health services, you know the argument.'

'A bit nationalist, fascist even, for my liking.' Sitting at the central wooden kitchen table with only a single light over their heads, they chat on and share a beer together. 'I've not had a beer for weeks now, that tastes good.'

'So how are those wounds, Hugo, are they fading?'

'Slowly, they'll never disappear completely.'

'Your hair is growing nicely, this side here is nearly covered,' and Garry points to Hugo's temple. At which point the lovely Angie wanders in wearing a loose white cotton nightgown and delicate pink shawl, in soft slippers. Hugo remembers her brown hair always draped around a smiling face. He rises slowly and she raises both arms up to hug his shoulders and neck and they touch cheeks.

'Angie, I'm sorry, did we wake you?' Hugo pleads.

'Only a little,' she laughs. 'I was not really asleep, I go to bed ridiculously early these days, the kids, they wake at night. How are you, Hugo? Oh, Hugo, you poor man. I was so sorry to hear about what happened. I visited you once in the hospital, you won't remember, and then I have been so busy: Chloe has been ill and I've had to take her to the doctors and then my mother had a small accident, and one thing and another...' Angie looks tired and sinks onto a stool next to Hugo.

They chatter on for a while about Hugo's attack, and his recovery in hospital and his two weeks in rural Wales; his journey back to London. And about Samantha: she has been so dedicated, you've no idea. And both Garry and Angie think, and have always thought, that Hugo and Sam should be together.

Soon after a light snack, all three traipse upstairs in search of sleep.

Prominent on a wall in the hallway, where a small angled light splashes across it at a sharp angle, Hugo finds one of his early paintings. Entitled "The Promise of Youth", signed and dated October 2005, it shows Garry's barge, resting on the tranquil waters of Limehouse, in the shimmering light at the end of a hot summer's day. The boat looks real and lived in, half submerged alongside the concrete towpath, with green and oily reflections off the still waters, some washing on a line nearby fluttering in the evening breezes, a geranium in a pot aft, the barbeque equipment on the path, a passing cyclist and his dog sniffing around. Started at the end of summer 2005, before he had had any work properly exhibited, he had almost forgotten it. He likes it. This is the copy, the one he had given Garry as a present, just before he met Angie. The original painting had been sold for a princely few thousand quid to an American tourist, one of his first sales and it was when he and Jake first worked together. Jake had created a deal with a gallery off Pall Mall and had copyrighted the work, had it printed on greetings cards, which helped with his name awareness and brought attention from art lovers looking for something different.

Jake had a knack and Hugo realised early on that he needed him for success, an agent to do the commercial fixing, while he got on with creating the passionate pieces he loved doing. Jake acted as an oil man, lubricating the joints, easing the way, fixing deals, fixing people and of course fixing the money. Often working with Jeremy Ashcroft, they steadied Hugo's charging energy, focused it for him, and channelled him in the right direction, sometimes tucking him up in bed at the end of the day.

This coming year was to be his busiest, with a series of interesting challenges, and real graft would be required to achieve everything they had set out. No wonder Hugo is experiencing bouts of panic, having missed so much time, worried by his schedules. There is the impending trip to New York City, where Jake strongly feels he would be well received, where audiences appreciate the tactile experience and honesty of real-life artists; followed by the Vienna Biennial and then later the Armistice/November Remembrance celebrations. All of this has been put at risk with his shooting and hospitalisation, and still further time will be needed to recapture his rhythm and full energy again. He needs a meeting with Jake and Jeremy urgently, to look at some rescheduling.

Even though the day is damp and overcast, Hugo takes a walk at a slow pace around the Common, while Garry is out and Angie otherwise occupied. On his own and glad to be out of the house, out of everybody's way, he feels better able to exercise, moving more freely than for a long time, without too many aches. He sticks to the paths, enjoying the relative peace, at least for an hour or so. He promises himself to arrange his follow-up appointment in a few days to see the trauma team again. In the rolling hills of South Wales, the air was clean and crisp, he felt it clear his lungs with its purity. In South London, Hugo is not so sure: there is a waft of diesel fumes and smoke in the air, and the persistent grumbling traffic is never far away.

He is hoping he has not upset Sam too much. He will go back to her again but he just had to have some of his own time away from her; her constant presence was overbearing, stifling, a bit like when he lived with his mother in the school holidays. You love them, these devoted women, but you just have to have some of your own space to breathe. Samantha is a terrific woman, he could not have managed without her and he told her so, many times. He showed her his gratitude, even though he found making love with her difficult. It must have been the drugs he had been on, the exhaustion, the strain of the operations, all combining to make him a touch incompetent in that department, he is afraid to admit. Still, she put up with that, not making a fuss about it. He wonders whether anything has been damaged down there; surely not, the doctors would have said. Something to ask them at the clinic next week.

When they first met, Samantha and Hugo, he was a penniless art student surviving on baked beans and Marlboro lights, she was a model on the make, although brighter than most. At somebody's house party, there she was among the boozy crowd, eighteen and exuberant, her brilliant auburn hair flowing around her, her wide mouth pouting with sensational lips, her breasts hooked up in your face and fuck the comments. Indeed they had, in a pitch-black upstairs room where all the coats had been thrown onto a spare bed. He lay back in a daze while she yanked his jeans down and pulled her skirt up. She wrapped her legs around the back of him like a vice and taught him a thing or two about rhythm and timing, while he thrust away as fast as he could. At the end, she was gripping his black wavy hair with both hands and giving off a prolonged low-pitched moan, like a tugboat on the river. After the tensions had subsided, she hugged and kissed him with gentleness and gratitude, while he laughed in uncontrollable bursts of pleasure.

He thought she was the best prize he had ever come across and he kept her existence from Gareth and his other friends a secret at first, afraid she might have been tempted elsewhere, or that they might have coveted her. Might have? They would have! But she was a good girl, loyal to him from the start. They shacked up together wherever they could find a bed, someone's spare room, a couch in the basement of a student's digs, a rented one-bedroom hovel in Brixton for a while. Later she got herself fixed up in a spare attic room of a friend in Muswell Hill and later moved to her own ground floor place that he used to visit on occasions, where she played her sophisticated music and kept cats. He found her exhilarating and they became long-term partners in a way, consorts for each other's needs, whenever they wanted. After modelling and casual work in a pub, she landed up in market research with some bloke she met in a bar and had been working for a big firm with offices in Euston recently. She had done all right for herself, had Samantha.

He sits on a bench for a while. There are few other people about; he watches with caution the occasional walker or jogger going past. Nearby an old woman with a shopping trolley that she pushes slowly in front of her stops to throw bread crumbs for the pigeons. She is mumbling to herself and appears to be wearing men's black leather shoes, brown stockings around her ankles. Her face is extremely lined and weathered, as though she is outdoors all the time.

He decides he prefers Hampstead Heath for casual walking, the terrain more interesting, the views from the top are better, closer to some restaurants and pubs, even if the traffic noise is always nearby. He leans back gingerly and closes his eyes. He and Samantha, friends for fifteen years or more, they have understood each other; they have been good for each other. But they have both had other friends; they have slept with other people, they both know that. She must have had other lovers?

He is so missing Lilly. He will get Garry to arrange something.

Garry always said Hugo may look laid-back, but do not be deceived, he remains sharp-eyed and alert. At Charterhouse, he used to gel his thick curly hair into a spiky mass, just to look a little different and to suggest a sense of rebellion that would take away his goody-goody reputation. He was not strong on sport, although became adept at defending himself and was hard to beat in the boxing ring, with his long reach and solid frame. He overcame the intense peer rivalry with ingenious displays of artistic talent, sketches of school life, the masters in full flow, plus some commanding roles in the school plays, including an oft-referred-to performance of Macbeth that was scarily realistic. When he could get away, he would wander the countryside of Hankley Common or trek through the nearby Nature Reserve, with a script for a play to learn or a sketch pad. His fingers were always black with charcoal or smeared with coloured paints from the art school.

Camberwell Art College had been hard work, always in tight black tops and ripped jeans. Then he did a short spell teaching at a comprehensive in south London. He soon linked up with Jake Preston, who had recognised his exceptional talent long before, and they agreed to work together to gain recognition, as Jake was developing his management agency. Hugo's first experience of exhibiting professionally in Camden had been briefly reported in the London Evening Standard as an exciting revelation and critics in general had shown support for his work ever since. Hugo remained rightfully grateful to both Jake and Jeremy, for the career planning, the negotiations, the business organisation.

Hugo is thinking of Lilly. Returning to the house, he finds Garry and presses him to drive him round to his workshop and studios and to Bermondsey South to snoop around Butler's Wharf, just to check it out. In the car later, they are chatting.

'Garry, I want you to get a girl for me. Bring her over, I miss her.'

'A girl? Not Sam, then? You're going to upset that woman, boyo.'

'Lilly Soames, who was in the car with me and was injured. I have not seen her for five weeks or so. I was with her in that flat, with Nika.' Garry promises to fetch her over one day this week when everyone was out of the house so that the two lovebirds could have some peace-time together.

Garry quizzes him on the shooting. 'Have the police come up with a better explanation?'

'I think it might have been a setup, this Midge Martin character, he's a clever bastard and the whole event has allowed him to escape police attention; he's well out the way, I guess. I don't know, there just seem too many coincidences.' Hugo remains confused.

They drop into the Elephant & Castle workshop first, behind the Buddhist Centre off Renfrew Road, where all is quiet. Tom, the elderly caretaker, who has been there for years, lets them in with a cheery welcome and then hobbles off to his corner for a fag and a drink. Hugo is pleased with the progress his students have made on the Remembrance and the Greece series. These canvases are large, six by eight feet, and a lot of coverage is needed, relentless repetitive work with background colours to fill in the spaces before Hugo comes in with the exciting details. The canvases are stacked around the room, dried and ready; the students must have finished and departed weeks ago. Gary is suitably amazed at their scope and dimension.

Then they head for Hugo's deserted Theed Street studio. He has his bunch of keys and opens up the wooden doors into his old world. The smell is stale and oily, the atmosphere dusty and cold. Weak light is glancing diagonally through the skylight from one side. Everything looks to be exactly as it was before he "disappeared". Although there has been some cleaning and sorting: the floor looks swept, used brushes have been cleaned and stacked in pots in rows along the trestle table; a pile of drawings and sketches is gathered neatly, the easels have been lined up along the other side, canvases stacked against the walls. The kitchen fridge has been emptied and switched off, plates and mugs stacked on the draining board.

Hugo wanders around like a child returning to his home after months away, recalling past moments, seeing friends come and go. He peeps around corners, upstairs, without touching anything, just reassuring himself that his previous coveted life is still there awaiting his return, anytime. There in the little kitchen, for no reason, he imagines Olivia, ever elegant and petite, exasperated as she struggles to concoct a cooked meal on his pathetic single hob, managing a roast in the tiny oven. The cramped space was always inadequate, the equipment old. Antique, she called it. Her lovely blonde hair is disrupted, her face is glistening in the heat.

Nothing has really changed.

By the black iron staircase, he sees Dominic, one hand holding the bottom bannister, exercising his sculpted limbs, his perfectly smooth chest bare, his face a picture of girlish concentration. Hugo relives his panic in his guts, looking at the dead face with its open eyes, while dark studio shadows hide unknown secrets, wondering what the hell to do next, the crumpled body sprawled at his feet. He is phoning Jake, Jake will know.

Garry parks his car a few streets behind Shad Thames, permit holders only, and for the next hour of that afternoon, he and Hugo stroll casually together up and down the towpath and along the narrow lanes, two friends taking the air, two businessmen in private conversation, stopping once or twice in the local shops to browse, leaning over the river wall to watch life on the waterways that never ceased to amuse them. Gareth waxes lyrical about their student days together on the canals and bemoans how difficult it was to persuade Angie to take to barge life.

'Used to the middle-class comforts, eh, Garry?'

'I suppose so.'

Both of them keep a watch out for anyone who seemed to be loitering with no purpose or watching with interest the comings and goings around the Butlers Wharf building. Apart from a skinny youth in a hoodie who spends time leaning on a wall outside the delicatessen, pretending to be really grown up reading the racing form before cycling away down Lafone Street, there is nobody particular of note.

'You don't want to go up, take a look round the apartments?'

'No, I've done enough for one day, thanks, Garry. I'm tired. I need to contact Dolce before I return.' He needs to talk with Jake and Jeremy urgently, he needs a list of his priorities. He's grateful, the exercise has done him good. Although not exactly brimming with confidence, Hugo says he feels ready to return to work and to his apartment, perhaps in a few more days (if that is all right with the Websters?). They buy coffees-to-go in Starbucks, before retrieving the car and returning to Clapham.

The return to Theed Street after his six weeks away, away from everything he holds dear, away from the centre of his being, has unnerved him. He saw some ghosts in the shadows, he felt a number of memories crowd around him. He recalled Olivia Truelove, no less, in all her glory; he had not thought about her for a long while. She had stolen his heart once with her looks and her cleverness, taking over his everyday thoughts after that New Year party, when she had stayed the whole night with him, and then struggled with his disordered domestic life, poor thing. But she had been brilliant, for the short time she had remained: she made the best of everything, she was so refreshing. He had enjoyed their discussions, long arguments into the night about politics and the City. And there was Sam mentioning her only the other day, something about Olivia concerned for his recovery and visiting him in hospital, although he was totally unaware of her.

Then there was that bothersome mincing Ukrainian, his body at the bottom of the studio stairs. What a time that was, a cascade of tragedies visited upon him one after the other, as if the Devil himself were out to get him. His father, the giant Barnabas, accused of fraud and corruption, having two successive heart attacks, and then dying; Dominic Lebelov, assaulting his woman, falling down the stairs and breaking his neck; Hugo's family in disarray, his mother hysterical and grief-stricken. And Olivia, dear girl, herself disappearing soon after. He could not have dealt with anything more.

Except then came his business failure and the sale of all the Pitsakis Corporation for millions of dollars that created him a rich man: a humble painter in oils worth millions of pounds – there was an irony in there somewhere.

Jake, he had been a godsend on the night. He calmed Hugo's nerves and applied his organising skills, as only he could. Jake was immediately concerned that the police would come snooping sooner or later, when Dominic was reported missing. He was thinking in business terms, appearances, reputation, the dangers to Hugo of being accused of a crime. He insisted that it would be best if they, Hugo and Olivia, were gone. While Olivia was shut upstairs in the bedroom, Jake and Hugo disposed of the body, cleaned up, leaving no traces. Hugo stayed with Olivia the rest of the night to comfort her and persuaded her to leave early the next morning for her own flat and to stay there for a while, to deny ever being in Theed Street that night, to ever seeing Dominic Lebelov there.

Whatever became of dear Olivia, he is wondering? When he finally returned to England, admittedly months later, it was the end of the summer and he had looked for her, but she was not around, in Theed Street or in West End Lane, she had moved out, but no one he spoke to knew where she had gone. Taken umbrage, he assumed, moved away, no forwarding address, no telephone number that worked. He waited for her to contact him, but she never did. He was sad but hardly lonely, he had friends to sustain him; he did not have time to feel heartbroken, perhaps he should have. So much had happened since they had seen each other, so many distractions. He had been disappointed; that was the word, disappointed.

Hugo's decision to sell all his father's inherited shipping and freight business, finally with his mother's approval, felt at first like a failure. That he had failed his father, his mother, all the employees. But cashing in on a surge of global interest, getting the best price, was ultimately the best thing for the business and its workers, so that it could be run by experienced private experts and its successes maintained. Hugo had some time to consider, while arrangements were being finalised and British and Greek tax authorities argued over details, and after he had paid whopping legal and advisory fees, what he would do with and how he would manage the unbelievable sums of money that were coming his way. What an amazing dreamlike situation to be in, to suddenly have untold wealth at your disposal, for you to do whatever you wanted. He could buy anything he wanted, live anywhere and possess anything, he just had to name it. The limits were the limits of his imagination and desires. He must capture the moment and not waste it, not see the money run away in ill-thought out ventures or ridiculous indulgences, in wasteful debauchery. He needed to make use of his good fortune, to develop something that could last and represent his father's legacy. He needed most important of all to consider how to conduct himself, how he would relate to others and want them to relate to him. These were difficult and troubling times.

The opportunity to obtain the leasehold on two adjacent penthouse apartment conversions at the top of Butlers Wharf, opposite St Katherine's Dock, was too much to resist. The views were spectacular, the lighting on a good day was remarkable and it placed him exactly where he wanted to be, in the middle of the city he had come to love. He created a massive art studio in one apartment, the size of a squash court, brickwork exposed, with pillars and original ironwork, a Manhattan loft look-alike. There were also a few rooms for storage, with washing facilities and guest bedrooms.

The second apartment became his new home, a sophisticated atmosphere of expensive calm. He had his king-size bedroom, two spare guest bedrooms, an open-plan kitchen and adjacent dining room where a dozen people could be entertained in a modern atmosphere, with southerly views across London rooftops. The front lounge, which held a collection of paintings and sculptures by his contemporaries, was furnished expensively, with Italian leather sofas, Danish wood, German fittings. It occupied the full width of the property, with north-facing terracing, from where he could spend endless hours observing the busy waters of the Thames six stories below.

The two apartments were linked through a short corridor. In the studio half, lived his Greek housekeeper, Dolce, who shopped and prepared his meals for him and generally kept the private apartment clean and well-stocked. She had her own living room/bedroom on site and she came and went as she pleased. A chunky black German SUV was in a nearby underground security car park and he sometimes used a driver, so he could be delivered or collected anywhere in comfort. And he was able to enter and leave the apartments from the underground, if desired, with elevators to all floors.

The refurbishment work had taken well over a year to complete satisfactorily and included huge sliding double-glazed windows along the front and extra skylight windows to provide as much light as possible. The outside views over London were ever fascinating, the changing light providing its own entertainment. The Thames, Tower Bridge and the Tower provided the main focus of attention at the front.

During lengthy reflection while recovering at Garry's place, Hugo remains baffled by events, frightened and a little vulnerable. The police attack still feels like a personal vendetta. A setup, a conspiracy played out against him. But for what purpose, he cannot say. People with a grudge, people he may have upset in the past, wanting to stop his progress, working against him, out to kill him? Greed, his newly acquired wealth, unexpected and undeserved, some would think; the facts were filtering out onto the street, difficult to hide fifty million pounds. Jealousy can be a powerful incentive. Causing such mayhem, accidentally or not, he surely did not deserve that.

His sudden wealth meant he was able to do what he wanted, help the people that he wanted, the struggling artists and their families that he knew; able to do the sort of art he wanted, and not worry whether it would be commercially successful or not; able to live the life he wanted. Not many people get that sort of opportunity and he was embracing it with gusto and vision. He did not deserve this police attack, mistaken identity indeed!

In the open bedroom doorway, Lilly Soames stands in turquoise balconette bra and pants and her best duck-face pout. With pigeon-toed cuteness and childlike naivety, a woolly teddy hangs by her side and she sucks deliberately on a forefinger distorting her crimson lower lip. To Hugo, she is divine innocence, augmented with awesome contours and that smouldering come-hither look.

A flimsy georgette blouse hangs loosely round her shoulders. She approaches in her bare feet, a model's walk, hips swaying, toes pointed in a single line, her lace panties hiding nothing. Her blonde hair bobs behind her, her bosom bounces and she drops the teddy on the carpet on her way. She swivels for him to undo her and peel her briefs down to her ankles; and then bends at the hips, her legs solidly straight, and wiggles her bottom in his face to show him a glimpse of her dusky lady garden.

She slithers ecstatically between the sheets, sliding against his course and scarred skin with the softness of her breasts, her thighs. He enfolds her, breathing in her smell, feeling the cold touch of her bare buttocks. Foreplay is short, their kissing noisy and wet, their restless desires sharpened by recent absence. He relishes her sheer nakedness, sucks at her nipples, crouches between her legs. Their loins collide irresistibly and conjoin in mutual penetration, that is as deep and meaningful as it is rewarding.

To Hugo, Lilly is a playful bountiful babe with generous attributes who fortuitously has come his way. He drools over her carefree and gratuitous approach. She is fun and undemanding; and delightful to study and to sketch, her classic form such balm to any artist and he uses his rare skills to celebrate it. Only a fool would resist the pleasures good fortune has passed his way. After his dreadful ordeal, from which he worried whether he would emerge unscathed, in that crucial aspect at least, her lovemaking became the pinnacle of all his most immediate desires.

To Lilly, Hugo is just a passing fancy. Wildly attractive, a swarthy hunk of manhood, sensitive to her feelings. He is charming and generous, and he makes her feel worthy, not just a cheap stripper. She is a touch bedazzled by his magical talent but genuinely loves his painting. He is sure to move on to the next floozy that flutters by when he becomes bored with her, but in the meantime, she is happy to associate with such a genius, to bask in the reflection of his growing fame. But when she discovers that he is boundlessly wealthy, she begins to reappraise her role, thinking that maybe she can become a more permanent friend and confidante, a regular muse for the artist during the most productive period of his career, and that perhaps their relationship might blossom into something more durable, much to her advantage, moneywise.

Part Four: Olivia and Hugo

1

Sunday, March 1, 2015

Samantha Little, true to her word, arranged the meeting Olivia Truelove sought with her one-time lover, Hugo Pitsakis, and it was to be at his studios in Theed Street, the scene of their first liaison and so much of their time together and the tragedy that was Dominic Lebelov.

So, a week after her meeting with Sam in Muswell Hill, Olivia finds herself feeling slightly nervous in the back of a black cab dawdling through the Sunday traffic towards the familiar quaint streets close to Waterloo Station, where she had not ventured for over nine years – not since she had walked away from his studio building with the last of her stuff, in a colourful wheelie case, leaving no note or explanation, and trudged to the station in a desperate retreat, back to her one bedroom flat, alone and wretched. It was a stumbling retreat, a humbling experience, leaving the once hectic exhilaration that was her emotional ride with Hugo towards the uncertainties of a vacuum, miserable in contemplation and from which she was unsure how she would ever extract herself or escape.

And it was not of her making. The whole thing, her thrilling and short-lived share in the chaos of his life, had just blown up, suddenly, with nothing left. She would not meet someone like that again, passionate, talented, generous she thought. Never had a dull moment, that was for sure; she was grateful for the short time they had had together. Although feeling suicidally wretched, she did not lose her dignity or disgrace herself, she walked calmly away looking straight ahead with dry unblinking eyes.

Her star would rise again, she told herself, she would emerge from the fog in time, and be stronger for it. Although her prolonged bout of sobbing once she had shut the front door of her pathetic flat and collapsed face down on her bed certainly felt overwhelming.

Yet here she is, nine years later, successful, confident and ready to come face to face with her past. She can handle it, she knows she can: she is a different person now, less impressionable for a start, more grown up. She is wiser, more self-contained, and she is not looking for anything other than a professional response. Hugo Pitsakis will mean nothing else to her.

She pays off the driver and stares at the outside of the building with its reddish-brown brickwork and tall windows with their iron grills. An unmarked white van is free-standing inside the metal fence on the stone driveway. The view down the street, of two-storey terraced housing, cars in the roadway and occasional forlorn trees, all looks the same. The heavy black doors have not changed, the weathered brass letter box, the bell button still loose in its socket.

The sense of *déjà vu* is not unexpected although the stab of empty nausea that hits her stomach is a shock, just as she is wondering, at the very moment of the door being wrenched open from the inside, whether she is doing the right thing.

Ever since Sam phoned her two nights ago, she had been excited. Sam promised that she would be there to help persuade Hugo to support her project and she knew that that would ease any tension that there might be between them. She had already spotted Sam's blue Renault parked outside on the road.

The benefits for her in kick-starting a fresh chapter in her life involving her writing, adding a new bow to her portfolio career, outweighed the small risk of an emotional battering that she might find too hard to handle. She feels certain that she will be able to resolve any issues from the past that still trouble her. And she will not fall for Hugo; she was not in love with him, the sight of Hugo was not going to knock her off her feet and change any of that; however captivating he might prove to be.

- Definitely not.

Hugo is concerned about Samantha. He cares about her, recognises her loyalty, and the long-term affection that they hold for each other. He called her last week, let her know where he was, that he was fine, that he would attend the hospital out-patient clinic on his own; told her he wanted to see her and all that. Samantha said she wanted Hugo to rehabilitate gradually and that she wanted to help in that process. She knew how difficult he found it to commit himself, to anybody; that he was committed to his work. But she could see him becoming even more hectic, as compensation for his experience and the time lost, and after coming so close to losing his life; all of which would drive his inner engine to work harder, with more enthusiasm. Which she saw as diminishing further her role in his life.

Hugo had to reaffirm that Samantha was far more than an extra to him, that the portraits he has of her were his treasures; that he would not have achieved any of it, without her. She brought up the question of a meeting with Olivia Truelove and said she would arrange it for the coming Sunday.

'She wants to interview you for a book, now that you're better. She wants to write a biography about you and your artistic life.'

'Good God, are you serious?'

'Yes, she was so enthusiastic.'

'You put her off, I hope.'

Hugo's initial reaction was not encouraging. But Samantha insisted, she had promised Olivia, at least an opportunity to talk to him about it. Hugo had been surprised and a little unnerved to hear from Sam when they were in Wales, that Olivia was back on the scene and wanted to meet him. It was after they had had sex one afternoon and they were drinking tea on her bed in the cottage, and he was feeling much relieved at his performance. His warm sensation of sleepy pleasure was disturbed by visions of Olivia, in her ripped cotton nightie, whimpering with shock at the top of his metal staircase in the studio, that dead naked dancer crumpled at the bottom.

'I was thinking of her only the other day, wondering whatever had happened to her,' Hugo responded, mildly irritated. 'What does she want, exactly?'

'I told you, Hugo, she was worried about you when she heard about the shooting and visited the hospital, regularly. Quite a few times, but you were asleep or having an op or something. She was angered by what had happened, you know, in broad daylight, the police shooting anybody they fancy.'

'Well, that's nice of her.'

'Yes and she wants to talk to you about doing a biography on you. The artist and his genius, you know the sort of thing. So she wants to interview you and see if you will agree.'

'And should I, do you think?'

'Hugo, you must decide. She is not putting pressure on you; you should listen to her and then make up your mind. I think she would be sympathetic and she writes this column in a magazine. I know it's about money and stuff, but she is obviously a good writer.'

'You like her, so I should see her. But I don't have to agree, do I?'

'No, Hugo, you do what you want. I know you are going to be busy, as you get back to your work, so now may not be a good time. Just listen to her, all right? It might help you rehabilitate.'

'I don't need rehabilitation, Sam,' he snapped back rather too quickly, 'you make it sound like another prison sentence.'

Hugo was thinking what his life would have been like had Olivia stayed? She might have become his new muse and regular lover. But then there would have been no room for the stunning Miss Lilly Soames, which would have been a sad loss. They agree on a date and time; Sam will arrange things with Olivia. 'Do you want me to be there with you, Hugo? I'm happy to come with her if you want.'

As it was, Sam had arrived separately an hour beforehand and had been helping Hugo organise his living space and tidy up the mess a bit. It is Sam in jeans and a loose red shirt who opens the main door and welcomes Olivia. They exchange a soft hug. Olivia sheds her winter coat and it is as if nothing has changed, as she steps through the entrance into the shadowy chaos of the studio. Classical music is playing quietly from the back. Wintery daylight tips down through the high ceiling picking out speckles of fine dust in the atmosphere; the steel pillars at intervals and white-washed brickwork walls, all in need of a paint; easels and tables, palettes and pots of brushes, canvases stacked against the walls, everything randomly strewn with papers. The wooden floor has been scrubbed in places with carbolic to get the spilt paints out, leaving its characteristic sharp tingle in the nostrils. And just below the pungency of the paint and oils, of spirit, linseed and turpentine, Olivia is sure she can detect a hint of human effort, the sweat of toil.

Hugo emerges from the cramped washroom at the back, rubbing his hands on a cloth. She stops abruptly, shocked by his appearance of weight loss and wasting. She struggles to speak, she cannot prevent her mouth stupidly hanging wide open, reminded of the ghostly images of him she had witnessed in the hospital. He is in the white tunic-thing he had always worn when painting, like a giant apron, tied with a cord around the waist. There are fingerprint smears of coloured paint on the lower sides and especially down the left edge, thick and twisted smudges of various oily colours caught in the cotton folds, where he had the habit of pulling with his right hand his thickly coated brushes through the cloth that he gripped in his left. There is a baggy black tee shirt underneath, with darkened chest hairs poking over the front, as ever, and a pair of jeans and school plimsolls without socks.

His curly hair seems to have lost its dark sheen and is cut so short his pale scalp shows through in places. He is shaven but already has a casual day's growth over his chin. His striking lack of bulk, the thinness of his limbs, the hollowed cheeks, give an impression of vulnerability and weakness, so removed from the stalwart bulk of the Hugo she fondly recalls.

On the other hand, Olivia looks so out of place, smart in a dark trouser suit and matching shoes, with a bright pink lipstick. She forces a quick smile but her voice sounds husky in the dry air. 'Hello, Hugo.' She looks at him shyly, searching for the misty brown depths in his eyes, from where he imbibes her, as he approaches, while he stuffs his cloth-wipe into the front pocket of his apron. His warm outstretched hands form a gentle clasp, just like the first time.

'Olivia. What a lovely surprise.' He sounds convincing.

'Long time, I know, sorry to intrude.'

His fingers are stained with charcoal and paint smears, despite his best efforts. He does seem somehow smaller, a bit shorter if that were possible, not such a solid presence, but still with his beaming smile and good teeth. He is dancing uncertainly from foot to foot, looking from Olivia to Sam and back, mumbling something about how different she looks.

'Had my hair cut for my holiday,' she offers coyly, 'the tan's more or less gone.'

'Come in, come along, Sam.'

'Sam has talked to you, yes? And been most kind; hopefully, you're happy for me to ask you a few questions.' Olivia is not sounding as formal as she had rehearsed, like she wants to. She wants Hugo to imagine that she is simply a woman at a routine business meeting, strictly in work mode. Except that she is so tempted to reach out, intuitively to clutch at an arm and offer him help, he looks so frail, to get across to the old couches, pushed up against the far wall, under the gallery. As if she was a goddamn nurse and he was some sickly old guy in a care home.

'Mind the pots,' he calls as she steps through the studio space, refraining from her urges, keeping her elbows tucked in, hands held together. 'We can go to the back, there are some chairs there. Sam has made sure that there is coffee and milk – although I seem to remember you have it black, is that still right?' Hugo quickly relaxes; he much prefers the company of women, especially beautiful and intelligent creatures who obviously admire him, which is simply how he is remembering her at the moment, as someone who was once his girlfriend. He almost winks at her.

- I am not going to let this man mesmerise me again.

'Yes, thanks,' she calls, walking firmly past the open metalwork staircase that descends steeply from the gallery landing above, without giving it a second glance. The carpet and the same old chairs at the back are arranged in the same way. The dirty little kitchen area is just through the open archway there, where she and Hugo had so often sat in the early morning preparing themselves for the rigours of their days ahead, still in their night clothes. The familiarity and emotions of that time, the smells and the feel of the place, threaten to engulf her and it is all she can do to refrain from flinging off her inhibitions and wandering around as she used to, as if she owned the place. She wants to venture upstairs, just to see what a holy mess Hugo was living in without her.

Instead, she sits down casually, determined to take it as it comes. Hugo emerges this time with a mug of black coffee for Olivia and Sam wanders behind with a bowl of soft fruits, offering her a colourful choice of grapes and various berries. Hugo drinks water from a bottle. 'I've gone off coffee completely since all the operations, just doesn't seem to taste the same. Just water for me.'

'Please, help yourself.'

'So how are you, now, Hugo? I was so sorry to hear about your injuries.'

'You visited me in Charing Cross, Sam says. But I was pretty knocked off most of the time, I expect.'

'Yes, I could never catch you awake. Never mind.'

'That was kind of you.' Hugo settles himself gingerly in an upright creaky chair, looking grateful, admiring Olivia's elegance opposite him. 'Well, I am recovering. I spent two weeks with Sam at her place in Wales, which was restful. Such a relief to get away from the hospital – those places terrify me, really. To be honest, I was worried about returning home; I felt sure I was being watched and had become quite paranoid. Hadn't I, Sam?' And he playfully pats Sam, sitting next to him, across her thigh. 'But I've learnt to accept what happened was a police mistake – just idiots getting the wrong guy.'

'Are you going to sue? I mean, they can't get away with this, can they? Will there be compensation?'

'I have been interviewed by the Police Complaints people, the Ombudsman, my lawyer, even Chris Jefferson, the local MP. I am told there is a compensation board and they will be offering a substantial sum in due course. We will have to wait and see.'

'Good.'

'And for Lilly, she was injured, with a bullet wound in her shoulder.'

'Good, she deserves something,' Olivia agrees, taking a handful of blueberries. For a few moments, there is silence between them, Sam sucking at the fruit, Hugo taking slurps of water, Olivia sipping carefully at her hot mug. Which begins to feel awkward for Olivia the longer it lasts. She is sure to avoid direct references to their old time together, with Sam present, and she wants to launch into her new ideas; she is unsure how much Sam has said to him already but is waiting for Hugo perhaps to make the first move.

They both speak together. 'So, what...' Hugo begins. 'Are you...' Olivia starts. They look across at each other making brief eye contact, then quickly flick away. They laugh.

'Sorry, go on...'

'Well, no, I was just wondering what you were working on at the moment. You seem to be getting back into the swing. Can't be easy, can it, after so much time away. Energy a bit low, I'd imagine?'

'I can show you if you like; some of them are here. But I need to get my organisation back together again, things have been shut down.' Hugo stands up and strolls over towards the centre of the studio. Olivia leaves her mug behind and follows him, watching his slightly laboured gait and studying the back of his scalp. He has switched on some of the ceiling spots to provide sharper lighting, as he stands among the jumble of canvases and easels.

'Things have changed a bit since you were here.' Olivia looks around, expecting to see something different, eager to peek at his new compositions. 'I often start new works at my home studio, where I shape the whole picture from early sketches, the main characters and the main action. Then I have some students and assistants who help, so I bring the canvases down here where they work on the fill-in and the background before I come to overlay detail, of the main action and so on.'

'You are as meticulous as ever, I see,' coos Olivia, admiring the nearest white canvas, a developing war image scene in a sepia hue.

'So I often return the pictures to my home where I complete them. They are always big and I need to get through them faster, so the assistants help with the turnaround. But now, after what happened I may have to rethink that and slow the whole process down, at least until I can cope with multiple projects. Jeremy sent the students away – they didn't know when I would be coming back, so we are gonna have to find some more or whatever. It's caused a horrible amount of disruption.'

Olivia watches as Hugo slides another canvas out of a stack and turns it round to face them, resting it back against a post. 'So this is part of a triple arrangement, this is the middle one.' It is at least six by eight feet and the sepia brown gives it an early twentieth century feel, like those old photographs that her granny would occasionally find in the bottom of a drawer. Although without any particular detail it looks flat, Olivia can anticipate the action and the human passions that will emerge. 'It's part of my First World War series, for Armistice Day 2016, one hundred years on from the Battle of the Somme. Plenty of time.' She can see the trenches and the churned earth, the explosive effects of artillery bombardment on farm buildings, as Hugo carefully points to the scenes, his voice rumbling on. 'In the distance here, is the village of Thiepval. These are inter-connecting trenches across the mud, with British soldiers on this side, beginning to pour over the front; up these rickety wooden ladders; others waiting, terrified. They're being caught in a mass of cross-fire, bodies already ripped apart by the heavy machine-gun fire from the German positions over here in the middle distance, on higher terrain – so they'll be on the next frame. The British seem to be rushing headlong into a suicidal attack, hoping to overwhelm the opposition by force of numbers.' Hugo steps back to view it all from more distance: 'the audience is watching in despair really because we know what happened: over 19,000 British soldiers killed in one day. So sad.'

Olivia reads the pencilled words of the title in a golden box along the bottom: "Seven-thirty, morning, July 1, 1916". Much detail is needed to complete the picture but she is moved by the impact and power of the piece, and she can visualise the final result that Hugo is painstakingly seeking. For a few solemn moments, they share the bleakness of history. Hugo moves on. There are other pictures in much the same vein and she is entranced by the action depicted, the perspective and the unique way Hugo brings it all to life. She wanders between the stacks of canvases in a sort of trance, letting the rumble of his mellifluous voice waft over her, like listening to a favourite radio programme, someone reading a bedtime story.

'Plenty of time to complete these. I have my Greece series in progress as well. There are several other commissions waiting, I haven't even started to plan them yet. And Jake will remind me again of the New York exhibition in the summer.' Hugo does look challenged, thinking about all the demands on him.

'A lot more ideas have been festering in my mind for a while, over these few weeks, you can imagine. It is now a matter of organising the time to transpose the ideas into real shape. That's how I use the sketches, as a sort of trial, seeing how things fit together.'

After their detour around the studio, they stumble back to their seats. 'That will be cold now,' offers Hugo, pointing to her mug.

'Oh, don't worry. Look, I have already talked with Sam about this; and I met with your mother recently, she's a lovely lady.' Hugo looks quizzically across at Olivia. 'What do you think? I want to write a biography of you, your life but, most importantly, about your passions and your work. We would illustrate it. Since I was here last, you seem to have developed into a business. I have met Jake and Jeremy. I would need to interview you and the others and gain a more detailed account. I have not found a specific publisher as yet, but a friend of mine who is a senior editor at the magazine I write for is encouraging and knows a couple of possibilities.'

'I am flattered that anyone would want to write about my life – really it's only creating some pictures.'

Olivia scowls at him, with pursed lips and then allows a smile to spread across her face. 'Yes, too right, just a few simple pictures, eh? Modesty, always became you, Hugo. You complained years ago about artists needing more influence and connection with society. Well, this would be a chance to connect.'

Sam, who has been watching the two of them walking around and chatting together, leans across and stretches a hand out to touch Hugo's arm. 'Well, the other thing, Hugo, was the reporting in the press about the shooting, it's been so awful, and so full of errors that we felt this was a way of putting right what they said; about you and your character; a way to publish your version, without getting directly involved in public argument or legal wrangling.'

'Yes, absolutely right,' says Olivia with some force. 'I wanted to correct so much of the crap reporting. And maybe question the police attitude, as if we live in a damned police state!'

2

Wednesday, March 4, 2015

Hugo has sent his driver to pick Olivia up from the Barbican, in a black German tank with cream leather interiors and air conditioning. His name is Jayden, a young Afro guy, with braided hair and a fuzzy beard, who wears loose and colourful clothes that flapped around him as he walked her to the car. She slumps gratefully with her own thoughts in the insulated luxury, watching the strong wintery sunshine which occasionally pierces through the grey afternoon, bouncing at low angles off the city buildings. But the outside world fails to intrude, and with the tinted windows, she is invisible to it.

Last night Louise had pressed her further on her relationship with Hugo, interested in how the two of them had not managed a longer-lasting arrangement. 'We were together about four months. Come on, he wasn't easy.' Olivia carefully filled in a few more gaps, as it helped her to clear some of her feelings, personal things that she had kept to herself. And Louise had agreed, that Olivia had done all that she could have.

This morning she had woken to the irritating sounds of cooing insomniac pigeons. She was only too pleased to get out into some fresh air, enjoying her morning commute by foot, although, with an atrocious queue at Starbucks on King William Street for her cappuccino to-go, she had arrived at the office a few minutes late.

She feels cocooned and safe inside the tranquil space and soon they are crossing the river at Tower Bridge and turning into Queen Elizabeth Street. 'You been at de Barbican long, Miss?'

'Oh, a couple of years now. It's convenient.' And when Olivia sees Jayden's round eyes flash in the rear-view mirror, 'I work in the City, so I can walk to work if I choose, when the weather's all right.' Jayden finds a tight alleyway between office blocks and then the car drops steeply down a slope and electronic gates at the touch of a remote button within the car sedately retract to admit them to an ill-lit and private underground car park.

Clearly visiting the new Hugo has become a more complicated procedure than before. Olivia's stomach feels churned with butterflies at the thought but is equally excited at seeing his new home at Butlers Wharf. This is a simple business meeting, remember, along business lines. She is aware they might be alone, or perhaps there will be a cluster of servants running around at his every command.

They ascend smoothly in a small elevator to the sixth floor and step out into a discreetly lit corridor, with shiny wooden flooring and whitewashed walls. Jayden leads the way to number 121 and buzzes the bell on the door post.

'OK, I leave you now. Farewell, Miss Olivia, I might see you later, the return journey perhaps.' He has a lovely smile.

'Yes, all right.' With her coat draped over folded arms, thinking only of her business remit, she stands straight and still, like a sentry on duty. The thick wooden door sucks inwards.

Hugo fills the doorway, a bashful smile growing across his darkened face. He is in a pressed shirt and Levis, looking surprisingly relaxed and clean, not the usual unremittingly tense artist of old.

'Hi, come in. Jayden got you here, no problem?'

'Fine. Very comfortable.' She smiles sweetly noticing the excitement in his attitude, and bowing her head, she slides past him into the serenity of a round hallway with a massive flower arrangement on a central marble-topped pedestal table at its centre under a cupula skylight.

In an instant, Hugo takes in her looks, her attractiveness, imbibing an intoxicating waft of subtle perfume: the neat blonde hair, with its parting and fine texture; the subtle make-up and coloured apricot lips; the expensive tailored black suit with its waisted jacket finishing just short of the taut roundness of her bottom; the apricot suede shoes and silk scarf to match; the restrained dangly earrings. All these things recall moments of times past, and compelling images of Olivia in the shower or at her dressing-table flash through his mind, to be just as quickly swept away by Oliva's bustling professional approach.

Again, having glanced around the entrance hall, noting the three doors that lead off, she stands upright feet together to one side of the central table, as a guest waiting politely for her host to lead the way. She admires the abundant collection of colours and scents, of white calla lilies, orange amaryllis, waxy red and white anthuriums and the orange plumage of a few birds of paradise.

Hugo closes the front door softly and skips across the soft carpet around the central arrangement on the other side, trailing a free hand over the grey marble surface. 'Do you like, fresh arrangement this morning?'

'Gorgeous.'

He opens the middle door into an impressive living room area that stretches all the way forward to the terracing at the front, it seems like the length of a tennis court away, where huge sliding glass doors frame the grey afternoon. Olivia follows him and is stopped by the sheer size and elegance of the surroundings. Halfway along on one side and two steps lower is a semi-circular area, with a man-sized bare brick chimney stack and open fireplace, and beautiful browned leather sofas in a horseshoe around. The whole room is softly carpeted with a separate dining area and further seating towards the windows.

'Oh my God, Hugo! What can I say?'

Olivia drops her coat and leather clutch bag on a chair as she strolls around, feeling she has entered a showroom or a luxury London store, admiring the furniture and the paintings on the walls, and is drawn towards the windows to catch the view. She presses her nose against the chill glass and stares out at the gilded turrets of London Bridge and the enclosure of St Katherine's docks opposite.

'What do you think?' Hugo is asking, close by.

'Stunning. How long have you been here?'

'About five years now, but there was a lot of planning involved and refurbishment work before I moved in. We can go outside if you like, but it's pretty cold.' He easily slides back a full-height glass door and they step outside onto the blustery terrace, broad enough for pine table and benches and a barbecue set over to one side. The floor is black, tarred and waterproofed, the front surrounded by a low brick wall, topped with a steel rail running full length. The cold wind blowing strongly up the river torments them. She watches flat open barges moving ponderously along the murky coloured water curving below them. An endless stream of traffic is passing over the bridge. Lonely sunlight reflects off the myriad glass and steel structures of the city buildings that rise up from the concrete jungle over the way, like plants thrusting skywards for their sustenance.

'Impressive view, isn't it? I never tire of it.'

Hugo is feeling confident in his attractive home, and delightfully proud to be able to show her the progress he has made since she was last in his life: the difference to the mess he generally lived in over at Theed Street, that she was accustomed to, is like chalk and cheese. Olivia takes in the beauty of Tower Bridge to their left with the chunky pale stone outcrops of the Tower of London beyond it, and opposite the dull block shape of the hotel and all the bobbing white masts like a small army gathering, in their protected waters behind the jetties of the dock.

Beyond the Bridge, HMS Belfast is moored silently and she can make out a few tourists moving in clusters over its decks. She leans further over to watch the little people below on the Jubilee towpath in front of the canvas awnings of a restaurant, pedestrians going about their business, tourists mostly, young lovers hand-in-hand, weaving between the lamps and the fixed benches, the occasional cyclist and jogger. The floating pier below has a walkway sloping down to its platform, where a couple of small pleasure boats are moored. And anchored a little way off down the river, there is a three-mast antique vessel, its wooden hull discoloured with age and neglect. Other familiar landmarks scattered over the vista she recognises: the Gherkin huddled with a group of skyscrapers towering over the old City buildings where she works, and she can just make out the familiar Barbican towers in the further misty distance.

'Amazing, amazing.'

'That's Le Pont de la Tour restaurant below,' Hugo shouts above the wind, 'the old Conran place, but not owned by him anymore. It's French, traditional. Great wines.' He is wrapping his arms around himself and blowing into his bare hands while Olivia holds her hands up to her face in astonishment, her eyes feasting on the view of famous landmarks that the wealthy pay vast sums to own.

She feels like a tourist and has real pleasure in her voice, almost singing out to make herself heard. 'You are so lucky with all this to look at. You're in the heart of London, Hugo, you could not be nearer the pulse of the city if you tried,' she exclaims. 'What you always wanted. King of the castle, eh? How did you ever manage this?' She turns to him, her expression incredulous and they move back inside to the comfort and warmth of the lounge, where the tones are neutral and restful, not what she would have expected from an artist so steeped in action and dramatic colour.

Hugo smiles broadly, basking in her admiration. 'Now steady on. I had to pay for all this and the renovations, like the floor-to-ceiling windows all along the front, and the arrangement here: there were originally three rooms, I had them opened up into one. I have the apartment next door as well, bought them both at the same time. That one is converted into studios. So, I kind of live in this one and work in the other one. They connect,' and Hugo points to a red painted door about halfway along the wall opposite the fireplace. 'Let me show you.' And he bounces off with all the excitement of a little schoolboy showing a friend his Christmas presents.

He guides her past bedrooms and through the kitchen, identifying the names of various artists on display, paintings and small sculptures. Through the red door and connecting passageway, to the next penthouse, she finds herself in a bright and broad space, an artist's studio, with three skylights in a row high above them and tall windows running the full width at the front with access onto the terrace, just like the residence next door. And just like at Theed Street, paintings on boards, blocks and canvases are leaning in stacks against the walls, and charcoal sketches, like fragments of scenes from Hugo's imagination, are scattered around, stuck to the walls or pinned to easels. There are a number of pictures in progress, in a line of wooden easels standing like soldiers on parade, and Olivia conducts the inspection, walking sedately and regally along the line with eyes left. Over in one corner, there is a stage covered in red plush carpeting, with heavy drapes either side, spotlights along a pole on the ceiling and a golden chaise longue in the middle. A backdrop of the Athens skyline painted in dramatic shadowy blocks.

'That's an area for make-believe, setting up a scenario for context, with special lighting if I need it. That's if I have models for sitting.'

Olivia can hardly absorb all that she is seeing, it feels almost fairy tale. She stops at the last picture in the row, a huge square canvas that attracts her eye immediately with its life-like surrealism. There stands the artist, in his crumpled overalls and mucky tee shirt, with paintbrush in hand and upturned jars of dozens of more brushes on a table with a palette of colours, standing in his socks, his big training boots on the floor to one side, laces curled. There is a hole in one of the socks and his big toe shows through. He is applying some touches to his picture, the figure of a young girl, leaping naked out of the flat canvas and throwing her arms around his neck, her breasts shimmering with excitement; she is attempting a full-on kiss and his expression is one of surprise. Even before the artist has completed her, her lower body just an outline and a blur without form, his subject has sprung alive. He is mostly sideways on, but you can feel his surprise, his hands thrown aside, and a paint pot is knocked over, just tipping off the table as you catch the moment and wait for the crash and the splash.

It's a painting of a painting, a surrealistic interpretation and Olivia is instantly absorbed by it, hooked on the storyline, just as she always was. It is a wonderful creation of colour and movement, of a beautiful blonde coming to life from the artist's imagination, even before he has finished creating her. Olivia immediately thinks of Lilly Soames as the girl, admiring her model figure, and she imagines the relish with which Hugo allowed himself to be carried away by her pleasing fleshiness. The paint is still wet and shiny.

She says nothing. She is laughing at the humour of it, the cleverness. 'Love it, Hugo, it's wonderful.'

When they are seated back in the lounge close to the burning log fire, with a drink each, Hugo begins to respond to her questioning, as he had promised. 'I inherited a great deal of money when my father died. It was so sudden: he fell ill and within a few days collapsed again with a second heart attack and died. I was deeply affected, I had never seen him unwell before, his great energy, his booming voice, gone, his body wasted. He died before our eyes. It was a shock. And there was this investigation hanging over him, accusing him of corrupting the results of council elections, for his own benefit. Mother thought it was brought on by one of his rivals; she thinks the stress set off his attack. I had to stay on and help. I was grieving inside, seriously. The thought that I was now the head man, as it were, was a heavy burden and I felt I could never master the way my father had conducted business, his bravery, his bombastic style, not to say bullying, that was not me. I was sure others would take advantage, rivals and competitors; so I would end up letting the side down, failing my father's legacy. And the employees, thousands of them. I tried to learn what would be involved, but the responsibilities would have been too much, for someone completely strange to that world.

'The whole family were there, grieving, hysterical; I stayed for a few months, to help my mother. My father had wanted me to run the business after him, he was always trying to get me over so he could teach me the nuts and bolts. But I was ignorant of the whole process, you know, I had never shown an interest, in oil transport and container ships and all that. The will left Loukas with the local building firm, the hotels and shops in Greece, but the main company, Pitsakis Corporation, was left to me. I stayed and worked with the management team and tried to learn, but I felt I could not take on the responsibilities. The Company employed over fifteen hundred people, I could not take that on. Besides, I would have had to live in Athens and give up my London life. It took me three or four months to come to that conclusion, but I backed off.'

Olivia is listening intently and wants to interject with questions but lets Hugo carry on talking. 'Our family solicitor and another director ran the whole

203

thing for a while and then I decided to sell the complete works. Just ahead of the crisis, the credit crunch, thank Goodness. A private equity group and a local Greek company that had been one of my father's competitors. My mother was livid, as you can imagine.'

In the kitchen, a light salad lunch has been laid out with various juices and bottles of wine. 'That'll be Mrs Brigossoulos, Dolce, my housekeeper. She's very good. I simply said I was expecting a visitor around midday. My mother found her for me, she had known her for years, in Greece before she moved. She's estranged from her husband and happy to live here.'

They settle on opposite sides around a mahogany table. 'Anyway, my mother moved away from Greece about six years ago, she said she would rather be here than left behind in Athens to watch her beloved Pitsakis empire sail on without us. Loukas was left with businesses that have struggled with the crisis of the Greek economy; but he has coped, he's not bankrupt. I was lucky; I think I did the right thing, in the end.'

They start to help themselves to cold meat, cheeses and salad, and Hugo pours some wine. 'Anyway, all that was shortly after we broke up, you know, 2006 whatever. I have moved on from then and had the delicious problem of how to manage fifty-four million pounds at my disposal. Or thereabouts.' At this point, Hugo looks vaguely lost, trying to show some humility at his lucky circumstances.

Olivia glances up with a look of puzzlement, her eyes narrowing. 'Broke up, erm, how was that? I seem to remember you just upped and left, without a message or explanation and I never saw you again.' She is holding onto her pleasant face, the smile still in place, but underneath she knows to be careful, to avoid an emotional scene.

'Well, sorry, yes, it was all such a blow and so sudden. I was overwhelmed when I got to Athens, the family were in a hysterical state, my mother especially. I…'

'It's okay, Hugo, I don't actually hold anything against you; not after all this time.'

- But of course I do; my love turned to hatred, remember.

Hugo does not rise to the bait but carries on chatting about his plans and further ideas, as they take their meal slowly. 'I had Jeremy here all morning, actually. You have met him, haven't you? Bright fellow. He looks at all the business aspects, and I do have a number of commitments, but with the hospitalisation, I have been out of action and so much has stopped. So he's working on some rescheduling.'

Hugo pauses, wipes his mouth. Olivia just listens, fascinated. She will have to reach for her notebook and pen soon and start writing.

'We run a gallery in Charlotte Street. We are starting a new art academy, it's a renovation of an old building just off Old Street in Shoreditch. A lot of new young company start-ups there and inspiration all round; the people work off each other, feed ideas off each other. It will have fees, like a small single subject university, starting with thirty to forty students but it could rise up to a hundred a year, we'll see how it develops. We market full reproductions of the most popular paintings, I mean copies of the originals, same size, oils, materials the same, the works. We host exhibitions, and, of course, we are exhibiting our own works, most of which are for sale at vastly inflated prices. I take commissions for even more; mostly organisations, charities, sometimes rich individuals. We also sell postcards, greetings cards and souvenirs, satirical cartoons, reproductions and other tat, you know. And I run a small school, where young artists just learning the trade work for me, helping me with the big pictures, speeding up the process. Now they have been laid off for weeks, they have moved away but Jeremy has started recruiting them again. They had become invaluable. And I paid them, apprenticeship-type money, less than the minimum wage but they were seventeen, eighteen-year-olds, just starting out.'

Olivia, at last, breaks away to recover her bag, to find her notepad. With her wine glass, she settles in the lounge in front of the fire, while Hugo pours coffee for her into a white cup that he places on a low walnut polished table. He asks her more about her biography idea, for which he has his doubts.

'I want to bring all this to life, Hugo. I want to show you off to the public, concentrating on your artistic instincts and genius, your techniques and the contemporary message in your work. I will present the life and times of an artist, with nice glossy illustrations, portraying your relevance to today's society.' She smiles at him, pleased with her oration.

Hugo laughs aloud, his beaming rumble that bounces back at her. 'Oh dear. Sounds ridiculously flattering. Will anybody want to read it?'

'I think so – especially if I include this shooting episode, how you managed to survive this brutal assault to carry on with your painting. It will do wonders for your PR, especially after such tripe has been written in some of the papers about you.'

Hugo stretches his legs and looks tired; a pause develops, while he watches her, liking her new hairstyle, the genteel way of sipping at her coffee cup. He always found her elegant, a model of understated beauty, contrasting with his more grotesque and less sophisticated habits. A lady in control, that was Olivia.

'How have you been getting on, Olivia, over the years? I mean with the crisis and all that, you survived, obviously?'

'I'm fine, thanks, doing all right. The credit crunch was a bad time for the City, for its reputation. A lot of adverse comment, blaming the bankers and finance people for all the money woes, the recession, poor growth, falling wages. But I was in fund management with Emerson's and we survived quite well; thrived with the takeover of Humbles who were struggling, but had a basically sound business, just ran out of cash; they had a decent list of customers and some nice funds. I live in the Barbican now, been there two years.'

'And you're not married to anyone, or betrothed, or anything? One so beautiful as you?' Hugo looks innocently across at her.

'I could ask the same of you, in one so eligible, especially now with tons of money.' Olivia decides impromptu to be bold and playful at the same time.

'How about Lilly Soames, she must be tempting? That's her in that painting, isn't it? And why have you not married Sam by now, you know she's devoted to you?'

Hugo stands up in a huff, looking embarrassed. He turns and wanders over towards the windows, so as not to show his annoyance. 'I did not invite you over here to discuss my love life, thank you. Anyway, you know me, I like my freedom, can't be tied down.' He does a slow circuit back to the fireplace, with his glass of wine refilled. He asks: 'how will you have the time to write this biography if you're working full time in the City?'

'Well, I could do the research and the write-up in my spare time, which I know would be difficult and would take a long time overall. Or I could take some time off work, a three-month sabbatical, or something. They know I write this money column and anyway I might want to leave my present job and take up writing full-time.'

Hugo nods. 'You want some more coffee?'

'No, I'm good, thanks.' She pauses and waits for Hugo to settle again. 'Can we talk about the family, a little? Tell me more about your father and growing up in Greece.'

Hugo hesitates, but after seeing Olivia's sweet expression, he returns his thoughts to his past. 'I had a good family when I was young, my parents were always there. My father was a big man, physically strong and he had a presence, not many people argued against him, he was used to getting his way. I told you about him. As his business grew, he became more involved, more powerful, so I did not see him all that much, I spent more time with my mother. Then I came to England at fifteen, went to a private school in Surrey for a while then art school, you know all that. Greece was a great place to grow up, the climate was always warm, it was an outside life for a boy, lots of adventures in the mountains or out on one of the islands. Even city life in Athens was good, food plentiful, jobs aplenty, good pocket money. And I was fascinated by history, the mythical stories of the Greek Gods and the conquering battles of old. I started doing theatre and drawing quite young. My parents were not posh, but my father, once he was making good money, moved in the richer business circles, mixed with local politicians. Greek business has its own way of working, you have to learn the system; my father was a natural, he knew which palms to grease and how to play his cards. We became gratefully middle-class, well-off, privileged, I suppose; but not showy. My father wanted a second home in England, in London: he saw property as being a good investment. I never realised the extent of his wealth; he never flaunted it, not really.'

'And when you realised you were going to inherit a lot of his money, how did you feel? What were your first thoughts?'

'Am I being interviewed here? Is this you taking on your researcher's role?' Hugo looks perplexed, and then his expression shows his amusement. 'We've agreed, have we?'

Olivia reacts innocently. 'Well, yes, I think so, you want me to do it, admit it. A high-profile book about you would do much to correct the injustice you have suffered. There would be a sympathy vote. You could have copies for sale at every exhibition and in your gallery. It can only do you good, and it may kick-start a new career for me, as well. Ha.' Looking rather smug, Olivia gives him a winning smile.

'All right. The issue of the money. I had no idea what would accrue to me. I had been left about 80% of the company, worth millions of pounds, but then the fees and taxation issues (and I only settled with Her Majesty's Most Gracious Tax Office in 2010). So it was worth about fifty-four million pounds. Staggering. For an artist who uses paint and brushes for a living, this was the most extraordinary thing ever. I mean, I could hardly believe it. And I quickly came to realise that unless I was careful this was going to change my life completely and for the worse. I thought if everybody I worked with or my friends found out about this money, I would not be able to have normal relations with any of them. They would be jealous or wanting a share, they would take advantage, I would not be able to trust anyone. Even if they weren't I would think they were. It would be awful. Not very generous of me, I know, but that's what I felt. I quickly became paranoid. I thought everyone would be asking for handouts and cheating me, it was difficult. I came clean with Jake and Jeremy, and they have been fantastic, helping to develop me as an artist but also in terms of delivery, getting to more people, more quickly and of course making a good deal from our business.

'My mother had already warned me, she knew what it was like to live with wealth and to deal with it. She said she expected me to spend it wisely, not to waste it on trivia and gratuitous pleasures, or my father would be turning in his grave. She said I must use the money to influence and persuade; use your talents, she always said. We helped a local charity set up a foundation in Athens to help with some of the struggle and the homeless, and that has started to go well, it is making a difference. I see that as worthwhile.'

Hugo stops, his throat feeling sore with all the talking and drains his wine glass in one.

'Bernadette was right.' Olivia was remembering Hugo's mother as a quiet but wise old woman. 'I mean the temptation to go and live on your own Greek island and lie in the sun for the rest of your life must have been enormous. I'm sure that's what I would have done.'

'Well, not exactly, but you're right. Ambition, incentive, sure. I have tried to concentrate on helping struggling artists here in London, encouraging more art in schools (and I was doing some teaching) and the new academy will provide a unique degree course for talented students, away from the traditional, away from the establishment. I spent quite a lot on these apartments, but I needed an inspiring setting, and I needed security and the right space, in the heart of London, as you said.' And he laughs his rumbling way.

'Ironic. The shooting in the street, when you have all this security.'

He grimaces with the hurt of it, reflecting. 'I did not want those two women coming here for that reason, that's why I went to their place.'

Olivia, thinking of Nika and Lilly, does not want to argue that point with Hugo at this stage. She moves to another subject. 'Now Hugo, when we were together, I can hardly ever remember you mentioning your brother or sister. Was Loukas not someone you were proud of?' With her feathery brows slightly raised, she glances across at him, to see his indifferent attitude. 'You never spoke about Hebe. Bernadette says she is a very pretty and charming girl?'

'I had not seen Loukas for over a year, but he came to the hospital with mother one time; he flew over when he heard the news, with Hebe. Probably wanted to check whether I was going to succumb and give him some more of my money.'

'Hugo, that sounds really unfair.'

'We never knew each other well. He was five years younger, so we did not grow up together, we were not at school together, and Hebe seemed even more remote. And he was quite different to me, we saw things differently. He lives in Athens with his wife and they have a baby girl, Lala. Hebe lives there as well, close by and she works with him, I think. I'm not sure whether she has a boyfriend, Loukas was a bit vague.'

'So, is Loukas still here in London? I would love to meet with him.'

'Yes, I think he is staying with mother.'

'I visited your mother a few weeks ago; she had seen him, but he was not there. He must have been pretty jealous of you getting the lion's share of your father's will. He must have felt entitled to more.'

'And then the euro crisis and the recession had such a damaging effect on Greek assets, but I could not help that. At the time his inheritance was worth a pretty penny, so he was grateful. I think he has accepted the luck of the draw really.'

'You surprise me; that's not what your mother felt. She thought there was some understandable resentment in Loukas' attitude.'

'I have already given Loukas a help with a sum to tide him over, but as always he will want more. I think you would be best avoiding any talk of the family in this biography of yours,' Hugo decides, knowingly. He considers a further refill of his glass but is feeling some uncertain effects of the wine, so decides to leave it. Olivia is writing some notes.

This time, it is Hugo who changes the subject. 'I have also remained quite close to Gareth Webster, Garry, you remember. He has been tempted into local politics, through some obscure right-wing party, not mainstream. We have often shared late-night arguments; he's quite anti-establishment. With the May election looming, he's been asking for donations for his party, the People's Popular Front. Not much but useful sums.'

'But you're a socialist at heart, or are you moving a bit rightwards, now that you've joined the wealthy elite?'

'Well, my political beliefs have always been a bit mixed, as you know. Not so sure they fit into any pure line for party purposes.' Hugo is still toying with his empty glass and draws a packet of cigarettes out of his top shirt pocket, lights up. 'Do you mind?' He blows smoke up towards the ceiling, preparing for his chance to indulge in socio-political debate, never far from the surface of his mind. 'Of course, I'm a socialist, I'm an artist! What else? I sympathise with the plight of so many people, brought to their knees by an unforgiving capitalist system; the sort that kicks these poor people when they are down. But for the wider good, socialism needs a capitalist edge, to use resources better.

'What I would like to see change is the party system. The single thing that alienates young people mostly from politics is the party system itself – the idea that only one party can speak for them or represent all their views across a spectrum of issues, like housing and defence, is ludicrous. People don't shop at one supermarket anymore, they don't just watch one TV channel all the time, they don't buy a whole album these days but download the tracks they want and compile their own playlist. Why should we be expected to sign up to one and only one political body to express or represent all our views? The sooner single party government becomes history the better.'

Olivia looks doubtful. 'You'll not see that change, not as long as these politicians go on being voted in; they all benefit from the two-party system.' Like Hugo, she loves these sorts of generalised arguments, philosophical appraisals which never lead to any real conclusion, the pragmatic always taking precedence over the theoretical; the *status quo*, in other words, always remaining unchanged. 'Politics is a machine that turns good people and good ideas into bad people with bad ideas. It does attract some people who want to help, but mostly who want to control. Once these people are in control, they use the machine to further their ends. This is not a flaw in the system, Hugo, it's how the system works.'

'I agree, I agree. Governments are overrated and usually do more harm than good. We should not encourage them by voting at all! Anyway, Gareth and I have these sorts of discussions all the time and he takes away some ideas, tries to argue for change. He is trying to get a candidate's nomination for the election with this PPF Party. He wants a London constituency.'

'Oh, well, good for Gareth. That's exciting.'

Hugo takes another tack before Olivia can start off with more questions. 'So what's wrong with working in the City? I mean, you are looking for something else, so…?

'Oh, don't get me started…'

'Or what's right with working in the City, we might ask?' There's a soft squeaking in the leather as Hugo sinks back in his chair, crossing his arms, and fixing Olivia with an eye-contacting stare. 'Or put another way, what is the City for?'

'Thought you'd never ask. A place for young men to get rich; a way of keeping London property prices among the most expensive in the world.' She laughs, triumphantly. 'Or a vehicle for raising capital for companies, promoting innovation and productivity. Sadly, in the last decade, the City has lost touch with all that. It seems to have little ambition left for improving existing companies and their global position; no one is arguing in favour of significant investment at the moment.'

'I'm baffled.'

'We all are, Hugo, believe me, but no one will admit it or jump off the carousel while it's producing the outrageous living standards that they have become used to.'

Hugo has puffed the last of his cigarette and stubbed it out. He leans back, his fingers intertwined behind his head, admiring the simple architrave design running along the edge of the ceiling. 'I like talking to you, Olivia, always did. You're refreshing. It's what we used to do, isn't it?'

'Yes. You like being provocative. But that's good; there is too much complacency about. It would be so good to see more of the young with new ideas being successful in politics and getting their voice heard.' Olivia is smiling. 'I think you are recovering, you seem happier.'

Hugo stands slowly and steadily. 'Yes, I think I am. Let's go for a little walk, along the river, shall we? You can hold my arm and make sure I don't fall over.'

The watery sunshine reflecting with a low trajectory off the river's surface is bright on the eyes. They start their stroll along the towpath away from it into the stiff breeze, like other couples, arm in arm in their winter coats. Hugo seems a bit nervy, looking about him suspiciously, eyeing other pedestrians going about their business. Every now and again they pause to take in the view, to point out something going on in the water or to pick out a new development on the other side that Hugo has not seen before. Their hair is blown about, their cheeks a healthy blush. They talk about Greece and its politics, the street riots, the food huts, the increasing number of homeless sleeping rough.

'The people burn rubbish and wooden doors to keep warm as they cannot afford gas or electricity, so there are constant palls of black smoke over the city every night.' Hugo talks about his visit to Athens just before Christmas: his time spent on the streets, finding inspiration in the desperate folk he met; seeing first-hand the police brutality and bullying.

Hugo's conversation frequently touches on politics, which suits Olivia fine, keeping them away from other potentially sensitive stuff, like catching up on their own personal lives. They lean together against the balustrade along one stretch of the towpath.

'The Labour movement and socialism in the UK,' Hugo intones, 'is a bankrupt ideology. Its welfare promises are economically illiterate, and Labour has no idea how to pay for them. Just like Syriza in Greece: the party of the desperate and dispossessed, they campaign against austerity, like the SNP, conveniently ignoring the fact that historically the UK is running its biggest budget deficit ever. They think they can spend and go on raising taxes forever. Labour's priorities would be to strengthen trade union rights, weaken the power of private companies and increase the size of the State.'

'It's totally delusional,' Olivia agrees, 'to think you can go on living on borrowed money all the time.'

'The Greeks are suffering because of all the cheap loans that came their way ironically from Europe during the good times.'

'It does not bode well. Do you think Loukas will survive? Would he do better selling up and moving here?'

'God, I don't think so. He would not get good prices for his businesses and properties, and the cost of living here would crucify him.'

'Unless you helped.'

'What, more handouts? Like the effing benefits system – reward for doing nothing.'

When they turn to follow the path back to Butlers Wharf, the bright light has faded somewhat and the rest of the afternoon is destined to be grey and overcast once more. Although Olivia has been dreaming of Louise, she wants to get back to the subject of his art. 'You talked about an academy in the early days, didn't you? So to see that idea blossoming must be so pleasing. The idea that you can put something of yourself back into the profession.'

'I've always wanted to explore something different, away from the traditional, away from the establishment. Art is able to teach us the value of things like love, grief, joy and compassion, which are the very points of being alive, aren't they?' Leaning against the white painted rails close to the wharf, they watch rubbish floating in on the tide below; a few boys down on the wet shingle picking up flotsam and throwing it back across the surface. 'Love for humanity, the world we live in, the wider universe and the miracles of science. All these things find expression in art. I want that message to fire up the young, with their new ideas; especially in this more technological age, it's more important than ever.'

The outer glass door to his entrance requires a security number punched into a pad, Olivia notices, and the elevator needs the swipe of a card, which Hugo also uses on his own front door. Once inside his private sanctuary, away from the hubbub of city life but perfectly placed to observe it from the sidelines, Hugo is able to relax again and goes off in search of some tea.

Olivia moves to take more notes, sitting on a stool watching Hugo, the artist, his passion imprinted across his face, in the muscle tension in his neck, in the expressions of his hands. He is bringing a wooden tray to the dining table, something else that Dolce seems to have fixed for them. There are butter-drenched hot teacakes and a choice of pastries. Olivia smiles and thanks him and Dolce graciously.

Daylight is beginning to fade fast when they return to the comfort of the leather seating by the fire. Olivia realises that their time spent together has passed quite comfortably; she is well pleased that they have conversed easily, without embarrassment.

'I still do not quite understand why, when you heard about your father's illness and you had to dash over to Athens to be with him and your mother, which I do quite understand,' Olivia emphasises, pressing the fingertips of each hand against each other, 'why you cut yourself off from London. You left no message and made no effort to contact anybody here, your home.' She pauses a moment as her mouth suddenly feels dry and her voice falters. 'There were no contact numbers. You walked out on me, more to the point, without any explanation.' Olivia's head is tilted to one side, her heartbeat has picked up a touch and she gently bites at a corner of her lower lip. Her eyelids are feeling heavy after the walk, the blustery fresh air, and now the comforting warmth of the fire in Hugo's vast lounge.

At first utterly confident taking her through his life with discussions aplenty about all his activities, Hugo now feels uncertain. Olivia is testing him over old territory, areas he felt she would not want to explore. He is looking for a way out. 'I was stressed out by the circumstances, the anxiety, it was exhausting. My mother was beside herself and she clung to me. It was as if I was trapped, my arms caught by my sides that I could not use my hands, or turn which way, they clung themselves around me, my mother on one side, my father on the other. He was most desperate about the inheritance, his legacy, worried that it would be broken up and so he made me promise that I would preserve it and keep everything running as he had planned it and that I look after my mother at the same time. He wanted to unburden himself of a few secrets, things that were hidden, some unfinished business, things my mother did not know about. Some people to pay off, debts from the past. He gave me a list of things he wanted me to do, it was ridiculous. This man had been like a rock to me, indestructible and then I saw the fear in his eyes. I was shocked and then terrified watching him die. The hysteria and grieving; I was exhausted by the time he actually passed away.' Hugo looks pained by the recollection of those moments, shaking his head, his voice rumbling then going quiet.

Olivia sits opposite him absolutely still, leaning in to pick up everything he says. 'For days I was trapped in the house, I could not think of anything else, do anything else. I thought of you, of course, I did, but I did not know how I would express myself, my anguish.' He looks hangdog into her face, although direct eye contact is avoided.

'Did you not think I might have been able to help you during this time? I could have come over to Athens to help with your mother or just comfort you, did that not occur to you, you could have asked? Would you not have wanted that, Hugo?'

'I... I don't know. Yes, but Jake was controlling things. He insisted I made no direct contact for fear of alerting the police, who were milling around after Dominic's "disappearance". I put messages out for you via Jake and Sam. Sam said she would talk to you, keep you informed.'

'Jake? I saw him once, when he told me not to worry and not to try to contact you. Sam, well, Sam never contacted me at all. She never said anything.'

'I am sorry, Olivia, truly I am.'

'I did not know where you were, exactly – I did not know when you might come back or if you would come back at all. Did you not think I deserved an explanation?' Olivia feels a shudder through her chest, a flutter of nerves. She looks sad, he can see that, her memories returning to haunt her, like his, memories of that terrible time.

'As I said, I thought Sam had reassured you.'

'At the time, I felt abandoned, I thought I had to find my own way. You put up barriers to people: when they get close to you, you walk away, don't want them to cramp your style, wasn't that it? Why is that?'

'No, no, I was frightened to admit to the weakness, the failure.'

'Of your father dying? How was that your weakness?' Her voice rises just a little. 'We all die sometime, Hugo.' Hugo hangs his head, making faces but not finding the right words to appease Olivia, as she picks away at the subject he dreaded. Meanwhile, Olivia is repeating to herself to avoid going too far, too deeply into this scenario. 'Were you surprised when you did return and found that I was not there?' she continues while insisting to herself to go easy.

'I did not come back for some time, three months or so. So much had happened in that time and I just wanted to get back to London and be an artist again, I just wanted to paint.'

'You treated Sam the same. She was terribly worried as well, you seemed to keep her away from you. Why do you do that, prevent people showing compassion or feelings toward you?' Hugo looks almost pleadingly into Olivia's face, wanting her to stop, change the subject.

But she carries on, she cannot help herself: 'I was pregnant, Hugo.'

The space around them is a vacuum, no sound, no movement and Hugo's fixed stare at Olivia slowly turns to surprise. Olivia remains quiet, her lips pursed together in a look of anger or is it her desperate attempt not to let her emotions overcome her, to keep calm? Her eyes are hooded, her glance is downwards at her feet.

'Four weeks after you left,' she whispers, lifting her head, 'I realised I was carrying your child.'

After a moment, Olivia brings her hands up to cover her mouth with her slim fingers, while still staring sadly across into the brown depths of Hugo's eyes, where she had so often before sought a response, a message of love or sympathy. Hugo has stiffened, his mouth opening, alert to the revelation, but unsure how to proceed. His eyes do widen a little and somewhere there, there is sorrow. Suddenly he fears in his belly that Olivia is going to tell him that he has a child somewhere, eight years old and unknown to him. He frowns, half stands up, leans toward Olivia, his hands outstretched, as if he really wants to comfort her; perhaps it is he who seeks the comfort?

'What? Pregnant,' he sounds aghast. 'What happened? You...?'

'I had an abortion, Hugo,' she whispers, not wanting to say the word out loud. 'I went to my mother's for help and stayed with her for a while. When I returned to Theed Street, you were still not there, there were no messages from you; it was as if you had vanished from the face of the earth, or at least from my world. I felt abandoned, so I removed the few things that I had there and left, returned to my flat on my own. I decided I did not want to see you again and proceeded to move on, so you wouldn't know where I was, even if you were interested.'

Hugo is stunned. He drops down again into a crouching position, his bottom on the edge of the sofa, lost for words. There is silence between them; not even the ticking of a clock or the sound of a distant London siren would have been registered in either of their minds, so locked were they into their own thoughts.

'It was horrible. The worst time of my life,' Olivia croaks dryly, 'but that was then, it happened and I am over it now. I don't blame you, Hugo, or hold a grudge or anything.' She slaps her hands together to break the spell and offers a meek smile for Hugo to work on.

Again, Hugo rises, instinctively wanting to console Olivia. He moves to be beside her, touching her outer arm, reaching for her hands, but she shrugs herself away to stand upright a pace or two away from him. 'Oh no, you cannot comfort me now, Hugo, that was nine years ago. It's…it's forgotten.' She rubs her fingers together as if trying to remove some dirt, looking nonchalantly at her coloured nails.

'I am so…sorry, Olivia, I had no idea. That wretched man, Lebelov. He assaulted you. It all happened at the same time. My mind was in turmoil. The call from my mother was the day after that, there was too much to deal with.' Hugo wipes the anxious perspiration off his forehead with tight pressing fingers, threading his eyebrows in painful memory; he wipes his nose. 'I am so sorry, I wish…I wish I had known.' He almost gives out an uncontrollable sob, as he pleads: 'Our baby.'

Olivia whips round to face him, her emotions controlled, in business mode once again. 'Hugo, what happened with Dominic's body?'

He gulps, almost chokes at the directness and swiftness of her thoughts. She wants tangible information; she really can be quite persistent. He walks away, over to the dining table to fetch his tea, his mouth uncomfortably dry. Still with his back towards her, 'I thought you might ask me that.' He moves over towards the uncovered windows, with the grey evening descending over London outside, appropriate to their mood. 'I disposed of it.'

'It was never reported, was it?' Olivia comments. 'I read in the papers some days later about the missing Ukrainian ballet dancer but that he was never found. The ballet production continued without him and I never read anything else. I dared not ask anyone.'

'I did not report it, no. Jake was very good. He came over, helped me think. We sealed him in some black plastic sacks and dumped him in a waste disposal truck. The police were alerted to his disappearance a day later and eventually went round to Theed Street (someone must have told them about the portrait painting), well after I had left, after you had left; someone showed them in and they looked around. I was interviewed about him when I returned to London, which was months later, but it was just some cursory questions and the police had no idea where he might be. They never found the body. That was the end of it. I have tried not to think about him since. The guilt and the confusion was another terrible burden, but I have got over it. Hopefully, you can too, and we can forget about him. His death was not our fault, he was assaulting you.'

'Yes. I know. I had my own guilt to live through.'

Another unwanted thought pushed its way to the top of Hugo's brain. 'Are you sure it was…?

'It was your baby, Hugo, yes. I was already six weeks. Dominic never, you know, in his assault, you interrupted him in time. For which I am eternally grateful.'

'Gosh, don't be silly, I…'

And at that precise moment, as if on cue, a message pings on Hugo's mobile, which has been lying dormant on the dining table, and he wanders over to it. Tapping in his passcode he recognises Sam's name and reads the message.

"We have Sam. Her life is in danger. We need to do a deal. If you mess up she's fucked, kaput. Say nothing. Contact the police and she's dead. Will be in touch."

Hugo's heart misses a beat but he manages not to wince or show any facial signs of panic, convinced it must be a hoax or a joke, and not wanting Olivia to see. He steadies himself with a hand gripping the back of a chair and shakes his head at the phone. He assembles a smile, as if to say that it was nothing, and concentrates on Olivia again. 'It was a ghastly episode, but we could not afford to be embroiled in a police investigation. He was dead, an accident, there was nothing to be gained by calling the police and all that. Jake reassured me and after I had thought about it a while, I didn't panic, it was a deliberate decision.' Hugo recalls having to dislocate Dominic's joints using his full crushing weight in order to stuff the body into a small enough package, inside three plastic bags, each taped tightly to prevent unravelling. 'We hauled him out to the van and in the early hours drove to that huge Asda store off the Old Kent Road, with disposable bins around their delivery backyard, and dumped the body in the bottom of a large wheelie bin – I made sure it was covered up. Nobody saw us and nothing was said about it since.' Hugo suddenly looks tired, older than before, as he has struggled with his recollections of that awful night.

Olivia recalls that night as well, often in horrible detail, sometimes in her dreams or in uncontrollable waking moments: Dominic trying to force himself on her from behind in her sleep; Hugo shouting and rushing at him, throwing him out; the fall down the stairs and that awful cracking sound of his broken neck, Hugo throwing his clothes down after him. Seeing the destroyed body in a heap at the bottom, she was distraught and felt hysterical, her breathing laboured. She returned to the bedroom to stare and shiver into the night for hours; sometime later to fall asleep in Hugo's large protective arms. She remembers thinking then that she loved Hugo and that she would gladly do anything for him, her hero. Which included lying to the police, if necessary. But by the morning everything had all been cleared up, sorted, the incident forgotten and not spoken of again. Hugo disappeared the next day, Jake came by sometime later to advise her to leave and that Hugo had had to rush off to his family in Greece, he did not know when he would be back. She never encountered the police. Nor did she ever suspect that Jake Preston had been involved in directly helping Hugo clear up the mess.

Hugo must have risen in the small hours before dawn, to do what he had to do and she did not want to think about it. She returned to her flat, she took a few days off work pleading sickness, to recover and recompose herself before returning as if nothing had happened. And she did not see Hugo again.

Not until recently, when she encountered his wounded body in intensive care shortly after his shooting by the police in Earl's Court nine years on.

Hugo and Olivia's guilty secret had been preserved and no one the wiser. Except Jake Preston knew as well. It was Hugo's argument that he received his mother's call about his dying father the very next morning, almost as he dumped the dead Lebelov in the chosen waste skip. He left London for Athens almost immediately, to become embroiled in his family's affairs and his father's illness and ultimate death; which worked as a useful distraction from Dominic's accident, but obviously was not what he would have wanted; and so he completely forgot all about Olivia, because of the weight of his intense family responsibilities hanging over him.

- Do I buy that? I presume I have to.

'I'll come with you, I have some chores.' Hugo has donned a tough pair of walking boots and a leather winter coat, battered and hard-wearing. He accompanies Olivia in the descent to the underground carpark, where Jayden is waiting, the car ticking over and warm inside. They drive north over the Thames, mixing with the rush-hour chaos in the descending gloom of the evening; comfortably conversing in the back of the car, watching the bustle of city life under sparkling street lights carrying on as always. Olivia thanks Hugo for his time and is dropped off along Beech Street.

They share a handshake. 'Keep in touch, Olivia. I'll be waiting for your next call. Take care.'

With the door closed and locked and the car moving off from the curb, Hugo settles back and retrieves Sam's text message on his mobile, rereading it with a growing sense of alarm, feeling desperate; and then baffled. He has tried three times this week to reach Sam by phone to discuss projects and generally catch up as promised, nothing urgent, but each time there had been no answer, which was unusual for her, not even switched to messaging. He tries her number again.

'Jayden. Take me to Muswell Hill, Sam's place.'

3

Weekend, March 6–8, 2015

Friday

The last two days have been fraught for Hugo, not to be alarmist about it; his painting routine quite disturbed by worry and distraction. Sam's flat had been locked and quiet when he arrived Wednesday, all appearing to be in order, no one answering his persistent ringing of the bell, and nothing untoward that he could see when he peered through the ground floor window into her front room. A long-standing elderly neighbour opposite said he had spotted a stranger in a hoodie hanging about along the street last week, and early on Monday, he heard Sam close her front door as usual when she went to work, but then there had been some unfamiliar male voices in the hallway and some scuffling, the outer front door knocking, but there was nobody there when he looked and Sam's door was closed. And the next day, he and his wife were sure they saw the same lad leaving the block with a bulky backpack, still with his hoodie up; said he looked gangly and seemed early twenties. Hugo had looked for any marks or signs, and scoured the pathways outside, finding a dark green leather ladies glove discarded some way up the street in the gutter, rain-soaked and muddied, and was not sure whether it was Sam's or not, but had taken it with him anyway. He also noted her blue Renault parked outside, undisturbed.

That threatening telephone message keeps coming up in his mind: was that a hoax or a joke? Was Sam genuinely in trouble? The message had come from Sam's phone, someone using her phone; or forcing her to send the message. What was he supposed to do? He has been trying to immerse himself in his painting, selecting the Remembrance sequence as his top priority to concentrate on, while waiting for events to develop. He thinks he should phone Jake, but he would probably argue for contacting the police. Following their deep conversation on Wednesday, his thoughts keep coming back to poor Olivia and the details of her revelation. Pregnant with his child and having an abortion; and him knowing nothing about it. He feels such an idiot; so cruel of him to have ignored her, but he was overwhelmed at the time – the assault by Dominic and the horrible accident, his father's dramatic illness.

It seems Sam failed to reassure Olivia with any of Hugo's messages. Why had she let him down? Jealousy? That's not like her. Olivia abandoned their love nest while he was away; she had to deal with her problems alone. He understands that now and is left wondering where he fitted in, in her scheme of things; having let nine years pass since then without any contact, she had clearly decided that he did not fit in anymore. Fair enough. But Hugo retains a soft spot for Olivia, so good looking, poised, knowledgeable and intelligent, able to argue politics with him. His earlier passion for her was genuine. He presumes she has a new set of friends, boyfriends; although not yet fixed up, he had dared not ask any more.

Alternating with Olivia on his mind is Lilly. He can hear her childish laughter, and a physical urge keeps catching him, as he works on his canvases, bubbling up inside, her agile body tempting him away, teasing him, playing her games, lying across a rumpled bed with her hair trailing over her face. She is scatter-brained and a bit young for him though, and she does not understand the driving forces and emotions involved in his art. He knows in his heart that she will tire of him soon and be off with someone more frivolous her own age.

And what about Samantha, good, reliable and beautiful Sam. What had Olivia said to him? He should settle down and marry her, she was in love with him and was devoted to him. He knows it, of course he does, but he hesitates, repeatedly, out of fear of capture, of losing his freedom to live as he wants. Selfish of him. But maybe Olivia is right: now is the time for him to grow up and take on some responsibility, to share his life meaningfully with someone else.

Except...

Another message pings in on his phone, from Sam's phone. He opens it clumsily with trepidation.

"Watch this – we have Sam. Do exactly as what I say understood. Or she gets it, across the throat. Wait for next message."

Hugo presses the forward arrow and a short video plays, with a soundtrack of muffled voices: a woman is being wrestled from behind, and forced to look at the camera, a man's muscly arm around her forehead. It is impossible to see who the man is, but the woman is definitely Sam, in a white blouse and she looks scared, she is crying. A steel knife is pressed aggressively under her jaw, creasing the skin. A fresh line of blood appears at its edge. Her voice is crying, 'Stop, stop. I'll do what you want. Please.' And then someone else nudges her, to prompt her. 'They want money, for my release or they will kill me.' She starts to whimper, as the knife cuts her skin and obviously hurts: 'They will kill me. They want money! And no police!' she shouts. Then the knife is lowered and the video stops, leaving a blurred orange-tinted image of Sam with her distorted face looking at the camera, her wild hair a mess.

The whole thing only lasts a few seconds. Hugo plays it again. It looks authentic, the blood looks real. Poor Sam. She is kidnapped, for a ransom. But who the hell would do such a thing? Not very articulate, the message or just made up like that.

All he can do is wait for further messages.

***

Midway through Friday morning in the office, and Olivia is in a rush to complete some jobs before the weekend, including her monthly column, which has to be submitted on Monday. This one is about the different approaches to the country's finances of the main political parties, as a *resume* before the May General Election. Her theme is "chaos versus competency", as the choice for the public between Labour and Conservative regarding their handling of the economy. Maybe an allegory of her own life, she ponders.

Her thoughts are interrupted by a message phoned through to her desk from reception downstairs to say that a young man wanted to see her and that he had some information for her that she would find most interesting; would she be able to come down to meet him.

Reluctantly she agrees and as she walks towards reception over the shiny marble floor of the lobby, she recognises the student with the red beard who had stopped her a few weeks ago, after one of her seminars. He had suggested a coffee somewhere, so they could discuss something or other, but she had been rather dismissive.

He steps forward with an awkward smile, as she reaches the security barrier. He offers a cold hand in a formal introduction. 'I am Edward Voight. I introduced myself to you a little while ago. I have something in my possession you should see. You will be interested, I think.'

'How do you do, Edward?' Curious and sceptical, Olivia retracts her hand, finding his accent jarring. 'Yes, I remember.' She has her handbag with her, but not her coat, although the coffee shop Edward points to this time is across the courtyard, a mere twenty yards away, and she agrees to walk over with him. He seems such an earnest fellow, a little shy in his appearance, but what did she have to lose? She takes a seat away from the door and Edward sits down opposite her, making no effort to join the queue to order any coffees.

They adjust their positions. Edward has an A3 size cardboard envelope under his arm. He lifts his unsmiling face and quietly accuses her: 'You don't remember me, do you, Olivia?'

She holds everything still, hands on the edge of the table, knees comfortably together, her gaze fixed on his thin mouth. She should be recognising him but is having difficulty.

'In the studios at Theed Street with Hugo Pitsakis. And Dominic Lebelov? You remember the Ukrainian ballet dancer, surely?'

A sudden shockwave of repulsion at the mention of the name sweeps up from Olivia's bowels. She must have sensed danger and was intuitively prepared and manages to stare him out, without any telltale hesitation. Her eyes are tracing the patterns of shadows across his face, under his nose; he looks so young under the thick hair of his beard, but once she strips that away, her recall instantly recognises the fresh faced teenager who had shared much time with the Ukrainian dancer, watching his every movement; and photographing him endlessly, wanting to record his life and activities whilst staying in London. She remembers a shy pretty boy called Eddy always lurking around the periphery of the group, saying little, fixated on but largely ignored by Dominic.

Edward clears the table with a brush of his arm, flicking some crumbs and sugar crystals away with the back of his fingers. He has adopted a grim rather embarrassed expression as he reaches into his envelope and retrieves a buff folder that he lays on the envelope in front of him. He opens the folder with meticulous movements and turns over a black-and-white photograph, an enlargement ten by twelve inches, rotating it around the right way to show Olivia as he lays it flat. 'I wanted to show you these pictures.'

He watches intently for Olivia's facial reaction as she glances nonchalantly down at the picture. It looks vaguely familiar: a man lying in a crumpled heap, filling most of the picture, on a concrete floor, a few black metal steps behind. He has no clothes on and appears lifeless, legs uncomfortably twisted under the body. Olivia leans forwards slightly as if she needs a closer look, and curious creases develop over the bridge of her nose as a questioning look forms across her pretty face. Edward pulls out a second photograph from under the first, before she can say anything, and turns it over, laying it flat on top. A close-up of the face of the naked man on the floor, his eyes open, staring into the camera. Black-and-white, long-focussed lens, good technique, sharp shadows, extra flash, she would imagine. Olivia has to exhale a snort of breath through her nostrils, as she has been unconsciously holding hers for some time, and brings a hand up to her mouth, wiping thumb and forefinger along her tautened lower lip, in a pensive sort of way, somehow buying her time. She notices the printed information at the bottom right-hand corner of the picture: 03:14 25-04-2006. Her brows relax and the skin reclaims its smooth outline once again. Her eyes fix for an instant onto Edward's cold expectant stare, with an immediate question.

'Why would I have any interest in these pictures? Who is this?'

'You know. You were there, at the top of the stairs.' Edward's voice with its accentuated Eastern accent is quiet, cajoling. Olivia wants to close the folder, hide the images, and walk away, pretending she has not seen them. She wants to smack his cocky little cheek.

'They mean nothing to me, Edward,' she insists, shaking her head slightly. She coolly makes a move to leave. 'So, if you'll excuse me, I have rather a lot of work on at the moment.' She stands up and turns away, managing a dignified departure through the thin cluster of customers around the doorway, and then across the windy forecourt to her building, without looking back and without giving away any indication of the trembling in her legs.

***

At the sports centre that evening, Olivia is involved in a tough foil match with a young opponent whose speed of foot is testing her skills to the full. The game is keenly played out by both competitors and looks like going into a fifth bout. Olivia's right arm is aching and her legs are tiring but she is aware of Louise watching from the small crowd at the side and finds some inspiration. A final burst of energy on her part gives her the upper hand and she wins out three bouts to one eventually. They salute each other, remove their helmets, their faces and hair wet with perspiration, and they shake hands kindly.

Dried and dressed Olivia walks comfortably with Louise under the street lights of Finsbury Park Road towards the Barbican. They kiss discreetly in the shadows of a deserted doorway before Louise reluctantly has to catch a passing black cab.

In the quietness of her own apartment, feeling some comfort in the familiarity of her surroundings, her pictures, her books, her clothes, and a bottle of wine to hand, Olivia has time to reflect on her meeting with Edward and his extraordinary black-and-white photographs, which quite disturbed her equilibrium all afternoon. What could he possibly do with them? Nobody would be interested, surely, not after all this time; the incident was forgotten. And those pictures could have been taken anywhere, there was no obvious link with Hugo's studios at Theed Street, although the date obviously coincides with Dominic's accident.

- Of course, we had no choice, Hugo had to dispose of him. It was not his fault, it was a complete accident; Dominic was crazy, self-obsessed and thoughtless.

She perches on the soft stool in front of her full-length mirror, creaming her face and then combs through her hair, while attempting reassurance. He will demand money, to stop him showing the pictures to the police. The bastard. Why has he waited all this time?

- Oh, Louise. You would not believe this. What to do?

While watching a television programme later about the natural world, cuddly looking lions in Africa, she thinks lovingly of Louise.

- Oh, am I smitten? How do I separate lust from deeper feelings of love? I have never had these feelings before.

She is continually amazed at how she and Louise gain so much pleasure from their mutual activities. This had never happened for her with men. Men are so self-centred, their physical side so dominant, their pleasure so wrapped up in achieving their climax, no matter what; do they ever have concerns for the pleasure of their female partners? Women on the other hand show kindness and thoughtfulness, understanding each other's sensitivities and needs. There is something so much more sympathetic about two women pleasuring themselves together; there is none of that brutal, rapid, "let's get it over" approach. Her whole relationship with Louise has been thoughtful and companionable. Should it continue?

Not for the first time, Olivia regrets that she has no sister to confide in or a really close friend to share some of her thoughts. Maybe she should give Beverly a ring, she would understand. She could ask about *her* new relationship, see how that was getting along. She should arrange to meet up with her, in a bar one evening and after a couple of wines, she would have the confidence to open up about her newfound lesbian tendencies and the love of her life, a beautiful, sexy Chinese Hong Kong teacher.

- Oh God, do I have the courage?

Should she tell Hugo about Edward? And how?

***

Saturday

Hugo wakes early, suddenly opening his eyes and looking up at the ceiling, aware of the wall-clock only showing just passed five o'clock. He reaches over to the bedside to check his mobile for more messages: nothing. He relieves himself in the toilet and then flops back into the middle of his bed face down, dozing for a little while longer.

With a pale dawn now spreading over the Canary Wharf buildings, he stares out over the misty river with a mug of tea in hand in the open doorway of his French windows, catching the blustery wind to wake him, noticing how wet the terrace is. Suddenly his mobile pings. Jumping out of his reverie, he grabs at it in his dressing gown pocket. Another message, again apparently from Sam:

> *"Sam is alive – I will cut her pretty throat if you mess up. I want*
> *two million pounds cash transfer to internet bank, details to follow.*
> *I give you deadline: 6 pm Tuesday, March 10. Wait for next call,*
> *Remember – no police or she is dead."*

My God, what is this? Who the devil is this? Hugo composes an immediate reply on his phone, an indignant text demanding to know who is sending these stupid messages and to return Sam to her home immediately; and presses "send".

For the next half-hour, he paces his apartment rooms, from studio to lounge, out onto the cold terrace and back to the kitchen, in a state of desperation and foreboding. Two million quid! He wants to talk to Jake, or Garry, or Jeremy, but thinks he will sound foolish, and in a moment of appalling paranoia, he genuinely worries about whom he can trust. Although these bubbles of doubt about his three most loyal friends bring almost an equal sense of disgust within himself, they seem so ridiculous. After a while, he decides there is only one other person he can trust, explicitly.

'Sam has been kidnapped, Olivia,' he bursts out almost before she has answered. 'I have had messages on my phone – someone wants a ransom paid into a bank, two million pounds, have you ever heard anything so ridiculous?' His voice is beginning to sound hysterical.

'Calm down, Hugo. Take it slowly.'

'I have a deadline, Olivia: 6 pm Tuesday to make this payment or they will cut Sam's throat. That's what the messages say. Three days to decide. I don't know who it is. It's a nightmare. Poor Sam.'

'How do you know Sam has been kidnapped?'

'They sent a video: I've seen her, being manhandled by some strong arm. I went round to her flat on Wednesday, there was no one there and she was not answering her phone for days and now these messages, sent from her phone to me. The last message was a few minutes ago – I have to wait to hear but they want a deal, an exchange for Sam for two million. She has obviously been snatched, kidnapped. I cannot contact the police.'

'Why not? They know how to deal with this sort of thing. Surely.' Olivia is trying to think clearly but is feeling too sluggish so early on a Saturday morning; and hopeless at suggesting anything useful, especially when she has been wrestling with her own "Edward" problem all night.

'The message said it would put her life in danger. The man was holding a big carving knife.'

'Oh, my God. Hugo, shall I come over?'

***

This time Olivia had rung for a cab, and Hugo had buzzed her in over the intercom. Dolce has made up the fire and she is preparing some breakfast for them. They are huddled together on the sofas, downhearted by the turn of events, weighed down by threats and fears. Olivia, in sensible trousers and a thick jumper, studies the messages and video on Hugo's phone. They keep asking who would want to do such a thing. For a while, Olivia forgets about Edward and his photographs, but then, just as she is tempted to tell Hugo, she feels she cannot burden him with this as well, not at least until she knows what the bugger wants.

'Whatever is poor Sam going through, what might she be thinking?' Hugo muses angrily.

'Did you notice anything at all while at Sam's flat?' Olivia is looking at Hugo's troubled unshaven face with some attention.

'Nothing really, I didn't go inside. Found this in the gutter outside, but I don't know whether it's hers.' He holds the dried-out dirty leather glove from his pocket and shows Olivia. 'Spoke to her neighbours, who said they hadn't seen Sam for over a week; that last Monday they heard some thudding and men's voices but there was nobody there when they looked – might have been from outside. There was no break-in or anything. Her car was parked outside, but she usually commutes by train.'

'Do you not have a key to her flat?'

'No. Why, should I have?'

'Hugo, I don't know. Should we not tell the police? They will be able to abstract more clues from these messages or from the flat than we could, surely?'

'You can see the message, Olly. It would be a horrible risk, Samantha's at the end of this.'

'We think, we don't know for sure. This video is grainy and blurred, terrible lighting, it might be someone else.' She knows in her heart it is Sam, the auburn hair, the face, that mouth.

'You mean a prank? No. That doesn't make sense. Sam has disappeared, and this is why,' emphasises Hugo tapping the little screen of his phone.

'Who would have use of Sam's phone? Sam is being forced by someone who knows about you. Could this be Nika, for example?'

'It's a man's arm in the picture.'

Olivia snorts. 'So, she has some unpleasant man friends, they are working together. She gets to realise you have a lot of money, and they decide they want some of it. She's from a dreadful background, right?'

'Nika would not be so vindictive; Lilly would never go along with that. She and I have been…close, you know, she likes me, I think.' Hugo looks genuinely confused and hurt.

'Who, Nika or Lilly?'

'Both of them, we came to trust each other,' Hugo stammers rather indignantly.

'But Nika under duress, from a tough boyfriend from Croatia or wherever?' Olivia stops, stares straight into Hugo's fearful eyes. 'Lilly has been here, hasn't she, in this apartment. She must have said something; she would have been impressed and said how well-off you were, living in luxury. They know about Sam, she said she had met them once or twice.'

'Not really, don't think so.' Hugo appreciates Olivia's growing strength and coolness under duress, rather like Jake, he thinks, whereas he feels he is floundering, losing control. His artistic urges are calling him back to his canvases to become absorbed once again into a make-believe story he can be in charge of. 'I need a drink.' And with a shrug, Hugo goes off to fetch two cool bottles of beer. 'Want one?'

'Er, bit early for me. There's coffee next door, shouldn't we eat something?' In the kitchen, she continues with her thought process. 'What about other personal enemies, Hugo? I don't know: business people, other artists? I mean, they can be pretty unpredictable, can't they? Someone realises you have lots of money. Who could pull this off, who would want to?' She pours coffee, strong and black. 'Family, jealous relatives? What about Loukas?'

'You serious? My own brother?'

'You said yourself he was pretty upset with the inheritance from your father, that he was jealous of you. Bernadette also confirmed his upset. He knows Sam, does he know where she lives?'

'You don't like him, do you?'

'I've never met him, do you mind!' Olivia is quick to reply, pulling a face at Hugo. 'I'm just trying to cover all possibilities.'

'Actually, my mother told me recently that Loukas is not my full brother, but a half-brother. We have the same mother, but Loukas is from another liaison, another father. I didn't know for such a long time, although I suspected something was a little different about him.'

Olivia is alerted. 'That's interesting. What about Hebe?'

'No, she is my sister, same mother and father.'

'Does he know? Loukas?'

'No, don't think so.'

'It's got to be some jealousy about the inheritance money? Loukas has to be the most likely, especially after what you have just said. Has he asked for money before?'

'Yes, many times. And I have given him a bundle on one occasion, that was last summer, some time. Three hundred thousand euros, to be exact. But he keeps asking for more, calls me names, blames me for his troubles! But the wishes of my father were clear, he had his chances with the businesses in Greece, all reasonably successful concerns and worth a deal of money. Why should I give him special treatment, just because it did not go so well for him, especially if he has been less than competent with his assets?'

'Well, he is half-related to you, so for your mother's sake,' Olivia rebukes. 'And also, you have been lucky and have a lot of spare cash; he has been unlucky, whatever you say about Greece, and he has less money – you can see the resentment if you refuse to help him with anything.' Olivia is surprised that Hugo has not shown a little more compassion, even for Hebe's sake. 'We ought to go and talk to him, you know. Talk reason with him. Offer him some monetary help as a solution.'

'What, a couple of million quid, it's outrageous?'

'You mean Sam is not worth two million pounds?' Olivia smirks but then immediately regrets her stab of sarcasm, knowing that Hugo's feelings will be hurt. After a few more moments of thought, sipping at her coffee, she continues: 'Would he do it, though? Hurt Sam? Surely not. And he knows how much you're worth, right? He would ask for more than two million, I mean, if he was going to do it at all?'

'Would he, I don't know. I don't believe this is Loukas. He is in town, we could go see him. I could ring him.'

'Let's just think. Are there any other dark relatives on your father's side who might feel they deserved some of his benevolence? Or hard-done-by employees, anybody having a grudge against your father?'

'Dozens, I imagine, but they've left it a bit late, haven't they?'

They both stare at the spread of toast and fruit and cereals laid out over the table but show little interest. Olivia continues in the same vain: 'Jake? He seemed a little unsettled when I spoke to him, perhaps frustrated that you had not done enough for him? His solicitor, he seemed to know about all the deals? Can he be trusted? What was his name?'

'Grout, Joe Grout. I've never thought about this, in this sort of way.'

'Jeremy, he knows your business. He knows Sam, he wouldn't want to harm her, would he? Anyway, he doesn't need the money and likewise would ask for much more than two million if it was him.'

Hugo is indignant and stands up for his friends. 'Look, Jake and Jeremy are friends and do well from the business, there is no way they would involve themselves in anything like this.' He reaches for a slice of bare toast and chews a corner off.

Olivia is rubbing a finger along her lower lip, in two minds about her next candidate for their inquiry. 'What about friends of Dominic, anybody felt that you were responsible or knew about it? Could it be related somehow?'

'I don't see how, there was nothing about him in the papers, he was a foreign visitor who disappeared without trace nine years ago. There was no obvious link with me, other than the commissions. There cannot be anyone who suspects I was involved after all this time. That would not make sense.'

Olivia is thinking directly of Edward, the shy obsessive teenager, sneaking around the downstairs studio in the dark, with his bloody camera and his telephoto lens, using a flash to snap his incriminating pictures, before slipping away unnoticed, and obviously before Jake arrived to help Hugo dispose of the body. Or had he in fact watched from a hiding place Hugo and Jake packing the body into black plastic bags before carrying it out to the van? Does Edward know even more about that night than he let on? She must definitely tell Hugo all about it but she was unsure whether at this moment it was relevant to the Sam kidnapping and it would serve only to distract and frighten Hugo even more when they both needed cool heads.

'What about the police? Revenge for the bad publicity and the compensation? You made them look bad – Inspector Mike Sanger orders the kidnapping of Samantha Little.' She snorts dismissively. 'No, that's ridiculous. Maybe he fancies her.'

'Jolly risky way to go about it. Would a policeman do that for the money? In England? Perhaps in Rio de Janeiro or Caracas. No, I don't buy that.'

'Garry or one of those political people of yours – again jealousy or something?'

'I can't see it, I mean we have heated debates, but that would be outrageous.'

Olivia walks off to the lounge, stretching her stiff limbs and aching back. 'I need the toilet.'

When she returns to the lounge, Hugo is pacing around. 'We need an action plan – you go talk to Lilly and Nika, if there's a police watch, they don't know you. Then we can both go talk to Loukas. I need to wait for the next message – I will have to comply. I need to talk to my bank, you cannot just transfer that sort of money in a few days. Whoever this is, they must have been watching me and Sam. Do you think they would be here, or at the studios? Am I being watched now, do you think?'

'Hugo, don't panic. We need to think this through logically.'

'I'm sure I noticed someone yesterday; I walked out to the deli for some milk and stuff, there was someone watching Butlers in Shad Thames, he was leaning against a wall a block away, hooded, I thought nothing of it, but he was there also when I came back. And I think I've seen him before, when Garry and I walked the patch, last week. Perhaps, Olly, you could wander down there and see if he is still there. They will not know you, so would not suspect you. You could walk the towpath side and then the Shad Thames side. If we find someone we would need to follow them and see where they went, who they reported to.'

'Hugo, we are not detectives. They're obviously nasty pieces of work, so you would be running a real risk of danger to yourself, which would not help poor Sam.'

Hugo moves towards the windows at the front and slides one of them sideways. The curtains flutter with the incoming breeze and he steps outside, moving with his back close to the building before stepping boldly towards the nearest railing. The wind is cold and tossing him about. He looks back at the window and imagines Olivia inside watching him but he cannot see her through the reflections of the glass. Then he leans gingerly over the front, pressing a hip against the metal rail for support, a small angle at a time, until he gets a view down to the quiet towpath and the restaurant awnings six floors below. The river is a dull grey sliding by serpent-like and the usual water traffic is seen at work. A couple of boys in anoraks are meandering over the wet stone and shingle, balancing along wooden beams at the water's edge, and Hugo can hear them calling to one another. Two men in business suits appear in conversation walking firmly against the wind towards the Bridge, their slicked hair ruffled. A jogger in the distance is slowly approaching. He sees nobody suspicious.

He returns to the lounge, closing the door behind him. 'It's perishing cold out there. Nothing. I am going to have a look from the back.' Rubbing his cold hands together, he goes out into the corridor and through a spare bedroom and then steps through another sliding glass door onto the rear terracing. Most of his penthouse neighbours have planted various bushes and miniature evergreens to shape into points or spirals or box hedges along their terrace space creating small gardens. Hugo's is confined to one large terracotta pot filled with yucca and trailing ivy in the corner. Cautiously leaning forwards over the parapet, he surveys the pedestrianised walkway below, with its cobbled and paved patterns and quaint doorways. There are iron walkways with latticed sides bridging the gap across to the buildings opposite, at various levels, not in use now, relics from the last century when the two sides were storage warehouses for tea and spices brought from the river barges, and workers could carry their sacks from one side to the other without being snared up in the passing ground level traffic. A few innocent looking people are passing back and forth, some shoppers, some workers, wandering tourists impressed with the clever gentrification of these historic wharfs. Hugo immediately spots the hooded figure he has seen before leaning with one leg bent against the building opposite, by the blue doors of a delicatessen. He is carrying a folded newspaper under his arm and looks to be studying a small A-Z map, as he glances up and down the street without conviction.

Hugo pulls back and calls to Olivia inside with an urgent whisper. She comes through, her soft soles quiet on the wooden floor, and steps close past him onto the balcony outside. With the wind howling haphazardly, she grips onto his arm. He stabs a pointed finger downwards over the edge and with raised eyebrows and pursed lips indicate there is someone for her to watch. She is not good with heights and with a look of terror leans stiffly a little way over the edge of the parapet; Hugo hangs firmly onto her arm until she has a view of the narrow streetway below. She scans the pavement quickly and sees the hooded man Hugo is interested in, ambling aimlessly, turning at the far end fifty yards away to retrace his steps. She catches little detail of his lanky appearance, possibly dark hair. They are both watching now, standing close together, tense and still.

They happily regain the warmth of the bedroom, Hugo sliding the door closed. Olivia uses both hands to smooth her hair back in place, preserving the parting. Hugo steps forward casually and holds both her arms and squeezes her gratefully. 'Thank you, for being here. For helping.' Her eyes open wide in mild surprise as she tilts her head back to look at him and does nothing to prevent him kissing her. Her simple pout accepts the pressure of his wide lips, as she watches his eyelids droop to enjoy the *frisson* of the moment. She lets it pass and pushes him away gently. 'Come on, we must formulate a plan.'

Hugo in his heavy wool coat leads the way out onto Shad, Olivia hanging back, watching from a vantage point in the doorway, three steps up from street level. Hugo is to stroll past the hooded youth, spotted with his head down in his newspaper, leaning in an arched entrance of the Valentina, and head west along the narrow lane towards Tower Bridge. If hoodie starts to follow Hugo, she will follow on behind him and then they will know. They might then accost this youth to find out more, although the thought that he might be armed with a knife or something slightly worries them.

She can see that he's a scrawny bloke in his twenties, with eyes close together and poor skin, wearing a brown leather jacket over his woollen hoodie. He looks up as Hugo passes close by, and then casually returns his attention to his paper. After a slight hesitation, he pushes himself off the wall and tucks the paper under his arm, stuffing both his fists into his jacket pockets as he moves into line twenty paces behind Hugo.

Olivia steps out from the porch, watching the two men walking away from her, before she, in turn, skips along in her soft shoes quietly a dozen paces behind. The hoodie boy's jeans are baggy over a flat bottom, the cuffs scraping over the paving stones with each long stride. She waits till they are past the heavy black gates of the porter's lodge alley and the Starbuck's coffee shop, with the stone archways and metal structure of Tower Bridge looming ahead of them, before she moves up just behind the youth and deliberately stretches a foot forward to plant her heel next to his rear foot, turning her toes across his path, tripping him. His trailing foot knocks across the back of his other ankle and he stumbles forward, trying to thrust his arms out to cushion the fall. Olivia walks into him, knocking her knee against his thigh and down he goes, with a groan, landing on a knee, then a shoulder as he twists before his head thumps sideways onto the hard paving stones. He grazes the one hand that he manages to get out of his pocket in time, and feels the hurt. And to add to his discomfort, the idiot woman rushing into him from behind and calling sorry at the same time has collapsed onto him, pinning him to the ground with a sharp stab of her knee into his chest. Then she thrusts the clasp edge of her clutch bag under his chin and her flushed face lowers down to his level, close to the side of his head. 'I have a sharp knife under your chin, so stop wriggling and I won't cut your throat open,' she murmurs with wild conviction.

Hugo has heard the commotion and has darted back to sit on the man's stomach, while Olivia with a vicious accent to her voice attempts to extract information from this dunderhead youth with his acned complexion.

'Who the fuck are you and why are you following Mr Pitsakis, Dickhead? Answer me now or my friend here will twist your balls off and stuff them in your mouth.' With that and with a certain relish, Hugo makes a grab at the man's crotch, and finding the soft contents between his legs, he starts to squeeze. The passers-by are either passing-by pretending not to have noticed the struggling threesome on the pavement in the middle of a Saturday morning, or are staring with astonishment completely transfixed by the odd sight of such behaviour.

'I will only ask you once more – who are you and why are you following Mr Pitsakis?'

Hugo applies more pressure and the poor boy with an ugly grimace and an open mouth half-screams, 'Okay, okay. I'm Jim. I'm nobody. Just doing what I'm told.'

'Who by?'

'Tommy, me dad. But he don't tell me nothing.'

'Where is he, where are you meeting him?'

'I report on the phone. He has a house on the Dogs.'

'Show me, your phone.' And the pressure on Jim is relaxed somewhat to allow him to move, and the passing pedestrians think that the poor lad is getting help after his fall. Olivia pulls the hoodie away from his ugly face to see him better, as he finds his mobile inside the leather jacket. 'Show me the number,' Olivia demands.

Jim swipes and taps a few times and turns the screen for Olivia to read. She copies the number onto her own phone. 'And this is Tommy, your father?'

The boy nods.

'What's the address?' When Jim hesitates to answer, Hugo applies some more twisting pressure on his groin, and he tries to scream, but Olivia has cramped a vice-like finger and thumb across his mouth and repeats into his ear, 'what's the address?'

Jim croaks. 'Stebondale Street, on Millwall Park, number 58. I have to report to him, usually, it's a message, every hour or so, if I've seen anybody leave Butlers or someone new come to the door.'

Hugo asks: 'There are three entrances fifty yards apart, you must find it difficult to watch them and be sure you miss nothing?'

'Yeah, but I know which is yours. Visitors is obvious, you can tell.'

'And who is this, Tommy? What is he to do with us? Why all this snooping, yeah, what's it for?'

'Don't ask me, lady, they don't tell me nothing.'

'They?'

'Tommy and me uncle, Midge.'

Olivia slowly turns her head to face Hugo. With a sudden realisation bursting simultaneously within both their heads, they stare at each other with pursed mouths and angry looks. 'Midge Martin?' they screech together.

And Jim nods: 'Why, do you know 'im?'

In that moment of subdued tension, he wriggles and rolls himself free, kicking out at Hugo across his back, and darts away, pulling his jeans up, nipping this way and that through the thin crowds. He is quickly lost to sight and neither Olivia nor Hugo have the will to pursue him, knowing that he would run faster than they possibly could anyway and that they would have no chance of catching him.

***

Olivia thinks they should talk with Loukas and Hebe. They agree on a meeting place over the phone, well away from Bernadette, and travel in Hugo's black SUV to Hampstead Village. After their earlier excitement on the open streets of Bermondsey, this is a steady trip through North London, time to let their feelings calm down. They walk through the old muddled streets with their uneven steep pavements and Hugo, still in his weakened state, is grateful for Olivia's presence. She hangs onto his arm and forces them both to stroll in a relaxed manner, although tensions are not far below the surface.

After the realisation that Midge Martin could be involved in the kidnapping, Olivia had argued persuasively that they should do some rummaging before rushing headlong. For one thing, it hardly seemed likely that Martin would go through the complicated and risky business of actually kidnapping someone, especially not Samantha Little, whom he did not know. And another, dashing over to Millwall might be gallant and all that, but dangerous: they should assess the situation fully first, make a plan that would work; maybe recruit some help, like Jake and Garry. Olivia thought they should see Loukas and talk with Lilly as they had planned to do, before deciding on their next move. Midge Martin and Jim just might be a complete red herring.

'So, what is Jim doing snooping for Midge Martin outside my apartment block? That was real enough, wasn't it?' Hugo had sounded increasingly anxious. Olivia tried to calm his nerves with a glass of wine, which he gulped down, while allowing her opinion to prevail. 'But we'll drive over to Millwall later and at least take a look from the outside, see how the land lies. Yes?' And Olivia had nodded her agreement as they prepared to leave his apartment.

Outside the coffee shop in the High Street, Hugo and Loukas shake hands and nod heads at each other and make the introductions. Loukas is a swarthy handsome man, shorter than Hugo by far but with similar dark eyes and heavy eyebrows. Hugo and Hebe hug affectionately. Hebe smiles a lot, which lights up her pretty face, although obviously shy. Having been careful not to imply any serious link between himself and Olivia, just long-lasting friends, Hugo trudges off to the counter queue to order some drinks, leaving Olivia to small talk with his brother and little sister. Hebe and Olivia share a gentle hug. She asks Loukas after his family, explains how Hugo is recovering from his ordeal, now back at Butlers Wharf, and how she has known Hugo and loved his art for ages. Hebe is a small and pretty brunette and she talks amiably about her life in Athens. Hugo returns with a tray, stripping his overcoat off over the back of the chair.

'So, Loukas, the issue is a difficult one – you know Samantha, my friend, my model, for years I have worked with her, she has disappeared and I have had messages that she has been kidnapped and the ransom is a large sum of money. Her life is threatened. We don't know where she is, or who the kidnapper is, although we suspect a villain called Midge Martin, who was the man on the run when the police ambushed and shot me, thinking it was him.'

Loukas and Hebe look on, wide-eyed and astonished at Hugo's story. 'Oh, my God, Hugo.' Hebe's lower lip quivers a touch as she tilts her head with a concerned frown across her features. 'That's so awful. Is it real? Or some joke?'

Loukas remains impassive, just a slight turn of the head, a questioning knit in the brow. 'That sounds bad, Hugo. I'm sorry.'

'Yes, too right, we are desperate and we are wondering if you know anything about it? I mean, you haven't heard any problems from anybody, threats or words, something said, I don't know, it's ludicrous.' Hugo struggles not to sound as if he is accusing his brother of complicity and stumbles along until his brother blurts out:

'Me? Why would I know anything about your private life? It is a closed book to me and Hebe. What do I know, Hugo, be honest?' Loukas looks aghast.

Olivia jumps in: 'Were you and Hugo not good mates as youngsters?'

'Hardly, he was much older, away at school or off to England. He never had time for us. We never saw much of each other – even less so with Hebe.' Loukas's face has reddened as he directs his answers towards Olivia. 'Hugo has never taken any interest in us even at the best of times, so why now?'

'Well, what about now? The inheritance must have been a problem, with Hugo going on to have lots of money to play with and you left to struggle with all the trouble in Greece?'

'Olly, go easy.' Hugo interjects, feeling she is overdoing the direct approach. 'We are just trying to piece together what may have happened to Sam. Whether you might have heard anything, or…' Hugo stumbles to a stop, not quite sure where to go.

'Look, this is all new territory for us. Your life is a complete mystery to me, to be honest. I shall be returning to Greece in a few days. With Hebe. I'm sure Samantha will turn out fine.' He makes ready to depart. 'Wish me well, Hugo.'

'Yes, of course, Loukas, I wish you well, as always.'

'Well, that didn't go too well,' Hugo remarks, sitting pensively in the car.

'I don't understand why you could not have helped your brother, Hugo? He has been going steadily downhill with the Greek crisis, businesses going bust, no free cash, his family struggling and Hebe as well, and he has asked you for some share in your inherited fortune. That does not seem unreasonable, does it?'

Hugo sits still, staring out of the front windscreen. 'As I said, he's not my full brother and my father's wishes were clear. I have already given him a sum to tide him over. Anything substantial he would probably blow. His assets were perfectly good when he inherited them; it's his bad management that has resulted in his difficulties. Why should I fork out more good money for him, when I know I will never see it back?'

'Hugo. He's your brother, half-brother. Your mother surely would expect you to help?'

'Olly, leave it.'

'It's not as if you'd notice, a million here or there. And this just may have been the powerful excuse that he needed to take some severe action against you, the last straw on the camel's back, or whatever. He seemed pretty resentful.'

There is a long pause, while Hugo remains unmoved, hesitant to switch the engine on. 'Loukas wasn't involved, I'm sure he knew nothing about it.'

Hugo finally starts the car and they move off, joining the busy traffic down to the Finchley Road. Olivia muses: 'what about Loukas working with someone else?'

'What are you thinking now? Loukas and Martin in league, enticing the police into that shoot-out situation? That is too far-fetched. How would Loukas ever have met a man like Martin? Loukas has been out of the country for years, only came here after the shooting, didn't he?'

'Yes, I suppose so.' She shrugs: 'Although I can't help feel that he has such a motive of resentment.'

They are heading westwards to Shepherds Bush but it takes nearly fifty minutes through the traffic before Hugo turns into Adelaide Grove. He drives slowly past the terraced rows of housing and the one he remembers as Nika's. He turns into a junction at the end, parking up on a grass verge out of sight. Olivia is going to pay a visit ostensibly to see Lilly alone, but Hugo will be watching from the pavement opposite, lingering under one of the trees in the street.

Olivia presses on the familiar doorbell at number 84. She can hear no sounds from within and is not sure whether anyone is at home. She has not seen the yellow Mini, nor signs of any watching police in unmarked cars. Suddenly the battered puce-coloured door opens a fraction and Lilly's small face appears, with her hair in disarray. 'Oh, hello,' she says quite brightly, in obvious surprise at seeing Olivia, whom she remembers for her elegance and perfect

232

blonde hair, on her doorstep. They had got on all right before and she opens the door wider.

'Hi, Lilly. I'm sorry to drop by like this, but I was sort of passing and wanted to chat to you. It's about Hugo again, I'm afraid. Can I come in...?' hesitatingly with as friendly a smile as she could muster.

'Yeah,' and Lilly steps back. She is barefooted, in a pair of old jeans. Olivia tries not to notice the free sway of her wobbling breasts and bumpy nipples beneath the tight white tee shirt with "RELAX" emblazoned across the front. She follows the young beauty along the bendy corridor to the lounge and kitchen area at the back, with its cheap lean-to windows and tatty decoration. Lilly is going to put the kettle on.

'I see you've got rid of the sling. Your shoulder better?'

'Yeah, a little. I got fed up with that friggin' thing.'

'Nika about?'

'Nah, she's been busy.' Lilly potters about by the sink and sideboard and soon slops over with a couple of mugs of steaming tea using one shared teabag, with a carton of milk. On the round table is a bowl of white sugar.

'Thanks. Hugo's friend, Samantha, you know, has disappeared and Hugo is worried sick, as you can imagine. He has received phone messages from Sam's phone, from some man who has captured her and is threatening her life if Hugo does not pay a large sum of money. Have you heard anything about this, Lilly?'

'Oh, Gawd, no!' She looks alarmed, and brings her dainty hands up to her face, eyes wide. From sitting hunched at the table, she pokes her chest out. 'I shouldn't tell you this. That bloody Midge Martin has come back and he's not happy with Nika. He thumped her the other day, bruise across her cheek. She's with 'im tonight, couldn't get out of it.'

'We thought as much; we think it's Midge who has taken Sam. But we don't know where. Have you seen him?'

'No, he won't come 'ere, he thinks the filth are watching. No, he meets Nika in various places, I'm not sure where, although she said his brother has a place on the Isle of Dogs somewhere.'

'Is that Tommy?'

Lilly shrugs. 'Yeah, could be.'

'Does Midge know about Hugo's place in Bermondsey?'

'Well. He made me talk about it and I had to show 'im, he took me there in a van and I had to show 'im. I'm sorry, I'm a bit scared of him, he can be quite violent; hell of a temper on him.'

'Where would Midge take Sam, as a prisoner? Where would he hold her and keep her hidden?'

'I don't know. He has another flat in Edgware but he has tenants, I think.' She looks about with a sceptical smile. 'Not here, I don't think.' Her blonde hair flops down to her shoulders and she frequently combs a hand back through it to keep it off her forehead. 'His brother's place: most likely? Or what about where Sam lives?'

'Do you know her place?'

'No. No idea. Just thinking that would be easier, no risk of taking her outside, bundling into a van or something with people watching.'

'Do you know Tommy's place?'

'No, never been there.'

'Look, Lilly, will you promise to message me or call if you see Midge Martin, or find out where he might be. Get Nika to tell you where he is holed up. Promise. You've got my number on your phone. We might go over to Millwall Park to look at Tommy's place.'

After Olivia's questions have dried up, realising that Lilly knows nothing useful, she leaves her tea undrunk and lets herself out. She meets Hugo further up the street and they return to the car. He shows some concern, asking how Lilly's shoulder is and Olivia reassures him. They head back across north London again for Muswell Hill, determined to get into Sam's flat and look about for themselves. They discuss how they might flush Midge Martin out of his hideaway, wherever he may be; they might need help, tracking him back to his lair. They know it might be dangerous, as they both know of Midge's violent past. They may need to have some sort of weapons, to protect themselves. The only thing Hugo can think of is his fire poker: 'It's heavy, steel and brass and the end is quite sharp,' he says proudly. 'Plus, I have an assortment of useful kitchen knives.' Olivia is thinking about Louise but says nothing.

It's another hour of driving before they find Sam's house and ring her flat doorbell. Nothing, of course. They try the flat opposite on the ground floor. After explaining what they wanted to Freda, the elderly lady, who remembers Hugo meeting her husband last Wednesday, they ask if she has a key. Surprisingly, she does, and she lets them into Sam's flat from the hallway. Freda knew something was wrong as Sam's black cat, Holly, was wandering around lost and she had started feeding her.

Inside everything looked the same as when Olivia had called a few weeks before; nothing was out of place, there was no sign of forced entry anywhere or of a struggle – nothing appeared to be amiss. They left disappointed, after giving their thanks to Freda with an exchange of wishes to keep each other informed if something came up or if Samantha magically reappeared.

***

In the middle of the night, Hugo suddenly awakes. It's pitch black; not a sound. Except he heard something, a thump, was it? Nearby, outside, above his head. He watches a single streak of outside light casting its line across the ceiling through a tiny gap in the curtains. He stops breathing, listens intently. All is quiet, as usual. He feels restless, thinking about Samantha in some horrible prison, against her will, being hurt. His anger rises, as he imagines indescribable things. He turns over, tries to relax back to sleep, but anxiety picks at his brain and he decides a stroll through to his studio will help. In bare feet, he creeps around in the darkness, comforted by the pungency of the odours that pervade everything here that he loves. In thin shadowy illumination from the skylights above, he stands among his collection of easels and canvases static like guests at a cocktail party. He fixes up a small arc lamp to cast a strong white light across his shoulders over the biggest canvas, a group of British soldiers in their heavy brown uniforms squinting into bright Flanders sunshine, snacking on chocolate from home, smiling and smoking freely, clustered around a battered artillery housing; a crumbling farm building and angular pine trees on the skyline behind. There is more detail to be added and the finer points to be finished, but for the moment and at three o'clock in the morning he is content to just fill in background in the hope of moving his thoughts onto other things. He returns to the raw umber and yellow ochre mixes on his palette from yesterday to capture the sepia hue of the time.

There it is again. He hears a thud, like before, like a footfall, somewhere outside, above him, on the roof. He is sure of it and freezes, mid-brush stroke to look across at the glass frontage. The sliding doors are closed and locked; he sees himself and the arc light reflected in the darkened glass, although if he moves a little to one side he can make out the twinkling lights strewn across the top of the bridge and across the city. Sometimes gulls swoop over the roofs and land with a bump. Not usually in the dead of night, though. Another sound, definitely a scuffled footstep, overhead, and then another, more of a scraping noise. He tilts his head, as if that makes his ears more sensitive, glancing up towards one of the panelled skylights five or six feet above him. He can see the clouded black sky through the glass, and then a shadow moves across like the whimsical swaying of a tree branch in the wind, except there are no trees growing on any of the roofs and the shadow is more of a solid image, a moving body.

Hugo places his brush and palette board down carefully on a table. He moves out of the lamplight, stepping deliberately into shadow, hoping to avoid kicking into anything. He edges his way towards the door, to switch the lights off entirely. A tingling sensation of fear passes from his loins into the back of his legs, as he listens intently, his body poised. He can hear nothing but his own shallow breathing. Then a faint scratching for a few seconds precedes the sound of sudden wrenching, wood splintering above, as one of the skylight windows at the back of the studio, not the one he was standing under, is forced up, open and outwards. In the darkness, Hugo feels a rush of cold air as a booted leg is lowered down through the gaping hole in the roof, followed by its partner; the feet rotate as a lithe human figure drops into the void, like an SAS officer on a mission. It hangs by its hands on the frame above, before neatly landing on its toes on the wooden floor below, feet together, knees bent, in a crouching position, arms akimbo, the position held firm. The man, Hugo assumes it is a man by his shape and attitude, is all in black, tight trousers and zip-up jacket, holding a long and spiked crowbar in one hand, his face covered in a balaclava, his hands in leather gloves. He is watching and listening, his head rotating to look around while adjusting to the darkness, but soon catches sight of Hugo's frame in dirty white tunic and pyjama trousers a few feet away.

The scary-looking figure slowly straightens up, tugging his woollen mask off from the top of his head, looking menacingly across at Hugo who is static by the door, shocked, mouth open, lost for words. The man with dark curly hair is impossible to recognise in the darkness, and Hugo is at a complete loss as to what is happening. Mesmerised, he eventually manages to splutter: 'Excuse me, what the hell do you think you are doing?'

The man approaches a step or two, holding his crowbar up threateningly. Hugo flinches and steps back against the wall, vaguely looking around for a weapon of his own, although all he can see close by are several glass pots with stacks of upturned paintbrushes.

'Switch the lights on,' a gruff voice says, 'then we can see what is going on.' Hugo fumbles for the switches and a series of downlights illuminate the entire studio space, shocking to the eyes at first after the previous darkness. 'You must be Hugo Pitsakis, if I'm not mistaken, the Greek artist who fucked my woman, in my flat, and then got what he deserved with the police. However did you survive?'

Hugo is even more shocked and flinches again, hitting his back against the frame of the door. He looks more carefully at the features of the figure in black still advancing towards him. He sees a good-looking bloke, with the hallmarks of an arch criminal, a menace in his eyes and a twisted smile. He is unshaven, about his own height and build, with wavy brown hair and Hugo suddenly knows exactly who he is.

'How many bullets was it they removed?'

'Nine,' Hugo whispers.

'Amazing. A miracle. Lucky man: except you didn't bargain for me, did yer, mate? Midge Martin, wanted for armed robbery and assaulting a police officer. As if you didn't know. You was mistaken for me, I don't know why. Except you was in my flat, with my woman. I wanted to have a look at you, see your face for myself, not just those awful newspaper pictures. See who I was up against. 'Cos I got your Sam, your lovely woman.' He smiled broadly, then turned it into a triumphant sneer.

'You bastard. You better not harm her, or I'll…'

'Yer'll what? You don't know where she is, and you wouldn't know how to harm me, would yer, you prissy little artist. You paint women with no clothes on, take advantage of them, don't yer? That's disgusting, that is.' And with that he swipes viciously with his metal bar at the pot nearest to him, smashing the glass and sending dozens of brushes flying about the studio floor. Hugo blinks his eyes closed, suddenly fearing he was about to witness his canvases being vandalised, and he wants to be sick.

He does not know whether to argue with him or try to cajole him or just ignore him, but he fears for what he might want to do, except killing Hugo would not exactly help his cause in extracting money from him. So why has he come, if not to harm him?

Martin advances even closer. 'I wanted to meet the man the police thought was me – and tried to silence, I mean they wanted me dead, all that wild shooting.'

'Well, now you have; what is it you want?'

'You going to get compensation or what? You got me messages, I take it,' he smirks. 'I want two million quid, mate, paid into my Spanish account. You can manage that, can't you. A man of your wealth. Or your Sam will have her pretty little throat cut. By the way, she is a ravishing beauty, isn't she? In bed, I mean.' And he sneers again, showing his uneven front teeth, gripping his crowbar tighter in readiness. Hugo winces at the smell of alcohol on his fowl breath.

'You little bastard, Martin. I suggest you get out while you can.' Hugo suddenly makes a dash through the half open door beside him and crosses through to his lounge, jumping over a sofa in desperation to reach the fireplace, where he grabs the heavy poker, the one he had been thinking of, a long iron rod with a heavy brass handle. He turns expecting to face his adversary behind him, but only to watch Midge Martin amble through from the studio in no hurry, shaking his head. 'No, no, mate, you don't want to be doing that.'

Martin stands with his legs apart, with his long crowbar gripped in both hands and ready to strike, and Hugo realises he would not stand a chance against him. Admiring the surroundings, Martin says: 'You got a nice place here and Lilly told me all about the dosh you inherited, so don't try to make out you ain't got it. You have your deadline to make the payment. I suggest you stick to it. Then we have three working days for the banks to do their bit. As soon as I know the money has been accepted, I will release Sam, not before – you'll get a message to pick her up. Damaged goods though, I'm afraid, the least you could expect for your crimes, Mr Prissy Artist Pittyakis. Get me drift. Account details.' And he places cool as you like a folded bit of paper onto the corner of the low shiny coffee-table.

'In case you doubt that I have her or doubt the serious nature of my intentions, I will leave you with this.' He is definitely smiling as he pulls a small package out from inside the front of his zip-jacket and places it over the piece of paper on the table: wrapped in brown paper, not much bigger than a packet of cigarettes. 'This should persuade you. Deadline: Tuesday six o'clock, pm, I won't wait any longer. Now, show me the proper way out of here, through the front door.' Midge Martin gives out a hideous coughing laugh and stands aside for Hugo to lead the way.

After the horrible Midge Martin has gone, skipping his way down the stairs as if he has been on a social call, Hugo is left in the shadowy hallway trembling with a mixture of anger and fear. He returns to the studio in a pair of shoes, to clear up the glass and his brushes and to inspect the damage to the upper skylight. Freezing air is blustering through the gaping hole. From a folding ladder he keeps in a cupboard, he is able to reach the frame with a pole and bring the broken window back into place, at least to seal the draught. He will have to contact a handyman to come to repair the damage tomorrow.

He looks at Martin's brown package on the table with suspicion, knowing its contents will be unpleasant. He hesitates with a pair of scissors to cut open one end: a used cardboard box slides out and Hugo stares at it for some time, willing for the courage to lift the lid. Crumpled white tissue paper covers a grizzly object, a short length of human finger, cut off amateurishly at the first joint leaving a bloodied and spiky bone end, the oval shape of a varnished nail preserved at its tip. Hugo lets out a cry of shock, turns away, nearly drops the box. He sits slowly down, screws his eyes tight, suppressing a desire to scream, and almost ready to cry, in anger and frustration, but most of all in sympathy and shame, that he could have allowed Sam to be subjected to such horror and torture.

As if to press home the message that this is Sam's finger and that Midge Martin means business, he also finds a short clump of auburn hair curled beside the stump in among the tissue.

He wonders painfully how this sorry saga could possibly get any worse. A film of cold sweat has gathered along his forehead and around the back of his neck. He feels nauseous again as he steadies himself at the kitchen sink to pour a glass of tap water.

He checks the locks on the front door, and the sliding glass window panels, he switches all the lights out and returns to his bed, carrying the grim little cardboard box with him. Dolce has not been disturbed in her room in the other apartment, which is a relief. He lies for a long time on his back, listening for sounds and watching the shadows shift, thinking of Sam and her ghastly ordeal and promising not to wake Olivia with his phone call too early, knowing that she needs her sleep to prepare for the day ahead.

***

Sunday

Next morning, Olivia lets Hugo into her Barbican apartment, the first time he has been inside. He had decently waited until half past seven to make his first contact with her and had explained on the phone that there had been developments and that he had had a visitor in the night.

Hugo looks pale, his lids swollen and eyes reddened, and Olivia knows he has had a rough night. She, on the other hand, has slept reasonably well after a quiet evening in – that is, after a quiet evening with Louise, who had come around for a drink but had not stayed long, as she had her brother over from Hong Kong dossing in her spare bedroom – and is looking fresh, eating a yogurt and a piece of toast, and is on her second black coffee. She pours for Hugo, who reaches for an apple from a pile of fruit on her kitchen table.

He places Midge's little box in front of him, looking at it with fear and hatred. He still has his big coat on, an old shirt underneath, jeans and his Timberlands. 'Sorry, I feel a little wretched this morning. I was disturbed in the night. At three o'clock, I heard someone up on the roof and a man broke through one of the skylights in the studio. He wrenched the frame open and jumped down inside. He was armed and threatening. And he left this for me.' Hugo pushes the box a few inches towards Olivia. 'It's horrid but you need to take a look.'

'So, who was this man?' Olivia sounds alarmed. 'How'd he get on the roof?'

'The delightfully horrid Mr Midge Martin.'

'God, Hugo; my God, were you scared?'

'Take a look,' indicating the box. She gingerly lifts a corner with one hand and pulls a disgusted face, screwing her eyes up; she stares in horror, blinks, slams the lid back down.

'There is absolutely no doubt who we are dealing with. He gave me his bank details and wants two million transferred electronically to an account in Spain, he said, by 6 pm Tuesday. He will cut Sam's throat if I don't comply.'

Olivia looks as if she will cry, her mouth is trembling. Hugo reaches a kindly hand to her face, holds her chin, runs his thumb along her lower lip. 'Don't, Olly, I need you to be strong.'

She sniffs, finds a tissue to wipe her mouth. 'Why the hell didn't you call me earlier, wake me?'

'What would that have gained? One grumpy tired lady this morning none the wiser,' Hugo scoffs gently.

'The bloody nerve of the man. What did he look like – did he look like you?'

'Er, I don't know, a bit, I suppose: same height, wavy hair, same age.'

'He wanted to frighten you.'

'He did that.'

'Hugo, poor you.' She steps forward to throw her arms around his broad shoulders and hug him, rubbing her blonde head into his neck. 'Poor Sam, that's her finger, her little finger. God, the brutality. She must be in such agony! What do we do?'

Hugo is upset and slumps on a stool. 'I rang Jake this morning and Garry and they are both coming over here, together, you don't mind, do you? They should be here soon.' He looks at his watch, a quarter after nine o'clock.

'That's good, Hugo.' Olivia makes sure he has a strong cup of coffee in front of him. 'Drink, it will help. Do you need to eat anything? Toast?' she asks.

'He insulted me, the bastard. Said he wanted to see what I looked like after all the fuss in the papers about the police mistaking me for him.'

'Bloody hell, Hugo. It's obvious now. It had to be Midge Martin.' Olivia is wielding a knife in her hand and shakes it like a wand as she goes through items one at a time. 'Using Sam's phone, he forced her. He found out about you and the girls from the papers, in the news, that you spent a night with his girlfriend, he is madly jealous, he wants revenge. Nika admits it to him, Lilly confirms and tells him everything. Lilly shows him your Shad Thames address.

He knows you have lots of money, now he's seen it for himself; he doesn't know how much, silly man, but two million pounds to him is an enormous amount. He'll never have to work again. Or rob again. And he might well have a mate in Spain with a legitimate bank account and they plan to split the proceeds and run away over Europe. He's obviously prepared to use a knife. Bloody Midge Martin.' She stares at the knife in her hand that is smeared with butter and drops it into the sink.

'How are we going to find her, Olly? Even if I pay this man and he escapes to Spain, there's no guarantee he will release her, is there?'

'Look, someone must be with her, making sure she is alive – giving her water, taking her to the loo, making sure she does not escape or shout out or bang anything. She must be in a place that Martin has or has easy access to. He has a flat in Edgware, but that has tenants apparently. His brother in Millwall seems most likely.'

'We must go there, we'll all go there this morning.'

'We need to flush him out from his hiding place, so we can follow him. Perhaps a message to say that you have a proposal and you should meet him. We could use a watcher, like Jake, again someone Midge does not know. And he could track him back to his hideaway.'

'All a bit wishful thinking. This guy seems to know what he is doing. What happens if he lies low now for the next three days, refuses to come out? The deadline will be reached before we have made any progress.'

'Perhaps we can use Nika to lure him to her place, for a night of unadulterated sex, where we can lie in wait and then follow him out afterwards back to his place,' suggests Olivia.

'We're talking about a real person here, Olly. This is not some crappy TV drama; you sound as if you're enjoying the intrigue.'

'Hardly. Look, where are the most likely places that Martin would keep her?' trying to get Hugo thinking straight. She holds out her fingers this time to count them off one by one: 'First place: Muswell Hill, Sam's flat. But we tried that and there was nothing.'

'Second, Adelaide Road, Midge's flat,' Hugo joins in.

'I was there yesterday, it's small, there were no signs at all of a prisoner unless they own the upstairs but that is a separate flat, isn't it?'

'Yes, I think so. We may need to investigate.'

'Third, Stebondale Street, Isle of Dogs: Tommy's place.' Olivia pulls her laptop towards them and shows Hugo the streets outlined on Google Maps. 'It's down Westferry Road from Canary Wharf into Millwall. There,' she points. 'It's likely that Midge's brother is helping and that Jim bloke; and maybe others.'

'We should all go there. But she may be at some other site altogether,' Hugo muses, 'somewhere completely remote, a disused building or garage somewhere out of town?' He sounds despondent.

Olivia needs to keep thinking positive. 'Why don't we try to enlist Nika's help; she must have no love for Midge, surely. She probably knows where he is or might find out for us – for a fee: she might give us the right information.'

'Okay. I need to meet her away from the flat, maybe at that nightclub in Whitechapel, the Nightingale – you could come with me.'

After another agonising period of silence, during which they are both engaged in unspoken and wild imaginings of the worse possible outcomes, without a solution emerging, Olivia reaches for Hugo's hands and looks closely into his eyes with sympathy. 'This is so awful, isn't it; poor Sam. What would you do, if you were Midge?' Olivia asks quite reasonably.

'Kill myself, with disgust.'

A few minutes later, Hugo's phone buzzes with a message. 'It's them, Jake and Garry together, they're waiting downstairs.'

***

The four of them are huddled close together in Hugo's black Mercedes, parked under a mature horse-chestnut alongside bare muddy playing fields in Stebondale Street, where a few kids are morosely kicking a football and yelling at each other. Notwithstanding the warmth and comfort, not to say, feeling of safety, inside, Jake and Garry are both keen to snoop around the dull prefabricated block down the road, where they believe Midge Martin's brother, Tommy, lives.

Jake is stroking his brownish goatee with one gloved hand while selecting the steel and brass fire poker for his weapon from the pile of objects on the floor behind the front seats. 'I've got a knuckleduster in my pocket as well, Garry, you may like to carry it.'

Garry is closely studying his choice, the longest kitchen knife Hugo could find, a well-built steel blade and handle all-in-one, Scandinavian, and single-edged razor sharp. He looks pleased. 'This suits me, boyo.'

They drove over from the Barbican in tandem, Garry following Hugo in his Audi, which is parked behind them. As suggested he has a supply of drinks and snacks in his car, bought quickly from a local supermarket before he picked Jake up from his place nearby in Battersea. Hugo has finished his quick briefing, so they are all up to speed. One problem is none of them knows what Tommy looks like, and only Hugo has seen Midge in person, although they all claim they will recognise him from the newspaper pictures they remembered from several weeks before.

Garry asks, 'How the hell did Martin get up on Butlers Wharf roof, anyway?'

Hugo has been pondering the same question all night and morning, and earlier conducted a little inspection himself. 'He must have climbed the old fire-escape: it's the original 1830's wrought-iron staircase, zig-zagging up at the west end of the building. It was encased in brickwork since Butlers was developed. At the bottom, it's fenced off to keep the public out and padlocked with chains. The chain was cut, I looked at it this morning. He would have got up to the terracing and then climbed along onto the roofs from there. He knew which were my apartments and wrenched open one of the skylights with a crowbar.'

Olivia has been sitting quietly in the front passenger seat, thinking tactics. She's wearing an old pair of tight jeans and a polo sweater with sturdy boots and a navy parka, which has a belt and fur-lined hood. She feels warm but is trembling with nervousness, secretly wishing they had involved the police. She is thinking of the severed fifth finger in its little box. They told the boys about Sam's specimen but did not show it to them.

Opposite the playing fields, there are a series of rectangular featureless blocks of flats over four floors, with pairs of green wheelie bins at intervals and off-road parking spaces, occupied mostly with a selection of unwanted furniture, abandoned bicycles and children's playthings, plastic slides, and a trampoline. The places look rather dilapidated but occupied, curtains at the small windows, trinkets on the sills and the occasional car parked on the road. Hugo and Olivia watch anxiously, as the two odd figures of Jake and Garry amble over the road to the ground floor property twenty yards up, their weapons secreted about their persons. Garry is in a bright red ski-jacket and bobble hat; Jake is wearing a tightly buttoned corduroy coat and trilby, both brown and terribly old-fashioned. They have promised to be polite to anyone they might meet, but there is nobody about as they approach the middle ground floor flat, number 58. They ring the bell and wait a while, start peering in through the windows, and then slip around the side to take a look at the back.

'And if Martin or anybody else who's working with him see us, or are suspicious, Samantha's throat will be cut,' Hugo moans, watching his team through the front windscreen.

'All right, Hugo. I know you feel angry but the deadline is 6 pm Tuesday, so we need some helpful, logical thinking at this point.'

'Martin is not logical, that's the trouble. Otherwise, he would not have broken into my apartment through the skylight.' Olivia looks at Hugo's hangdog face with her own hopeless expression.

'Think positive.'

'Doesn't appear to be anyone there.' Jake is leaning against Hugo's open window, giving him the lowdown. 'I can't see anybody inside, but it is occupied. It's all quiet in the other flats as well. What do people do around here?'

'Can we break in around the back?'

'There's a kitchen door, down the side, looks easy.'

'Garry, you stay here, with Olivia. Come on, Jake.'

Hugo is desperate to be doing something, so he wanders over with Jake to the building, with a hefty jemmy plain as daylight, Jake with his poker hidden. Weeds are sprouting out between the cracks in the pathway, some of the wooden window frames look rotten. He pushes Jake forwards through a narrow archway between blocks and they put their shoulders to a flimsy-looking side-door. Jake smashes his boot at the lock; with just two thumps the lock rips through the wooden jamb and the door flies open.

The place smells musty, unaired. There are signs that someone lives there, like an open box of Kellog's cereal on the table, a half-empty bottle of milk in the fridge, neglected remains of heated baked beans in a not-too non-stick pan on the stove. There are dirty dishes and cutlery in the sink and general clutter everywhere, the bin overflowing.

With their weapons at the ready, they tour the cramped place, creeping into every room, including two cluttered upstairs bedrooms, bathroom, downstairs toilet, living room, everywhere smelling stale. It looks like a dosshouse for untidy men, no signs of any woman present, no dressing table with lady things about, make-up, mirrors, clothes or drying underwear. There are no hiding places either that they can make out, no secret basement, nothing to suggest a kidnapped woman in distress.

'Fuck.'

'Are you sure this is the right house, Hugo?'

'Number 58, that's what Jim said.'

'Maybe he lied?'

'Maybe.' They sloped away outside. 'Shame about the door.'

Back in the warmth of the Mercedes, Hugo suggests one person remains in Garry's car to keep an unobtrusive lookout, just in case someone returns; that might prove helpful. 'Would you mind, Garry? Just for today up until, say seven, eight o'clock? Ring in with updates. You've got some snacks and drink in your car.'

'Yeah, fine. No problem, anything to help.'

'Okay,' continues Hugo, 'now what?' He turns towards Olivia.

'We either sit and wait for the next message. Or we can try to provoke Midge into doing something, making a mistake. Send a message to say you cannot get that sort of money in the time available. You want to meet with him, somewhere to discuss it?'

'And we follow him afterwards – could be really difficult. I can see that going horribly wrong. The longer it takes, the longer poor Sam has to suffer – and a threat of delay may provoke Midge to get angry and chop off another finger.'

Sitting in the back, Jake and Garry both wince at the thought. There is silence in the car as the four friends slump in despair, knowing they have not really got a workable strategy.

'Okay,' Olivia carries on, thinking. 'Contact Nika, plead to meet her, and see what she knows. Then use her to entice Midge away from his hideaway and we challenge him, threaten him to reveal where he's keeping Sam.'

Jake pipes up, 'I could ring her, like a business call. Then work on her, offer her money, arrange a meet? She might know where he is, even where Sam is.'

Hugo asks with some venom, his lips tight: 'What if she is in cahoots with Midge?'

'A risk worth taking?'

***

Olivia returns home, midday Sunday. She needs to freshen up, change her clothes, eat something.

Samantha's phone was not picked up when Hugo rang through, and so he messaged it, directed at Midge. He drove them back from the Isle of Dogs, leaving Garry alone in his Audi for a boring day of watching, and dropped Olivia off at her entrance. On the journey, Jake quietly made several calls from the back of the car. Hugo and Jake would stick together and inform Olivia as soon as anything else was planned.

Like Hugo, Olivia is fraught with a deep anxiety in the pit of her stomach, remembering the sight of that fingertip and wondering what the unpredictable Midge Martin would do next. She cannot begin to imagine what Sam is going through, physically and mentally. She has tried to suppress her true worries, but still feels they should have contacted the police. Whatever Hugo has said, the police do have experience of this sort of situation, and Sam would probably be in no more danger than she already is, with at least some possibility of finding her before further disaster happens. Olivia had picked up Inspector Sanger's contact card from where she found it, tucked under a glass pot in Hugo's studio, and she has it slipped into a back pocket of her jeans. She turns it over between her fingers, contemplating whether to make the call.

Later, frustrated and unable to remain calm on her own, she rings Louise, begging her to come over. She has some serious talking to do. She needs to share her concerns; she needs someone she can trust.

There are bright wintery views over the estate, the damp forecourts reflecting the afternoon's sunny light. The fountains are glittering as the wind whips them into erratic patterns, splashing water far and wide. Louise has sprinted up the stairs, fresh and cheery, in a sporty tracksuit. Olivia is unsupported in a loose white tee shirt and clinging black leggings as she welcomes her with open arms. They share a passionate full-on kiss, their lips picking up the sparks of their passion, stirring the embers. She imbibes the smell of her lover, subtly perfumed, as she unzips her top and holds on to her with tight desperation. They snuggle close, slouching across a sofa in the lounge, with wine poured close to hand.

'What is it? You sounded scared.'

'I need to talk with you; I need your help.' Louise starts to finger trace with tenderness over Olivia's face and neck and Olivia, as if no longer able to hold back the flood, bursts out with all her worries, one after the other tumbling out, somewhat incoherently. Louise has to slow her down. Tears have welled up in

Olivia's eyes and she gives a little laugh, dabbing at her lower lids with the back of a finger.

'Sorry.' Louise kisses her friend's warm cheeks, licking the tears.

'It is fine, you tell me, tell me slowly. One at a time.'

She starts again, explaining some of the finer points of the Midge Martin scenario, at least as best as she understands it. She describes how Hugo had found himself in Midge's flat in Shepherd's Bush, with Midge's girlfriend and her buxom blonde friend, Lilly Soames; how the police shooting happened by mistake. She talks about Hugo's recovery in hospital, his escape into Wales with Samantha, and now Samantha's disappearance, her kidnapping by Midge Martin, his break-in to Butlers Wharf and his threats, including their discovery of Sam's cut finger.

'He is demanding a large sum of money for her safe return, deadline is this Tuesday 6 pm.'

'Can Hugo pay this money, to get her back?'

'Oh, yes, I think so, but what guarantees are there that Sam is returned, or not further harmed?'

'Have you called the police?'

Olivia looks guilty, kissing her friend's lips again and touching her with her fingers. 'No.'

'That is okay. Police can be heavy handed.'

A little later, on the settee in the broad afternoon daylight, their clothes easily discarded, they attempt to make love gently and quietly, but unconvincingly, ineffectively, their pairing missing its usual passion. They rest naked in each other's arms, allowing the emotional fires to stutter, their warmed perspiring skins to cool. Olivia is resting her head on Louise's cushion-like stomach, licking her salty bellybutton, while Louise caresses her hair. They drift through a languid half-hour of sleepy conversation, about themselves and the love of women and what might become of them. Olivia even tells the sad tale of the oversexed self-centred male dancer from the Ukraine, who years ago had fallen down Hugo's studio stairs and broken his neck.

***

For the next 36 hours of waiting, nerves are fraying. Tempers are stretched. Appetites are spoiled. Sleep is casual and interrupted. Plans are put aside, although Olivia has to go to work Monday morning, as usual, the only antidote to her nervous tension.

Garry had nothing to report from Millwall. Jake had spoken to Nika eventually on the phone, finding her late in the day, not sure where she was; they had agreed to meet in a nightclub off Leicester Square later; Jake was going alone and would report back as soon as he was able.

Hugo had not received a reply from Midge all day and had taken refuge in his studio, with his paintbrushes, immersed in his own imaginative world.

Olivia messages Lilly to find out what is happening, and the answer is a load of nothing, except that she had managed a photo-shoot in a studio in West Acton, topless but tasteful and good money; Midge had been in the flat and had been angry with Nika, pushing her around a bit; Nika was off to a club in the West End to get away from him.

Olivia has been dreaming about Dominic Lebelov and his prancing walk and pouting lips looking like a fancy pantomime joker; a self-parody that she never found funny, although the younger men around the studio at the time would imitate him with raucous laughter. She sees his broken body at the bottom of the stairs and the young besotted Edward, clean-shaven and innocent, creeping out from the shadows with his camera to record the incident. Dominic had spent time with several of Hugo's friends, male and female, and had acted pretty loosely with either sex, but with Edward, he had always seemed indifferent, showing him no particular favours.

She did not mention Edward's black-and-white photographs to Louise.

***

Charles Treadwell sits chipper as ever in his glass-walled office at the end of the row, comfortable in dark pinstripes, his jacket slung over the back of the swivel chair. His blue braces don't match the pink socks, but he has a bright shine on his black brogues this morning, matching the brightness of his mood.

'Olivia, come in, come in.'

All morning, Olivia has been jumping with shock, waiting for news, irritable, expectant at the sound of any phone ringing or buzz of a mobile, even the call of the post arriving in Emerson's lobby. She had contributed next to nothing at the weekly headline meeting and now advances uncertainly towards the spare chair by his desk in her neat ruby-coloured trouser suit. She sits demurely, unsure of what to expect. Her division boss is often in a good mood, even on Mondays, but today he does seem to be especially buoyant; perhaps he has had sight of this winter's bonus scheme, she wonders. Actually, she decides, given the strange life of a quite ordinary citizen she seems to inhabit out there, as far from the unfathomable world of quantitative easing and binaries trading as one can imagine, she does not really care. Even if he is planning to sack her for some odd misdemeanour, she doubts whether that would register above 1 on her Richter scale, given the weight of other worries that are pressing in on her right now.

'How's life? Good, yes?'

Never sure whether he wants a reply to his small talk or just a sycophantic nod in support, Olivia delivers a non-committal smile.

'Conservative Party office has been on the blower. You've been spotted in high places, Olivia. Joss Arnold, their press officer I know from old: interested in your chaos versus competence economy theme for their manifesto, a nice soundbite. The PM might want to lead with that one. Would you believe? They want you to work with them on this, short-term, quick bit of collaboration. Good for the firm; good for you. What do you say?'

'Oh, fame at last,' she shrugs with a dull laugh and a slight flutter of her lightly mascaraed lashes.

'Absolutely. With the election three months away, they are looking for the perfect slogan. They need to finalise pretty soon, he said. So they would appreciate a rewrite specifically for their manifesto, in a way that the lay public can understand. Do you think you could do that?'

'Yes, I'm sure I can,' wondering exactly what she may be letting herself in for.

'You may need some seconded time, to be part of their manifesto team and all that. Quite exciting, don't you think? Might get to visit Number 10. Who knows where it might lead in the future – you may end up writing the Prime Minister's speeches, if he wins the election. Ha!' Charles always was a bit of a comedian.

'Ha, indeed. Wouldn't that be something?' Olivia is flattered but clearly needs to give it some more thought and remains underwhelmed. 'When do they want it by?'

'The deadline is tomorrow, I'm afraid: Tuesday, close of play, 6 pm.'

Olivia makes a half-grimace, as if in pain, but Charles Treadwell would not have understood the irony.

4

Deadline – Tuesday, 6 pm

Tuesday dawns for Olivia rather as Monday had, too soon and with meagre hope. There is no fresh information or new idea emerging. There have been no sightings of Mad Midge; Garry, who returned to watch the run-down Stebondale Street on Monday, reported zilch, as if the place had been abandoned, and nobody he asked could provide a possible reason. One neighbour had volunteered that he had seen the main man, Tommy Martin, and his son, drive off in their van loaded, looked like camping gear, boxes; provisions, maybe; beginning of last week, he thought, hadn't seen them since. Jake phoned to say that Nika had been unhelpful, she had no idea about any kidnapping, or where Midge might be when away from their Adelaide Grove flat, and that he had been cross and pushed her about in the flat on Saturday accusing her of being unfaithful; she did not think she would be able to lure him anywhere, sex or no sex. Jake is struggling to think of anything else they could possibly do, except perhaps to call the police.

Hugo is going crazy. He spent yesterday talking with his bank, trying to convince a sceptical central manager of the integrity of his wishes with a load of boloney about a business deal and the impending deadline, and he is waiting to receive confirmation today.

Olivia forces herself into activity and arrives at work looking her best, but with an empty sick feeling in her guts. Elegantly made-up and dressed comfortably in her navy trouser suit with pressed pink stripe blouse, she sets about her routine, dealing with e-mails and internal reports, and ensures her phone is fully charged. She completes her final draft of her "chaos versus competence" manifesto article, sending it as an attachment to Charles's friend in Whitehall. She is enduring an hour of her research team discussing youth unemployment across Europe and the lack of a credible EU strategy to deal with the refugee crisis, when her phone vibrates on the papers in front of her. She taps the screen a couple of times: "Lilly Soames".

"Midge is here ranting at Nika, v. angry and drunk. I'm scared. Chance for you to catch him. Lilly"

Olivia is immediately alert. She knows what she has to do. There is danger ahead, but her senses all point in the same direction. Lilly agreed to alert Olivia as soon as Midge made an appearance and now she has. Olivia promised a quick response. Lilly herself could be in danger and she is relying on her.

There is no time for explanations. She slips out the back of the meeting room, looking as unhurried as she can, and strides along to her office. She logs out and shuts down her computer, shoving all her papers in the central drawer of her desk and locks it. Her tuna coleslaw salad lunch is dropped in the bin. Grabbing her parka and bag, she walks briskly through the trading floor, dismissing with an upraised hand the approach of a secretary and a work colleague, and exits through the automatic doors at the end of the corridor. She descends the stairs two at a time and shouts for a black cab.

She messages Hugo *en-route* and they arrange to meet at Shepherds Bush Green, where she is picked up forty minutes later in the Mercedes, Jayden driving.

'The arrangement is that at one minute before 6 pm tonight,' Hugo explains, 'I will make the bank transfer, electronically and ring Midge on the number written on his piece of paper. He will wait three days to see the transfer details in his account, before releasing Sam. He will message me then with her whereabouts. No discussion.'

'So whatever, you must be back in front of your computer before six o'clock?'

'Yeah.'

The chance they are looking for is to follow Midge away from his flat to wherever he might be keeping Samantha. They park as before up on a grass verge along Sawley Road and leaving Jayden to mind the car, stumble nervously down Adelaide Grove from the north end to pass number 84 by the street bollards, Hugo in his big duffle coat and walking boots. They have both remembered to bring gloves.

Having been here twice in the past two weeks, Olivia is becoming familiar with the drab appearances of the street. Most of the houses have a neglected look, old doors flaking, window frames rotting with untended gardens and broken brick walls. She wonders why more people cannot look after their places with a bit of pride, a paint-over occasionally, a tidy-up around the front. Number 84 is particularly drab, and they stare up at the stuccoed frontage and in at the ground floor windows, either side of the adjacent puce front doors: the left-hand one is 84a for the ground floor; on the right is 84b, leading to the flat upstairs. All is quiet. They can see nothing inside, the filthy windows and drawn net curtains combining to obscure any view.

What should they do if Midge decides to stay in the flat all day and goes nowhere? They step past the broken front gate, their hearts racing. Olivia is poised to message Lilly, hearing her plea in her head about being scared of Midge and his hell of a temper. She is thinking that a bleep on Lilly's phone, if she is hiding, might alert Midge to her whereabouts, but that is a risk they have to take, hoping she will have the phone on silent mode.

"We are outside. Where are you? Are you safe? Where is Mad Midge? Olivia."

Standing together at the front door, they feel exposed for what seems like ages, but not a soul walks along the street on either side and only one car has passed by. There is no response coming from Lilly. Hugo retrieves his steel and brass poker from inside his coat. Olivia feels pulses thumping in her neck, as she watches Hugo step up to the front door, pushing his gloved hands against the woodwork. He then unexpectedly takes a step back, raises his right foot to waist height with his big Timberland boot and aims it hard at the edge of the door by the lock. The frame splinters easily with a wrenching crash and the door shudders. A second shove and it swings open freely.

They step inside, pushing the door closed to behind them. The corridor ahead is dim and smells of sweat. The place feels cold and there are no sounds of movement or voices. The first door on the right, the small room used by Lilly, is closed. A step or two further on is the bigger front bedroom, that is Nika's, on the left. Creeping under the edge of her door, which is slightly ajar, is what appears to be a spreading puddle of dull congealing blood, that has advanced a curving line of trapped dust ahead of it. There are bloodied footprints on the lino leading away from the entrance. Olivia is not sure whether Hugo has noticed but she now sees further blood smears along the corridor with plenty of finger marks on the walls.

Just then, from the darker depths within, they freeze at the sound of something dropping and then rolling, like a bottle, and Hugo hears a man swearing under his breath. He steps carefully forwards, further into the darkness towards the bend in the corridor, ready to confront whoever might be there. He has caught a strong whiff of alcohol and sees the bloodstains along the flooring, which he tries to avoid. He senses being watched, expecting Midge Martin to be waiting.

Olivia moves along behind and tries to push open Nika's door but it feels jammed against something solid, on the floor. She steps cautiously up to heave harder with her shoulder. Once the gap is widened she is able to peer around the door into the dimness of the bedroom.

Hugo is brandishing his steel poker in front of him, as well as holding a vicious looking kitchen knife, which he had concealed inside his coat. Unexpectedly there is a gruff shout from the back of the house, the male voice again, sounding angry, followed by shuffling footsteps. Hugo stands still, poised but uncertain.

'Oy, you. What the fuck?' Mad Midge sways unsteadily towards them from out of the shadows, shouting and swearing liberally, his voice sounding tipsy. 'It's piss-pot boy. Pisskaris, the man who fucked my girlfriend and thought he could get away with it!'

In panic now, Olivia sways away from the doorway to look over Hugo's shoulder and sees Martin with his long crowbar braced. He has not shaved, his wavy hair unruly and messy. Hugo, without flinching, his rising anger giving him a boost of courage, faces up to his drunken adversary, although he realises the full weight of Martin's crowbar, at twice the girth and twice the length, will be, when it arrives, far more robust than his own fire-poker. Hugo is going to have his work cut out defending himself. He feels the painful judder in his right hand as the metals clash and he almost drops his wretched poker. Remembering his kitchen knife, he swipes it with his other hand across the front of Martin's body. Martin is surprisingly alert to the threat and leans back to avoid the sharp point, which misses him only by an inch. He seems to be fortified by his beer, keen and agile, his face lit up and shiny, and when he smiles Olivia can see the resemblance to Hugo, the shape of the brows, the roundness of the cheeks. Perhaps he will be more foolhardy. Hugo is trembling, nervy shocks still resonating painfully along to his fingertips, but he grips both his weapons tightly, making them perfectly visible, still standing his ground.

A cigarette butt dangles from Martin's mouth and smoke swirls around his face. He stumbles forwards again, in a heavy thigh-length leather coat, open at the front which reveals a once white shirt that is darkly caked with reddish muck. 'And who's this tart with you? Another of your models to paint without clothes on? What the hell you doin' here, anyway? Looking for Samantha?' He tries with a posh voice, 'Oh, Samantha darling. You'll not find her here, I'll tell you that for free,' and he laughs and coughs. He appears to have blood in his hair and smears over his cheeks and hands. His boots are smudging blood stains all along the corridor.

Olivia fears the worst. All this blood.

In the front room, she has already cast her eyes over the mess, the body on the floor, the knife. Somehow, she has suppressed her screaming, but inside, she is in turmoil. Instinctively she wants to rush in; and then she wants to turn and run out. Instead, she has to hold back a sob, as she presses her weight against Nika's door, pushing against the limp leg. A dirty bare foot flops against the wall at the skirting board, toes curled, turquoise nails scratched. She slides through the gap twisting herself against the wall. She cannot step inside without treading on something she would rather not tread on but adding more smudges to the mess already there will not make any difference.

In the corridor, Hugo has found his voice. 'You've got blood all over you, Midge, what have you been doing?'

'Wouldn't you like to know? Samantha might be next. You got my money yet?' He is laughing again and looking about for the bottle of beer he dropped. 'What are you doing here, you idiots?'

''Course I haven't got your money. It's not your bloody money. Where is Samantha? What have you done to her? If she is harmed again in any way, you bastard,' but Hugo is unable to finish his threat.

'What you going to do, pisshead, tick me off, call me a naughty boy?' Sneering, he throws the remains of his cigarette aside and hefts the crowbar above his head preparing for a strike, rather like a golfer in his backswing. Hugo steps aside to avoid the attempt to crush his skull, and the crooked end of the crowbar crashes against the wall next to him, potholing the plasterwork. Martin heaves the bar away from the damage and with surprising agility, catches his elbow fully across Hugo's jaw. He then shoves him in the chest with both hands holding his bar, pushing Hugo backwards against another door, pinning him against the frame and preventing him from using his own arms effectively. Their faces come close together. Some filtered daylight from the bathroom shines over the corridor scene for the first time, showing Martin's dirty, smeared and unshaven appearance, his facial muscles screwed up and tense with sneering hatred. His breath is beery warm and a few drops of his spittle pop across Hugo's mouth. The two of them struggle for a while, grunting and shoving, each trying to overpower the other, but their strengths are evenly matched, and in the end, Martin has to back away to give himself room for a further swing at Hugo's head.

Hugo ducks and moves away, while Martin charges forward, swiping across his legs with a boot and then another shove and a kick into Hugo's midriff. Another pothole is taken out of the plasterwork as Hugo ducks again from another full swing, but this time, Martin has the advantage and is able to quickly readjust his holding position with both hands grimly gripping his weapon as he smashes it down vertically with as much force as he can muster. The blow grazes along Hugo's scalp, catching his ear and crashes into his shoulder with a thumping pain. Hugo stumbles and sinks down to one knee, unaware for a few seconds of the full impact. Immediately he is reliving his fall to the tarmac with police bullet holes and a wound to the temple with warm blood gushing across his face, and he realises with brutal clarity that he must resist and fight this man, or he is dead.

Horror-struck by the violence of the scene in the bedroom, Olivia stands motionless amongst it, the concern of dirtying her nice navy work shoes long gone, holding a hand to her mouth. The room is icy cold. The dressing table is knocked aside and everything on it swept to the floor; a stool is overturned; there are clothes strewn haphazardly, shoes thrown around, the bed a dishevelled mess of crumpled blood-stained sheets. The smell is getting to her, a sweetness and a fetid mix that catches in her throat and makes her want to throw up. There is a pool of thick and dark semi-coagulated sludge spread widely across the floor, still spreading out at a snail's pace, and lying supine on the ruined carpet, her feet pointing towards the door, her head towards the middle of the room, is the naked body of Nika, an horrendous knife handle protruding elegantly from her abdomen. One of her legs is bent at the knee and propped against the corner of the bed, a pair of cotton blue knickers still hanging around the ankle. The other leg is stretched out behind the door, hence the earlier resistance. There are cuts across the palms of both hands, stab wounds over her chest, cuts that have dribbled and coagulated; and there are cigarette burn marks too, on her breasts and arms. Her body is pinned to the floor by the steel blade that has passed through her guts. Olivia wonders at the strength needed for such a blow and she wonders where Lilly might be thinking her slaughtered body must be in the little bedroom opposite.

It is not the nakedness particularly that shocks. Olivia does not focus on the soft fleshy belly and the pallor of the fatty skin around the protruding blade, or the rouge-coloured pointy nipples or the bushy pubic triangle atop the dusky exposed pudenda at her splayed legs. It is the fearful look on Nika's face, her open grey eyes glazed and unfocused and her sunken cheeks giving the impression of seeing a ghost, that will haunt Olivia's dreams. Her head is flung back, her short brown hair stuck with dull sludgy blood off her forehead, her mouth open and lips a deep blue. There is extensive bruising across one cheek spreading around the nearby eye socket, starkly purple against pale skin.

The lifeblood has drained away through the body wound like a tap and she is left deflated and ceramic white. Olivia bravely bends to press her fingers down to close the eyelids. The face is ice cold already.

She wants to cover the body.

Mad Midge, drunken and angry, must have let his wild temper get the better of him. Maybe Nika taunted him, but he stripped her, tortured her, wounded her again and again to inflict maximum pain and humiliation. Heaven knows what ghastly demons were passing through his mind or what he was planning.

Olivia, her breathing jerky and uneven, steps over the body, avoiding as much of the gooey mess as she can, and yanks a mucky sheet off the bed, which she throws over the gruesome figure of Veronica Secola from Croatia. She feels rather sick.

She needs to rescue Hugo and find Lilly before Midge does something more dreadful.

Olivia is petrified as she steps out into the corridor and stares fearfully at Lilly's closed door, anxious to check inside. Suddenly Martin jumps forward and grabs her arm at full stretch, dragging her backwards off balance in a tight grip. She yells and tries to wriggle free and kick out at him. He tries to get his arm around her neck, but she twists and hacks at his shin with her foot. She loses a shoe as he deals her a glancing blow with his fist across the top of her head and she shouts, ducks and forces her body against his bulk, pushing him back against the bathroom entrance. She is wondering what has happened to Hugo, she cannot see him. The smell of beer on Martin's breath is full-on as she grapples with his crowbar arm, but he is strong and throws her sideways into the bathroom, where she knocks her hip painfully against the sharp edge of a radiator. From a coat pocket, Martin now has a six-inch pointed steel blade in his left grip. He prods her in the midriff with the sharp end of his crowbar and then lunges at her, catching her with the knife in the upper chest under the collarbone. She tries to swivel around sideways in the narrow space but Martin stabs her again, through her jacket and deep into the flesh. She feels the blade scraping over sinews and bone. She feels immediately faint. The back of her heels hit the side of the bath and she tumbles backwards, falling, crying out, cracking the back of her head on the tile surrounds behind her, and crumples onto her bottom in the bath with her legs up in the air, so pleased she chose to wear trousers, one shoe hanging on.

Hugo was down and hurt, but he swiped his poker across Martin's shins, which checked his attack, giving him just the chance to scamper away down the corridor to regroup in the kitchen. He has a look around at the mess, the overflowing bin, the empty beer bottles, the pizza packaging slung on the floor. He recognises his old wooden easel propped up in a corner. There is nobody else here, no Samantha tied up in a corner. His shoulder is hurting like mad, his ear is cut. He advances back into battle with his poker and kitchen knife, and with as much fear as determination.

He approaches behind the shambling figure of Mad Midge at the bathroom entrance, thwacking him across the back of his neck with the poker, but the blow is poorly directed and deflects less effectively across his shoulders. Martin turns with a grunt and Hugo catches him on his return swing in the face this time, across his right cheekbone, and blood splatters, a drop catching Hugo in the eye. The short steel knife with Olivia's bloodstains on the blade drops to the floor. Hugo has to blink and wipe at his eye with the back of his gloved fingers, as Martin charges him like a bull, bellowing loudly and forcing him backwards at a pace to crash down the corridor into the kitchen door frame. They both sink to the floor in a huddle, both feeling hurt. They grapple and wrestle, grabbing at anything they can get hold of, rolling over, trying to get on top of the other, trying to force an advantage. Hugo's knife is somehow lost amongst the folds of their coats.

Olivia is feeling light-headed, but her body is heavy, curled into a ball at the bottom of the hard bath, like a wounded spider. All sense of energy has drained away. The back of her head hurts. A fresh swell of blood is spreading down the front of her nice parka, soaking into the material, getting into the teeth of the zipper, making it sticky. She can feel the wet warmth on the inside over her skin, inside her bra. The pain makes her cry out, feebly. She thinks of Louise, her beautiful Louise. So thirsty, she wipes a gloved hand under the dripping bath tap and wets her dry lips, falling back against the side of the bath exhausted by the effort. After a moment, she manages to tweak the tap a little and a gush of cold water runs over the stained enamel around the plughole and swirls away. She leans into the stream and licks and sucks at it, letting the refreshing water splash over her drained face and hair.

The pain in her shoulder is so acute, yet her arm feels numb. Wondering how deep the stab wounds went, what possible damage they could have done, she wiggles her fingers tentatively. She wants Louise to be with her. She feels so weak. If she is going to die here, she wants Louise to hold her hand, to be with her. She cannot face leaving her, without an explanation or an apology for spoiling things. She wants to say goodbye, to her face.

She manages to pull her gloves off, feebly fiddling for her phone deep in a jacket pocket, which all takes ages. She tries to focus, to concentrate; thank goodness she does not have to remember the number, just has to tap on the relevant contact. She leaves a smear of blood across the tiny screen. Her lips are so dry, she can hardly speak. Amazingly the buzzing is answered after only three rings. 'Loulou, I am wounded,' she cries softly, 'I am hurt. Can you come? I want to see you.' She is sobbing and can only faintly hear a woman's voice. She tries to think what she has to say. 'We are in the flat. Mad Midge is dangerous. You need a weapon.' The voice she can hear is soothing, reassuring. 'Nika is dead. Can you come? I love you.'

'You won't want Sam back,' Martin is shouting, 'when I've finished with her. Damaged goods, mate, she is, been violated. Ha ha.' Hugo sees his poker on the floor close by but cannot reach out for it, his arms are pinned down. The knife seems to be lost as well. He wants to smash Martin's mouth for his disgusting words. He manages a thump into his face with his elbow and a punch to the side of his head and then a better swing with his right fist with angry power.

The blows knock Martin's face into distorted grimaces but he has brought a hand up to catch Hugo's arm and as their heads clash, he tries to butt him on the nose. Hugo pulls away and forcibly gets his knee up into Martin's body and then up onto his mucky chest, leveraging himself onto his feet, gaining some room to kick him hard in the groin, not a perfect blow, but enough to gain a temporary advantage. Both men are winded and breathing heavily, but Hugo manages to wrench the crowbar that is still in Martin's grip, whipping it viciously across the man's ankles, where the bone is so close to the skin. Hugo sinks against a wall for support, feeling exhausted, panting. Martin is screaming in agony, swearing furiously as he tries to reach for his shin to soothe it. Hugo's kitchen knife drops from the folds of his coat onto the floor and he finds the resolve to grab it and hold the sharp point to Martin's neck. His whole body is shaking as he screams at him.

'Now, you bastard, why don't I stick this in you, eh, eh?'

***

The knocking on Inspector Michael Sanger's office door is urgent. DI Wade puts his head round, noting the warm fug inside and the substantial pile of files and folders on the desk in front of his boss. Sanger is up to his neck in paperwork, as usual, and has at least three more reports to have on the Commissioner's desk by the end of the day. The last thing he wants is any more interruptions.

'Thought you would like to know, boss. A disturbance has been reported at Adelaide Grove, number 84; we're sending a car down there to take a look. The suspect Midge Martin has been seen, we think. Thought you might like to be there.'

Sanger is immediately alert, his eyes widening at the mention of his mysterious adversary, the elusive Midge Martin, and he swings himself up into a straight position.

'You bet, Wade. What sort of disturbance are we talking about?'

'Shouting, screaming, banging. An altercation of some sort, with lots of thumping, according to a Mrs Eadie Balding (Wade reads the name off a piece of paper in his hand), who lives next door but one. She said it started in the morning, then went very quiet for a few hours, before it all started up again. She thinks she saw Martin in the street outside first thing.' Even Wade is feeling excited at the prospect of nailing the infamous Martin, whom he has never actually clapped eyes on.

'We need the firearms team – officers primed?'

'Absolutely.' Wade holds up some other papers in his hand. 'I have the forms, boss. And the ARV has been deployed as we speak.'

'Good lad. Let's do it.'

***

As Louise listened to Olivia's list of worries, her confessions almost, only last Sunday, when she had unburdened herself of so much – about how Hugo had been shot by the police by mistake, how he had recovered miraculously in hospital, how he was looked after by his long-term muse, Samantha; how he had got himself involved with two models, Nika and Lilly; the kidnapping of Sam and how they were trying to track the man Hugo was mistaken for, Midge Martin, as they think he was responsible; about the death of a male ballet dancer they knew years before – well, she realised how intimate were these thoughts, how trusting Olivia had become. She felt privileged and was keen to support her lover in any way she could. At the talk of action against this Midge creature, and his deadline, Louise wanted to be involved, but Olivia advised she should hang back, as a second layer of support, if needed. Olivia had called her earlier to say that Midge Martin had been sighted and she was going over to Adelaide Grove with Hugo to find out whatever they could, at least to help Nika and Lilly.

Louise senses danger instinctively and finds the address Olivia had scribbled down on the corner of a magazine, preparing herself for the adventure that she foresees ahead. From wall fittings above her fireplace, she unhooks the heavy steel sword in its sheath of leather and brass that had been handed down through past generations of unknown warriors and apparently was presented to her father for services to the independence of Hong Kong, when the territory was handed over in 1997. It was a relic from the China-Japan wars of the 1600's, she was assured, and Louise had acquired it on the death of her father from silicosis. She has kept it close with her on all her travels and, although as far as she knows, the sword has never been unsheathed, except during formal ceremonial occasions, she is looking forward to putting it to good use. Her make-up is soft and natural, slight darkening of her pencil-thin brows, black mascara and an oxblood lipstick. She dresses neatly in tight black pin-cord trousers and black ankle trainers, with a white crewneck sweater over sweatshirt and sports bra. She slips on a black zip front waterproof blouson and black beanie to restrain her hair, and with dark glasses in place, in the hall mirror she looks like Jackie Chan on a martial arts gig.

The Lexus navigator directs her towards Shepherd's Bush. Olivia comes on the line, crying, sounding hurt and in trouble. She parks up in Sawley Road, behind a black German SUV, where Hugo's driver gives her a curious once-over from inside his car. She pulls on a pair of skintight leather gloves and grabs her precious instrument. Dashing down Adelaide Grove, counting off the house numbers, she turns in at 84. The front door is hanging open, swinging slightly in the breeze and she steps over the threshold without hesitation. She removes her glasses and it takes her a moment to adjust to the dim light. She is alerted to the red stains along the lino corridor and under one door. She hears moaning coming from the back, a man's voice. She silently unsheathes her sword, which then feels a might lighter, but at 75cm long of tensile polished steel, is still somewhat unwieldy. The blade is narrow with a pleasing curve and a single cutting edge; much heavier than her usual foil, and with a hand-guard of shaped brass and a leather strapped grip, more designed for a larger male hand than hers. She wishes she had given herself some practice beforehand but remains ever confident that with her fine fencing skills, it will do her proud. It glints even within the dim unpleasant surroundings she finds herself.

There is a horrid gut-wrenching smell of sickly sweet drains, which seems to emanate from the door ajar on the left, where a messy dark puddle has collected on the floor. Carrying the sheath in her left hand, she advances up to the corner of the corridor, like a warrior soldier, poised, weight forwards on bent knees, her senses alert.

Some daylight from the open bathroom shows a man with unkempt greasy hair in a dirty leather coat huddled against the skirting and mumbling to himself. There is an empty beer bottle nearby. He is reaching down to his leg with both hands, rubbing the shin repeatedly, mouthing obscenities, his eyes squeezed closed. Louise can see a nasty cut and bruise with swelling over his cheek, and his face and hair are messed up with dried and fresh blood. She assumes this is the murderous Midge Martin.

She places the point of her blade across Martins's shoulder, ready to sever his jugular vein at a moment's notice. She leans forward and speaks with her slight Asian twang. 'Where are my friends, big boy?'

The moaning stops and Martin's eyes suddenly open wide and swivel around in panic. He lashes out an arm, protected by the thickness of his coat, knocking the blade aside and rises up on his haunches so quickly Louise is taken by surprise. 'Aha. Another tart, a bitch for the taking,' he shouts. He has grabbed his trusty crowbar that he was lying on and faces Louise with menace in his eyes. 'Who the fuck are you?' Louise has herself leapt backwards to be at a safer distance, but equally stands up to face the threat of Martin, who waggles his iron rod like an amateur swordsman. They start to joust, her using the ceremonial shiny steel and him his jobbing workman's length of iron ore. Both employ a remarkable amount of skill to fence, keeping each other at bay, within the narrow confines of the corridor.

Martin is bouncing on the balls of his feet like a boxer in the ring, despite the agony of his battered shin. Louise is *en garde* in the correct fashion, and she lunges and parries with her weight forward on her bent leading right leg while maintaining balance with her left arm out to the side, on a straight trailing left leg.

Olivia, semi-faint and half asleep, is alerted by the voices and clashing metal sounds nearby and cheered by the familiar voice of Louise, who seems to have responded to her call with wondrous haste. Slumped in the bath, where she thought she had died, she summons a huge effort using her good hand to pull herself up and somehow roll and flop over the edge, moaning with the stabbing pain, and thump onto the floor. Then she starts the slow crawl on her stomach over the lino, leaving her own smears of water and blood, towards the open door of the bathroom. Glancing up, she sees her beautiful Chinese lover taking larcenous stabs at Martin, trying to penetrate through his thick leather coat with a long sword, her mighty blade clashing noisily against Martin's iron bar. She seems to be toying with the bulkier man, being quicker in her movements and thrusting elegantly in perfect balance at full stretch of her right arm, just as Olivia has watched her do so many times before on the foil piste.

Martin is shouting obscenities once again, with misplaced confidence. Olivia finds the six-inch sturdy-looking Scandinavian double-faced blade, still smeared with her own drying blood, lying where it had been dropped close to the door frame and she grabs it, holding it in her good fist like a dagger. Once again searching for the effort required and with a deep inspiration that ignores the pain in her shoulder, she swipes the blade in a vicious downwards arc with all her might, plunging the point in line through the top of one of Martin's feet, conveniently and only for a second still at an arm's length from where she lies. It cuts easily through leather, sock, skin, muscle and sinews, passing between metatarsal bones, piercing more muscle, fascia, fat and skin and even the sole of the boot, and out into the wooden floor beneath. She releases the black gripped handle and watches it reverberate from side to side in its fixed vertical position. The resultant human scream is delayed, as there is a finite time between the blade first penetrating the skin and Martin's mind registering the unpleasant event, despite him looking down at it. But when it comes, it is as lancinating a bellow as Olivia has ever heard, a distressing animal sound that must have been registered all the way to the Shepherds Bush roundabout.

Hugo had staggered away, retreating hurt, to the back of the house, almost overcome by the heat and the exertion, after taking so many knocks. He had a fresh blow across his cheek that had disarmed him just when he thought he had Martin to himself. He attempts to revive himself, with a slosh of cold water from the sink tap. There is blood on his gloved hand. Among the filth of several days' neglect in the kitchen, as he is feeling so uncomfortably hot, he discards his thick duffle coat onto a chair, all the easier to move and fight effectively. He needs to save Olivia, aware that she is hurt. He is desperate to find Lilly and unaware of Nika's fate. He emerges into the corridor still with his pathetic fire-poker, determined to complete the business, just at that moment of Martin's guttural suffering. He is surprised to see a knife sticking out of the top of his foot, pinning him to the floor. He is even more surprised to come upon a slim Chinese woman all in black wielding a shiny steel sword at Midge Martin's chest.

'Oh, hello. You on our side?'

'Louise Li, friend of Olivia,' she nods, saluting Hugo with her sword raised vertically in front of her, her feet together. She notices the thumb of her right hand is poking through a split in her leather glove. Martin, shouting obscenities at the world and Hugo in particular, is clearly going nowhere and Hugo pounces with his own knife to his throat, screaming in his ear.

'Where is Samantha, Martin, so help me God?'

Louise presses the tip of her sword into Martin's chest, indenting the brown leather. 'Now is your chance to redeem yourself – tell us where she is and ring her guard to release her, now!' She applies further pressure. 'Tell him the deal is finished. Return her to...' and Louise looks at Hugo for help.

'Her flat in Muswell Hill.'

'Her flat in Muswell Hill.' Olivia notes with some pride how Louise's pronunciation has improved immeasurably in the short time she has known her. 'This minute, you hear.'

Even a mad Midge Martin, wild-eyed and grimacing, with tears running down his cheeks, knows when he is beaten. He bends down from the waist and clutches the knife handle, wedged through the top of his foot. He takes a deep breath and closing his eyes, applies constant upward force. Steadily the blade emerges, releasing a well of fast flowing garish blood that floods over the floor. The tip pops out with a jerk and he drops the offending blade, sinking to the floor, exhausted and quietly howling.

Louise bends to comfort Olivia, helping her to her feet and they hobble off to the kitchen. They hear Martin's gruff voice speaking to someone, over a phone. 'It's over, it's done. You hear. Release the woman, return her with her stuff, to her flat. Muswell Hill, yeah. Right? Do it. Now, dunderhead!' Hugo in some sort of subdued triumph trots into the kitchen to tell the two women of their success. 'What shall we do with him?' nodding back towards the corridor.

'We must get Olivia to a hospital, she has lost a lot of blood. Stab wounds here,' pointing at the soaked parka on the left side of her chest. Olivia looks pale, her head propped against Louise's shoulder as they rest on a tattered couch.

'Oh, Hugo,' Olivia whispers, 'I'm so sorry.' She is crying, her chest heaving rapidly between gulps of air. Her eyes and mascara are wet and smudged, a streak of blood smeared across her cheek and her blonde hair wet and flattened against her skull. Louise Li is holding her close, squeezing her to her bosom, and she keeps kissing her forehead, in between soothing words of encouragement. Hugo fetches cold water in a glass and finds an old towel among the mess, to affectionately clean Olivia's face in between her gulps.

'You'll be okay, we'll get you out of here.'

She looks pleadingly up into his eyes. 'Lilly, where is Lilly?' When his face stiffens and he is about to bound out of the room in search of his younger lover, she touches his arm. 'Nika is dead, in the front room, don't look.' She sobs, 'stabbed, don't go in, she is very dead.'

Suddenly there is another grizzly howl, as a bedraggled blood-stained Midge Martin has come alive again, and with idiotic superhuman effort, limps into the kitchen with his wretched crowbar in his hands, wielding it dangerously at Hugo's head. In surprise, Hugo turns and stumbles over a chair leg, while Martin towers above him. His face is bruised and bleeding, his foot is pouring blood, his shin is exposed to the bone, yet he still finds the vitriol, the anger to ride through it all and wrestle with Hugo, who has grabbed him around the waist with his big arms. They circle around the confined space, watched aghast by Olivia and Louise. Martin smashes the bar against the central hanging lampshade and then into plasterwork above the table, as he spins around, but cannot get a shot at Hugo. Hugo finally rams him into a corner by the stainless-steel sink and jutting wooden cupboard, the bar crashing anew into a glass-fronted wall cupboard, before dropping onto the floor out of his reach. Hugo slips aside with exhaustion, as Martin turns to the pile of assorted dishes, and burnt frying pans draining in front of him. He grabs a heavy pan firmly by its handle and is ready to swing around with it from high above his head, to swipe at whichever of his adversaries he can reach.

But Louise has reacted instinctively, has reached for her precious sword laid flat on the kitchen table and has stepped nimbly forward centre stage, right leg in advance, bent at the knee, left leg trailing, having chosen her favoured plane of delivery to take Martin's raised wrist. Mad Midge has foolishly placed all his weight on his damaged left foot, the one still floridly oozing, to give his planned spring some force on the offensive, forgetting his injury in his moment of madness; which foot collapses under him, the tendons damaged by Olivia's earlier well-judged strike. He slumps forward onto his arms, which he uses instead to thrust himself back up from the edge of the sink, to gain his full commanding height before attacking, emitting another raw howl of pain. His last, as it happens, as Louise's cross-strike from ceiling height in a perfect arc descends, originally to disarm him of any kitchen utensils, instead to cut cleanly through his neck from back to front, with a single uninterrupted swipe, so razor sharp is the blade. The gristly severance is followed by a resounding metallic clash as her steel hits the stainless-steel of the draining board, and Louise's immediate worry is for any damage she might have inflicted to the cutting edge of her invaluable ceremonial sword.

Midge Martin's head topples forwards without ceremony and plops with a squelchy thud into the middle of the sink, as accurately as if you had tossed a basketball through its hoop. Midge Martin's torso remains standing for an agonising few seconds, tilted towards the sink and cupboards, while his carotid arteries ceaselessly pump his cardiac output into the far corner of the room, flooding the floor at his feet when the sink starts overflowing.

'Oh fuck,' says Hugo.

'Shit,' says Olivia.

'A perfect riposte!' Louise observes.

While Louise cleverly upends the headless torso by its ankles, before it collapses, and positions it front down along the cupboard top, with its severed neck still draining into the sink, Hugo dashes back along the corridor, kicking in the doors of the bathroom, the toilet, a cupboard and then the bedroom on his left, calling Lilly's name. He picks up Olivia's lost shoe. He pushes on the other door, from where the smell is strongest and the entrance is soiled, learning all he wants to learn from a short glance around the door. Lilly does not reply.

Louise picks up a dirty towel and pulls her messy blade full length through the material, sharp edge facing away. She inspects the perfectly shining steel blade with a critical eye and is satisfied, before returning it to its sheath.

Hugo is the first to hear the distant police sirens, and the howling noise becomes suddenly much louder as he peers carefully past the damaged front door to see a convoy of noisy white BMW's approaching down the road with their reflective yellow and blue squares and lights flashing. He returns to the kitchen, uncertain what to do next.

He looks directly at Olivia. 'No sign, she must have scarpered a while ago.' Olivia looks relieved.

Louise has opened the back door from the kitchen onto the yard and signals that they should leave. Hugo collects up his coat and struggles with Olivia outside. Together they move to the low brick wall at the back, which they scale, by stepping up onto a discarded refrigerator, and wriggle over clumsily into another garden, then through a rickety wooden gate, into an alley that leads between two end-of-terrace houses to the next adjacent street, Oaklands Grove. Louise has found a wooden-handled broom. She walks to the sink and carefully picks out the severed head floating in its own sticky blood by grabbing its clump of thick hair. Outside she balances the broom against the back wall, holding Midge's head as far away from her side as possible so as not to contaminate her own clothes, and spikes the mushy innards of his spinal cord and midbrain onto the end of the handle, ensuring it stays upright leaning against the brickwork and facing towards the open door of the kitchen. She paces back to the sink to rinse off the filth from her gloves under a running tap, wipes them dry on the used kitchen towel which she drops on the floor before leaving, closing the door behind her.

Hugo, Olivia and Louise depart the scene of slaughter the back way, while numerous officers of the law begin to explore the unexpected scenario by the front way.

***

The carnage confronting the armed response is surprising even to a hardened police officer like Detective Inspector Michael Sanger. After all, he's seen it all before. The front door has been kicked in, splintered and hangs loosely on one hinge and there is a single bloodied male sole print on the stone step, apparently leaving.

The first wave of heavily armed and body-protected policemen disperses itself rapidly throughout the flat, front to back, to secure the site. The leader reports two bodies down, one terrified blonde under a bed and no other signs of activity. When Mike steps in, the house is quiet, although he can hear a vague dripping sound. There are blood puddles and smears everywhere, churned up by the heavy-footed, along the lino corridor, thick and runny in places, and on the emulsioned walls, hand and finger marks, most like a man's. A horrible glutinous pool of blood has seeped out from under the first door on the left, which bangs against a woman's leg as he pushes it inwards, the foot flopping against the peeling paintwork of the skirting board. The painted toes are curled and filthy and a thin gold ankle bracelet incongruously twinkles in the gloom. In his blue plastic overshoes and blue rubber gloves, he pokes his head around the door to look into the darkened airless bedroom, the curtains still pulled across the window despite the time of day, and steps carefully inside. He is hit by the pungent smell that cloys in his nostrils. On the wall opposite, Elvis Presley looks down from a giant poster. There is a once-white now bloodied sheet, with a tented appearance from its middle, covering he presumes the rest of the woman's body. He bends down to reach for an edge and slides the sheet towards him, slowly revealing the naked woman, supine on the floor, with the black handle of a large kitchen knife protruding from her abdomen. He can see other cuts and burn marks. Her head is wrenched backwards, but her eyes are closed in some sort of repose. There is thick blood smeared everywhere around her and in her hair. The blade has been plunged to its hilt straight through her, nailing her to the floor, leaving a thin trickle of ruby blood to contour over the fleshy stomach and spill over at one side. A massive pool of coagulated blood spreads from under her and across the carpet covering some distance. He looks at her tortured body, the deflated breasts splayed across her chest and her tangle of brown pubes with a sense of imagined horror, hoping that she had died quickly, for her own sake.

He retreats to the corridor, stepping carefully between the smears where he can, feeling slightly sick. In the open doorway opposite, he sees a young woman in a thick white paint-stained sweater sitting huddled on the edge of a bed, with tangled blonde hair tumbling to her shoulders and hanging over her face. She is crying, her shoulders quietly shaking, fiddling with her hands held tightly in her lap. A bulky figure of public security in black combats and yellow reflectives stands over her, his big boots spread apart, his automatic carbine in active service position. DC Wade joins Sanger for the rest of the walk through the flat, inspecting the damaged plasterwork, stopping to look in the bathroom, noticing more blood smears on the floor. In the bath itself there are some fresh bright red dollops. And a discarded pair of woman's black leather gloves, which have retained the shape of their owner's hands, still warm on the inside. There are more puddles of fresh blood in the corridor approaching the back room.

Standing in the back kitchen are two further figures in black, motionless on opposite sides. Sanger stares across at the body lying on the cupboard top. A stream of bright gooey blood is trailing down the door fronts like a waterfall from the edge of the overflowing sink, splashing into a growing pool on the floor, with a definite dripping noise. The body is of a heavy man in a leather coat with boots and jeans, lying face-down so to speak with one arm hanging limply towards the floor.

As Sanger approaches, he sees that the shoulders are level with the side of the sink but he cannot quite see who it is. Craning himself a little nearer, he realises with a slight start that there is no head, just a decapitated clean cut, a gaping wound across the middle of the neck, from which the lifeblood has all but been pumped out, the final remains draining slowly away and continually filling the sink to the brim.

He swallows hard and leans over to look, wondering whether the head will be there, floating just beneath the surface of the mucky liquid. Wade catches his outer arm. 'Boss.' Sanger turns with raised eyebrows and sees Wade pointing outside and nodding his head towards the yard. There is a trail of wet blood that seems to lead from the sink round to the back door and Sanger follows it with his eyes. Through the murky glass, he can make out the spiked severed head of Midge Martin looking back at them from the other side of the yard.

'Oh my God.'

The hair is wavy and dishevelled and matted with goo, but the face is unmistakable behind the cuts and the dirt and the unshaven chin, grimacing in a sort of ironic way, the eyes wide open. They both wander outside, horrified at the audacity and viciousness of the attacks.

'So, we finally meet,' murmurs Wade. 'Shit. If he killed the woman in the front bedroom, how did he manage to decapitate himself and place his own head on a spike?'

Wade has to retreat in a hurry to the toilet and vomit copiously down the bowl. Sanger studies more bloodied footprints across the concrete yard and a few possible stains on the brickwork of the back wall. He stands perplexed in front of the spiked head and speaks aloud to it. 'So finally, you seem to have met your match, Midge Martin. But whoever could that have been?'

***

They find Jayden standing on the corner of Sawley Road, looking extremely anxious along the length of Adelaide Grove, which is now blocked halfway down by numerous flashing police vehicles.

'Am I glad to see you, Mr Hugo. You are hurt, are you all right? Miss Olivia, can we help?'

Olivia and Hugo stand together, supporting each other. Louise clicks open her boot and reaches for a roll of black plastic, shaking a bag open. 'Okay, folks. Shoes off and then gloves, into here.'

Olivia thinks Louise is pretty clued-up about these sort of procedures, thinking of everything. She keeps crying out with the pain in her shoulder as she hops from foot to foot, as Hugo helps her off with her shoes. He kicks his own boots off and then drops everything he can into Louise's bag. He helps Olivia over to Louise's car, where the front passenger seat has been covered by a plastic sheet. He helps her settle in and kisses her cheek. She hooks her right wrist around his neck for a moment and whispers: 'Make sure Samantha is all right. Give her a hug for me. Hope to see her soon. Yes?'

They smile weakly at each other, their faces close and he kisses her mouth. 'Love you, Olly. See you soon.'

'I take Olivia to Royal Free Hospital now,' Louise calls, throwing the screwed-up black bag into her boot. 'Hugo, you get to see Samantha – she need hospital too, about the finger.' She reaches up to Hugo's shoulders and they cheek-kiss both sides. 'Good luck,' she whispers.

'Thank you, for your help,' Hugo murmurs, in astonishment. Louise nods at him and walks around in her bare feet to the driver's side to start up. Hugo hops painfully across the road in his socks to his black car where Jayden settles him in the back. He suddenly feels weak with exhaustion, his body bruised and aching all over, his face sore and cut. He sinks down into the leather seat and dozes fitfully during the smooth journey to Muswell Hill, wondering where the Chinese lady in black had come from, wielding her ceremonial sword.

5

Clearing Up

Olivia Truelove found herself on the seventh-floor Trauma ward of the Royal Free Hospital later that day, with a short blood transfusion running, recovering from a surgical approach to her chest wound. Louise and Olivia claimed the cut was caused by Olivia tripping forwards when they were stupidly practising their foil manoeuvres with sharp knives, which was a complete accident, and, whether anyone believed them or not, the hospital took it no further. The doctors reassured Olivia that no deep damage had been done, the nerves appeared clear, and that it was mostly blood loss and bruising and a fractured rib with muscle damage that would repair in time. She would be able to return to normal activity in a few weeks, they had no doubt, but it would probably remain stiff for quite a while. A course of physiotherapy was recommended. Her right side, her foil arm would be fine.

Louise Li visited regularly and remained supportive during her four-day stay until Olivia was discharged for at least two weeks' rest before her expected return to normal work activities in the City.

Samantha Little, pushed out of the back of a white van with little ceremony, found herself standing exhausted thirty yards from the front of her flat in Muswell Hill. She was confused and frightened, her left hand wrapped in makeshift bandages. She felt dirty and dizzy and started to cry when she saw Hugo waiting on the front doorstep.

He drove her to the Whittington Hospital straightaway, where she had an operation the next day under antibiotic cover to repair the stump of her damaged fifth finger. Hugo claimed she had had an accident with an electric mixer, you know how sharp the blades are these days. The two distant metacarpals had been severed, but the clever surgeons would not be able to reattach the recovered specimen, which Hugo presented in its cardboard box, as there had been too much tissue death.

A small skin graft was required, and apart from the unsightliness, her hand would function extremely well again in time. Her mind, on the other hand, had been severely traumatised, and she remained in a state of shock for some weeks, living with Hugo and his housekeeper in the secure luxury of his Butlers Wharf apartments.

***

A bruised and terrified Lilly Soames was found cowering under her bed, in her small room at the flat in Adelaide Grove. A potential witness, she was consoled and questioned by a stocky, unsympathetic policewoman, without saying anything, before being accompanied, tearful, trembling and shocked, to her parents' home in Stanmore. She later confided in them how she had been hit by Mad Midge, trapped in the flat, and then had had to listen to his raving temper and vicious attack blow-by-blow on her friend Nika. She slipped her hidden mobile phone out from her knickers gusset to give to her father for him to destroy, in case of any incriminating links to others, and it ended up in bits in a supermarket waste bin.

Lilly stayed indoors with her parents for many weeks, before shyly venturing out to look for a fresh direction in her life.

***

After a monumental quantity of forensic material had been obtained from the scene of the Shepherds Bush slaughter and sifted without much hope of identifying anything useful, a thumbprint found on the doorknob to the outside yard at the house in Adelaide Grove was finally identified by the team at Vauxhall Cross as that of an officer of the People's Republic of China, working in the diplomatic core as a secretary on a temporary visitor's visa. Ostensibly teaching mandarin to Chinese children in North London, MI6 recognised her as an appointed secretary to the Ministry of Foreign Affairs; in other words, a spy. Louise Li was summarily arrested, denied immunity, and after four weeks' intensive interrogation and diplomatic wrangling, while held in isolation with no allowance for visitors, was quietly deported to Beijing.

Detective Inspector Michael Sanger was fascinated by the ornate ceremonial sword in its leather and brass sheath found hanging above a fireplace in her flat. He examined under a microscope a tiny chip and some fine scratches on its gleaming razor-sharp edge, indicating recent usage and a heavy clash. There were no fingerprints. Although his team were unable to find a definitive link between the sword found in Maida Vale and Midge Martin's decapitation in Shepherds Bush, it was their working hypothesis that it had been used for his murder, after he had put to death his Croatian girlfriend Veronica Secola. Quite how or why this Chinese woman had come to be involved in his execution remained a complete mystery.

***

On May 15, 2015, the Conservative Party claimed victory at the UK General Election, having won a small and surprising overall majority. Olivia was congratulated by several Emerson seniors for her contribution to the party manifesto and its thinking on financial governance, with her well-received slogan "Chaos versus competence".

Olivia spent election night at her mother's house. She continued to work hard at Lombard Street and was soon putting her name forward for promotion, which seemed to everyone who knew her a mere formality. Even after Louise had disappeared without explanation, she persisted in rejecting all offers of romance from male suitors and colleagues. Her left shoulder remained stiff for many months as her interest in foil fencing waned somewhat.

***

The wedding of Hugo Pitsakis and Samantha Little took place on Friday, July 10, at Lambeth Register Office, in Kennington Lane, only a short distance south from the MI6 headquarters building. A small reception was held at Apartment 121, 36 Butlers Wharf Terrace, and the guests included: Bernadette Pitsakis, Henry Little (brother), Loukas and Salma Pitsakis, Hebe Pitsakis, Garry and Angie Webster, Jake Preston, Jeremy and Sally-Ann Ashcroft, Alicia Arundale and Rob Black, Elaine Greening (cousin), Linda Porter (best friend), Dolce Brigossoulos and Jayden Dawson. And Olivia Truelove. The bride wore white with cream and bronze trimmings. A short honeymoon holiday was planned in one of the remoter islands of the Seychelles.

Olivia's plans to write a biography about the life and times of the Greek artist, Hugo Pitsakis, were put on hold pending developments.

***

After being admonished at a Police Complaints Tribunal, Detective Inspector Michael Sanger retired quietly to Dorset after thirty-two years in the Metropolitan police. Detectives Finch and Jardine were suspended for six months and then returned to non-firearm duties at Shepherd's Bush Police Station. Compensation awarded by the Police Federation to the tune of £15,000 was paid to Miss Lilly Soames, of Craigwell Drive, Stanmore, for her shoulder injury; and £135,000 to Mr Hugo Pitsakis, of 36 Butlers Wharf Terrace, for his mistaken shooting entirely the fault of the police.

***

On returning to her apartment from work one summer evening, Olivia picked up a handful of post dropped through her letterbox. After changing and preparing her supper in the kitchen, she extracted a large, brown stamped envelope from the collection with her name and address clearly typed on a sticky label. Inside were three black & white photographs that were by now familiar to her: the pictures Edward had shown her in that café. Pictures of the studio stairs and the crumpled naked body of Dominic Lebelov. There was also a single sheet of notepaper with a typed message, no signature, no contact number or address:

"Olivia.
I enclose these copy photographs for you to ponder over.
My conscience is pricking me. I am not sure what I should do with
them. I think we should go to the police, don't you?
The least we can do in respect for the late, talented Dominic
Lebelov. Or I could give them all to you – for a price.
I give you time to think about it. I will telephone for an answer at
the end of the week: Friday at 8 pm.
That is your deadline."

THIS COLLECTIVE REPORT HAS ATTEMPTED TO PUT THE RECORD STRAIGHT OVER POLICE FAILINGS AND THE TRAGIC SEQUENCE OF EVENTS THAT LED TO LOSS OF LIVES IN LONDON IN 2015. I HAVE TRIED FAITHFULLY TO REPRODUCE THE COMPLEXITY OF THE STORY AS I SAW IT AND AS IT WAS DESCRIBED TO ME USING PERSONAL ACCOUNTS AND THE OBSERVATIONS OF THE INDIVIDUALS WHO WERE PRESENT. I HUMBLY LAY THEM BEFORE THE PUBLIC TO ALLOW IT TO DECIDE FOR ITSELF THE RIGHTS AND WRONGS OF THE CASE.

Detective Inspector Michael Sanger
Metropolitan Police (rtd) January 2016